THE
DAYS
BETWEEN

THE
DAYS
BETWEEN

A NOVEL

ROBIN MORRIS

LAKE UNION
PUBLISHING

Published by Lake Union Publishing, Seattle

www.apub.com

Amazon, the Amazon logo, and Lake Union Publishing are trademarks of Amazon.com, Inc., or its affiliates.

ISBN-13: 9781662520341 (paperback)
ISBN-13: 9781662520358 (digital)

Cover design by Faceout Studio, Molly von Borstel
Cover image: © Martin Barraud / Getty; © m-agention, © nevodka, © overlays-textures / Shutterstock

Printed in the United States of America

For Lex. I love you, sweetheart, more than words can tell.

CONTENT NOTE

This work of fiction includes mentions of the following topics: infertility, self-harm, racial intolerance, substance abuse, and suicide.

CHAPTER ONE

Friday, March 24
Andrew

The only thing Andrew had found to love about his new house sat outside the front door: the deserted stretch of beach that was his to run alone each morning before the world woke. That day, as a sorbet glow parted the sea and the sky, Andrew's footfalls found their rhythm beside the breaking waves while his heart hammered in his rib cage, and he licked the sea spray from his lips. He fought the urge to glance at his watch; the distraction would cost him precious seconds, and he could feel it in the blood pumping through his body; today was the day he'd finally clock an eight-minute mile.

Only four hours before he was slated to give Larry a final answer regarding the promotion.

When his boss had announced his retirement, Andrew had been certain his decade-and-a-half of busting his ass for his firm meant he was due to step into Larry's shoes. The interview had been a mere formality, and the subsequent job offer and breathtaking compensation package commended his years of sacrifice, but Andrew had avoided his acceptance—or his rejection—for as long as he could.

He had awakened at the witching hour, countless versions of the conversation spiraling in his mind until his alarm had crowed and he went through the motions of beginning a new day, rolling from bed, lacing his sneakers, then swallowing two tablets from the orange bottles beside the sink.

The day had come.

His sneakers ground into the sand with newfound ferocity, his collar clinging to his sweaty skin. When he reached his finish line—four wooden posts that jutted from the waves, remnants of an old dock, carpeted with jade moss—his feet sank to a stop in the sand, and he drew ragged breaths, blinking the sting of sweat and salt from his eyes. The screen of his watch rewarded him with a spiral of neon-green sparks. Three miles in twenty-three minutes and fifty-eight seconds, his best time yet. Andrew set his hands on his hips, relishing his two-second triumph, and appraised the restless sea.

On his return, he fell into a slow jog in the damp sand, and an odd sense of gloom overtook him with every step. In the three weeks since they'd moved in, each time his house came into view at the end of his morning run, Andrew swore the windowpanes were glaring at him, like the house knew he was running away from everything it held inside. And everything it lacked.

He took his time climbing the steps. Inside, Amy's keys dangled from their hook. He'd been hoping Amy's shift would have run long and they'd have missed each other, but she came home earlier since they'd moved; they were only minutes from the hospital, so now Andrew shouldered a thirty-minute commute. Amy's existence outside their home was something Andrew knew only in theory; he didn't know how many lives she touched, how many people walked the earth because his wife held the delicate thread of life at the end of a scalpel. A stab of guilt; when Amy worked late, it often meant someone was living their worst day.

He stepped into the kitchen, the first hint of a headache drilling at his temples. Amy was at the island, dressed in her seafoam scrubs, sleek black hair pulled into a short ponytail, unpacking her lunch bag.

"Morning," Andrew said. "Want me to make you a coffee?"

Amy shook her head as she lined her stackable lunch containers on the top rack of the dishwasher. "I want sleep."

He fished in the silverware drawer for a spoon.

Amy glanced over her shoulder. "Before you leave work today, don't forget to remind your coworkers about the barbecue." She pressed the On button and closed the dishwasher. "Sunday. Two o'clock."

Andrew shut his eyes. The barbecue. The fucking housewarming barbecue. "We're still doing that?"

She turned to face him. "Of course. We already invited everyone."

The previous Friday, when Andrew had come home with news of the job offer, he and Amy had exchanged careful, practiced *this makes me feels* that had been nothing but sparks on the kindling of an argument. They'd gone to bed, left it to smolder, and in the week that followed they'd tiptoed past one another in the vast, unfamiliar hallways of their house, electricity between them, like the first crackle of a thundercloud.

Now Andrew closed the silverware drawer harder than he'd intended and faced his wife. "Amy, if I turn this offer down, it's going to be mortifying. Why would I want to have everyone here to celebrate?"

"It's a housewarming, Andrew. We planned it before the offer. We can't cancel now."

Nothing but the hiss of the dishwasher.

"I thought we were on the same page," Amy said. "I just started this new position, and I have to work several graveyard shifts every week." Her palms were flat on the counter, like she was in her operating room, in control, where her decisions would never be contradicted. "If I get pregnant . . . it just isn't the right time for you to take on more work."

So she expected to keep her job, but he had to sacrifice his career to stay home and pace the empty halls of this massive house with a fussy infant? "If I accept this position, I'll try to work my travel around your schedule," he pushed. "And it's not like we can't hire help."

Amy's jaw clenched. "I'm not letting a stranger stay with my baby overnight."

"And what if there is no baby?" The words hadn't left his mouth before he regretted them. Amy's reaction was subtle. He caught the way her eyes narrowed, darkened. He'd touched her deepest fear: that he couldn't—or wouldn't—manifest the resolute snapshot of the life she'd planned. But that was what he'd been aiming for, hadn't he? And then that tick of fear, this time his own. He raked a hand through his hair. "It's something we have to consider. We need to face the reality of our situation—"

Amy straightened. "The reality of our situation is that my husband seems to have given up on this before we've even met with the specialist. Dr. Cassidy is the best fertility doctor in the state. She made an exception to get me—to get us—moved to the top of her very long waiting list." Her voice was as hard as the granite countertops. "My OB and your urologist both agreed there's no medical reason we can't conceive."

Like he needed another reminder of the creased ten-year-old titty magazines he'd been offered alongside the little plastic cup at his appointment. "This wasn't the plan, Amy."

Amy leaned forward, wispy flyaways framing her face, smudges of purple beneath her eyes. "If you don't want children, you need to be honest with me. The time to tell me is now."

The time to tell his wife the truth had long passed. Before they'd moved out of his condo in downtown West Palm, before they'd committed to thirty years of staggering mortgage payments for this sprawling house in the suburbs. If he came clean, she wouldn't want this life they'd built together.

The first tremors crept into his hands.

No. No no no.

Andrew balled his fists, pushed on. "Why are you putting yourself through all this?"

Her tone dropped an octave. "You know why." Almost pleading.

"We agreed to adoption—"

Amy recoiled. "We're both over forty—it could take years to get through all the red tape just to sit on a waiting list. Then one day we could have a kid dropped in our lap. A kid, Andrew, because we'll be pushing fifty and they'll never give us a baby." Her voice ratcheted up, a version of his wife Andrew had never met. She'd never before raised her voice to him; he'd never seen her controlled facade crack. He stepped back like he feared getting burned. "People get pregnant left and right without even trying, and you and I are in a position to give a child everything they could ever want," she yelled, red-faced.

That electric tingle surged up his limbs as his lungs constricted. He recognized the signs that he was past the breaking point, all control slipping away.

But Amy was oblivious, and she stepped closer, in his face. "We have it all. We're ready. And now you're getting cold feet?" She sucked in a desperate breath. "That's not fair to me. You know this is what I want and why I—*I need this.*" Her eyes narrowed. "Do you not want children, Andrew, or is it that you don't want them with me?"

Amy's face melted from his vision, and the kitchen faded into a sea of crimson.

◆ ◆ ◆

After making a sharp turn off Worth Avenue, Andrew maneuvered his car into the parking garage and into his assigned spot. The engine ticked and he settled into his seat.

After his fight with Amy, he'd forgotten about his coffee. He'd showered in a rush, reversed out of the driveway with his hair still damp, his headache now viselike, and he was left with that depleted feeling, the way he always did when it happened. When he lost control. In his four years with Amy he'd never faltered, never given her a glimpse of the vein of weakness inside him. But that morning he saw fear in her eyes.

He swallowed. He couldn't have another slipup like that. He had to be more careful.

The floors above him were home to Andrew's firm, Goldman Investments, where an imported espresso machine sat perched atop the kitchen counter. Andrew pictured his colleagues at that very moment, standing in a semicircle, swapping their usual Friday-morning one-upmanship while tearing through a box of greasy Breaker's Market doughnuts. They would pepper him with questions about the promotion.

He ran a palm down his face and glanced at his phone. Over the snapshot on his screen from his wedding day—he and Amy looked like tiny cake-toppers in front of a watercolor sunset—the time read 9:00. One hour before his meeting with Larry.

Andrew climbed from the driver's seat and made his way out to the street. The day was blazing hot, the sun a hazy white ball. He weaved through the throngs of shoppers, pulled the Starbucks door open and ducked inside, AC washing over him. Bodies were packed together, the air alive with chatter, rising steam, and the heady smell of espresso. He took his place in line while around him groups of people in discount designer suits hunched over their phones, taking small steps side to side, the crowd an entity all its own, inching closer to the counter. Andrew pushed his hands into his pockets. The harried baristas, their brows dewy with sweat, scribbled names onto paper cups in permanent marker.

The woman in front of Andrew surveyed the crowd on either side of her, tapping a toe on the tile. Maybe she was meeting someone. Maybe she was late. She scratched one calf with the toe of her shoe. Red bottoms. Sapphire-blue dress. Sunglasses perched atop her head, glossy chestnut hair spilling down her back in waves. After pulling her phone from her handbag, she scrolled through emails with a manicured thumb, not bothering to pause on any message long enough to read. Andrew's own inbox and voicemail were likely bursting with clients demanding his attention, but he shrugged away the thought. Sandwiched between his meeting with Larry and his fight with Amy, thoughts of email seemed trite, pointless.

He and Amy had always been civil to the extreme; Amy spearheaded their household with logic and order. The show that morning wasn't in their nature, and Andrew couldn't shake the way it had rattled him, and the creeping sensation that it was the prequel to something much larger, something catastrophic. He tried to wrangle his thoughts.

The woman slung her hair over her shoulder, and a hint of her perfume—warm . . . vanilla?—brushed his nose, stirring something that clenched his stomach with a tickle of excitement.

The line shuffled closer to the counter, the woman stepped forward, and Andrew followed. Her phone chimed in her hand, and she held it up. A video call. Max, the name on the screen read.

She answered with a clipped "Yes?"

Andrew yanked his eyes away to afford the woman some privacy and scanned the menu board behind the baristas. From her phone, a male voice cut through the clatter of the coffee shop. "I had a missed call from you." The voice was flat, impatient. White noise whipped in the background, like the caller was outside.

"You didn't text me last night." The woman's voice was familiar somehow, though he couldn't place it, and something rippled down his spine, like the first fingers of fight-or-flight.

"Chill, Mom. Javi got his hands on the new PlayStation." The boy's voice held its touch of indignation. "We played it all night, then got up early to surf."

Oh, to be a teenager again, careless, a late night with a friend—and likely a six-pack the boy hadn't mentioned—washed away by the cool water the next morning. At that age Andrew had dreamed of the life he now had. The good job. The massive house. The sleek car. He'd imagined the feeling when he'd made it. The security. He'd never pictured this . . . whatever it was. This ache.

"Listen. All I ask is that you check in." She sighed. "I was worried."

"I'm nineteen. You don't need to worry about me." The way the boy spoke the seven words sent a message. A message the woman received, Andrew noted in the straightening of her spine.

"That was our agreement, Max." Her voice was hard. Andrew's neck prickled.

Silence. Andrew wondered if one of them had hung up. Behind him, the door opened, and Andrew was nudged closer to the woman, nearly touching her. She shifted, her elbow grazing his shirt, and before Andrew could stop himself, his gaze dragged across her glossy phone screen.

A white-hot jolt of recognition sparked. Those narrowed brows, the shade of the boy's blue eyes, the texture of his sandy-blond hair. And that scowl. It was like Andrew was staring at himself twenty years in the past.

Andrew drew a sharp breath close to the woman's ear. She spun around, and he lifted his gaze from her phone to meet her eyes. Her lips parted with a soft gasp.

Everything that had happened since the last time Andrew had seen Kathryn Moretti flashed before him. He would know her anywhere. Across time and space, he'd know her.

Andrew shuffled backward, colliding with a man behind him. His heart fluttered like a bird in a too-small cage, and a moment flooded his mind of his lips meeting Kathryn's forehead, pressing the tender spot where her hairline began, waking her. He watched the blanket fall from her bare shoulders before the image slipped away, just as Kathryn had slipped away all those years ago, first from his bed, then from his life, leaving nothing of herself but her fading scent on his bedsheets.

Kathryn jerked away, her phone slipping from her grasp before it clattered onto the floor.

CHAPTER TWO

Friday, March 24
Andrew

Kathryn snatched her phone from the tile, the screen smashed beyond repair; then, without a word they moved away from the line, a single unit, the space they'd occupied swallowed by the crowd. And just like that, Kathryn led him, as she had all those years ago, and Andrew followed, out the door, now propped open, a braid of confused tourists and harried businesspeople spilling onto the sidewalk. Kathryn stopped halfway down the block beneath a narrow strip of shade provided by a palm tree and turned to face him, her phone clutched to her chest. "Andrew." It was like his name took all the breath from her.

The years, the distance between them, and everything that had taken place had given Kathryn Moretti a mythical quality. But now she was here . . .

Andrew had forgotten how tall Kathryn was; she towered in her heels, her face level with his, so familiar yet so different. She was stunning, maybe even more so than the day he'd spotted her on their college campus, a single moment that had sent their lives spiraling into motion, culminating under this tree, his heartbeat booming.

The boy's face strobed in his mind. And his age. The possibility notched into place, but he pushed it back. It couldn't be. The stress of the morning had left him seeing things.

Andrew shoved past the shock of having Kathryn a few inches before him to say something, anything, fumbling the words. "I haven't seen you in—twenty years?"

Kathryn gave a terse nod. "Twenty years and two months." Her cheeks flushed. So she'd marked the time that had passed, too.

"Why are you here?" he asked. Another choppy question. A flash of the boy's face again.

Kathryn stared. "I work for Rowan and Price."

"Since when?" Andrew demanded. The Rowan and Price offices sat just a few miles from his office. So close.

Kathryn's jaw tensed as she swallowed. "I've worked at the Boca Raton office for almost a decade." She batted an invisible strand of hair from her face, then flicked her hand toward the end of the street. "But I occasionally come to West Palm to meet clients."

For eight years, Kathryn had zipped in and out of Palm Beach, a few miles of distance between them. "How have we never crossed paths?"

"I made sure of it." Her voice was a hard wall. "I usually avoid places like this." She gestured to Starbucks. "But I had a long night."

Andrew thrust his hands into his pockets. The few times he'd dared type Kathryn's name into social media, always when he was racked with insomnia, he'd scanned hundreds of beaming, toothy thumbnail photos. Blond mom with three kids. A Realtor in New Jersey. But it appeared Kathryn had never created any social media profiles, at least none she intended for him to find, and he'd set his phone on the nightstand and rolled over, his mind swimming with disappointment, guilt, and—relief? Now he was slapped with a cold realization: she'd been avoiding him, had successfully camouflaged her secrets against the backdrop of the concrete buildings and glittering sea of cars, until moments ago.

Kathryn's eyes narrowed. "Nick hasn't mentioned me to you?"

Andrew's best friend's name on Kathryn's lips sliced through the anesthetic veil of shock that had fallen over him. The hair on the back of his neck spiked. "What? No. Nick and I haven't discussed you since . . . When did you talk to Nick?"

Kathryn's gaze fell on the blue swath of ocean across the street, her forehead pinched.

The tiny bits of information Andrew had just extracted from Kathryn piled onto his suspicions. The hiding, talking to Nick behind his back. The question—the accusation—boomed in his mind like fireworks. "Kathryn." He pointed at the phone she still clutched. "The boy—how old is he?"

Kathryn switched her phone to her opposite hand, and when she did, he saw she was trembling. He'd forgotten her intense green-eyed gaze until they locked on to his face. "Nineteen. He'll be twenty in the fall."

The gravity of her words settled over him, and something clicked into place. A certainty. Andrew's equilibrium wobbled, like the ground beneath his feet had quaked. "He's mine." It wasn't a question.

"Yes," Kathryn whispered.

A trembling heat rose inside his body, and Andrew stepped back.

"I'm sorry." The words erupted from Kathryn like they'd been held behind a dam, ready to burst. "I wasn't going to keep it—him. At least, that was my first plan. Back then." Again, she swallowed hard. "And when I didn't . . . do *that*—I just—it was just easier for me."

Andrew's frustration was instantaneous, springing from an almost primal place. "How was it *easier* for you to hide this from me?"

Kathryn's eyes rimmed with tears. Andrew drew a deep, forced breath, jerking his shoulders to loosen his sweaty shirt adhered to his back. He didn't want to scare Kathryn away.

"I'm sorry," she said again, a whisper.

Andrew held up a hand, a rush of blood beating in his ears. "I need a minute."

Kathryn nodded and fell silent.

"Why?" The single syllable was all he'd ever wanted to ask, and it held so much more than the need for an answer about the boy. Kathryn knew it, too. Her eyes swept the sky before falling to the ground, her jaw tightening as she swallowed. A single tear broke free, spilling down her cheek.

"Max." Kathryn cleared her throat. "Maxwell."

Andrew's phone buzzed against his thigh, the shock of the movement shooting through him, along with a bolt of irritation. He withdrew the device from his pocket and squinted in the sunlight to make out the screen. One missed call from Amy.

A text message appeared: Call me.

At the thought of his wife—and the helpless look in her eyes that morning—acid rose in Andrew's throat.

If Amy learned he had a child out in the world, she'd be devastated. Kathryn's revelation would shatter her. But if she found out about Kathryn . . . well, it would change everything his wife thought she knew about him. Amy wouldn't want the life they'd built together if she found out who he really was.

He couldn't lose her.

Andrew's heartbeat doubled. Kathryn standing before him was a reminder—a warning—of the spiraling darkness that awaited him on the other side of heartbreak. His windpipe narrowed, familiar, unwelcome.

An electric tickle coursed down to his fingertips. His sympathetic nervous system was already in overdrive from that morning, he knew. The clinical terms had been explained to him, but he couldn't let it happen again. Not now. Not here, in front of *her*.

Andrew forced his focus onto his breathing, the seconds ticking by as he waited for the tablets he'd swallowed that morning to work their magic. Then, with an unsteady hand, he slipped his phone back into his pocket and asked, "Does he know about me?"

There was a flash of something in Kathryn's eyes, like she was frightened. "No."

"Does he have a father?" He scanned Kathryn's fingers for a wedding ring and found none, just a stack of gold bands on her index finger and a ring with a dramatic blue stone on her right hand.

Again, Kathryn shook her head. "I raised him on my own. He's yours, biologically. But he's *mine*." Her hand tightened around her phone. Kathryn drew a breath, and when she spoke again, her voice was softer, her eyes avoiding his. "I never wanted to tell you this way."

"Can I meet him?" The question surprised Andrew nearly as much as it did Kathryn, apparent when her eyes widened.

In a harsh whisper she said, "Absolutely not."

Andrew hadn't expected her answer to be so swift, and a stubborn defiance slipped out before he had a mind to stop it. "Why not?" If it was true, if this kid, Max, was his, he could answer the millions of tiny, fractured questions that had lurked in the background for Andrew's entire life.

"It's not a good idea, Andrew. He's . . . we're sorting through some personal things at the moment," she finished curtly, her jaw set with finality. This Kathryn, with her clipped words, was not the woman he remembered. When they were young, Kathryn had been like autumn light filtering through the trees—warm and bright and comforting, like coming home. Andrew allowed the brief indulgence of remembering the feel of her skin, the smell of her neck, the taste of her on his lips, before he pushed it away. This Kathryn's eyes were deeper, like she concealed a heaviness from the rest of the world. He ached to get past what she kept so carefully hidden and find the brightness he'd once known. He searched her face for a hint of the person he'd loved so fiercely.

Back in his pocket, his phone buzzed insistently, but he ignored it.

They stood for a beat, the morning sun beaming down. Above them, the Worth Avenue clock tower loomed, a pillar of white stone coral. The minute hand moved silently behind its glass dome, and Andrew stood straight. "Fuck. I have a meeting with my boss in five minutes." But he didn't move. His feet were rooted in place.

"Okay." Kathryn's eyes danced across his face, then traced him up and down. Something shadowed her expression. A longing. Sadness, maybe. "You look good, Drew." Her brows narrowed, her words almost an accusation. *Drew.* For a moment he was twenty again, his naked body tangled in hers. His mouth was dry. She straightened. "I mean, you look like you're doing well." Kathryn lifted her eyes, looked as if she was about to add something. He watched her recalibrate. "It was good to see you. Take care of yourself." A beat before she turned to leave.

He reached an arm into the empty air. "Kathryn, wait."

She turned back to face him.

"Can I—can I reach out to you? I have so many questions."

Kathryn clutched her phone tighter, seemed to consider his request. She nodded, hesitant. "Okay, I'll give you my number." She held up her smashed device, pink flushing her cheeks. "And I'll buy a new phone today."

Andrew tapped the number she gave him into his phone. Was it her real number? Would he drum up the courage to contact her? Then he looked up. The hardness in Kathryn's eyes ebbed and a hint of—what was it, amusement?—played at the corners of her mouth. "You were the last person I expected to see today," she said. A twitch of a smile.

Kathryn turned, and Andrew watched her hair sway as she strode down the block.

This woman had no idea how she'd once broken him. And if he hadn't craved coffee, hadn't run away to fucking Starbucks, she'd still be a ghost teasing him with regret for a life he'd almost had. Now, having Kathryn so close was like having a sweating glass of whiskey set before him on a hot day, dancing the dangerous line of *what if* only addiction and love could.

The buzz of his phone again hauled him back to the present. A new message from Amy blinked across the screen: Dr. Cassidy had a cancellation. She can get us in on Monday. Call me as soon as you get this.

CHAPTER THREE

Saturday, March 25
Emmy

Emmy Silva woke with a jolt, her vision calibrating to an unfamiliar space. The previous night replayed in bursts. The fight with her mother. The uncomfortable car ride with Kathryn.

She found her bearings: Kathryn's guest room, the pink and blue cotton-candy clouds floating by the window. A few more steadying breaths, then she completed her morning ritual: wiggling her fingers under the duvet to the count of twelve. Twelve weeks until her eighteenth birthday. Twelve weeks until the day she could board a plane to Seattle and never look back, never again see her mother, and never, ever, *ever* again have to lay eyes on her nasty bitch of a grandmother.

In late January, Emmy had returned from school to find a thick white envelope tossed on her bedspread. Three dirty lines ran down the front, marking its journey, and the logo in the top left-hand corner rang as clear as a bell: the University of Washington. Emmy knew by its weight she'd been accepted before she tore it open, leaving shreds of manila confetti on her bedroom floor. Since the fall, she'd watched her classmates celebrate their college-acceptance letters. Some were showered with parties or lavish dinners, sandwiched between their glowing parents. Others were whisked away on vacations, gifted cars. The sky was the limit at Saint James Academy, where both GPAs and celebrations were equally competitive. But when Emmy had intercepted her mother, Harper, in the kitchen to share her acceptance letter, Harper had frowned thoughtfully, as if she hadn't considered that her daughter wished to attend college. "Right," Harper had said. "I'll arrange to have your deposit paid this week." Harper had plucked the letter from Emmy's fingers, then disappeared down the long hallway toward the wing she shared with her dull-as-a-board husband, Joshua, without further comment.

There was no celebration, no acknowledgment at all, and Emmy felt silly for expecting anything. In her fantasies, Emmy never dared dream she'd be the hopeful freshman in a collegiate sweatshirt, decorating her dorm with the help of a weepy mother. Harper's approach to parenting consisted of sporadically whisking Emmy away for lunches on Worth Avenue or for exhausting shopping dates followed by long stretches of silence. Sometimes weeks stretched on and Harper didn't venture from her bedroom at the far end of the cold, marble estate owned by Emmy's grandmother Nora. Like all the residents who hid behind the gilded gates of one of Palm Beach's most exclusive neighborhoods, Nora scrutinized the landscapers and housekeepers while Harper, Emmy, and Joshua stayed out of her way.

Since her college acceptance, Emmy had counted down the weeks until she could leave her family, like a prisoner hashing their days to freedom. Emmy soothed herself with daydreams of lush greenery against foggy Seattle skies, of rainy days and long afternoons spent in the warmth of a Seattle bookstore. Her vision of the future had steeled her resolve, and she passed time in her bedroom, lost between the pages of a romance novel, in dewy worlds of lust and promise, where happy endings existed, where love always found a way to win. Emmy had dodged any arguments with her grandmother for nearly three months—a record, really. That was, until the previous night, when the familiar sound of arguing floated in from the hall outside, drawing her attention from her book. It was soft at first, like music, until the pitch and tone spiked. Emmy listened for Harper, her voice soft and pleading, between Nora's jabs. Harper spoke exactly the way she presented herself: delicate, like words could physically break her, while Nora took great care to give off the poised air of a Palm Beach socialite. Nora was manicured and graceful in the public eye and appeared as if the slightest upset might shatter her like a Fabergé egg, but behind closed doors, she had the personality and bite of a rabid dog.

"This is why I warned you not to run off with *the help*." Nora's voice pierced the air. "This all could've been avoided, Harper."

The help. This was how Nora saw Emmy's father, as if he'd never been a person with his own life, his own dreams, just a faceless figure who had once served Harper and Nora lunch at their country club. Lucas Silva had been a few shades too brown for Nora's taste, as was his inconvenient offspring. Nora never bothered to conceal the fact that she was bitingly racist.

And worst of all was Harper's response: nothing.

The way she always responded to Nora.

Then Nora's sharp "Are you going to spend your whole life paying for the mistake of marrying that man?"

The words sliced through Emmy. She'd heard her grandmother berate Harper over Lucas before, and on a few nights Emmy had slipped into the bathroom and unwrapped a razor blade she kept in a tissue under the sink, which she held to the side of her wrist. At first she'd been scared to press too hard, but when the sharp point broke her skin and tiny pearls of blood seeped out, a blissful rush of adrenaline neutralized her pain. Each time, she wallowed in shame the following day, concealing her secret under a stack of beaded bracelets, and promised herself she'd never do it again.

But this time Nora's words broke something inside Emmy, something that had been fraying like an old rope her entire life. In a single moment of clarity, she knew her time in her grandmother's house had come to an end. She'd reached for her phone and called Kathryn.

Kathryn had once been Harper's closest friend, had lived with Harper and Lucas until Emmy was three, when *something* dramatic had imploded their relationship. Emmy gathered it had something to do with her father but had never been able to extract any details from tight-lipped Harper. The bitterness between the two women was so complete, it was palpable on the rare occasion they were in each other's presence. Kathryn sent cards like clockwork on each of Emmy's birthdays until they'd evolved into text messages in recent years. They were always the same.

Happy birthday, sweetheart! I love you. Call me if you need anything XOXO

Emmy had never called. She'd been keenly aware that Harper had invited Kathryn to her wedding only to prove to Kathryn she was worthy of remarrying. At the reception, while Harper was distracted with Emmy's so-called stepfather, Kathryn had pulled Emmy into a dimly lit space outside the bathroom and clutched her.

When she finally pulled away, Kathryn made earnest eye contact. "Oh, honey, look how grown up you are," she gushed. "You can call me anytime. Seriously. For *anything*."

After overhearing the fight between Harper and Nora, with her phone trilling in her ear, Emmy hoped Kathryn's promise had been sincere. "I need to get out of here," Emmy begged Kathryn the moment her breathy voice answered.

"Put Harper on the phone," Kathryn said without hesitation. Sharp. Assertive. So unlike Harper. "And pack a bag. I can meet you in an hour."

In the hallway, Emmy had thrust her phone into Harper's hand. "I'm going to stay with Kathryn." Reaching out to Kathryn was the ultimate act of sticking it to her mother, which held an appeal all its own.

Harper's face was alabaster white but registered her shock. "Absolutely not."

Emmy pointed at the phone. "Then I'll find somewhere else to go. But I'm not staying here."

Harper drove Emmy to meet with Kathryn, looking small and fragile, her shoulders hunched. "Take some time away." Harper's voice was raspy, just above a whisper, and Emmy wondered whether she'd been crying, whether she had brushed her tears away before they'd climbed into the car, like it would kill her to show even a shred of emotion. "You may feel differently in a few days."

Her mother was supposed to stop her from leaving. That was what mothers did. Instead, Harper agreed they needed time apart? All they'd ever had was time and space between them. "I won't." Emmy crossed her arms, her body angled toward the passenger door. "Grandma hates me."

"She doesn't hate you."

"She hates you, too," Emmy snapped.

Harper swallowed but didn't respond.

"I'm nothing but a reminder of Daddy, anyway. For both of you." Harper stared straight ahead on the winding road, where the headlights illuminated the tunnel of greenery. "You aren't anything like the parents of the kids at my school. Nobody in our house even talks to each other. Why did you even have a kid if you didn't want one?"

That had struck. "Emmy," Harper gasped. "I—we wanted you more than anything."

"Well, you don't show it. All you do is mope around." When Emmy spotted Kathryn's car idling in a cone of yellow light in the parking lot where they'd agreed to meet, she'd slammed the door.

Kathryn waved to Harper as Emmy climbed into her car. Emmy watched her mother's car with bated breath, waiting for the dome light to burst aglow, for Harper to step out and beg her not to leave. But there wasn't so much as a flicker of movement, and finally the red taillights spilled onto the pavement as Harper maneuvered out of the lot and disappeared down the street. Emmy had turned away, her eyes stinging.

"Oh, honey." Kathryn reached out. Her body was warm and unfamiliar, but Emmy let herself lean into her hair, where a hint of her spicy perfume still lingered. When she pulled back, Kathryn appraised her in the dim light. "Whatever's going on between you two, your mom will come around."

Emmy had never seen a shred of evidence to prove this. "No, she won't," Emmy said with certainty. Kathryn had been Harper's best friend, but maybe now she didn't know Harper at all.

Emmy watched Kathryn's face concede.

"Sweetheart . . ."

Emmy waited for her to tell her she was wrong. But she didn't. To be fair, Kathryn didn't seem like the type to bullshit. Instead, she said, "Come back to the house and get some rest. You'll feel better in the morning."

All Emmy could offer was a nod, and the two fell into silence as Kathryn drove south along Ocean Avenue, the world passing by. There were no streetlights on the east side of the road, just stone walls and tall gates, concealed in thick vegetation. On weekdays, the gates stood open, and on the sprawling lawns the roar of lawn mowers rose in the air. The yards and gardens were peppered with tan men in stained white coveralls who ate their lunches out of paper bags under the shade of palm trees to escape the hot afternoon sun, people like Emmy's father, who had once worked for the wealthy residents of Ocean Avenue. Lucas had likely never believed he'd reside in one of the towering properties one day. But he had, and when the brass numbers marking 228 Ocean Avenue glinted in the dim light, Emmy craned her neck to catch a glimpse of her father's house in the darkness.

Kathryn chewed her lip, and Emmy wondered what might be troubling her. They turned right on Atlantic Avenue, the street that bisected Delray Beach, meeting Ocean Avenue to form a T. Two blocks inland, in an entirely different world, smaller homes lined a quiet street. There were no fences here, no stone walls; the properties were divided by high shrubs, and Kathryn turned into the driveway of a two-story house that looked like the others. They came to a stop in the garage, and Kathryn led Emmy inside, then offered a brief tour, gesturing toward the bathrooms and the kitchen. Emmy had the feeling Kathryn's *Seriously, sweetie, help yourself to anything* meant she'd be left alone most of the time, which brought some comfort.

Now, the following morning, Emmy was tucked under the white duvet in Kathryn's guest room. She'd done it. She was free of her family. But her eyes stung. Harper hadn't put up a fight. Her own mother didn't want her around. And why was Kathryn certain Harper would come after her?

Emmy swallowed and narrowed her focus, let the picture of her future bloom, clearer than it had in as far back as she could remember. She could crash at Kathryn's house until her birthday. That allowed Harper twelve weeks to prove Emmy wrong and Kathryn right, to offer a single hint that she cared. Otherwise, Emmy would leave for Seattle and never look back.

Emmy slipped from her bed and ventured into the hallway, where the aroma of coffee floated up from the kitchen. She'd kill for a cup, but first, more practical matters needed to be addressed. She edged toward the bathroom, her bare feet silent on the hardwood floor.

"All I ask is that you tell me you're okay." Kathryn's voice, dripping with unease, rose from the first floor. "Nothing more."

Emmy tiptoed to the top of the staircase, cloaked in shadows, peering down at Kathryn standing in the doorway to the kitchen. Max stood a few feet from his mother.

Max. She hadn't considered him when she'd called Kathryn. In the years since Emmy had seen Max, he'd sprouted and now stood a few inches over his mother. Emmy's childhood memories of Max were too slippery to grasp; what she recalled was splashing in bright ocean waves together, that they'd adored each other. Max was two years older than she was, so that made him, what, nineteen now? Why was Kathryn drilling him about a few nights out?

His shoulders squared. "I don't ask you to text me when *you* spend the night out." A beat of silence. "Just because I got into a little trouble doesn't mean you can stop me from having a social life."

"A little trouble?" Kathryn scoffed. "You could've killed someone—you could have killed yourself. If Nick hadn't intervened, you could be looking at jail time right now."

"You think I don't know that?" Max snapped. "I don't need you throwing his *favor* in my face every chance you get. I'm not a kid anymore; you can't keep tabs on me every single second, and you can't *ground* me."

Tension reverberated upstairs into the hallway. Emmy knew she shouldn't be eavesdropping, but curiosity tickled her, and she didn't move.

"Max." Kathryn's voice was almost pleading. "Nick says since you got that car, you've been speeding around—"

A strangled groan from Max; then his footsteps pounded up the staircase. Emmy's options forked before her, her brain screaming at her to run, but her body froze. Max reached the hallway and stopped. His gaze fixed on Emmy, looking at her—*through* her—for an intimate, unsettling second.

Neither said a word; they just stood as the air around them grew still. A vivid memory flashed of his face illuminated by the glow of fireworks at her mother's wedding.

Kathryn's voice rose from downstairs. "You need to be careful, Max."

Max's eyes darted to his left, over his shoulder—a subtle movement, almost protective. Kathryn's shadow moved toward the kitchen.

"Well." Max cleared his throat, slipping past Emmy. "It's good to see you again." He disappeared into his bedroom, the door closing with a click.

The hallway was heavy in Max's absence. Emmy's heart drummed, her chest and face hot with mortification. She slipped into the bathroom, working the lock behind her.

She hadn't meant to impose on Kathryn when there was drama with Max, hadn't considered it. All she'd thought about was getting away from her grandmother and Harper. Maybe it was a mistake to come live with these people she hardly knew. It hadn't been twenty-four hours, and she was already invading their privacy. And why did Max's presence—and his penetrating stare—rattle her that way? It was . . . uncomfortable. Inconvenient.

Maybe spending the night at Kathryn's had been enough of a lesson for Harper. Emmy's fingers found the doorknob. She'd go into her room, call Harper, tell her she'd changed her mind. Maybe Harper would be relieved. Maybe she'd realize Emmy was worth keeping.

She recalled Harper's indifference. Seventeen years of it.

No. She couldn't let anything derail her plan to move to Washington.

Emmy's heartbeat slowed, and she moved away from the door, met her eyes in the mirror. She couldn't go back to her grandmother's house, back to the stony silence Harper had let grow between them. No way.

Emmy switched on the tap and splashed her face with cold water. The night before, when Harper had stayed still behind the darkness of her windshield, that was the last chance.

She had to stay with Kathryn. And with Max, if that was how it was going to be. How had Max earned the right to have any bearing over her life, her decisions? He hadn't. She wouldn't allow it.

Kathryn and Max certainly had their own things going on, and no time to worry about her. Emmy could stay out of their way.

It was only twelve weeks. She had to make it work. She had nowhere else to go.

CHAPTER FOUR

Saturday, March 25
Kathryn

In just over one month, Kathryn's life had collapsed into shambles.

And that was before she'd spun around in Starbucks and locked eyes with the man she'd been avoiding for twenty years.

"I always thought I'd feel, I don't know, different somehow," she said to Nick. With her back against the bedpost, she could feel his eyes on her from the other side of the bed, where he was propped against the headboard, one hand resting behind his head. In the solitary light from his nightstand, where Nick's empty wineglass sat, his features were dramatic and defined, his skin fair. Even sitting naked in his bed, with his neat haircut and stocky frame, Nick looked as much a cop as he did in uniform, though in the moment his brown eyes were soft and showed no hint of the blaze he veiled behind them.

He arched a brow. "How *do* you feel?"

Kathryn stared into the dregs of her cabernet. "Guilty."

Nick responded with a soft exhale, but Nick so often let silence speak for him Kathryn hardly noticed.

She'd always imagined that unburdening herself of her largest secret—certainly the most life-altering one—would alleviate the weight she'd carried for so long. But the memory of Andrew's eyes boring into hers the previous morning replayed on a continuous loop, along with his desperate questions, and shame roiled inside her.

She'd let her guard down. When Max hadn't come home the night before, Kathryn had rolled around in her bed until dawn, alternating between blinding fear—*He's dead in a ditch*—and blinding rage: *He's out drinking again, ignoring my texts.* Kathryn had flipped her pillow, then pressed her face to the cool side. *When he has the audacity to show his face here tomorrow morning, I'm going to kill him.* The last time Max hadn't come home, thirty-seven days ago, all her maternal nightmares had nearly come to fruition. The night he'd wrapped his car around a light pole. The night she'd nearly lost him. The night she'd realized that no matter how hard she'd clung to him in his nineteen years of life, it was futile. She could lose him in a fraction of a second. The realization had shattered everything she'd ever known to be true, that her love for her son could be enough. In those thirty-seven days, Kathryn had felt like she was holding a breath so hard her chest burned, but she didn't dare exhale.

When sunlight had peeked through the crack in the curtains, Kathryn rose, her body aching with fatigue. That morning was a perfect storm: she'd sniffed the vanilla creamer in the fridge to find it spoiled. Then a wreck on I-95 had snarled traffic and left her pressed for time. She'd finally caught a break on Worth Avenue when a black sedan pulled out into the creeping traffic in front of her and Kathryn glided into the empty space it left in front of Starbucks, twenty minutes still on the meter.

She'd scanned the crowd for anyone resembling Andrew, a practice so embedded within her it had become encoded in her DNA. At every coffee shop, every restaurant, every school event she'd attended as Max grew, she'd scanned the crowd for a tall man with blond hair, for danger. And he'd never appeared, until that morning, at Starbucks of all places, when Kathryn was sleep deprived and distracted. She hadn't vetted the person directly behind her, and she'd spun around to meet his crystal-blue eyes, her secret already laid bare.

Kathryn tipped the last few drops of wine onto her tongue and handed Nick her glass. "I appreciate you breaking out the good stuff tonight," she said. A half bottle of cabernet had dulled her nerves, but she was still rattled. Kathryn had navigated the raging misogyny that infected the law world and risen to the top of her firm, but Andrew's pleading gaze had dissolved all the confidence she'd worked so hard to practice.

Nick offered a soft grunt of acknowledgment that was just so . . . Nick. His apartment was sparsely furnished with black, rectangular pieces she was sure he'd put together himself, but his bedroom was cramped: three walls housed bookshelves, sorted in some way only Nick was privy to. His stiff black uniform was draped over his hamper. When he'd undressed, she'd watched him remove his firearm and place it in his nightstand drawer.

"Drew called me as soon as you left." Nick shifted on the mattress. "I haven't heard him that keyed up in years." He picked his cuticle, which was already cracked and ragged. It was one of his most irritating habits, but Kathryn ignored the urge to tell him to cut it out. "Are you going to see him again?" She clocked his veiled concern.

This was why she'd dreaded recounting the encounter to Andrew's closest friend. Some wounds gouged so deep they never healed.

"I'm not sure." Kathryn stared at the far wall and answered just as carefully. "He asked if he could meet Max."

"Are you going to let him?"

"Are you serious?" Kathryn turned, meeting his eyes. "Max barely talks to me as it is. His list of reasons to hate me is endless, and getting longer every day."

Hiding her son from Andrew had been Kathryn's sole focus since Max was forming inside her, when she could shield him from the consequences of her decisions; it had become a natural appendage to her parenting. She regretted not pushing Max harder to apply to college. He'd be safely tucked away at a tree-lined campus somewhere, instead of zipping around Delray, where Andrew now lived, leaving the potential for her secrets to be exposed, laid out like a live wire. Telling Andrew about Max was one thing, but telling Max about Andrew . . . it wasn't possible.

Nick slid his hand across the sheet and laced his fingers with hers, then leaned in to press his mouth to her collarbone. It was so easy for him to lose himself in her, placing light kisses up her neck. But she couldn't lose herself in him. Not this time.

Andrew's face flashed in her mind, along with pulsing guilt. Over the years, when she'd idly pictured what Andrew might look like, how he'd aged, it was easy to tell herself he no longer resembled the man she'd loved with a life depth all those years ago. But when he'd turned to look at the Worth Avenue clock tower, alarm ringing on his face, this was the Andrew she remembered, and her mind had flashed to the morning twenty years ago when she'd stuffed her belongings into a bag and fled the apartment she'd shared with him and Nick. The day she'd derailed their lives, all their carefully laid plans.

After that morning, she hadn't seen Nick or Andrew for nearly eighteen years, had begun to let herself believe she never would again. Nick was the first to resurface, when Max had just started his junior year of high school and was still a model student, still a source of pride, and each of Kathryn's days were indistinguishable from one another: coffee, work, motherhood. She was sitting at a small table at a bustling deli during the throes of lunch hour, had speared a fork into her kale salad when she looked at the dark-haired man two tables over. Nick's deep eyes were familiar, and a wave of recognition stole her breath. He waved her over with a warm smile. She rose, an inferno raging in her as she approached. "What are you doing here, Nick?"

Nick had dabbed his lips with a napkin, then balled it and discarded it on his plate atop a sandwich crust. "Well, it's good to see you, too, Kat." A smirk. "I took a job with the Delray PD."

"You're a cop?" She'd never pictured the Nick she'd known all those years ago working a government job. He was a painter. A poet. She'd imagined him in a far-off European town, imprinting his mark where eons' worth of other artists had before him. And, of all the towns in the world, in Florida, even, why Delray? "In the town where I live? Where my son lives?"

Nick's jaw had dropped open, and he looked like he was about to speak, but instead he closed it and nodded.

"Did you tell Andrew?" Kathryn had demanded.

His expression fell, serious now, and he answered, "I told you I never would."

The words washed over Kathryn, a puzzle piece snapping into place, answering the one question that had haunted her for decades, and a hint of a reprieve from her ever-present guilt. *Andrew never found out about our son.* For years she'd lived in two alternating realities: either she'd been successful in keeping Max a secret from Andrew, or Andrew had learned about their son but hated her—which was understandable—too much to reach out. So when Nick's words confirmed the former scenario, she'd taken a few beats to reframe her reality. Kathryn dropped into the chair across from Nick. "Are you and Andrew still in touch?"

"Of course," Nick said with a hint of force. "We shared an apartment in downtown West Palm for the last few years, until his fiancée moved in."

A lightning bolt of fear. "He's been in Florida this whole time?" The last time she'd gotten close to contacting Andrew—a call so disastrous it had sent a shudder through her when she recalled it—she'd learned he had returned to his hometown in South Carolina, and as the years had passed, she'd imagined he'd stayed, planted roots near his family, that a safe buffer of time and distance sat between him and Max. But Andrew lived just twenty minutes away from where she did. She'd told herself she was being paranoid every time she scanned a location, but she'd been justified all this time. The thought did not bring comfort.

"He has, mostly. We both have." Nick's forehead crinkled. "You seem surprised that we're still friends."

She was, though she felt a tug of guilt admitting it.

A fuzzy voice blared from Nick's radio, and he cocked an ear, then gathered his empty plate and rose. "I gotta go. But listen, are you busy tomorrow? We could grab a drink, catch up?"

"Of course, yes." Her pulse ticked.

Kathryn had rushed from the deli back to her office, where she shut her door and tapped Andrew's name into Google. Of the twenty-four matches in Palm Beach County, only two corresponded in age, and one worked for Goldman Investments on Worth Avenue. And there was his photo on their website, with his brilliant white teeth and his *trust me with your money* smile. Bile rose in her throat; his face was strikingly similar to her son's.

They'd cross paths eventually; she'd felt it in her core.

The evening after she'd run into Nick, the two had settled into an isolated booth at the back of a moody wine bar, where he said, "You look great, Kat. And you did it, you finished law school. You seem like you're doing well." Nick's black T-shirt hugged his arms. Her fear ebbed, and a tickle of warmth crept in.

"You look good, too." And she'd meant it. The years had matured Nick, providing a confidence he hadn't had in college. He was more focused, it seemed, though his deep eyes still held mysteries from the world.

He gazed at her. "And you're—forgive me for saying this—more beautiful than you were in college." They sat on the same side of the booth, leaning against the Naugahyde, their bodies angled toward each other.

She was used to men complimenting her. But this time, a ripple ran through her. "Thank you."

Each time she'd inquired about Andrew, Nick had nudged the conversation back to Kathryn, but Kathryn managed to extract answers to some of the millions of questions that zoomed through her mind. Andrew had recently married, Nick revealed, and didn't have any children. Though it was absurd, the word *married*—the permanence of it—stung like a barb. But the news Andrew remained childless brought a measure of relief. It had been far too long to justify these feelings, she thought, and pushed them aside as she sipped her wine.

"I'm glad we ran into each other," Nick said. The candle flickered between them, and his lower lip was stained purple from the wine.

"Don't tell Andrew we saw each other," she pleaded. "Don't tell him anything, please."

"You know me, Kat. You know I won't." Nick set his hand on hers.

Maybe she hadn't ruined all their lives with her decisions after all. She'd inched closer to him in the small space.

The following morning, Kathryn had awoken to the pale light of Nick's bedroom, a pinging headache, and a swell of regret. She'd untangled herself from Nick's arms and fled.

After their date at the wine bar, Kathryn had avoided Nick and the ghosts he'd brought back into her life. They'd coexisted in Delray for a year without friction, nodding hello when she passed his Delray Beach Police SUV on the street. One morning, while she waited for her vanilla latte at Deja Brew, she glanced up to see Nick leaning against the counter, his eyes on her. He was in uniform, *Officer Nick Keegan* embroidered on a strip of Velcro on his chest. He narrowed his focus onto his phone, a tickle of a smile on the corner of his mouth. Kathryn took him in; his uniform suited him, she realized with a tug deep inside.

A gaggle of stroller moms buzzing around a table eyed Nick, too. *Hot Cop,* one mouthed to another, fanning her face, and they stifled giggles. Kathryn peeked at Nick again, with a flash of a memory, his strong chest rising above her, her fingers twisted in his hair, his mouth open, hungry, on the valley between her breasts. That familiar shudder.

Walk away, she told herself. It was against the rules she'd constructed: never date anyone with strings attached. If Nick gave her all of himself, she could never give him what he wanted in return. Nick had guarded her secrets—and Andrew's, she was certain—for two decades. He had found a way to love them both, despite the unfair dichotomy that was his life.

Nick collected his coffee, gave Kathryn a nod, and left the café, the bell above the door chiming, the sunshine making his hair glisten as he crossed the parking lot.

Learning Andrew lived nearby, and the search that led to his photo on his company's website, had sparked Kathryn's curiosity. She dug deeper. Andrew had only a sparse Instagram, just a photo with his family at Thanksgiving, and another, Andrew's arm around Nick at a police department fundraiser at the Breakers, the two of them on a terrace, a brilliant sunset over their shoulders, cherry red grading into cobalt. But a tag led Kathryn to a page, a few glossy tiles laid out by his wife, Amy. And, occasionally, in moments fueled by chardonnay and regret, Kathryn scoured Amy's photos. Of course Andrew's wife was gorgeous; of course she spearheaded fundraisers for her hospital. Of course her fitted strapless wedding gown fit her like a dream, and she beamed at her new husband. Kathryn zoomed onto Andrew's face. His eyes crinkled in the corners, but there was something there. Something darker. Whatever it was, Andrew concealed it carefully. Kathryn was certain Nick knew exactly what Andrew hid behind his smile, but he'd never share.

Kathryn maintained her self-control, avoiding Nick until that February night, thirty-seven days ago, the night Max had downed a frat party's worth of liquor, then skidded his car off the curve on Ocean Avenue. The chime of her phone had sliced through a dreamless sleep, and when she'd answered, the voice at the other end was unrecognizable, and the only words she gathered through the beating in her chest were *car crash*. It wasn't until Max's strained, raspy voice choked out the words *Mom* and *help* that she gathered what had happened.

She'd dialed Nick's number without a second thought. He'd instructed her to stay away from the scene, to avoid attracting attention, and had delivered Max to her door, surly and intoxicated, but alive and whole.

For a week following Max's accident, Kathryn had managed to doze only in sweaty fits after finishing a bottle of wine or popping a sleeping pill, sometimes both. She woke, her chest aching from her racking sobs, and sneaked to Max's room to peek in, to make sure he was there, alive. Nick's actions had spared Max the consequences of his behavior. And they'd spared Kathryn the public embarrassment, kept Max's name out of the news. And for all of it, she owed Nick everything. On her eighth sleepless night, she had dialed Nick's number. He asked her to meet him for a drink, and she showered and coaxed her hair into long, glossy waves. She swiped on crimson lipstick and drove off into the night to meet him, to thank him for saving her son the only way she knew how.

A week later, Nick had invited Kathryn for hibachi to celebrate her forty-third birthday, an event that left their clothes smelling of grease and onion. That night, Nick announced Andrew and his wife had bought a house in their suburb of Delray Beach. Nick broke the news casually, though there was a subtle quaver to his practiced, police-officer tone.

The news had sucked the air from her. "I can't have him and Max living in the same town. I need to tell Drew," Kathryn told Nick, and she'd practiced the conversation in the lost hours of the night, how she'd finally tell Andrew about Max. But she'd never let him uncover the reason she hid her son.

Never.

It was ridiculous, but Andrew's move felt like he was encroaching on her territory. Logically, Delray Beach was a natural choice. Kathryn could picture Andrew and his wife cruising down Atlantic Avenue, taking in the canary-yellow facade of the Colony Hotel, the charming boutiques and sparkling nightlife, all within walking distance of the cozy suburbs. The beach was pristine, the neighborhoods zoned for the best schools in Palm Beach County. I-95 provided a twenty-minute jaunt north to the city of West Palm Beach, and fifteen minutes south to Boca Raton. It was a gem, sure, but sharing it with her ex made Kathryn feel as if the walls of her secrets were closing in on her.

Then fate had intervened in the form of an empty parking spot in front of Starbucks. She'd answered Andrew's questions, carefully concealing how completely she'd failed their son. Beneath that palm tree, with Andrew inches from her face, her mind had swirled with a thousand thoughts, but one struck her: if Max had died that night on the side of the road, Andrew would never have known of his existence. Her beautiful, brilliant child. Of all the guilt she'd shouldered over the years, this was the heaviest.

In Nick's bedroom, a long sigh drained from her, and she turned to him. "Tell me about his wife."

Nick groaned. "Why are you doing this to yourself, Kat?"

"Sick curiosity, Nick. Humor me."

He exhaled. "She's a surgeon. That's why they moved here; she took a position at Boca General."

Andrew's wife was a surgeon at the very hospital where Max was born. Kathryn didn't know why, but the thought stirred unease inside her. Life certainly had a twisted sense of humor.

Nick adjusted his shoulders against the headboard. She'd taken all he was willing to give that night.

Kathryn plucked her dress from the chair and tugged it over her head. "I couldn't avoid him forever, though God knows I tried." She spoke as much to Nick as to herself, then perched on the edge of the mattress, giving him her back. "Zip me?"

Nick's fingers worked her zipper. "Twenty years later and we all find ourselves living a few miles apart." He grunted. "What's the worst that could happen?"

Kathryn didn't answer, just stared at the rug beneath her feet.

"I have a barbecue to go to tomorrow afternoon," Nick said. "But I'm around at night if you want to swing by."

"I shouldn't." Kathryn turned back to him. "Last night, a friend's daughter called me. She's having trouble with her mom, so she's staying with me for a while."

Nick's eyes lifted, giving her his full attention. "Who is this friend?"

Kathryn stifled a groan. In his time in town, Nick had learned the who's who of Delray Beach, was privy to the darker sides of everyone's personal lives. "Harper Silva."

Nick's brows arched. "Damn, Kat. I didn't know you cozied up to the Palm Beach *elite*."

"Yes, well . . ." Kathryn didn't take the bait, didn't elaborate. "I hope Emmy's less of a hellion than my foulmouthed son. If I have two of those in my house, it might kill me." She sighed. "Anyway, I should stick around in case she needs me. And I'm going to take the longest bubble bath of my whole goddamn life."

The corner of Nick's fingernail was now raw, a red drop of blood pooling on his skin. "Why would you let a random kid stay at your house?"

"Stop that." Kathryn reached out, grabbed Nick's hand, stopped the incessant picking. He met her eyes. "Emmy's not a random kid. Harper's . . . well, ultimately, she's the reason I kept Max from Andrew."

CHAPTER FIVE

Sunday, March 26
Andrew

When Andrew returned from his run Sunday morning, Amy was haul-ing bags from three different gourmet grocery stores into the kitchen. He'd awoken to an empty house, a Post-it scribbled with one word beside the coffee maker: *shopping*.

"You slept late," Amy said as Andrew lifted a case of wine from the hatch of her Volvo.

Over the two nights since his encounter with Kathryn, Andrew's mind had spiraled between restless fits of intermittent sleep. Why wasn't Nick returning his calls? He'd dialed Nick the moment Kathryn had walked away and unloaded the story as he rushed back to his office, sweating through his suit jacket, but hadn't heard from Nick since that conversation. They usually spoke every day.

Andrew tossed on the mattress as Kathryn's words echoed in his mind along with flashes of her face, and the boy's, the image on her phone screen. He'd finally drifted off, the lines of dreams and lucidity blurred, and he'd woken disoriented, the blankets in a knot at his feet.

"Nightmares." Andrew leaned against the countertop as his coffee brewed and Amy unpacked her grocery haul. When she didn't respond, he asked, "How can I help?"

Amy held a mesh bag of potatoes aloft. "I got everything you need to make your potato salad." A smile parted her lips. A truce.

Relief sparked within him. "You got it, little lady," he drawled in a South Carolina accent. "It's not a barbecue without a real southern potato salad."

Amy's smile spread and she shook her head, and in a practiced movement, Andrew pulled her to his chest, and Amy wound her arms around him, pressing her forehead into his shirt with a sigh. This was his Amy. This was *them*. The them they'd built.

He'd met Amy in the dark. It was a Friday morning, and just as he'd stepped into the office of a car rental shop to return the minivan he'd been issued while his car was being serviced, the lights flickered; then the room fell into darkness. Beyond the window, the traffic signals and storefronts were lifeless, lending an apocalyptic feel to the world. Frazzled employees scrambled behind the counter.

Andrew caught the panic on the face of the woman in line before him. "Blackout," he declared. "Happens a lot."

It seemed fated in the ease of it. Andrew introduced himself, if anything, to distract the woman, to soothe her nerves. Amy slipped a warm palm into his hand. She was in town to view apartments, he learned. New job.

"The power should come on any minute," he assured her.

But when the darkness held steady and the room grew stifling, Andrew shifted. "I could show you around town?" He braced for rejection.

"Are you a serial killer?" she'd asked. "I like *Dateline*, but I don't want to be on it."

A shared laugh. The spark of something more. Of promise.

Andrew cherished the flashes of that weekend. Amy was stiff in the passenger seat as he drove her to her showings. Then she'd unwound as the day wore on, as he zipped over the bridges that arched the waterways, an exaggerated tour of Palm Beach. She'd leaned over the console to kiss him the following night after a seafood dinner on the water.

On Sunday evening, before Amy caught a red-eye back to California, Andrew brought her to the beach, the sunset catching the puffy clouds, glowing pink and lilac. "I signed the lease for the apartment on Rosemary," she said. "Is it okay if I call you in two weeks when I get here?"

He reached out, found her hand. "Can you call me when you land tomorrow?"

Amy had found him in the dark, but he fell under her spell in the light. On a Saturday afternoon one month later, after Amy had settled from her move, they'd wandered the butterfly aviary, sun beaming down in columns, warming the earthy air. Andrew had watched her take the stepstones, her sleek black hair brushing her shoulders. She weaved between the lush ferns and bromeliads, careful not to disturb the vegetation. Andrew knew, watching butterflies dance around her hair, he'd always be inferior to her. But instead of feeling a shred of insecurity, this fact made his heart swell with pride. Amy was a natural leader, had to be in her line of work, and he was content to follow her not just down those stepstones, but into a life he could be proud of. Something stable. Solid. Something he once thought he'd never have.

He vowed to himself that if he allowed their love to bloom, he'd give this woman a life she deserved. Those dark things he'd locked away would never come to light.

That was what their partnership was: Solid. Practical. Before he'd cracked the box on that two-carat ring and asked her to merge her life with his, they'd had the necessary discussions, checked the boxes: money, religion, politics. Check, check, check. And children. Adoption, Andrew had said. He'd told her of his panic attacks. That he was prone to anxiety. Depression. He took medication for both. Family history, he explained.

Amy's forehead had pinched, but she considered, then a simple word: "Okay."

A surge of relief. He could give her everything. And he could protect himself, too.

Until a year ago, when Amy had gotten the news her mother's breast cancer had metastasized. One morning at breakfast, she'd lifted her espresso. "I'd like to try naturally." It wasn't a question. She'd made up her mind.

"Amy, we talked about this."

"Andrew." Her deep eyes met his. "There are things in my family history, too: doctorates. We both have strong, loving families. A predisposition for depression is something to keep an eye on. I'm a physician, leave that up to me." Her lips lifted into a smile, and she found his fingers on the table, squeezed. "We have so much love to offer."

He'd promised to give her the life she dreamed of. So he'd conceded. But with each passing month she failed to conceive, he harbored a relief he couldn't share with his wife. Amy's frustration bloomed until the blowup that Friday morning.

In the kitchen, Andrew cupped her head and pressed his lips to her crown. He hadn't realized how much he missed this until he didn't have it. "I'm so sorry, sweetheart," he said.

"I am, too." Amy's voice was muffled by his shirt. She took a step back, her eyes glassy. "I'm sorry I lost my cool."

He tipped her chin upward. "I never want to fight with you again."

Amy nodded and stood on tiptoe to bring her lips to his. He drew her in, her familiar softness, her delicate, soapy scent. In the very place they'd fought, they came together, and Andrew felt the balance between them restored. It was as if he'd woken from a deep sleep, refreshed. The fight was a fluke, a smudge on their otherwise impeccable slate.

"Dr. Cassidy will help us tomorrow," Amy said, turning to the counter. "We'll have good news soon."

I have a son. And she doesn't know. The thought boomed so loudly he was surprised Amy couldn't hear it. And it was on the tip of his lips; he could tell her, rip open the wound, get it over with. But that electricity awoke in his fingertips. He couldn't tell Amy about Max without telling her about Kathryn. Without telling her everything. She wouldn't want this life with him if she knew.

Andrew snatched the bag of potatoes from the counter and wrangled his focus, tapped into the most deep-seated of southern coping mechanisms: masking guilt with rich food.

They fell into familiar choreography; Andrew knew his way around the kitchen, but he was happy when Amy took charge, delegating tasks the way he imagined she did in the operating room, with total control. As she mixed a marinade, Amy chatted about work, as if she was in a rush to share all the events she'd withheld from him after their fight all at once.

It was exactly two o'clock when the first guests arrived. Andrew had just stepped out of the shower and was buttoning his shirt in the dim bedroom when voices floated from downstairs.

Fuck. It was a barbecue, not court. Couldn't people be fashionably late?

He straightened, softened his jaw, relished the final moments of his solitude before he prepared to play the part of the perfect husband Amy deserved. Downstairs, his boss, Larry, boomed a greeting. Dread swept over Andrew and he cringed; he hadn't faced Larry since their formal conversation on Friday morning, when Andrew had stoically rejected the promotion. He drew one more breath, then jogged down the staircase. Amy's delicate hand rested on the front door as she welcomed Larry and his wife inside. Behind Larry, Phil and his wife—Andrew had forgotten her name—called a greeting. Then the hallway was bursting with bodies, bottles of wine and sealed plastic containers swapping hands, cheek kisses, and chatter. Andrew watched two more cars turn into the driveway. That itch in his palms. Heat rising in his neck.

"Hey." Amy met his eyes. "Look at me. Are you okay?"

The group moved deeper into the house, away from them, and Andrew's system settled.

Andrew reached out and set a hand on her arm, craving her skin against his once again. "Yeah, I'm good." She glowed in a strapless lavender sundress. "Honey—you look beautiful." Amy's cheeks warmed a rosy tint, her lips lifting into a smile.

Ten minutes later the men stood on the deck, clutching cold beers, swapping competitive small talk, sweating in their linen shirts. Amy guided the wives on a tour of the house while Andrew busied himself with prepping the grill. On a trip into the kitchen, Andrew filled a highball with iced tea, then collected a foil-covered plate of kabobs from their massive Sub-Zero.

The gaggle of wives trailed Amy up the hallway. Lilly Pulitzer sundresses and glossy nails, heels tapping the tile, their veneer-smiled compliments laced with envy.

Andrew stepped onto the deck, into the sticky heat, where Larry intercepted him. A knot braided in Andrew's stomach. "This house is really something, Andrew. And the view, damn."

Andrew squinted from behind his sunglasses at the layers of crystal-blue water glittering between the palm fronds. He tipped his glass. "Thanks."

Larry's stance was wide. "I can't lie, I was shocked when you turned down the offer. Shocked doesn't do it justice. Since you walked in all those years ago, bright eyed and bushy tailed, you've been laser focused on this position. I didn't picture anyone else taking my place. I don't have a plan B."

Andrew felt his smile harden. "Yeah, well, like I said, Amy and I discussed it at length, but with her working nights the travel wouldn't be feasible."

"I get it, man." Larry clapped a hand on Andrew's shoulder. "You're married to South Florida's hottest trauma surgeon."

Andrew forced a smile. "That I am."

"When kids come along, priorities change, but they'll be worth the sacrifice," Larry said. "Well, mostly." He motioned to his dome of a head, shining in the sunlight. "Some men would kill for the chance to let the missus rake in the cash while they play Mr. Mom."

Andrew was about to tell Larry he didn't *let* Amy work, but the patio door glided open, and Nick stepped outside, the gel in his hair glistening. Andrew excused himself from Larry, the knot in his stomach twisting. Since the moment Nick's name had appeared on Kathryn's lips, questions had mounted in Andrew's mind, blooming into suspicions during those nearly sleepless nights.

Amy had given Nick a beer, and he greeted the men on the back porch. They'd met; Nick popped into Andrew's office for lunch at least once a month, but the Tommy Bahama–clad men offered Nick aggressive handshakes.

"I didn't do anything, Officer, I swear." A voice sailed over the yard, and the men bellowed.

Nick ambled away. "Your friends are fun, as always," he said as he approached Andrew, brows knitted.

"I know." Andrew gestured to the small crowd gathered on his deck. "The only break I get from these guys is on the weekend." He peeled the foil away from the tray. "Nice of you to return my calls yesterday."

Nick tipped his beer to his lips, the glass beaded with condensation. "I had company."

The kabobs sizzled as Andrew laid them across the grill, and the smell of onion rose in the air. "Whatever. We need to talk." Nick's mouth hardened, and Andrew set his foot on a stone that wound down an uncertain path, one he'd been avoiding for twenty years. He drizzled marinade over the meat, making it sizzle. "Kathryn asked if I knew, if you'd told me." He gave Nick the space to explain Kathryn's question. She'd seemed so certain Nick had broken the news about Max. When Nick didn't respond, Andrew's suspicion ticked up a degree. "She knew where I worked." Andrew held his tone steady.

And there it was, revealed in a subtle nod of admission from Nick. "I ran into her a little while after I moved into town."

Andrew's stomach dropped.

"You knew." When the words left his mouth, it was as if he had no more breath in him. Andrew leaned forward. "You knew I had a kid, and you didn't tell me?"

Nick folded his arms across his chest. "Kat made me promise I wouldn't."

Kat. Andrew hadn't thought of her that way in years. "Do you talk to her? Like, regularly?"

"Here and there."

Nick's admissions crashed over Andrew. "And—you told her I was moving to Delray?"

Nick nodded again. "Yeah."

Amy stepped onto the porch and looked in their direction. Andrew's throat constricted, but one of the wives touched Amy's arm and pulled her into conversation. His heart thudded, and he leaned closer to Nick, decades-old suspicions nudging their way to the surface. "You promised her, but what about me? You didn't think to warn me we'd all be living in the same town?"

The day Andrew had told Nick their offer on the house had been accepted, the phone line had gone flat. Andrew blamed a spotty connection, a dead zone, maybe, but now that silence rang in his ears.

"She made me swear I wouldn't say anything. She wanted to be the one to tell you." Beads of sweat formed at his temples.

Nick had always kept certain parts of himself private. Andrew knew in a sort of process of elimination that there were large parts of Nick's life he never talked about. Andrew had learned of relationships Nick had had well after they'd ended. He took long international vacations, often alone, and returned in a pensive mood that lasted for weeks. Andrew chalked it up to the fact that Nick valued his privacy.

Andrew leaned closer. "I would think your relationship with your best friend would take precedence over . . . whatever Kathryn has on you."

Nick might value his privacy, but after two decades of friendship, Andrew was familiar with Nick's short fuse, recognized in the narrowing of his brows that his limit was near.

"Listen," Nick said. "I'm going to tell you the same thing I told Kat: I'm not going to get in the middle of this. Do I need to remind you what happened the last time you went down this road?" Andrew held Nick's gaze, waiting for his friend to drag up the ugly silt they'd let settle at the bottom of their relationship. "When you got serious with Amy, I told you to tell her everything. I told you keeping things from the woman you were planning to propose to would blow up in your face."

"It's a little late now, don't you think?" Andrew snapped, shutting the grill with a bang.

Nick responded with steely silence.

"Fuck, Nick, the timing literally couldn't be worse. We just moved, Amy started a new job, she's waited months to get an appointment with this doctor. And her mom is sick. This is just . . . the timing sucks." Andrew had nothing left with which to finish the sentence but a thousand different nightmares rolled into one.

Andrew looked at his wife, the afternoon sun warming her face. When Amy had come into his life, she'd filled it with promise and light at a point when he never thought they could exist in his universe again. When she made a decision, she never deviated from the path, while Andrew had been white-knuckling his life, trying to stay the course. Amy was meticulous, from the way she tucked the corners of the bed, to the way she filled his space with a softness it seemed she reserved for him, to the way she wiped the porcelain basin dry after she used the sink. Even the way she loved him was precise.

Andrew's relationship with Kathryn had been passionate and intense. Amy was sunshine, was the fresh air after a storm had cleared, when the world felt clean with renewed promise. She was safety. He was so close to giving her the life he'd promised, the life he'd promised himself. So close.

"You're not going to tell Amy, are you?" Nick didn't bother to hide his surprise, or his judgment.

Andrew shook his head. "Maybe. But not yet. We just had a huge fight, and for the first time, it made me question us."

Nick frowned. "If you're looking for my advice—"

"I'm not—"

"Tell Amy about the kid and let it go. You have everything you could ever want." He gestured around them. "Get it out in the open and move on. And stay far away from Kathryn Moretti."

Andrew rounded on Nick. "Stay away from her, like you did?"

"We went out for a few drinks. It's not the same."

A few drinks. Andrew's chest pulled when he imagined Nick and Kathryn together, sharing his secrets, discussing his son without his knowledge. Andrew hadn't expected Nick to defend Kathryn, and unwelcome jealousy surged. "And Max? Have you met him?"

Nick's eyes flicked up, and Andrew knew the answer in an instant. The envy he felt when he imagined Nick meeting the son he didn't know took him by surprise. A rush of questions vied to escape his lips. How did they meet? Did they talk about him? He wasn't sure he wanted to know.

Biological. Kathryn had used the word, which invoked images of test tubes and medical settings, of control. But he had no control over this situation. Kathryn had stolen it from him. A long minute stretched before Andrew spoke. "Tell me about him. Is he . . . okay?"

Nick's jaw tensed. He shrugged, the way he often did. "He's a trust fund baby. Spoiled, does whatever the hell he wants. Kat lets him get away with murder."

Max sounded like a teenager. Not far off from the way Andrew had spent his youth. And something sprouted in him. If Max was fine, a normal kid, maybe his fears about any children he and Amy may have had no footing. The thought soothed him, a lifetime's worth of concern melting away.

"Tell me about Kathryn."

Nick's eyes again flicked to Andrew's face, and he shook his head. "I don't want to get involved in this."

"I don't know anything about her. Please."

An exasperated sigh from Nick. "What is it you feel like you need to know?"

"What's she like? What's her life been like since . . . ?"

A sigh of surrender from Nick. "Listen, don't tell Kathryn I said any of this."

A flicker of hope. Andrew would agree to anything if Nick would give him any bit of information. And tell Kathryn? The idea of speaking to Kathryn again sparked something inside him, deep, primal. Terrifying. Thrilling.

Nick's fingers were white as he clutched his beer. "She lives over on Cherry Street. Made partner at her firm a few years ago."

"Is she married?"

Nick paused. "No. There was someone a while back—a long time ago—but that's over now."

"Is that why she left me, for him?"

Nick's shrug was slight, dismissive. "I don't know."

But Nick's words had flared something else to life. Something dormant. He needed answers from Kathryn. He had to know what she'd been hiding from him that morning she'd disappeared, and everything that had happened in the days between the last time he saw her and that moment. It was all he'd wanted for twenty years.

CHAPTER SIX

Sunday, March 26
Kathryn

The clock that hung on the burnt-orange wall at Deja Brew had the word *coffee* scribbled in lieu of each of the twelve hours, the kind of intentional whimsy that made Kathryn's caffeine headache rap harder at her temples. She'd pushed herself at the gym, tried to run off her stress, tacked on two extra miles on the treadmill. Now her legs were rubbery, and she needed at least half a latte under her belt before she had to face Harper.

"Regina!" the barista shouted and set a cup on the bar. "Nonfat latte, one pump of sugar-free hazelnut."

Kathryn shut her eyes. It couldn't possibly be the same Regina—

"Oh, hi, Kathryn." That voice. That tone, like a flat Diet Coke.

Kathryn opened her eyes to her neighbor Regina Wilson in her tennis whites, collecting her latte. "Regina. It's been a while."

Regina's eyes panned to the crowd, like she wanted to run, then thought better of it and looked back to Kathryn. "I heard about Max's little mishap." She twisted a strand of her hair around her finger. "Is he okay?"

Great. Now the whole town knew about Max's accident. Kathryn bristled. "He's fine, thankfully."

"Good to hear," Regina offered with a veneered smile.

Regina had put the money she'd been awarded in her divorce to good use, Kathryn noted, in the ample breast implants bursting from her tank top, the key fob that dangled from her hand to the pristine Mercedes that Kathryn saw gliding from Regina's driveway.

"On the bright side, he got to replace that clunker he'd been driving."

Kathryn had selected the red Audi for herself, fully loaded, and had driven it for two years before she'd upgraded and gifted the car to Max on his sixteenth birthday. It was hardly a clunker. She could feel her mouth turn into a frown before she had a mind to stop it.

"Anyway, it's been fantastic chatting with you." Regina glanced at her Rolex, her slim, tanned legs already aimed at the exit. "But I've got tennis in ten, gotta run—"

"Regina, wait." Kathryn's swallow was dry when Regina turned around. "Maybe I'm being paranoid here, but ever since your divorce, I can't help but think you've been avoiding me."

"Well." Regina lifted her chin, her voice clipped. "I saw you and Dan together at the Rosses' barbecue."

"Excuse me?" Kathryn's mind spun. Two years earlier, when an invitation to a Saturday-afternoon "luau" had been deposited in her mailbox, Kathryn had reflexively tossed it in the recycle bin, but the hibiscus-print card had snagged something in her. She'd lived in the neighborhood for twelve years without socializing with her neighbors. So she'd tugged on a sundress and crossed the street with a Tupperware of broccoli salad in hand and a scowling Max at her side. She'd planned to down a mai tai, exchange pleasantries, alleviate a decade's worth of neighborly guilt, then retreat to her bedroom and her sweatpants before *Law & Order* began. Three drinks later, the sun had dipped behind the horizon, and with a cheap plastic lei scratching the nape of her neck, Kathryn had made her rounds, chatting with her neighbors. Now, in the coffee shop that morning, bathed in Regina's accusatory glare, Kathryn searched her memory for Dan Wilson, until all that remained was Dan's face in the flickering light of a tiki torch. They'd talked for a while, though Kathryn couldn't recall anything more, and certainly didn't remember Regina watching them, her mind churning with suspicion. "Regina, I had nothing to do with Dan."

"Oh please. He was sleeping with half the neighborhood. I saw the way you looked at him, and everyone knows your reputation."

Reputation. The word jangled in Kathryn's mind in time with the bell above the coffee shop door, leaving bitterness in her mouth. When men dated without forming attachments, they weren't vilified, but she always would be. For Kathryn, attachments weren't an option.

"Karen!" the barista called. "Iced vanilla latte." He handed Kathryn her cup, *Karen* scrawled on the side. Kathryn scowled. This wasn't the first time this had happened.

When she looked up, Regina Wilson was gone.

The bell above the door chimed once more, and Harper stepped into the crowd, her jaw tensing when she laid eyes on Kathryn. So much for properly caffeinating. Kathryn waved Harper to a table at the back of the café.

"Thank you for meeting me." Harper's voice was stiff as she settled across from Kathryn, her hair pulled into what looked like a painfully tight ponytail. Despite the priceless jewelry on Harper's thin fingers and her flawless silk blouse, she looked fragile. Between Andrew and Emmy, the dam had burst, and the ghosts of her past now paraded through her life. It was more than she could handle. Kathryn stabbed a straw into her drink and jostled the ice. The first sip was cool, creamy, a balm on the sting of reality and Regina's accusations, and she let the heavenly liquid soothe her for a moment before she spoke. "What's going on with Emmy, Harper?"

Harper shook her head. "I don't know. I don't think she's happy living with us, with my mother."

"You think?" Kathryn hadn't thought to reel in her sarcasm until after the words passed her lips.

A small sigh escaped Harper. "She just . . . she pushes me away. I don't know what to do."

It had been only two days, and Emmy had spent hours in her bedroom, the TV blaring, surviving on turkey sandwiches and cereal, but maybe she was uncomfortable in a strange place. Still, the previous evening, when Kathryn had knocked on Emmy's door and asked her to bring her hamper to the laundry room by morning, Emmy had complied, deposited her wicker basket of dainty pastels and florals in front of the washer. A text to Max with the same request had gone unanswered. Why was Emmy so amenable, and why did Max leverage any available opportunity to give Kathryn gray hair?

"She's a teenager, Harper. But she seems like a good kid. Well adjusted, given everything." Harper's brows lifted. Kathryn took another long sip of her latte, caffeine working its magic to alleviate her headache. "She's way easier than Max, that I can tell you. Are you interested in a trade?"

Kathryn thought Harper's lips might twitch into a smile, but instead Harper frowned. "It's just like you and Luke planned. She ended up with you."

A barb. Fourteen years later and just as sharp. Kathryn swallowed, this time her throat tight. Between Regina and Harper, and seeing Andrew in person (she'd given him her number; *Would he call, would he not?*), her rope snapped. "Nobody planned anything that happened, Harper."

Harper's eyes locked on to Kathryn's. "Luke asked you to look after her. I know he did. And he paid you for it, too."

Kathryn steadied herself. When she'd spoken to Emmy, the girl's eyes had hit Kathryn like a slap—two different colors, one brown, one lighter, with a cluster of gold. Like Max, Emmy had her father's eyes, a sight that proved to be far more haunting than Kathryn had anticipated. "We've been through this." A flash of a memory. Broken glass glinting on the floor. "That's not true."

Harper's lips trembled, and her eyes misted. Kathryn gripped her cup, silently begging her not to cry. Kathryn huffed a sigh. "Harp, let me talk to Emmy. I'll see what I can do."

To Kathryn's relief, Harper accepted Kathryn's twig of an olive branch and gathered herself with a small nod. Over the two nights that had passed since her encounter with Andrew, the hours stretched by insomnia, Kathryn had ached for a girlfriend to confide in. She and Harper were here, seated across from each other, a stone wall between them. In another life maybe they could have ridden the tides of life united. Instead of years of silence between them. Of suspicions. "Andrew is back," Kathryn blurted.

Harper's eyes rounded.

"I mean, I saw him. Face-to-face. He moved to Delray."

"Did you tell him?" Harper's words came out in a whisper.

Kathryn nodded. "I told him about Max."

"Kat . . ." That one syllable and Kathryn was snapped back in time. They were eighteen, she and Harper whispering about their crushes. The first time Harper had mentioned Lucas, Kathryn could see in her friend's eyes that this boy was different. This was the one who would change everything.

But this wasn't that Harper. This Harper had sad eyes, crinkles at the corners, frown lines around her lips. She sat back, eyed Kathryn with apprehension. "Don't do it to him, Kathryn," Harper warned. "Not again."

◆ ◆ ◆

Emmy

The afternoon sun glittered off the surface of the pool as Emmy spread her pink-and-white-striped towel onto a lounger. She wrestled her ringlets into a topknot, popped a piece of strawberry bubble gum in her mouth, and settled onto a lounge chair. With the palm leaves swaying above her against a cloudless sky, and beams of sun cutting across the yard, she peeled her book open and relaxed her shoulders. Emmy sailed through one chapter, then the next, the pages sticking to her sweaty fingers.

The rattle of the patio door snapped her attention from the story. Max stepped onto the deck, a towel slung over his shoulder. "Morning."

Emmy tapped her phone. "It's twelve thirty."

"Afternoon, then." He tossed his towel onto a chair, then dove into the pool, shattering the surface before he pulled himself onto a blue inflatable raft. He brushed his hair from his face, settled on his back, and shut his eyes. From behind her sunglasses, Emmy watched droplets run down his lean, toned torso, noting the way his skin was a few shades lighter around the waistband of his shorts. Something stirred inside her. A memory of his invasive eyes boring into hers in the hallway the day before. It was hard to reconcile this Max with the boy she'd known, who, like most things in her childhood, she recalled in idea more than practice, a vague recollection of warmth toward him.

After overhearing Max's argument with Kathryn, Emmy hadn't seen him for the rest of the day. She'd waited for the house to fall silent before tiptoeing into the (thankfully) deserted kitchen. Kathryn's house was the opposite of Emmy's grandmother's; it was welcoming, smelled of coffee and dish soap, the open-concept first floor light and airy, all hardwood floors bathed with sunlight that spilled in from the southern-facing windows. The coffeepot was full, and she'd gratefully filled a mug, poured a bowl of cereal, and then returned to the guest room, where she'd burrowed under her duvet and spent the remainder of the day watching trashy dating shows. She tried not to look at her phone, but when she did, the blank screen screamed her mother's rejection, and Emmy stuffed it beneath her pillow.

In the evening, Kathryn had knocked on her door to say she'd be going out for a few hours, and to ask Emmy for her laundry. "There's sandwich stuff in the fridge," Kathryn had said apologetically. She was intimidatingly pretty, even without makeup, though shadowy purple half circles smudged beneath her eyes. "I'm sorry, I'm not much of a cook. Max is better at it, but only when the mood strikes him." Kathryn nudged a shoulder toward Max's closed bedroom door. "I'll bring home a rotisserie chicken tomorrow when I go shopping; that's kind of our Sunday ritual." Kathryn gave Emmy a weak smile. "Is there anything you need?"

"I'm okay, thank you," Emmy said. She and Harper had never had a Sunday ritual, or anything close to it.

Aside from their brief conversation, Emmy hadn't spoken to Kathryn for the remainder of Saturday. Apparently it was a house of closed doors; everyone stayed in their space and interacted only occasionally, which suited Emmy.

At the pool Emmy narrowed her focus onto her book. She'd been engrossed in—okay, obsessed with—the first three books in the series since January, enough to distract herself from life at her grandmother's house, but now she found herself skimming the same line again and again.

Eventually, Max sat up, slipped off the raft, and swam to the edge of the pool. "How's your book?"

"Ugh, amazing." Emmy let a dreamy sigh drain from her. She'd fallen hard for the male protagonist. Max's eyes matched the color of the pool water. She snapped her gum; she had no intention of letting him know she hadn't read a word since he'd come outside.

Max rested his tanned arms on the edge of the deck. "Let me guess: innocent girl meets bad boy, boy acts like he isn't interested and treats her like shit, but she falls for him anyway, and he goes all soft and they live happily ever after?"

Emmy considered the cover of her novel, a silhouette of a boy and a girl, their lips a few centimeters apart, and frowned. "There's more to it than that."

Max rolled his eyes. "Please. It's a predictable formula, always a happy ending."

"You're not a fan of happy endings?"

"Life rarely—if ever—results in a happy ending."

"So cynical," Emmy teased. "Sometimes love wins, Max."

Max scowled but didn't retort. "Aren't you hot just roasting there in the sun?"

Beads of sweat rolled down her skin. She set her book down and rose. She felt Max's eyes follow her as she walked to the steps, then dipped one toe into the water. The chill was shocking, but Emmy found her footing and lowered her body in. It was cool and refreshing. She approached Max, noting his widening grin. "Is this what you do all day, sleep until noon and then work on your tan?"

Max stirred the water around him. "Sometimes."

"Do you have a job? Go to school?"

"No." He dipped under the water, surfacing an arm's length away. "So did you have it out with the infamous Harper?"

"Something like that." Emmy tried to curb the venom in her tone.

Max seemed to know better than to push the subject. Instead, he said, "You look different."

Again, the image of his face glowing under an intense flash of fireworks. "Well, the last time I saw you I was thirteen, at my mom and Joshua's wedding. Believe it or not, you look different, too."

Max smiled like he possessed a secret. He still had a boyish face, but he was calm and confident, not forceful, loud, and awkward like the boys Emmy went to school with.

"I didn't realize you were still living at home when I asked Kathryn if I could stay here." She didn't want to bring up the moment Max had caught her eavesdropping in the hallway, but maybe acknowledging it was a tiny shred of an apology. "I hope I won't be in your way. Or Kathryn's."

Max smirked. "Aside from the fact that you've already covered every surface of my bathroom with your girly things, I don't think it'll be a problem."

It was Emmy's turn to roll her eyes. She'd charged her electric toothbrush and left her face wash, a bottle of petal-pink nail polish, and a handful of hair ties on the shelf above the sink. Her things hardly covered "every surface."

"You go to Saint James, right?" Max asked.

Emmy nodded. "For a few more weeks." She realized she might have to share the house with Max in the afternoons, and it might be awkward. Sure, her solitude stung at times, but it also came with privacy. "You graduated last year?"

Max nodded and ran a hand through his hair. "From Delray High. You don't have a car; how are you going to get to school?"

"My grandmother confiscated my keys when I left. My mom didn't try to stop her." That familiar spike of rejection. Harper didn't care whether she had transportation, whether she had a way to drive herself back to the house if she wanted to. Which she didn't. "Kathryn said she'd drop me off in the mornings."

"And you're going to walk home?"

"I guess." Emmy shrugged. "It's only like a half mile."

"It's almost summer; it's hot as fuck." Max wiped water from his face. "I'll pick you up. Just don't say anything to my mom."

Emmy hadn't anticipated his offer and took a beat to consider it. She didn't know how to say no. She didn't want to say no, though the thought of even a short car ride with him made her jittery. But why didn't he want Kathryn to know? What was their deal?

Max seemed the opposite of jittery, and with the matter settled, he dipped into the water once again and surfaced, wiping his face once more before he made his way up the steps and wrapped his towel around his waist. "I'll see you later," he called as he left wet footprints on the deck.

After he disappeared inside, the lapping of the pool stilled, leaving Emmy feeling . . . alone. She'd spent so much of her life on her own, but this was different, like when Max had left her in the hallway, like she wasn't ready for him to walk away.

Emmy climbed from the pool and wrapped her towel around herself before she gathered her things and opened the patio door, stepping into the kitchen. Kathryn stood at the counter, tipping the coffee carafe into a Deja Brew cup, and she looked up. "Hello, sweetheart."

"Hi, Kathryn." Emmy watched Kathryn reach into the cabinet above the stove for a small pill bottle. On the top shelf, a white coffee mug caught Emmy's eye, tucked between rows of spices. A smiling yellow sun peeked back at her from its lacquered surface, summoning a whisper of recognition she couldn't place. Kathryn tapped two blue ibuprofen tablets into her palm, then returned the bottle to its shelf and closed the cabinet. She downed the caplets with a swig of her coffee, then turned to Emmy, leaning against the counter. "Is your room comfortable?"

"It's fine, thank you. And thank you for letting me come stay." Emmy took a good look at Kathryn in the long rectangle of honest light that fell through the patio door. She wore black leggings and a workout top, her hair pulled into a high ponytail. Like Max, Kathryn was tall, but aside from her height, she hardly looked like Max's mother. Her olive complexion was darker than her son's, and he hadn't inherited any of her features. She still looked tired, maybe more so than the previous day.

"I had coffee with your mom this morning," Kathryn said.

Emmy clutched her book to her chest and thought of her phone. Blank. Not a word from her mother. Had Harper asked for her?

"You probably don't remember when I lived with your family." Kathryn shifted from one foot to the other. "But I know what a bitch your grandmother is." Emmy was struck by the brashness of the word, and the way Kathryn used it so casually. "And your mom—" Kathryn caught herself and paused. For a moment, she looked like she was thinking more than she said aloud. "I'm just surprised you didn't want out of that house sooner. Your dad told me you'd call, so I've been expecting it for years."

Emmy drew a tiny breath. For a moment the only sound in the kitchen was the far-off thump of the dryer. Kathryn was right: her grandmother was a bitch, and Harper was too weak to stand up to her. The fact that Kathryn knew this once again reminded Emmy there was a vast expanse of time when their lives had crossed that she was too young to remember.

Emmy's father was a forbidden subject in her family. Kathryn was right, Emmy had no tangible memories of Kathryn and Max living with her family. Emmy recalled her father's house as a vast castle of secret hiding places. Flashes of slivered memories—curtains rippling in the sea air, wicker furniture beneath her legs, blueberry pancakes on a griddle—were recalled in a dreamy haze, but it was impossible to distinguish which of her memories were real and what her imagination had created. Kathryn might be able to paint a clear picture, to explain how they'd all turned into the people they had, to explain why Harper was a shell of a person, why she seemed to fear loving her daughter. But Emmy wasn't sure how to approach the subject.

"So," Kathryn said, "stay here as long as you'd like."

"Twelve weeks." Emmy felt her cheeks flush. "Sorry, that's oddly specific—I'm moving to Seattle the second week of June. On my birthday. I got into UW."

Kathryn's eyes broke away, like Emmy had touched a nerve. Again, she seemed lost in her thoughts for a moment. Then, as if shaking off a trance: "That's incredible, Emmy. Congratulations." Her voice was heady, genuine, and Emmy absorbed the recognition. It was sweeter than her classmates' brand-new BMWs. If only it had come from Harper. Kathryn took a few steps closer. "You stay here as long as you'd like, but please reach out to your mom."

Emmy bristled. Harper had time for coffee but couldn't text her daughter? "I'll think about it."

Kathryn's eyes narrowed. "I saw you and Max outside." Emmy's pulse ticked. Kathryn's green eyes, her energy—her entire presence—was intense and electric, sending a tingle of nerves up Emmy's arms. "He was in some trouble recently, and we're working through it. If he's not friendly, don't take it personally. He needs to work on his attitude." Kathryn tilted her head. "Do you understand?"

Emmy did not, but she nodded. With a tight smile, Kathryn turned and left the room, leaving Emmy's mind to spin with her words, to flash with Max's bright smile in the pool.

Emmy was used to her family's particular brand of icy distance. When she'd come to Kathryn's house, she'd braced herself for boredom in an unfamiliar environment, for a long gray period before she'd finally leap and begin her own life. But she'd stepped into the middle of something between Kathryn and Max. And Max certainly wasn't unfriendly to her. Now Emmy saw color creep into her existence. Maybe living with the Morettis would prove to be more interesting than she'd expected.

CHAPTER SEVEN

Monday, March 27
Amy

Dr. Evelyn Cassidy's office was more impressive in person than on its sleek website. In the waiting room, Amy leafed through a magazine beside the floor-to-ceiling waterfall while Andrew stared at the far wall, bouncing his knee. It seemed, for a small fortune, the practice fell just short of a guarantee of a pregnancy, evident in the smug smile from the petite blonde seated across from Amy, her phone perched atop the globe of her belly. Amy smiled back, fingering the stitching on the leather armrest. An impostor, noticeably *un*pregnant.

"Relax, honey," Andrew murmured, setting a hand atop hers. His hand was everything Andrew was: strong, yet tender. Warm. Supportive, nearly to a fault. She squeezed back, relieved by his capacity for forgiveness. Every marriage has its challenges, she knew. And theirs had been so smooth until that fight, aside from Andrew's vague aversion to parenthood. That was all this was, a blip. She'd make sure it didn't happen again.

Amy's residual guilt over their fight sat, unsettled, in her belly. She hadn't expected Andrew to take it so hard. The argument felt disingenuous; they weren't *those* kinds of people. Andrew's expression, the primal fear in his eyes, was seared into her mind. That morning, his breathing had started coming in short, desperate bursts before blotches rose on his neck; then he'd slumped to the floor. Her brain had switched tracks when she recognized he was having a panic attack, from fuming spouse into physician mode. She knew he'd been prone to them, but his medication seemed to quell his symptoms, and she'd never witnessed an episode. She guided him through his breaths, asked him to identify something he could hear. Something he could see. Something he could taste. Until he grew still.

Then he'd rushed off to work. Andrew came home that night shell-shocked, worse even than when he'd left. He was jumpy, restless, had spent the weekend wounded. Sullen. Embarrassed, maybe. Certainly hurt. On Saturday, the day before their barbecue, Andrew worked in the yard most of the day. Amy had watched him from the windows, considered him, the way his backward baseball hat made him look like a teenager, the way his T-shirt was pulled by the breadth of his shoulders as he stacked stray palm fronds at the end of the driveway. They had landscapers to do the work, so when dusk fell and Andrew came inside, his shirt soaked with sweat, Amy couldn't help but think he'd been avoiding her.

And before their barbecue, Amy had basked in relief at his strong body wrapped around hers.

Dr. Cassidy's nurse guided them to an exam room, where Amy was instructed to change into a flimsy gown. Andrew seated himself in a chair in the corner, clutching her handbag as if he feared someone was going to snatch it. He scrambled to be helpful: accepted her jeans, her top, folded them on his lap, asked if she was warm enough. The white paper crackled when Amy lowered herself onto the exam table, and they fell silent. Andrew's eyes darted around the room, at the diagrams of fetal development, a scale model of female reproductive organs, pamphlets touting fertility drugs. Her gown fell open at the back, letting the chill of the air-conditioning creep across her bare skin. She tugged it over her shoulder. Why did doctors always make patients wait so long? She swung her feet, clad in white socks.

A rap on the door preceded Dr. Cassidy's entrance. "Welcome Amy, Andrew," the doctor crooned. Andrew sat straight, cleared his throat.

Dr. Cassidy instructed Amy to settle on her back. Her palms were sticky when they brushed the paper beneath her. "How long have you been off birth control?" Dr. Cassidy asked.

It was all there, detailed in her chart, but Amy blew a steadying breath. "One year."

In those twelve months, six nurses at Amy's hospital had gotten pregnant. They'd waddled through the halls and chatted together at the nurses' station. They'd thrown six separate baby showers, and while Amy had scraped a pink buttercream flower off a slice of sheet cake, a nagging concern grew inside her. Each month became a roller coaster of hope, disappointment, and simmering resentment at Andrew's inexplicable but palpable relief when her period came. Before either of them had tested out the *I* word that buzzed between them, *infertility*, Andrew had suggested Amy attend a meeting, some type of support group, but she had imagined a circle of teary-eyed women sipping watery coffee from Styrofoam cups, taking turns sharing heartbreaking stories of miscarriages, cancer diagnoses, rare genetic glitches. When it was her turn, she'd say, *I'm Amy. I've never lost a baby. I've just never had one to begin with.* In their expectant eyes they'd see her for the impostor she was. She had resolved to handle it on her own.

Amy tilted her head to catch a glimpse of the monitor above her shoulder, which glowed in tones of red, yellow, and orange. By the looks of the screen, her uterus was on fire. *No wonder nothing can grow in there,* she thought darkly.

Dr. Cassidy's practiced smile spread across her face. "Try to relax."

That word again. It started to grate on her. She should have frozen her eggs when she'd gotten into medical school, she conceded. Her mother had nearly begged her, and though the advice carried the weight of experience, Amy had brushed it aside, as children do. Her parents had emigrated from China when they were young and were now two of the most well-respected doctors in Pasadena, California. Her father was a cardiologist, her mother a dermatologist, and through the eyes of their only child, their union seemed simple and balanced. In their sun-drenched home, Amy had watched her parents rise each day, go through the motions of the morning, don their white coats, peck each other on the lips, and take each day in stride.

As the studious daughter of two doctors, Amy was aware at an early age she was a living stereotype, and she'd openly—almost defiantly—embraced this identity. *How does it all come so easily to you, Amy?* She'd heard the line from her friends and classmates so many times it began to itch under her skin like a rash. But she sat down each day in the library and unpacked her case of highlighters. She made rainbow stacks of sticky notes next to her textbooks. It wasn't easy, any of it; it took preparation and organization. A plan, carefully executed. Small, deliberate steps led her where she needed to go.

She'd imagined her parents' delight when she announced her intention to pursue trauma surgery, but instead, her mother's face had fallen. "You won't have time for a family, Amy." Elena had squeezed Amy's hand across the table. "It's too much stress. You need to choose which is more important to you."

This new challenge had struck a particular nerve in Amy. She'd leaned over her lab table and sutured her grape with precision while her classmates watched with burning envy. Amy had had no desire to prescribe pimple cream all day like her mother did; she'd craved the type of heart-pounding surgery that danced the line between life and death. The fact that she could sway fate, pull a person from the brink of nonexistence, had drawn her in like an addiction. She could help people and raise her family while she did it. Two pillars, balanced and equal.

Dr. Cassidy weaved her gloved fingers together. "I agree with your OB: there are no physical issues preventing you from becoming pregnant." Her tone, meant to sound soothing, was laced with a veil of condescension. "We still have a lot of options at this point—"

Amy propped herself up. "I'd like to start preparations for IVF."

Andrew's chair creaked as he crossed his legs.

Dr. Cassidy's tight expression made it clear she didn't like being interrupted.

"I'm forty. Time isn't in my favor," Amy added.

"I understand you're eager." Dr. Cassidy peeled her gloves off and tossed them in the stainless-steel trash can by the door. "But it's only been a year. You're ovulating normally. There's nothing in either of your test results to indicate you're not able to conceive naturally. I recommend we begin with less invasive steps before we resort to IVF, which is the most aggressive—not to mention the most expensive—option." A small laugh, a chuckle, really, a sound that boiled Amy's patience like lava. The same chuckle of condescension she'd encountered countless times during her education, then her career, unstanched by her own white coat.

When they rolled out of the parking garage into lunch hour gridlock, Amy's anger burst over the dam of her control, and she gripped the steering wheel. "Can you believe the way she completely blew me off, like I'm stupid, like I have no idea what I'm talking about?"

"I know, sweetheart," Andrew soothed. Was he placating her? "But the good news is, there's nothing wrong with either one of us."

That was exactly the problem, the infuriating thing about the entire visit: how *routine* it was. There were no answers. No major breakthrough. There was nothing wrong, nothing to diagnose.

"These things take time—"

"Time is the one thing I don't have, and you know that," Amy snapped. Wind rushed past the windows. "My mom's cancer is stage four."

Andrew's face paled. "I realize that. But her doctors are confident the treatment will buy her months. Years, even. Maybe you should consider pulling back at work. None of this is good for your stress levels."

Amy had been in her position for only three weeks, but the job swept her in like a riptide, and nothing in her experience had sufficiently prepared her for how difficult, how physically and emotionally draining trauma would be. Her previous hospital saw a quarter of the patients Boca General did. Now she hardly had time to breathe. Every shift ran long, sometimes double her scheduled time. The hospital paid no mind to the rhythm of the world outside its walls. When she tried to sleep, racing images of bloody gloves and endless white hallways circled her mind. Amy often reminded herself why she'd taken the job: that she felt needed, that she was making a difference. But her colleagues were right: she never forgot a patient she lost. Each one's name stuck to her like bloodstains on her scrubs. But her job was a part of her, a pillar, as much as motherhood was a pillar, not yet come to fruition. "I'm *not* stepping down. I worked for years to get *this* job at *this* hospital because of the trauma center."

"You worked sixty-hour weeks in your last position," Andrew said. "Now you're required to take on night shifts, too. You're never home. It might be too much. Something has to give." His words buzzed inside the car like an angry beehive.

Amy's mother had found the lump in her breast six months after Amy and Andrew were married. Three doctors in the family and there was nothing any of them could do. Andrew didn't grasp what it meant to create a being that was *hers*, that was *his*, from nothing, as if it were magic. Her grandparents and parents had worked hard to make a country that wasn't their own feel like home, had fought against all odds. Amy had tried to explain how much it meant to her to give her mother a chance to see their dedication embodied in the eyes of a child, carrying little pieces of each of their stories forward. The pressure had doubled with the arrival of Amy's fortieth birthday.

Amy could give her mother *this*. She needed this.

"Tell me what this is all about, Andrew. Tell me why you're so scared to do this with me."

"I'm not scared." But his voice said the opposite. His shoulders sagged. "You know my reservations. And, sweetheart, pregnancy is dangerous. The side effects of IVF—"

"I know all about the side effects of IVF. And pregnancy. I know the risks."

Andrew faced the window, defeated. Amy didn't have to see his expression to know a shadow had passed behind his eyes, the way it did when he retreated inside himself. Sometimes she thought it was his medication that left his words hanging in the air when she needed him to speak his mind. Her world was clinical, her *whys* answered with tests, with evidence. This unanswered *why* itched in her. Why didn't her husband tell her what scared him so badly?

Andrew was everything Amy could've wanted in a partner: he was responsible and kind. Playful smile. Good genes, she'd thought the first time she'd peeled off his shirt, then felt guilty for being superficial. Though she'd never depended on anyone, at six-two Andrew stood a full foot taller than she did, and when she came home from a grueling day, she craved his strong arms around her. Andrew's years of bachelorhood had taught him well, and he dutifully managed domestic tasks without complaint. He cooked meals and loaded and unloaded the dishwasher. He stripped the sheets every Sunday and ran them through the wash. He greeted her each day with a hot meal and a glass of wine.

Amy never saw any fault in her family's lack of physical affection, but Andrew reached out to her at idle moments, stroking her arm while they read in bed or caressing her hair as they watched TV. She craved this, too, as if he were extracting the stress from her body. Andrew's presence was the antidote to the chaos of her job.

But as her frustration with their situation bloomed, Andrew's calm demeanor had started to grate on her. He took each day in stride. He ran each morning. He wiped water spots from glasses before putting them away and polished the marble countertops. Was she being unreasonable for not entertaining his desire to pursue adoption? All she wanted was what came so easily to others: the choice.

"Can we just take a break from all this?" Andrew asked. "A breather? A month or two until we settle in the new house, and into your job?"

She wanted to snap at him. But a seeping thought crept into Amy's mind: What if her mother and Andrew were right—she wasn't tough enough for the job, and the stress was affecting her body in ways she couldn't control, while driving her husband away? It was the first time she'd ever doubted herself. Could she sustain the career she'd chosen, nurture her marriage and be a good mother, or even be a mother at all? "I'll think about it."

Relief painted his face. Amy pulled over to the curb in front of Andrew's office, and he leaned over to peck her on the cheek and said, "Have a good shift. I'll see you in the morning." He closed the door, and Amy watched his back. This wasn't how it was going to be between them, she decided, watching him move farther away from her until he disappeared from her sight. She was going to fix this.

CHAPTER EIGHT

Monday, March 27
Emmy

Just beyond the squat stone wall that enclosed Emmy's school, Max leaned against his car, his hands pushed into his shorts pockets. When Emmy spotted him, her breath caught in her throat, and she paused at the top of the stairs, letting the mass of students move around her. He'd shown up, as promised.

The walk across the pavement took an eternity, with Max's eyes watching her approach, a grin splitting his face. Emmy's palms were sweaty on the straps of her backpack, and she wondered whether she'd developed an awkward gait.

"Hey." Max opened the passenger door. "You ready?"

Emmy slid into the leather seat and clipped her seat belt. "Thanks for picking me up." Max's Audi was spotless. The space still held its new-car smell but had also taken on Max's scent, like sea salt, an ocean breeze on a warm day, with a hint of his bodywash she'd opened and smelled in the shower. Emmy didn't know anything about cars, but she could tell by the interior Max must've custom-picked every detail. She rolled her eyes. Boys and their cars.

Max merged into traffic. His white sneakers were as immaculate as his car, and he wore a simple mint-green V-neck. "You don't have to come get me, you know," Emmy said.

"It's no big deal. I'm not doing anything else, Emmy."

It was like she'd never heard her own name before. It had never sounded the way it did when Max said it, like he was directing her to trust him with her own identity.

"How was your ride to school with my mom?" Max asked.

"Short, but awkward." Emmy had woken to a single text from Harper, and a surge of hope had sprung into her chest. The message read: How are you?

That was all her mother had to say? It was just so . . . Harper. Distant and infuriating. And Emmy again remembered the way Harper had backed her car out of the spot, had abandoned her, over and over, in words and actions, her entire life. Emmy left her mother on read, tossed her phone onto her bedspread, out of her own reach. When she'd climbed into the car beside Kathryn, she'd thought of asking questions. What had really happened between Kathryn and Harper that made Harper a shitty mother and Kathryn an attentive one? But Kathryn maintained her far-off look, visibly distracted, so Emmy watched the passing green lawns and said nothing.

At a red light, Max glanced over. "You hungry?"

At lunch, Emmy had picked at a dry bagel while leafing through her novel. She'd grown up with the pool of students from Delray Beach's wealthy families, and she and her best friend, Maggie, had enjoyed an easy friendship that evolved from childhood. But when Maggie's father had accepted a job in New York the previous summer, Emmy had found herself alone. She was hardly a pariah; her family was well respected, but she had no close friends. So Emmy dove into novels to battle the tedium of high school. Maggie's texts first came in flurries, then tapered off as she made new friends, then found a boyfriend. With the culmination of high school and her impending move on the horizon, during her lunches, Emmy chose to read, ignoring the roar of the students behind her. "I'm starving."

"My friend Javi is having some people over while his parents are in Colombia. I said I'd drop by if you want to come with." Max's face turned toward her, but he kept his eyes on the road. "We could grab a burger first."

She'd been planning to put away a few bowls of Lucky Charms in front of a toxic yet addictive dating show, but the alternative Max presented seemed interesting. "I would kill for a burger right now."

Max's face came alive when he smiled, open and broad.

At the corner of a strip mall dotted with scrawny palm trees, Max looped around the narrow U of the drive-through and pulled up beside the speaker. With one arm resting on the open window, he called out their order. The attendant's voice was garbled through the tinny speaker, and an amused smile crept across his face, and Emmy felt herself slipping—uncontrollably—into a bout of giggles.

Stop, Max mouthed, but it was too late. She pressed the back of her hand to her lips.

"Yeah, sounds good," Max called into the speaker, and they rolled forward. "I guess we'll get . . . whatever we get." He turned to Emmy, who'd slid down in her seat, her sides aching with stifled laughter. When Max pulled up to the window, the attendant eyed them with a raised eyebrow, and Max bit his bottom lip as he gathered their bags and parked under the shade of a tree. Emmy drew a steadying breath and settled into her seat. Max passed her her strawberry milkshake, the Styrofoam cup cool in her hands.

Max fished for stray fries at the bottom of the bag. "Jesus Christ, we ordered enough food for fifteen people."

"I told you I was hungry." Emmy peeled back her wrapper and sank her teeth into her burger.

"So is Harper's husband the reason you wanted to get away?" Max pulled a pickle slice from his burger and flicked it onto his wrapper.

Emmy chewed. "Why do you say that?"

Max held a fry and shrugged. "I only met the guy once, but he seemed like kind of a tool. And if some random dude showed up in my mom's life, I'd be pretty pissed."

Emmy mulled this. "No. Joshua may be a tool, but he's okay. He's scared of Nora, so he keeps to himself. I could've been nicer when they first got together, I guess, but I was thirteen, so I made it my mission to make his life as miserable as possible. I must've done a good job, because he barely talks to me now. Like, he was my mom's therapist; how gross is that?"

Max's brows arched. "Wow, that's pretty messed up. I'm sure it violates all kinds of doctor-patient rules."

"I know. Ew. But he's not the problem. It's my mother. She chose him. She moved to the other side of the house. They have their own kitchen, their own entrance, so I don't see her for, like, days or weeks at a time. She doesn't give a shit about me." Emmy let the cool milkshake melt on her tongue. "She's nice to me when she's in a good mood or when her meds are right, when she wants to take me to get our nails done and stuff. But she always gets depressed again. The higher the highs are, the lower the lows."

"So what made you decide to leave now? Why not wait it out a few more months?"

"I tried to wait it out. My mom already paid for my first semester of college, so I tried not to make waves. But the other night, my mom and grandmother had an argument. Nora said I'm just a mistake from my parents' marriage."

"Shit," Max hissed.

"I've always felt it, but it was different to hear the words, you know? And, worse, my mom didn't stand up for me. I'm just, I—" A lump formed in her throat.

Max's eyes locked on hers. "What is it?"

"I just—I thought my mom might try to stop me from leaving. I thought maybe if I did what she's too scared to do—put my foot down to Nora—it might be the wake-up call she needed to get away from her, too. We could move. I don't care if Josh comes, too. But I wanted my mom to choose me—" The knot was harder now, painful when Emmy pushed away the threat of tears. "Now I'm worried she'll pull the plug on college. And then what?"

"Do you really think she'd do that?"

"I don't know, but if she does, I'll never talk to her again. And I'm going to move away, going to have my own life. I'm seventeen—I don't even know if I want a husband, or kids—but if my mom doesn't choose me now, she's not going to be there for any of it—"

"Hey." Max leaned in. "Breathe."

Emmy hadn't realized her words had gotten choked with tears. Max shifted and slipped his hand over hers, and when their skin met, his hand was gentle and warm, welcoming, and she let her fingers relax, let him slide his palm around them. His brilliant blue eyes held hers. "You don't have to figure any of this out. She's the parent. It's on her."

Emmy swallowed again and drew a breath, her heartbeat slowing. When Max withdrew his hand, she felt the warmth where his fingers had been. "I'm never going back there," she said. "I can't. I won't."

"You don't have to. Kathryn might think I'm a demon spawn, but she thinks you're an angel. She'll let you be."

Emmy cleared her throat. She felt her heart harden the way it did when she allowed herself to feel the pain of her mother's absence. "I don't give a shit if I never see any of them again."

Max looped a finger around the steering wheel. "I wish my mom would show less of an interest in me. She wants, like, proof of life every few hours. It's exhausting."

"Don't say that; you don't want that. At least she cares."

Max's gaze returned to her. "I guess, but growing up, it felt like she was too worried about what everyone else thought about us. She didn't let me do sports; it felt like she didn't want me to go out. But, on the other hand, she goes wherever the hell she wants to. And one day I just snapped. I told her it's my life, I can do what I want."

They sat with his words for a moment. Emmy sucked her milkshake. "I guess what they say is true, the grass isn't always greener."

"I guess so." Max gave a resigned nod, looking out the windshield. "Do you remember me from when we were kids?"

A spark of curiosity. Emmy hadn't considered Max might be the source of answers to the questions that itched her. "Not much, I was too little. It feels like all of you—my grandmother, my mom, Kathryn—live in the 'after,' and I'm the only one who doesn't remember the 'before.' Does that make sense?"

"It does," Max replied gently. "I *loved* living with your family. That house, right there on the beach. It was sick."

"Do you remember my dad?" she dared.

"Kind of." Max was quiet. "You don't?"

"Nothing detailed, just little things." Like so many of Emmy's memories, those of her father had an untouchable dreamlike quality; emotions attached to brief images. "It sucks, what happened between our moms. I mean, I don't even know—it's not like Harper tells me anything—but I can tell she's sad about it. And who knows, maybe you and I could have been friends growing up."

Max seemed to consider this. "Maybe. I think Kathryn's sad about it, too. She's too stubborn to admit it, though." He swallowed. "Nobody explained anything to me, either."

A twinge of disappointment in Emmy. Max wasn't a source of answers.

"One day we just packed up and we were gone." Sadness fringed his voice, and Emmy realized that at five, though Max had been witness to things too distant for her to remember, a collective shattering of all their lives, things he didn't recall, the consequences were imprinted on him. By the time she'd formed memories, the shards had settled, but Max's eyes held more than the words he spoke. Something in Max's life had taught him to conceal this sadness artfully, and she wondered how she hadn't noticed it before.

Max lifted his chin. "Moms, huh?"

"Yeah. Moms." Emmy chewed her straw.

Max's sadness was broken with a smile that chased away the shadow she'd seen before, and he leaned one shoulder into his seat. "So why didn't you talk to me at your mother's wedding? We were the only people there under sixty. I was bored as hell."

Emmy recalled observing Kathryn at the table beside hers. She could still see Kathryn's formfitting dress the color of cranberries, the champagne flute perched in her fingertips. It had occurred to Emmy this woman and her son held some significance in her life, had been close with her father, and she had watched Kathryn, intrigued. This woman who had known a different, unshattered version of Harper. A version Emmy was desperate to know. The seams of Emmy's dress had itched her sides, and she'd squirmed in its confines the entire evening. While guests danced to a string quartet and the sun dipped behind the ballroom windows, the sky had surrendered to a deep midnight blue. A beautiful night for an unholy union, an angsty Emmy had mused. Beside his mother, Max had extracted a sprig of sage from the centerpiece. When he'd looked up, he'd met Emmy's eyes for a moment, taking a long sip from a tumbler of amber liquid, and suddenly the room had been too warm.

"Well, I was in middle school, so at that age talking to a high school boy was . . . terrifying."

"Fair enough," Max said.

Talking to Max was easy; he didn't pry, just took in everything she said without judgment. "But I have a confession."

Max arched a brow.

Emmy pointed at him with her straw. "I looked at you while everyone else was watching the fireworks." She'd discarded her shoes, and she'd stood in the surf, watching Max's profile come aglow with each burst that thudded inside her chest, the same thud she felt now, looking at his face.

Max leaned back in his seat and brought his straw to his lips. "So you were staring at me all night?" His face bloomed with a smile. "That's not creepy *at all*."

A giggle rose in Emmy, and the sting of her mother's distance ebbed some, replaced with the warmth of normalcy, of laughter, a lightness she hadn't felt in as long as she could remember.

◆ ◆ ◆

After Max had gathered their stray wrappers and napkins, seemingly satisfied his car had survived their greasy meal unscathed, he cruised back to their neighborhood and pulled up to a two-story house two blocks from their own. Emmy followed him when he opened the front door and entered without knocking. "Javi!" Max yelled into the space. A group of people milled on the other side of the patio door, and one of them slid it open, the sound of voices spilling into the house.

"Maxwell!" The boy pulled Max into a side hug, and one of Max's feet lifted off the floor.

"Javier." Max motioned with his arm. "This is Emmy."

Javi gasped. "Did hell freeze over—Maxwell Moretti brought a date?"

Max shot a playful glare at Javi, but Emmy saw his neck flush. Javi's skin was deep and rich, his warm brown eyes pulled up at the corners, and his genuine smile set Emmy at ease.

The three of them stepped onto the patio, where four twentysome-things circled a table littered with red plastic cups.

"Everyone, this is my mostly hetero life partner, Max," Javi said to the group.

"Mostly," Max said with a wave, his expression not offering a clue to what *mostly* meant. Had she misread Max's friendliness toward her? Was Javi Max's boyfriend?

"And this is Emmy," Javi said, then motioned to the group. "And these are the best coworkers in the whole goddamn world." The group cheered, and Javi pumped the keg and filled plastic cups. Emmy took hers, foam rolling on her tongue at the first sip.

The group arranged a volleyball game, and Emmy opted out. She kicked off her sandals, weaving her toes into the rough grass while she watched the group organize into two teams. Max took a deep swig from his cup, then handed it to Emmy. The boys stripped off their shirts, and when one of the men served, they all dove after the ball. Javi was muscular with tattoos on his biceps, and was shorter and stockier than Max. The boys were tan, and their sun-bleached highlights told Emmy they spent a lot of time outdoors. The ball bounced over the net, making a soft, satisfying thump each time it met skin. With Max's back to her, she took him in. She'd seen him shirtless twice in as many days, and she shamelessly noted his broad shoulders, and the controlled way he moved with athletic ease. He brushed his hair back and dove for the ball, sending it sailing over the net.

With her empty cup dangling from her fingers and the warm afternoon light falling between the branches, Emmy's shoulders loosened. This group of people—she'd forgotten their names—didn't look at her the way people at school and the country club did: they saw her without any expectations. Though she was just a few miles from her grandmother's house, she was a world away. Is this what it was like to feel normal?

Emmy caught Max's gaze on her, but they didn't break away, he just smiled like they shared a secret from the rest of the world. Javi eyed the exchange, and his relaxed smile faded.

When the opposing team huddled, Javi tugged Max's elbow and led him away, where they exchanged jagged whispers beside a hibiscus bush. Javi set his hands on his hips, and Max crossed his arms. Emmy struggled to read their lips when Javi pointed a sharp finger at Max. When the boys broke away and rejoined the game, their argument hovered over them, their movements lacking fluidity, and their team lost the match. Max snatched his shirt from the grass and tugged it over his head, then said something pointed to Javi. Javi had been so warm to her. Was he jealous that she was there?

But when everyone refilled their cups and gathered around the table, Max scooted his chair close to Emmy's and leaned back, ankles crossed. Javi sat at Max's other side. The group swapped battle stories of restaurant work. The end of March had ushered in the offseason, and their restaurant, like most in town, closed on Mondays for the summer, so they'd procured the keg to celebrate their first collective day off. It had been a long winter of serving nasty snowbirds—now flown mercifully back to their homes on Long Island.

The sun dipped and the beer flowed, and voices rose, filling the yard. Emmy hadn't realized how heavy her limbs had become until she stifled a yawn. Max leaned forward. "Wanna get out of here?"

"Don't go, we're about to order pizza," Javi said.

"We ate Good Burger before we came," Max said. "Unless you're hungry again," he added, looking at Emmy. She shook her head.

"Wait—Good Burger?" Javi turned to Emmy, his cheeks flushed pink from the beer. "He let you eat in his car?"

Emmy's cheeks warmed.

"Oh shit, man." Javi turned back to Max. "You're done for." The crowd howled. "I swear to God," Javi continued. "After we went surfing last week, I had like three grains of sand on my feet, and I thought he was going to make me walk home."

Really, Max had allowed her to risk his immaculate car interior, but not Javi? This fact, and the beer, bubbled within her, warm. She shot Max a smug smirk.

Max stood and pulled Javi into a hug, and mumbled something that included the word *asshole*; then Emmy followed Max out of the gate into the front yard. The noise of the group faded as they made their way down the driveway. The evening air was heavy and warm, the sky dimming with twilight. Max pulled Emmy's messenger bag from his trunk and slung it over his shoulder before they walked toward the street. "I'll come back for my car tomorrow."

Emmy was tipsy, and she focused on the sound of their mismatched footsteps scraping the asphalt. As they passed houses, windows glowed in warm yellow, offering a glimpse of private lives: bright dining rooms, colorful flashes of TV screens. There was a sense of security, of trust, in the way newspapers rested against front steps and recycle bins were deposited at the foot of driveways.

"It's cool to have you here," Max said, breaking their comfortable silence. "And Javi approves, so I won't have to kick you out."

"Does he? He seemed kind of pissed."

Max shook his head. "Nah. He's just protective."

Emmy thought back to the conversation she'd overheard between Max and Kathryn, and her stomach panged. Why was everyone so anxious around Max? "How long have you and Javi been friends?"

"Since first grade."

Max's romantic life was none of her concern. But their argument itched at her, and the beer made her brave. "Have you and Javi ever dated? Are you dating?" Then, a rushed "I'm sorry, that's not my business."

But Max's smile was calm. "No, and no. Yes, Javi's gay. But we've never . . . Javi's my brother."

"But you . . ."

Max stopped and turned to face her. "Look. When I like someone, I like them, that's all I know. Sometimes it's when I first meet them, and sometimes . . . when I haven't seen them in four years." With a wink, he continued walking.

Her pulse doubled, and warmth spread through her, a tickle of exhilaration.

"Anyway," Max continued. He motioned toward Javi's house. "I spend most of my time here. Javi's parents are awesome. My mom worked a lot, and kept me on a short leash, so I practically grew up in this house."

Javi's house was familiar to Max, a safe space. This was his world, and he'd invited her into it. She smiled at the pavement, and for a moment their footsteps scratched in unison. When they turned the corner and their house appeared a few yards ahead, Emmy felt a tug of regret. She would've been happy to continue walking beside him under the yellow streetlamps, where it felt they were the only two people in the world.

"So," Max said as they started up the driveway. "What are your plans after you graduate?"

"I'm starting college in Washington in the fall, but I want to leave on my birthday in June and wait until school starts."

"Three months . . ."

"Two and a half," Emmy said. "Well, eleven weeks and two days."

"How many minutes? Seconds?"

She shoved him. "Are you making fun of me?"

"No." Max's grin was open and broad in the glow of the porch light as he punched his code and unlocked the front door. "I want to know how much time we have together."

CHAPTER NINE

Wednesday, March 29
Kathryn

Dusk settled over Hollywood Beach as Kathryn squeezed into a too-tight corner spot—the jackass beside her had parked over the line, and her passenger door brushed against the shrubs.

She flipped down her mirror and checked her teeth, her makeup. The thought of seeing Andrew face-to-face again had left her so jittery she'd wiped away her eye makeup twice to retrace her eyeliner with a shaky hand. Her mind careened with everything she had to tell him. And everything she could never share.

Don't do it to him, Kathryn. Not again. Harper's words burned. It had been so long, but Harper still had precise aim. And fucking Regina. Their accusations only strengthened Kathryn's resolve to keep her relationships distant.

With two minutes to spare, Kathryn shut off the engine and tapped a text message to Max: Let me know if you're not coming home tonight.

It was a lost cause. If she held her breath for Max to answer, she'd die of asphyxiation. What had she done for him to punish her this way? All she needed to know was that he was safe. Why couldn't he be a sweet, cooperative kid like Emmy?

Kathryn had hoped having Emmy in the house would be a distraction from her encounter with Andrew, but the girl seemed content to keep to herself. Aside from their conversation on Sunday morning, Kathryn had caught only glimpses of Emmy's messy bun as she scurried between the kitchen and guest room. She had suggested to each of the kids they have dinner together that week, but her text to Max had also gone unanswered, and Emmy seemed to be satisfied eating cereal in her bedroom.

Sunday afternoon, when Kathryn had peeked out her bathroom window and spotted Emmy sprawled on a pink towel by the pool, the image had jarred her, and bright flashes of the summers she and Harper had spent lounging beside the glittering pool of the Delray Country Club had rushed back. Suddenly Kathryn could taste a sharp, bubbly sip of Coke on her tongue, could feel her wet fingertips sticking to the pages of a gossip magazine. Kathryn should have known then, the way Harper was giddy some days, morose and snappy others, that something was amiss. By sixteen, Kathryn had learned to read men. She'd learned to give a wide berth to those whose eyes lingered a few seconds too long, leaving her with a dirty feeling, as they had since the summer of her twelfth year, when her body had blossomed against her will. By the end of high school she'd learned to harness the power she had, to wiggle out of a speeding ticket or into a movie for free by tugging her blouse a little lower on her cleavage, while shy, shaped-like-a-breadstick Harper frowned at her.

At sixteen, when Kathryn had lost her virginity, an awkward, surprisingly sticky exchange with her neighbor's grandson who was visiting for the summer, it was hardly the earth-shattering event her *Cosmopolitan* had led her to believe. Kathryn had buzzed with excitement to autopsy the event with Harper, but Harper's disapproving frown had struck Kathryn with a barb of judgment. So, for the remainder of that summer, when Kathryn had engaged in casual bed-hopping with said neighbor's grandson, she failed to mention it. She'd enjoyed the sex as much as she liked cheeseburgers or a pedicure, and she hadn't been about to let Harper, or anyone, judge her for it.

The following summer, when Kathryn had worked the hostess stand at the Delray Beach Country Club, she'd scrounged cash and treated herself to a mail-order electric-pink swimsuit from Victoria's Secret. When it finally arrived, she'd admired herself in the full-length mirror on the back of her bedroom door, the way the color made her sun-kissed skin glow, the way the hip-hugger bottoms accentuated her curves. One of the lifeguards, Sam, had been smirking at her, and she'd known he'd appreciate it. She'd worn her hair down that day, donned her oversize sunglasses, but when she'd approached Harper, all her friend had said was, "This is why everyone at school thinks you're a slut."

The words had sliced deep. Maybe Harper's period was due, Kathryn reasoned, because just as Harper had sunk into her dark mood, the bubble popped, and she'd asked Kathryn to go shopping like nothing had ever happened.

Harper's mother, Nora, had one unrelenting message to her daughter: nothing she did would ever be good enough, so Kathryn gave Harper grace, instead choosing to skim over their bumpy moments to enjoy those carefree days of turquoise pools and aggressively air-conditioned malls.

Kathryn remembered the exact moment she'd met the man who would become Emmy's father. The summer they were eighteen, Kathryn had been promoted to waitress at the country club. The day Lucas had arrived, buttoned-up in his server uniform, with his warm skin and light eyes, a silent competition had initiated between the waitresses to see who could earn his attention. Kathryn had ignored the chatter; she had one month left to scrounge away her tips for college, had her sights set on bigger things than what Delray Beach held. But when she had spotted Lucas in the dancing sparks across a staff bonfire one night, she'd been taken aback when he crossed the sand to sit beside her. And she'd clocked the way he didn't gawk at her body like other men did, a simple act that set her at ease. They'd chatted for hours, her skin warm from the fire and the buzz of rum.

And then something shocking had happened. Lucas had met Harper. Kathryn had watched the transformation in her friend; as she fell for Lucas, Harper held her head high for the first time, even seemed resilient against Nora's criticism. Pride had swelled in Kathryn, and she and Harper had maintained their sisterhood well after Lucas and Harper had married, well after Kathryn and Andrew had collided, when the plans the two couples made had nearly come to fruition, until the fingers of jealousy had pried the cracks wide open. Looking at Emmy basking in the sun, the memory had left a tight knot in Kathryn's throat. The girl was the physical manifestation of everything they'd all lost.

But she had more pressing problems at the moment. Seeing Harper in person had dragged back memories of Lucas—compounded by her run-in with Andrew—it had all left Kathryn pouring her anxious energy into cleaning all day Sunday until her body ached. It occurred to her, as she'd stood barefoot in her spotless kitchen late in the evening, that getting her house in order had done nothing to remedy the fact that her personal life remained a disaster.

She'd run a hot bath and slid the cork from a bottle of cabernet with a satisfying pop, then sank into the warm water, her lips meeting the delicate rim of the glass. She'd closed her eyes as the first sip of sweet, acidic wine ran across her tongue. Her phone had buzzed angrily against the cold marble of her vanity. An unknown 561 number. She'd answered with a shaky *hello*.

"Kathryn. It's Andrew." That voice. She'd nearly dropped her phone in the bathwater.

Andrew had spoken in a hushed tone, his voice heavy with hesitation, and asked her to meet him the following night. And within her, that flicker, like the spark of a match. When she'd hung up, she'd closed her eyes and rested against the porcelain. *He's married,* she'd reminded herself. *You aren't the same people you were all those years ago.*

They'd agreed to meet at a nondescript taco joint forty-five minutes south. A safe distance from inquisitive eyes. Now Kathryn opened her car door and stepped out into the night. There was a noticeable shift in the atmosphere the last week of March as it slipped into April, when the heat no longer dissipated when the sun went down. Kathryn ran her fingers through her hair, the strands getting coarse and wavy, and realized it was a lost cause; the hour she'd spent styling it had been a waste of time. Motels lined the street, giving the neighborhood a worn-down beach-town feel, a more relaxed vibe than Delray Beach. The lot was full, littered with a colorful array of license plates from northern states and Canada.

Andrew appeared from between the parked cars a few rows away, and her pulse quickened. He paused, seemed to consider her for a beat before he slid one hand into his pocket and strode across the asphalt. Then he was in front of her, occupying the same space, the sleeves of his pale-pink button-down cuffed at the elbows, and he leaned in to kiss her lightly on the cheek.

They swapped obligatory *how are you*s and *how was your drive*s as they made their way up the stone path toward the restaurant patio. Fans stirred the heavy air, and the hollow legs of their chairs scraped painfully across the concrete. Kathryn took in the brick wall beside them, where a weathered mural featured a large mahi of greens and blues. Andrew settled, but his tight smile told her he was nervous, too.

While Andrew spoke to the server, Kathryn studied him, the way his subtle South Carolina accent slipped through, though it wasn't as pronounced as it had been in his twenties. He stood an inch or so taller than Max and had twenty pounds on her son, but their faces were eerily similar. Kathryn found herself marveling at the wonders of DNA. But physical similarities aside, Andrew's mannerisms unnerved her. His smile and Max's were the same, as was the tilt of their heads when asking a question. She'd forgotten how perfect Andrew's teeth were.

Max was five when everything collapsed between Harper, Lucas, and herself. It was then Kathryn realized she couldn't protect her son from the darkness life dealt, no matter how she ached to. As his childhood sped on, Kathryn had done everything in her power to shield him from anything that might harm him further. Max was resilient, sure, and as he grew into his own person, Kathryn had marveled at him, in awe of the way he learned and grew, at the miracle of his existence. But their gears never aligned, and the friction between them only intensified as Max got older.

The summer Max turned sixteen, he'd accompanied her to Publix, and while Kathryn had waited for her half pound of sliced turkey, Max had leaned against the shopping cart, wearing his teenage boredom. A girl in a pale-blue sundress had passed, and Kathryn had watched a playful smile lift her son's face. Max had recently reached the end of his package of pricey dental aligners and had just aged out of his early-teen lankiness and was now six feet tall. He'd spent the summer surfing, and a smattering of freckles had appeared on his nose and shoulders. The girl's cheeks had flushed, and Kathryn had realized her son wasn't shy or awkward. He was aware of his charms, and how to use them to his advantage. Anyone who fell for him was going to be in trouble. It was then she looked at him and saw not her son, but Andrew.

It was the following fall that Max's behavior abruptly changed, seemingly overnight, when her son guarded his life like a fortress. Kathryn always looked back to that afternoon at the store, worried Max had sensed a shift in her that day, that her regret for everything she'd done to Andrew had surfaced and poisoned her relationship with her son as subtle as mold spores, only visible when the fruit was rotten.

Andrew sipped his iced tea. "So you're a lawyer. Like you planned."

Andrew was more direct than Max in the way he spoke, maybe something that came with maturity. Her fingernail loosened the label on her beer bottle, separating it from the glass. "Yes. Real estate lawyer. Mostly corporate, very boring."

"It can't be more boring than being an investment banker."

There was something there, in his eyes and tone. A grittiness. Was it regret? Resentment?

Andrew cleared his throat. "Don't get me wrong, I like my job. My colleagues are tolerable, I guess, but if I never saw them again, I wouldn't miss any one of them. And the work, after all these years, it's very . . . one dimensional."

His words conveyed how she felt about her own career. She brushed the condensation off her beer bottle, and in a flash, she was entwined in his arms all those years ago, mapping their life. She had seen it then, tangible: the house. The pool. And she lived it again, the way Andrew had laced his fingers with hers and pressed a kiss to her earlobe, sending that tingle through her body. "I can't wait to share my life with you," he'd said, his breath warm in her hair. He'd rolled her onto her back and met his mouth with hers, and as he melted into her, she'd believed they'd never spend another moment apart.

How naive they'd both been. She sipped her beer. "Did you end up going to grad school?"

His forehead pinched. "No."

"Oh." Surprised, she recalculated. "Well, I'm glad we both found the fulfilling, world-changing careers we dreamed of when we were in school." She peeled the label from the bottle in one clean sheet.

Andrew's smile was resigned. "It pays the bills, though."

"I suppose it does." With her beer nearly finished, her body felt lighter, and a swell of camaraderie washed over her, a fleeting moment in which, despite the time and distance between them, they had something in common. But apprehension swirled in her stomach. "I have a question."

Andrew nodded. "Sure, go ahead."

"How did you take it when I left?"

Andrew tore a shred of his napkin, rolled it into a ball between his fingers, his expression hard. "It was tough," he said, guarded. "I'm not going to lie; I wasn't okay for a while."

"You look good now," she rushed. "No, I mean, you look—you're successful. You have it together." It was what had struck her that day outside Starbucks, how normal he looked. It was what had planted the seed inside her. But she couldn't ask him for a favor yet.

A blush rose from his neck to his cheeks. "Well, thanks." Andrew didn't meet her eye, just shrugged one shoulder. "It took time."

Time. That word held so much.

The waitress set two plates between them. Kathryn lifted her fork but found she had no appetite.

Andrew poked at his food. "I'm not going to tell my wife about this, about him, just yet. I can't—she's just started a new job and she's under a lot of pressure with some family issues; it's not a good time to unload something like this on her."

"Okay." Kathryn leaned back. It wasn't what she'd expected. Would this be the last time she'd see him? Would he get what he needed from her and then move on with his life, his wife none the wiser?

Andrew's face shifted as he mulled his next question. "I have to know why you ran away when we were so—happy? It made me question everything, our whole relationship, it made me question myself. Did I miss something? Was it not what I thought it was? Weren't we good together?"

Her throat was a tight, painful knot.

"I—I just have to know why you didn't tell me you were pregnant."

Kathryn drew a shaky breath. "I was young. I was confused. I didn't know what I was doing until after I'd done it." She'd rehearsed her answer, casting a tiny shred of light onto the truth.

"Was there someone else?"

"No." She forced another painful swallow. Her eyes drifted to the parking lot. She wasn't ready to open that door with him, shine a light onto everything that had happened between the morning she'd left him and the moment they'd locked eyes in Starbucks. "I had my friends, and my mom, until she moved away. And now it's just the two of us, and that's how it's been for a long time." Kathryn hadn't realized how lonely her life was until she had to put it into words.

Andrew set his taco down. "When exactly did you get back in touch with Nick?"

Kathryn swallowed. "Two years ago? A few weeks after he moved to Delray. I was surprised when he said you two were still in touch. You never had much in common."

"He stuck by me, even when I didn't deserve it. He was the voice of reason when I was acting like a stubborn jackass. May have saved my life, even, if I'm being honest." Andrew dropped his eyes. Shame. It prodded her deeply, and all she could offer was a nod. Andrew pushed his plate aside. "Tell me more about Max."

Relief rushed through Kathryn when he didn't ask any more about Nick. She'd braced herself for Andrew's questions, reminding herself she didn't have to tell him anything she didn't want to, but her hands were still sweaty against her thighs. "What do you want to know?"

Andrew shuffled the salt and pepper shakers beside the hot sauce caddy. "I'll take anything, Kat."

She drew a deep breath, her thoughts churning. "Well . . . he was an easy baby. He was so *cute*. But parenthood is hard. And the teenage years are no joke." She gave a nonchalant shrug, though she knew it wasn't convincing, and she bristled when Andrew's eyes narrowed. She wasn't going to betray her son's flaws to someone who didn't know him. Kathryn collected her thoughts, then continued. "He's like you, in a lot of ways." Andrew was still fixed on her. "He was never as studious as you were, but in school everything came easily to him. He tested at a moderately gifted level and took some advanced classes." Her tension eased as she spoke of her son, and she swelled with pride. "But being an only child wasn't easy for him. His best friend, Javier, and his parents live down the street, and he spent a lot of time there. It took a lot of guilt off me, knowing Max had somewhere to go after school every day. He and Javi grew up on the water; they spent their whole life on boats, and learned to surf when they were in middle school. It was so cute, they'd get up at the crack of dawn and go down the street, barefoot, with their surfboards under their arms." She felt lighter, drained, as if she'd finished a long cry. All of it almost made her seem like a good mom. Probably the biggest lie she'd ever told.

Andrew leaned back in his chair and exhaled, the sadness in his eyes stabbing the place reserved for the deepest of her guilt. "Do you think he'd be open to meeting me?"

Kathryn's pulse doubled. "Andrew—"

"Please." He leaned forward, his forearms on the table. "He's a *part* of me. It's driving me crazy—I can't sleep—I just have so many questions."

"I acknowledge this situation isn't fair to you, but . . ." If Max learned the truth about Andrew and slipped back into his reckless behavior, she could lose him this time. With each unanswered text, each therapist he'd written off, each night he spent out, he slipped further from her grasp.

She'd already stolen so much from Andrew, she could never let him find out what a terrible mother she was. Hot tears burned her eyes, and she closed them—closed them to the image of Andrew's gaze on her probing her guilt, a reminder of everything her son had lost because of her decisions.

She felt Andrew rest his hand on top of hers. "Hey, it's okay. Just consider it, please." His voice was gravelly.

She opened her eyes as her hand jerked from his. "I've already told you no."

Andrew's hand fell to his lap.

"It's getting late," she said. "I should get home."

"I'm sorry." Andrew leaned closer, the thump of far-off music bouncing between them. "I didn't mean to push you like that. Seeing you has brought back so much, things I never thought I'd think about again."

That certainly was the truth.

"I'd love to keep talking to you. Let's get out of here, take a walk?" he offered.

A short while later, in a convenience store, Kathryn plucked a can of beer from a bin of crushed ice before stepping out onto the pavement where Andrew waited. "I've never been down here before," she said as they set off on the stretch of pavement beside the beach. The moon reflected in the ripples out across the water, and acoustic guitar flowed from a tiki bar. Families with squirmy children chatted on benches, eating soft-serve ice cream. The back of her hand brushed Andrew's. She yanked it away and swapped her beer to her other hand. "You don't drink?"

"No." The stiffness in his tone made it clear he wasn't open to any more questions on the subject.

When Kathryn had moved into the apartment Andrew and Nick had shared in college, beer had been a staple in their fridge. On weekends, they'd partied until early morning with friends, a cheap, greasy diner breakfast the cure for a hangover. But there had been fractured bursts of his bitter words, of arguments, of the darker side of himself that alcohol revealed.

"You don't mind if I drink this?" She held up the can.

"No." His voice was soft. Sad. Kathryn turned to look at his profile as they passed the warm glow of the restaurants. This Andrew, handsome in his early forties, had long shed his sophomoric college-boy persona, and in his maturity the gentleness she'd loved in him all those years ago had blossomed. He was exactly the man she'd pictured growing old with.

On an outdoor stage, a high school choir sang to a patchy crowd. They sat on a concrete bench in the last row, where they took in the night and each other's presence in the ethereal bath of voices.

When they were finished, Andrew walked her to her car. "I'm sorry I pushed you that way. I won't do it again."

Again. This wouldn't be the last time she'd see him. The thought warmed in her chest, and the little seed that had sprouted inside her cracked open. Maybe Andrew could be that missing puzzle piece that showed Max he would be okay, that he was worthy of the love she tried to show him.

"Thank you for dinner," she said. From the restaurant, the quick, repetitive beat of house music floated to them on the wind.

"My pleasure." Andrew stepped forward and took her in his arms, his body strong and welcoming, and she settled her head on his shoulder. Amid the sea spray, his cologne—a hint of cedar—clung to his shirt, and she drew it in, drew him in. His scent held a comforting familiarity, like she'd come home.

"I'm glad you called." She sighed into his shirt. So much had changed in just a few days, and she was drained, body and soul.

"I am, too." Andrew's breath was warm on the top of her head. It may have been the sea air, but his voice was different, deeper, the facade of politeness gone.

His lips brushed her forehead, light as a whisper. Another memory flooded back. When they'd dated, he'd kissed her at the base of her part, more intimate than sex. She wondered how the memory had burrowed itself so deep inside her that she hadn't recalled it in years, decades. Now it rushed through her, to her core; stirring something that shouldn't be there. A concerned look passed over Andrew's face. But she didn't pull back, just stood, his face a few inches from hers, his eyes catching the light from the streetlamp, until his shoulders relaxed. He squeezed her hand. "Have a good night, Kathryn."

When she closed her car door, Andrew's scent lingered on her shirt, and she leaned against the seat. *Oh no,* she thought. *Not again.* But she sat alone with it in the quiet for a long time before she drove home.

CHAPTER TEN

Thursday, March 30
Andrew

From behind his desk, Andrew watched the 11:00 a.m. drawbridge reach into the morning sky, while his thoughts circled around the son he'd never met. He recalled himself at nineteen—horny, arrogant, naively optimistic—before he pulled his laptop across his desk and tapped Max's name into Google. When he located the boy's social media profiles, they were sparse, the most recent posts from over a year before. He clicked on an album aptly titled *Salt Life*, and a dozen or so tiles lined up on his glowing screen. Andrew recognized Max among a group of five boys in their midteens, smiling back at him from the immaculate white deck of what looked to be a thirty-foot fishing boat. The boys' tan arms were draped over one another's shoulders, and all wore crisp white T-shirts silk-screened with various vibrant swordfish and marlin.

There were a few far-off shots of choppy, slate-blue waves dotted with surfers beneath a low, threatening sky. Then a close-up of Max beside another boy, holding their respective surfboards, flashing beaming smiles.

The pictures ignited an insatiable curiosity in Andrew, and he scooted his chair closer to his desk. Rapidly clicking through the slides animated the images, and Andrew watched as Max ran a hand through his wet hair and turned to laugh at the boy beside him. This must be

Javi. Andrew's best friend was dark haired and shorter than he was, and it was like looking at Nick and himself two decades in the past, leaving him with a cloudy sense of déjà vu.

His fingertip crept across the trackpad. The next set of pictures had been taken in the backyard of a sprawling stone house, in a lagoon-like pool built out of the same gray stones as the house in the background. It was filled with a dozen or so teenagers, and Andrew recognized the same group of boys mixed among bikini-clad girls. The boys were noticeably older, the party time-stamped nearly two years after the photos on the boat. In one of the pictures, Max stood in a swimming pool, his arm resting on the edge, a red plastic cup in his hand. Beer cans littered the side of the pool, along with more red cups. The glass table behind Max housed half-empty bottles of clear and dark liquid. Andrew zoomed in on the image, over his son's shoulder, and shuddered, the memory of the warm burn of a healthy pour of hard liquor spreading in his belly.

Still zoomed in, Andrew passed over Max's face. The boy's eyes were shadowy and unfocused, and a weight—solid and heavy like one of the stones surrounding the pool—settled in Andrew's stomach. He recognized his own face in Max, from the period when he'd passed through each day in a drunken haze, detached from the world around him.

Andrew snapped his laptop shut. He'd thought gaining insight into Max's life might quell some of his curiosity, but the expression on his son's face in the pool etched in his mind. It was such a stark contrast to the carefree boy on the boat, and he wondered what had happened that had left Max so deeply unhappy. A picture of his son had started to form. Max was a whole person, faceted and complex, and Andrew had gotten only a tiny glimpse into who he was. It wasn't enough, not by far, but with every detail he learned, he craved more.

He's like you, in a lot of ways. Kathryn's words whirled in his mind. The most intimate parts of what made Andrew who he was had been replicated without his knowledge, and he wondered what other parts of himself existed inside Max that couldn't be captured by the shutter snap of a photo. The boy who shared his face seemed to also share the darkest parts of him, the part that had nearly taken his life.

His phone buzzed, and Andrew startled. Kathryn? He snatched it. Nick: Lunch?

Andrew's palms tingled, but his mind switched tracks. An olive branch from Nick? And a tick of curiosity: Nick's job allowed him insights into the lives of the residents of Delray Beach. Nick must be privy to Max's activities. Likely privy to things even Kathryn may not know.

An hour later, Andrew and Nick piled out of Nick's SUV in front of their favorite Cuban hole-in-the-wall. The bell on the door chimed while Nick nodded at the owner, a man with a bald dome of a head who sat at a corner table, reading the newspaper. The sunlight was muted through the grimy window, scrawled with faded chalk paint.

Nick didn't waste time. "You've been talking to Kat?" he asked after they'd ordered. They each sat with a tiny Styrofoam cup of sweet coffee before them.

"Yup." Andrew forced indifference in his tone, concealing his excitement.

Nick's eyes were shadowy, and he wore a few days' worth of stubble. "You look tired. What's going on?" Andrew probed.

Nick rubbed his eye with the heel of his hand. "Some shit's going on at work."

"Again?" Andrew hadn't meant the word to come out pointedly. Nick stopped rubbing his eye, but didn't respond. Andrew asked, "Care to elaborate?"

The bald man sat Cuban sandwiches before them, the bread glistening with melted butter, then shuffled back to his seat in the corner and unfolded his newspaper.

"Not really." Nick yanked a napkin from the caddy. "Just more bureaucratic bullshit. Not everyone gets to work in air-conditioned offices, kissing rich people's asses like you and Kat do."

You and Kat. The first bridge between Andrew, Nick, and Kathryn. Somehow they'd all found their way back into one another's lives. Only now Amy was in the mix, too. "You don't think I have to deal with bureaucratic bullshit at an investment firm?"

Nick made a noncommittal noise. "You don't have to see what I see at your job. The violence. Blood literally on the street."

That was true, Andrew conceded, but only to himself, and sipped his coffee.

"So." Nick shifted. "Kat won't let you meet the kid?"

A muted TV bolted to the ceiling played a silent soap opera. "Max has had a rough time recently, and Kathryn doesn't want to do anything to upset him."

"Yeah. Rough." Nick snorted. "You obviously don't know Kat. She's good at stringing things along for as long as it suits her."

Irritation brewed. Just because Max was rich didn't mean the boy hadn't struggled. And Nick insulting Kathryn flared something deep within him. But he bit back his words and chewed. "I still can't believe you didn't tell me."

Nick closed his eyes. "Look, I'm sorry, all right? Is that what you want? An apology. But I told you, Kat told me not to."

Nick's loyalty to Kathryn still burned.

"And the kid he . . . got in some trouble recently." Nick looked at his food. "Drinking and stuff."

A hot spike of fear. "What else?" Andrew pushed.

Nick shrugged. "Spoiled-rich-kid shit. He runs around with these other brats partying. Popping pills. None of them ever face any consequences until they end up dead or in rehab . . ."

Nick's words faded to a din, and Andrew's palms tingled, a familiar, panicky heat rising in his chest. Acid burned his legs, like he'd run a marathon. He raked his fingers through his hair. "The drinking. The drugs. Was it just high school–kid shit? Or is it—is he—like me?"

Nick's eyes danced across Andrew's face. "I don't know," he finally said. "But trust me, Drew, it's best to stay far away from Kat and that kid." Nick was almost begging, but his desperation didn't register; heat rose in Andrew's face, and the undercurrent of fear rushed to the surface. He thought of Max's eyes in the photos by the pool. The resignation behind them. Andrew had spent years running from the darkness inside him, but if it was alive and well inside the son he'd never met, it could be for any future children Andrew and Amy may have. The secrets he was hiding from his wife were adding up, each one a stone on a wall, getting higher between them.

"When are you going to tell Amy?" Nick asked, as if he could read Andrew's guilty thoughts.

Amy was so absorbed with her job, she hadn't suggested another visit to Dr. Cassidy, hadn't raised the subject of IVF again. Andrew gripped his Styrofoam cup. "I need to find the right time. It's a delicate situation—"

"Which you're making less delicate by going to dinner with your ex?"

Andrew dropped his arms into his lap. "Amy's under a lot of pressure. I'm . . . I'm trying to learn everything I can about Max before I tell her. It's twenty years of my son's life that were stolen from me."

"If it were me, I wouldn't waste my time."

And there it was again: something in Nick's tone that spiked the hair on Andrew's arms. But he told himself it was the proximity to Nick's firearm, strapped to his side, which had always made him uneasy.

"What else do you know about him?" Andrew asked, suddenly desperate for any details about his son. "Where does he hang out?"

Nick dabbed his lips with a napkin. "Why?"

Andrew's curiosity was insatiable, but he tried to hold his tone steady. "It drives me crazy that everyone knows this kid, *my* kid, but me. I'm sure you know what he's up to. Something. Anything."

Nick's face tilted toward Andrew; then he gave a sigh of surrender. "He doesn't go to school, doesn't have a job. His best buddy is Javier Quintero; he's the one with that obnoxious orange Jeep, and his parents own a handful of nightclubs in Miami Beach. They spend their time surfing and cruising around town with fifteen-dollar smoothies from Juice Papi."

A dusty fan stirred the still air above them. "What else?"

"They belong to the gym on West Atlantic, a different one than the gym Kathryn goes to—I guess he doesn't want to work out with his mom—but don't go looking for him there. Stalking is a crime."

"I'm not going to look for him."

"Anyway." Nick balled his greasy wrapper. "Stick around this town long enough and he'll pop up. Delray is full of gossipy people, and sooner or later, everyone's secrets come out."

But Andrew was soaking in the details. Max's world sat a few miles from Andrew's house, his beach the same Andrew ran each morning. The backdrop of Max's life was vibrant Atlantic Avenue. His son was so close, yet untouchable.

A memory of Kathryn leaning into his chest in the parking lot of the Mexican restaurant rose to his mind with a bubble of optimism; maybe in time Kathryn would open up, she'd let him in, and he could finally get the answers he'd always needed from her. There was a chance he could get to know Max—all of him.

And maybe he'd find the courage to tell Amy all the things she didn't know about him.

At home that evening, Amy stepped through the garage door into the kitchen, fatigue emanating from her body, her eyes sunken. "Bike week is officially upon us. The ER is overwhelmed, and it's going to be a long weekend. I'm going to get a few hours of sleep and head back in."

"You're going back to work? Babe, you look exhausted."

"I am exhausted. My back has been throbbing all day," Amy snapped, a hand on her hip. "But this is the job. We both knew this when I accepted."

The crackle of a disagreement brewed. Andrew relieved her of her lunch bag and pressed a kiss to her forehead. "Take a shower, dinner's almost ready. I'll pack extra for you to take to work."

He slid chicken breasts into hot oil, his thoughts circling back to every word he and Kathryn had exchanged when they'd met for dinner, examining them like stones found on the beach. The inertia of the things he was hiding from his wife swelled through him.

Andrew's life had collided with Kathryn's on a spring day at the tail end of his junior year of college. Carlisle University sat just outside Gainesville, and on that Friday afternoon, after their final class of the week, he and Nick had meandered the shady grounds, giddy with freedom, the weekend stretching before them. A keg had been procured by a nearby frat house, and Andrew had been in the midst of coaxing Nick to join him that evening. It was their dance: Nick would come out; Andrew just needed to work him. Yes, the frat bros were *douchebags*, Andrew conceded, but the draw of free beer could not be ignored.

In the crowd ahead, a towering girl caught Andrew's eye. Her long chestnut hair spilled in waves down to the middle of her back, the April sunlight infusing it with a honey-red glow. Andrew nudged Nick and motioned with his chin. *I'll get her number, just watch.*

Andrew called out, and the girl turned her body halfway to regard him, and her full lips pursed. The gentle tilt of her head and a blush to her neck nudged his confidence. "I'm sorry, my watch broke." He motioned to his wrist. "Do you have the time?"

It was a lame excuse, they both knew, but the smile she gave him—curious, full of possibility—told him it had worked, and she didn't concoct an imaginary meeting to escape. Instead, she fell in step with him and Nick and the three chatted as they strolled across campus. When they parted ways, Andrew asked Kathryn for her number, and though he was the one to call her two days later, she led the relationship in every way from that day forward.

Kathryn was basking in the freedom of her last few weeks of college before she earned her business degree, while Andrew had one more year ahead of him before his graduation, which felt like an eternity. Kathryn merged into his life seamlessly. Her smile was electric, her laugh unapologetic. She was confident in her place in the world, yet grounded. She was assertive in the way she introduced herself into his life, into his group of friends, even in the way she'd unbuttoned his jeans when they made out two weeks later, the way she wrapped her hand around him with a gasp of approval. Kathryn kept him out late on school nights, pulled him from his studies, kissing his neck until she had his undivided attention before she dragged him down on the bed with her.

In the summer, without the distraction of school, their days flowed together. They packed his car with their friends and drove to the beach, where they hauled a red-and-white plastic cooler full of beer across the sand. They spent the entire day there, lounging in cheap plastic chairs, Andrew's eyes on Kathryn's bronze skin against her sun-faded beach towel. When the sun set and the air grew chilly, they built a bonfire, the sand around them littered with empty beer cans. Andrew grabbed a sweatshirt from the trunk of his car, and Kathryn pulled it over her head and wrapped her arms around him, her delicate fingertips poking out of the sleeves.

They slept until late morning, the curtains drawn, and he flipped pancakes with Kathryn perched on the kitchen counter. She reached out, pulling him close, her long legs wrapped around his waist, and when Andrew turned back to the frying pan, smoke billowed in the air.

Andrew's mother and stepfather were an aggressive picture of toothy-smiled upper middle class, and had modeled an affectionate, polite partnership, focused on the logistical aspects of raising Andrew and his younger brother, Timothy. Andrew fit into their portrait of glossy suburban life with his toothy-smiled, blond-haired, blue-eyed, middle-class Americana physicality.

In his mother and stepfather, Andrew had never seen the fire that existed between him and Kathryn, hadn't known of its existence outside of a movie screen. When his love for her took hold of his life, he was blissfully surprised, and that summer he surrendered, letting it blind him to the realities of life. By July, those romantic movies and sappy love songs started to make sense, and he'd begun to believe the things he'd only read about before: that people were *fated* to meet, that their love was *written in the stars*, had existed long before the two of them had locked eyes.

Their future was a stretch of nothing but promise; he pictured the house they'd buy, the sparkle of a swimming pool, a lush lawn he'd obsess over. They would have it all, the summer vacations, the envy of their coupled friends. In the meantime, Andrew indulged himself in her exquisite body between his bedsheets. He was sure he had all of her, that Kathryn loved as much of him as she knew, that she might have the capacity to love all of him entirely. In the limited scope of a twenty-year-old boy, he attempted to articulate his feelings, reducing his sentiments down to two promises: I'll study hard to build us a solid future. Then I'll marry you.

Now, twenty years later, Andrew stared at his backyard, at the dull glint of his stainless-steel grill in the floodlight. This magnificent house was his. The living room window offered a stunning picture of a blue ribbon of the Atlantic. The world on the other side of the paned glass seemed alive, from the cadence of the tides to the towering palms that yielded to the whims of the wind, even if, inside, the space was still and sterile. He had everything he'd imagined, all the trimmings life could offer. Only the woman he'd envisioned sharing it with had changed.

He had Amy. He was the luckiest man alive. So why did he feel that flicker, like a dream he couldn't remember, of what it would be like to throw it all away, just as he had all those years ago? Andrew had heard the time it takes to get over a relationship is half its length, but he knew that wasn't true. Did he still crave a sense of closure he'd never gotten with Kathryn, or had he never truly gotten over her?

Amy's footsteps came from behind, and he set two steaming dishes at the table and brushed his thoughts aside.

Amy lifted her fork. "I got tickets for the breast cancer research fundraiser. First week in May, just like last year."

When he married Amy, he'd anticipated, in some form, the long hours, that he'd have to share this brilliant woman with the people who needed her. He didn't mind carrying the bulk of the household tasks. But he hadn't imagined donning a tuxedo and smiling for local newspapers at multiple charity events each year. The crowds. The cameras. His neck grew hot thinking about it. But after their fight, he had no interest in making waves. He speared a piece of chicken. "Pink tie again?"

"Pink tie." A smile teased her face. "You know I can't resist you in a tux."

Andrew smiled at his plate. Amy filled the space, chatted about the hospital. Andrew knew she held back, that she spared him the most heartbreaking aspects of her job. He could tell when she lost a patient by the haunted look she'd carry for a few days and wondered when she would come across the case that would break her. He hoped he'd be there to catch her when it did.

After dinner, Amy went upstairs to shower, and Andrew loaded the washing machine. A white scrap of plastic fluttered from that day's scrubs, and he bent to collect it from the cold tile. A corner, corrugated. A tampon wrapper? It wasn't Amy's usual brand, not a cheery yellow. Maybe she'd had to make do at the hospital. A deluge of relief. He'd been bought another month—another month to learn what he could about Max. Amy hadn't agreed to take a break from trying to get pregnant, but she hadn't raised the subject since the day of their appointment with Dr. Cassidy.

Andrew slipped between the sheets. Beside him, Amy dozed, and he worked his way close to her body, settling his face in the crook of her neck, relishing the time he had with her beside him before her alarm would blare and she'd slip away, leaving him to wake in an empty bed. Amy's hands were rough from washing, despite the greasy, minty salve she applied each evening, but the rest of her body was impossibly soft, and Andrew let himself sink into her velvety warmth. In that moment, weighing everything Amy was facing—her mother's cancer, her job— the idea of sharing the news of his secret son seemed downright cruel.

Andrew had collected tiny bits of information about Max, but the evidence of the striking similarities between the two of them was already manifesting. The vivid image of Max's expression in the swimming pool again slipped into his mind, and the draft from the air-conditioning vent sent a shudder through him, lifting the hairs on the back of his neck. Nick was right—Andrew couldn't let Amy discover this secret by accident.

As he grew drowsy, a final thought slipped into his mind: he knew for certain no amount of time would help him get over Amy. It would be like his house burning to the ground, everything he'd worked for reduced to ash. So why did he feel like he was standing in front of his life, holding a lit match?

CHAPTER ELEVEN

Thursday, March 30
Emmy

Emmy spent the evening burritoed in her duvet, devouring *Grey's Anatomy* reruns. When she heard Kathryn come home just after ten, she decided to brush her teeth and go to bed, or risk being a zombie at school the following day. She finished in the bathroom, and tiptoed toward the sliver of light that fell from her bedroom door.

Max crept from his room and pressed a finger to his lips. "Wanna go outside?"

Emmy glanced toward Kathryn's bedroom door just as Max slipped his palm into hers, and warmth spread from her fingertips at his touch. He tugged her toward the staircase and moved through the dark house with stealth. Emmy was certain he'd sneaked in and out of the house undetected countless times before. The patio door glided open, and they stepped onto the pool deck, the trees above illuminated in a flickering turquoise glow. They crossed the grass and pushed the netting on the trampoline aside so he could help her onto the smooth surface, the old springs stretching beneath them.

Emmy wanted to pull at the fabric of her tank top where it hugged her breasts, but Max's face tipped upward toward the sky. He reached into his pocket to retrieve a rolled joint and a lighter. A glow flicked on in Kathryn's bathroom window, startling Emmy.

"She's not coming out," Max said before the tip of the lighter sparked to life, and he took a long drag. "She knows I'm home, so we're good. As long as you tell her where you are, she'll stay off your ass."

"She's concerned with safety," Emmy said before she inhaled, the smoke burning her lungs. She stifled a cough; she'd gotten high only twice before, but she didn't want Max to know she was an amateur.

Max grunted in response.

"Thanks for inviting me to Javi's house the other day. It was fun." Her voice was raspy, and their fingers brushed as she pinched the tissue-thin paper and handed it back to Max, white smoke curling into the night air.

Max's smile lifted. "I'm glad you had a good time." The ember at the tip of the joint flared orange when he inhaled.

Emmy's next drag was smoother, and the adrenaline rush of sneaking out with Max slid away, replaced by something gentler, soothing, like sinking into a warm bath. "Why aren't you guys away at college?"

"Javi wanted to take a year off to work, save some money."

"And you?"

"I don't need to save money," Max said, like it was obvious.

"What does that mean?"

There was a slight narrowing of Max's eyebrows, and he considered her. "Nothing." He coughed, then shrugged. "Anyway, I left school last April."

"April? What, were you expelled?"

"Not exactly." Max's voice was hard, and Emmy recalled the argument she'd heard between Max and Kathryn, the tension that hovered between the two of them. "It was the end of my final semester my senior year, and I had all the credits to graduate, so I was given my diploma, but I wasn't allowed to walk at graduation, which sucked, because I was supposed to give a speech."

"What kind of speech?"

"I was valedictorian."

Emmy reeled. Valedictorians didn't get expelled unless the situation was severe. She took Max in in the white light of the moon, noting the shadow that crossed his expression. He seemed calm, in control of his emotions. Emmy considered the way the people closest to him handled him, the way he got under Kathryn's skin, the playful warmth emanating from Javi's eyes when they'd arrived at his house, then the whispered argument between them. Max seemed socially confident, but so far Javi was the only person she'd met in Max's inner circle. He spent his time zooming around behind the anonymity of his tinted windshield. There was so much to this boy she didn't know, and suddenly she wanted to, wanted to peel away the layers and find who he was.

"Was," Max repeated. "The title went to that dipshit Lance Bromley after I got the boot."

"What'd you do to get in that kind of trouble?"

Max's stare drifted to the starless sky, a haunted expression lingering on his face. "My mom was always in my business. *Always.* But at the end of junior year, I realized she couldn't stop me from going out, so I did. A lot. At first, I was partying with my friends on the weekend. Then it turned into weekdays, then every day. Then alcohol turned to pills. And other stuff." His eyes darkened. Emmy saw a tiny crack in the wall Max had built, and she remained silent, let him give as much of himself as he was willing to give. "I guess I just wanted to lose control. To let myself fall, and I didn't care where I landed. Then, it all"—he paused, as if searching for the right word—*"culminated* when the school decided my conduct was unbecoming." He swallowed. "Without school, I had the time to do what I wanted all day. So I mostly surfed and drank and partied. Until a little over a month ago, when I wrecked my car."

Emmy thought of the time she'd spent with Max so far, how gentle he was with her, and how alive he'd seemed on that sunny afternoon, diving for the volleyball with Javi. But there it was again, that sadness in his eyes. "So that's what Kathryn meant when she warned me about you."

"She did?" Max scowled. "Kathryn doesn't know anything about me or my life." His words held a sharper edge than they had before.

"And she has her own mess of shit going on. She's been going out with this dick of a cop."

"She has a boyfriend?"

"'Boyfriend' is a stretch. Don't expect him to come over for dinner or anything like that. He fudged the police report about my accident so I wouldn't get in trouble."

"Why would he do that?" Emmy gasped. "Why risk getting fired—or worse?"

Max grunted. "He's shady. I heard he got suspended once for excessive force during an arrest. Apparently he beat the shit out of some guy during a routine traffic stop. He claimed the dude resisted, but the guy was hospitalized for a week and the family sued." Max's eyes were round. "Anyway, he wasn't doing me any favors. He wanted to screw my mom." The warm breeze rustled the palm fronds in the moonlight. "After my accident, Kathryn snapped. She tried to force me to go to rehab, drove me to some sketchy clinic for tweakers. I refused to get out of the car."

Emmy caught the way his eyes dulled, even in the darkness of the backyard.

He shook his head. "There's no fucking way. She made me agree to a bunch of ridiculous rules: no drinking, no smoking, no driving over the speed limit. Sent me to therapy. She's been on my ass, texting all day long."

"But I've been here for a week," Emmy said. "And all we've been doing is drinking and smoking."

"I'm just living my life. Flying under her radar. And this?" Max held up the joint. "Helps me sleep. I like to come out here at night and smoke and watch the stars. I just need to keep it away from Kathryn until she settles down." He passed Emmy the joint one more time. "I figured you already knew most of this from spying in the hallway the other day."

Emmy's mind flashed back to Max's eyes holding hers when he'd caught her at the top of the stairs, and her cheeks burned. "I'm sorry, I didn't mean to—"

Max's smile broke through, crooked and amused. "I'm fucking with you."

Emmy slapped her hands over her face and dropped onto her back. "So embarrassing," she mumbled through her fingers.

"Stop it." Max tried to pry her hands from her face, but Emmy held them tight. "More embarrassing than everything I just told you?"

Emmy dropped her hands to her chest and met Max's eyes. "I don't think any of it's embarrassing."

"No?" Relief flushed his face.

"Everyone has their shit, Max."

"Well, I have extra shit."

"Maybe, maybe not." She looked at him a few inches above her. "Is that why you don't want her knowing you pick me up from school?"

"I don't want her involved in my life. And if you don't want her sending you back to live with your family, it's probably best if she doesn't know you're hanging out with me. Since I'm a bad influence and all."

"I agree," Emmy said, and his shoulders relaxed. "So what's next for you?"

"Culinary school," Max said without a beat.

Emmy sat up. "You cook?"

"Among my many talents." His secretive smile returned when he looked at her again, and her heart skipped. And it was as if the pieces of her life slotted into place for the first time. The sting of her mother's absence dulled until she could no longer feel it. Everything in her life had led up to that moment beneath the stars. She didn't want to go home, didn't care about Harper. The weed settled in her brain like a cloud, and she took Max in, suddenly taken by the absolute cliché of his beauty, of his perfect teeth and the way the breeze rustled his hair.

"What?" Max's smile bloomed, like he was in on her joke. His head cocked to one side, his eyes glazed, and the corners of his mouth tugged upward.

"This weed is . . . *good*." A tiny laugh slipped from her lips before she could stop it, and a grin cracked across Max's face. Emmy shook her head, but it was useless. When the giggles got her, they didn't let go, and she melted, leaning back onto the smooth surface, and slapped a hand over her mouth, and Max joined her as they melted together.

The trip indoors was decidedly less graceful. The kitchen and staircase filled with their stifled giggles and mismatched footsteps. "Good night," Max whispered when they reached the hallway.

"Good night." The giddiness of their time together faded, leaving a vague cloud of disappointment with each step toward her bedroom; a realization that the whole encounter had been anticlimactic.

Emmy reached for her doorknob, determined to open it without a sound. She felt his hand on her lower back and a deeper breath fell from her. She turned. Max's face was serious, his body close to hers, in her space. She could feel him, the tingle between them, again. Max brushed her hair from behind her ear, sending a shock down her body at his touch. He ran the knuckle of his index finger down her arm, from her bare shoulder to her wrist, then took her hand, his palm flat against hers, and wove their fingers together. Emmy's heart thudded and her palms tickled. Max moved swiftly, taking her face in his hand, and pressed his lips to hers. His kisses came soft and gentle, three times, their lips parted slightly, before he drew back for a moment to regard her, then moved in again. When his tongue met hers, her body awoke— the hint of electricity buzzing between them had finally caught a spark. Fire blazed through her as she leaned into him, and he pushed back, pressing her against the wall with his hips. She gripped the fabric of his T-shirt and drew him in, closer, hungry for something she'd never known existed inside her.

Finally, Max stepped back and loosened his grip. He smiled before leaning in one last time, meeting her lips again, with a whisper. "Good night."

He retreated to his room. With her back still pressed against the wall, Emmy closed her eyes and took a few deep breaths, dizzy, aroused.

CHAPTER TWELVE

Saturday, April 8
Andrew

Andrew navigated the unfamiliar streets between the frantic laps of his windshield wipers. Guilt wrenched at him as he pulled into the driveway on Cherry Street and double-checked the address Kathryn had provided. "Do you mind picking me up?" she'd asked when they'd spoken. Her request had swept him with surprise. "People in my neighborhood . . . they talk." The words were strained. "So I'd rather leave my car here. Do you mind driving? Park on the street. Do not get out. And pick somewhere to eat in West Palm or Lantana or something—not in town."

"Okay." Andrew had let her instructions process, chased by the thrill of having Kathryn in the passenger seat beside him. But that night, the rain came in angry sheets, and he didn't want Kathryn to get soaked, so he rolled into the driveway. But there was another pull, a magnetic tug of curiosity, when the house came into view. Andrew leaned forward, taking in the two-story structure that held the secrets he kept from his wife. The home his son had grown up in sat unnervingly close to his own. Max had come home from school every day, eaten dinner, completed his homework, living a parallel life so close to Andrew's, just beyond his reach.

Again he saw Max's smile, dewy with youth, in the photos with his friends on the fishing boat, and the familiar course of emotion rose once more: anger, resentment, betrayal, jealousy. Andrew wasn't a monster; he wasn't abusive; he belonged *here*, the three of them living their normal, suburban lives. For a moment it were as if he could erase everything that had happened and slip into this parallel universe, before their lives had fractured, sending them in opposing directions.

Since the night they'd gone to the Mexican restaurant, each time his phone had pinged, his breath caught in his throat, and he brushed aside his disappointment when the messages were from anyone but Kathryn.

Andrew settled back into his seat. With his eyes closed, he drew a breath and tried to gather himself. On an inhale, he concentrated on what he did have: a successful career; a home; a stunning, brilliant wife. It was a practice he'd learned in addiction counseling, an exercise of gratitude. A thought bubbled in him, warm, with a sense of excitement. Sure, he had everything he'd ever wanted, and now, through some twist of fate, Kathryn had come back into his life, very much the woman he'd once loved, and yet so different. He realized that he had—at least in this delicate moment in time—the best of both worlds. And he did appreciate that.

The front door swung open, and a figure darted down the driveway, yanked the passenger door, and climbed in. This wasn't Kathryn. Andrew tapped the dome light, illuminating the space. A petite teenage girl sat before him, and she looked around the car, then up to Andrew's face. She had warm, golden skin with strange, light eyes, and her lips were parted slightly in confusion. Rain thudded the roof. Andrew's eyes darted up to the address. Was it the wrong house? "I'm here for Kathryn."

The girl didn't speak, just opened her door, rushed back into the rain, and disappeared into the house.

A disorienting beat passed.

Andrew reached for his phone just as the front door opened once again. Through the rain, he could tell this wasn't the girl from before but someone taller, dressed in dark clothing.

Kathryn climbed into the seat, pulling the door shut, and set her umbrella between her feet. "I told you to park on the street." Her long hair fell down her shoulders, and she brushed it away from her face, her perfume filling the small space, sultry and rich.

"Uh, yeah—the rain—"

But Kathryn swiveled to regard his car. "This is so strange. Max has the same car."

"Really?"

"A different color, but otherwise exactly the same."

The young girl's expression was burned into Andrew's mind, almost scared. "Maybe that's why—a girl got into my car a minute ago; then she ran back into the house."

"Emmy? That's weird, I didn't see her." Kathryn bit her lip, as if considering more than she was saying.

"Who is Emmy?" Andrew asked.

"My friend's daughter. She's staying with me for a few weeks." Kathryn didn't offer more.

Andrew scrambled to break the tension. "Your house is nice," he said, failing to secure a better word. His house, like the others in his row along Ocean Avenue, was custom built and uninviting. The elusive neighbors he and Amy had didn't walk their dogs or chat at the end of their driveways, but Andrew could picture people living real, messy lives in this neighborhood.

"Thanks." Kathryn frowned up at her home in the shroud of rain. "I guess when I bought it, I thought I'd get married someday, maybe have more children." Her eyes were sad and faraway. Maybe she, too, was imagining another version of her life, one where the space between them didn't exist. "But it's a little late for that now."

Andrew reversed into the street. As he shifted into drive, a car approached, and he stopped, blinded by the oncoming headlights. The car rolled to a stop, and torrents of rain fell in the space between them. The silver car turned into the driveway, and the red brake lights illuminated when it stopped. It wasn't until Kathryn drew a gasp that Andrew realized Max must be behind the wheel. Andrew craned his neck to get a glance of his son, but between the rain and Max's tinted windows, it was impossible.

Kathryn's hands balled on her lap, and she shook her head. "It was a terrible idea to have you pick me up."

"I don't think he saw us," Andrew said. Kathryn gave a small nod, but her hands didn't unclench. He let the rain drum on the roof for a long moment before he proceeded down the street.

◆ ◆ ◆

Emmy

Darting into the rain, Emmy yanked the door handle of Max's car and climbed into the familiar black leather seat. Her breath caught at the sight of him, fresh faced and handsome, one hand on the steering wheel. Max leaned in to place a soft kiss on her lips. "You're all wet." He switched the heat on, and the seat warmed beneath her legs.

Over the last few weeks, slipping into Max's car each afternoon was like passing into a different universe. Something had shifted in Max; he was lighter. His smile had changed, no longer secretive, and it reached his eyes.

Harper sent Emmy an increasingly desperate string of texts, but Emmy had left her mother on read. It felt good to punish Harper with silence the way Harper had always done to her. A new source of resentment bubbled up; Harper had kept Emmy from Max and Kathryn her entire life for no reason. Maybe they could have been friends, been *normal*.

Emmy's world was now painted with color, a delicious secret blooming between her and Max, dulling the sting of Harper's indifference.

In the afternoons, Max drove to the beach lot and cut the engine. In a fluid movement, they unbuckled their seat belts and moved into one another, as if they couldn't bear the space between them any longer. Kissing Max was electricity; it was fire, all-consuming, like warm honey running down her body. It was a million times hotter than any romance novel she'd ever read. The way he drew in made her feel like he craved her more than anything else in the world. Emmy slid into his lap, and Max slipped a hand under her shirt, sending a rush through her; it was empowering to be wanted this way. She shifted her hips against his. Max let out a sharp gasp before pulling back, pressing his forehead to hers, and in his expression, Emmy saw it took every bit of his restraint to break away from her.

One day, Max had brushed her bracelets aside, his forehead narrowing when his eyes fell onto the four straight lines marking the edge of her wrist. The oldest scar had faded to white, the other three were still an ugly, raised purple. "What's this?"

"Nothing." Emmy's pulse thrummed. She slid her bracelets back into place. "Just something I used to do."

Max laced his fingers with hers and lifted her hand, letting her bracelets roll down her arm before he pressed his lips to the tender, vulnerable skin of her wrist. Nobody had ever touched her this way. It was addictive. "Promise me you won't do it again?"

"I promise." She meant it, vowing as much to herself as she did to him. She'd spent so much of her life narrowing her focus onto an unspecified future, an escape. But she'd never imagined this, something in her life she didn't need to run from. A brighter world.

In the driveway, as the rain washed over the car, Emmy tried to shake off the experience with the man with Max's eyes. It was absurd; her mind had to be playing tricks on her. But the encounter replayed in quick, disorienting flashes. The man had Max's face, remarkably similar, though with no trace of Max's boyhood. In the moment she'd frozen and studied him, determined to commit each detail to memory, the way she would cling to a dream she desperately wanted to remember. She considered telling Max what had happened, but what if she was wrong about what she'd seen?

"Kathryn just left," she said. "Do you want to go inside?"

Max mulled this as he leaned over to kiss her once more, his hand gliding up her thigh, sending a ripple through her body. She didn't want anything to extinguish this flame that raged between them. "No," Max said. "Kathryn's been blowing up my phone. Let's go somewhere else."

A realization sparked inside her. "The tenant moved out of my dad's house a few weeks ago. It'll be empty until early summer," she offered, shy, her body buzzing. "Nobody will bother us there."

A smile tugged at the corners of Max's mouth, and he shifted the car into reverse. He didn't take his hand off her leg as he drove, and she set her hand on top of his. Neither felt the need for words; the only sound was the rain and the rhythmic thump of the wipers. Max turned onto Ocean Avenue and made his way under the passing streetlamps until he came to a hidden driveway, the headlights illuminating a dark wooden gate. He rolled down his window and reached out into the rain to punch in the security code Emmy gave him, and they passed through, the low-hanging palms brushing the roof of the car. A chill rippled through Emmy when she looked up at her father's house.

"Okay." Max turned to her. "Ready?"

They threw their doors open and ran through the rain and up the stone path on the side of the house, their sneakers splashing in the puddles. A bright flash lit the sky, and thunder boomed around them as Emmy punched her code into the panel beside the door before she pushed it open. They ducked out of the storm into the house.

Max found a light switch, and the house came aglow, while thunder echoed in the upper levels. Emmy had been inside the home only a handful of times since her childhood, whenever Harper had to oversee some sort of repair or delivery, and each time Emmy tried to let the space revive memories of her early life but was left empty handed. She now walked over to the swath of windows before the sunporch and watched lightning bolts dance white and yellow across the ocean, momentarily revealing the low, heavy clouds above.

Everything had begun here. Emmy heard it: ghostly laughter on sunny days. Then, sharp words. Screaming. Broken glass. It could have been imagined, but she was sure it wasn't; she felt it, the fear visceral. She watched Kathryn disappear out the back door, watched Harper collapse on the floor.

Emmy slipped her phone from her pocket, scrolled to "Kathryn." **Spending the night with my friend Maggie. I'll be back tomorrow.** She ended the message with a heart. She should feel terrible about lying to Kathryn. But she saw it again, the man's face. Maybe Emmy wasn't the only one with something to hide.

Max switched on the fireplace before he came up behind her, slipping his arms around her waist. She turned to face him. The fire grew, the room flickering with strange shadows.

Max rubbed her arms and whispered, "Before this . . . continues, we need to talk." His face was serious. "If Kathryn finds out we're . . . she'll send you home. And if you do anything to upset your mom, she might pull your school funding."

Emmy didn't know how to respond. Everything was spinning so fast. She'd been in Kathryn and Max's house only a few weeks, but they'd been the best weeks of her life. And the draw toward Max was magnetic. Something tugged deep within her at the feel of his body underneath the fabric of his T-shirt.

"I have nothing to lose." Max pulled back a few inches, his body rigid. "But you have everything. So, if you want to, let's stop this now. Before it grows into something larger. Before anyone gets hurt."

Her stomach dropped when she thought of her mother stopping her from going to Seattle. Her future would be dead before it began. "What's that going to be like for the next two months? I can't go back to my grandmother's house, Max. Ever."

Max offered a shrug. "I'm not home much. I can control myself. I'll give you space. We can be cordial."

"*Cordial?* Not even friends?"

"Emmy." Her name fell away from him on a breath. "There's no way I can be friends with you."

Her world spun. She was standing on the precipice of something much greater than herself, and if she followed the path, her life would never be the same. She had to focus. Her mouth was dry, her throat tight, and she shook her head. "That's not what I want." Looking at Max, there was nothing she wanted more than him. She was in deep, and she suspected he was, too.

"I won't let you ruin your future for me," Max said.

"Let me decide what's right for me." She held out her palm, and Max's half smile lifted in surprise, but his hand was sweaty when he reached for hers. Why was he so nervous?

Emmy pulled him into her, and she knew it the way she knew her own name: her love for Max had been there all along, flaring to life the moment she'd allowed it to breathe. It may have been there in those days she hardly remembered, splashing in the sun. Or when she'd watched him at her mother's wedding. But it was there, weaved into the fabric of her being. She didn't need to speak the words and didn't need to hear him speak them.

Her body was alive, buzzing with possibility, with yearning. Was this the part of her romance novels where the heroine went against all common sense, all good advice, because of a love that burned so hot it blinded her? How much was she willing to sacrifice for him? Scrapping all hope for a relationship with Harper? Betraying Kathryn's trust?

And was this what happened to Harper, maybe in this very house?

"Yes, Max. This is crazy. It's dangerous. And I'm freaking out right now, but all I know is I want *you*. If it grows into something larger . . ." Emmy let the words fall off her lips, possibilities blooming. What if she and Max found a love like her parents once had? Was it worth the risk?

In the reflection of his eyes, she watched lightning flash just beyond the windows, and behind his eyes—excitement. He leaned in, bringing her face to his. "Then we'll be careful." His tone was low, sultry, with a note of delicious secrecy. Emmy nodded, and Max took her face in his hands. His mouth met hers, hungry, wet, desperate. And she gave in, surrendering all control. Her hands snaked across his back as his lips traced down her neck and across her collarbone. "I didn't expect this to happen between us," he said softly, and stepped back to look at her. "But I knew it the minute I saw you standing there in the hallway. I knew I'd fall in love with you. And it scared me. It still scares me, but you're the best thing that's ever happened to me."

Emmy took a moment to grasp the gravity of his words. She'd felt it, too, but couldn't allow herself to presume Max's feelings for her were so strong. But she knew he meant every word. To have Max return her love was more than she could have wished for. She leaned into him, his hand slipping between them to undo the buttons on her shirt. Her heart thudded when he took a step back, still kissing her as he moved upward, and peeled the wet fabric away from her skin. Max lifted his own shirt over his head, then reached for her face, tilting her chin to kiss her. "I want you."

Her body awoke, and she was aware of every inch of her skin where it pressed against his. This was *her* life; she was going to do what she wanted.

"Is that okay?" He kissed her neck, and his hands glided to the small of her back. When she didn't answer, he paused and met her eyes. "Emmy? Say something."

She nodded. "Yes."

Max's grin spread, and he pulled her in again, pressing his lips onto hers. "Come over here." He took a blanket and some of the pillows off the couch and set them on the rug, and the warmth of the fire blazed onto her skin as Max guided her closer. Emmy lowered herself onto the blanket before he joined her, tracing kisses down her neck. Max reached for the waistband on her skirt and unbuttoned it, letting it slide to the floor. Her fingers traced along his skin until they found the buttons on his jeans. Max slid out of his pants and cast them aside with her clothing. Then he carried on, kneeling over her, engrossed in her neck, kissing her down her arms to the tips of her fingers. Emmy glanced over at their clothing piled on the floor next to them, the weight of the situation dawning on her, and her body tensed. Feeling her reaction, Max pulled away once more, this time more gently. "Are you okay? You're shaking."

A rush of panic slipped inside her, and her eyes panned down her body, exposed in the light of the fire. "Max. I've never—"

"It's okay," he said, his swift body moving over her again. "Just tell me if I do anything you don't like."

◆ ◆ ◆

Amy

After being rebuffed by Dr. Cassidy, she had sketched out a three-step plan to fix her life and her marriage.

Andrew had cold feet about parenthood. So many men, and women, did. She couldn't waste time massaging his feelings. She saw it in him, in his patient, nurturing demeanor. He would love their child with all his heart, she was certain. If only she could solve the problem without burdening Andrew. She'd find a way to bridge the obstacles, would lean on her nature, run every test, adjust any variable to achieve the desired outcome. It was what she did best.

Step one was completed over a cold cup of coffee in the lost hours of her night shift: she'd dug deep in the web pages on her phone for a "drugstore" in North Miami she'd heard about on an infertility message board: a small rented space tucked into a nondescript three-story office building that advertised all manner of "supplements."

The next morning, she executed step two. She'd set her alarm for 10:00 a.m., but as the rising sun pressed against the curtains, she couldn't rest, her heart fluttering against the mattress as Andrew returned from his run and showered. He tiptoed across the carpet, and she willed her face to relax. She knew his routine from the muffled sound of fabric: he slipped into his boxer briefs, then tugged a white V-neck over his head. The drop of his weight onto the bed surprised her, and suddenly he was close, his face against the crook of her arm. She thought of leaning into him, of pretending to wake and reaching out, but he'd been so careful not to disturb her that she realized this moment was for himself. He rested his face against her arm, nuzzled her skin with a featherlight touch. Andrew placed a kiss on her head, then pushed off the bed, leaving her with an ache for him to return.

Once Andrew left for work, Amy had gotten up, showered, filled a travel tumbler with coffee, then merged onto I-95. The day was blazing hot, white popcorn thunderheads floating offshore. Amy found she relished her illicit task the way she had felt as a child, having successfully swiped a cookie from the kitchen under her mother's nose. But the sensation faded, dulled by the reality of the countless tiny tragedies she faced each day, leaving a bitter taste in her mouth. She shouldn't have to operate in this clandestine manner; she should have her doctor's support. But Amy had encountered people who doubted her over the course of her career, her life. Professors, fellow doctors, patients. If Dr. Cassidy was the best, and the clock was ticking, she was left no other choice.

The hour drive provided time for her mind to wander, to examine her marriage. Andrew had been upset about turning down the promotion. Could they have adjusted their schedules to accommodate one another's additional hours? Her guilt throbbed. If she'd been more flexible, maybe the seat beside her wouldn't be vacant; she and Andrew would be united in their mission to eschew the snobby Palm Beach fertility "specialist" and find success by way of a seedy backdoor shop in Miami beside a KFC. But a cushiony barrier had formed between them, like two opposing magnets, held together by force. So Amy needed to smooth this rough patch. It could be done.

She'd been raised with a near aversion to drama. In the mornings, her parents watched the weather and traffic. Then, lunch bags in hand, they shuffled out the door to face the day. In the evenings, Amy's father helped her complete her homework while her mother, Elena, prepared dinner. On Saturday evenings, they all paused, watched a movie of Amy's choosing with a bowl of popcorn between them. Their lives were calm, predictable, focused.

Until one afternoon when Amy was thirteen, and her algebra tutor came down with strep. Amy came through the back door early and saw her mother at the kitchen table, her cheeks glistening with tears, eyes red rimmed. She straightened at the sight of Amy, but Amy caught it: the anguish in her mother's face, the cordless phone discarded on the table. This wasn't something simple. It was as if a piece of her mother was missing, and in its place, a hardening. Elena rose, moved to the stove, switched it on, sniffed. And, like that, the mother Amy knew had returned. In that moment Amy realized people could hide parts of themselves from those around them.

The dinner table was quiet. From her parents' bedroom door, Amy heard harsh whispers late into the night.

Her father moved differently. He was stiff and doubled his attention to Amy's studies. Something softened his eyes. Remorse, maybe.

He hired a new receptionist at his practice.

Then, five months after she'd caught her mother crying, Amy came downstairs on a Saturday evening to the smell of microwave popcorn. Her parents were settled on the couch, a blanket tenting their legs. Amy rushed to them, wedged herself between them, and felt their bodies on either side of her, both of them relaxed for the first time in months.

She'd dedicated her entire life to fixing problems. She could mend her marriage while the wound was still small.

And it seemed to be working. There was a lightness to Andrew since their appointment with Dr. Cassidy, one Amy hadn't seen in him for as long as she could recall.

The first time Amy had slept with Andrew, they'd been dating for two months, and he'd invited her over for dinner. It was clear the evening would end in his bed, and Andrew's smile was replaced by a sheepish grin as he poured her a glass of her favorite pinot grigio and set two steaming dishes of chicken marsala between them.

"No wine for you?" Amy asked.

Andrew examined his plate. "No." She could have sworn she saw a tiny tremor in his bottom lip. "I run six miles each morning. It's best with a clear head."

A dash of concern. He'd seemed perfect over the last eight weeks. Kind, gentle, genuine. She twisted the stem of her glass. "Is there something I should be worried about?"

"Absolutely not." The conviction in his voice was fleeced with something hard, a decision made long before they'd met. He looked up. "I promise you that."

Amy operated on facts, on evidence. She clocked the fear in Andrew's face. But aside from that conversation, the sum of all his parts left her with a different conclusion; they moved around one another effortlessly after dinner, Andrew's hands submerged in soapy dishwater while Amy toweled drippy plates. To Amy, it made him even more desirable, this control of his own life. A spark of desire crackled in the room.

Amy realized Andrew was waiting for her to give him a signal, and she relished the power she had over this gentle man twice her size. She set her towel on the countertop and gripped his T-shirt, pulling him in to kiss her. It was all Andrew needed to break his restraint; she could feel it in the way his strong body gave in to her, and he lifted her onto the kitchen counter, where they peeled their clothes away and left them strewn on the kitchen floor before he carried her into his bedroom, slamming the door behind them.

Afterward, he'd opened the balcony door, and the lights of the high-rise buildings around them glowed like so many stars from where they lay in his bed. Andrew had his face pressed into her arm, curled on his side. "You can be any kind of surgeon; why choose trauma?" he asked, his fingers stroking her hair.

Amy considered for a moment. "I always loved the idea that I could fix someone when something awful has happened to them."

Andrew made a soft noise but didn't add anything, and Amy listened as his breathing slowed. The curtains danced in the breeze, and it occurred to her she was fixing something damaged in him. The evidence was there in his apartment: the lone bedside table, the single towel hung in the bathroom. Though she was sure he'd brought women there, there were no stray toothbrushes or shampoo bottles, as if nobody had returned often enough to leave belongings behind. Andrew's phone calls with his family were polite and formal; they stuck to safe, almost preapproved topics. Amy was introduced to his roommate, Nick, who eyed her with caution, and she realized he was the only person Andrew had allowed into his orbit until she'd arrived. Andrew lived a careful, solitary life. If he was protecting himself from something, it was concealed by success and privilege, by hard work and focus. He didn't let any hand life had dealt him become an excuse, which made Andrew a rare find.

Four years later, on that sunny morning, Amy's car glided onto the off-ramp in North Miami. The robotic navigation led her to a desolate parking lot dotted with potholes. Inside the building, the elevator door was smudged with fingerprints, and the air smelled sickly sweet of bargain all-purpose cleaner. The attendant didn't pry, just gave Amy a curt nod as acceptance of the code word she'd been provided by the ladies on the message board, then handed her a paper bag. It wasn't until her drive back up the highway that the weight of potential consequences rode in on a wave of panic. If she was caught purchasing drugs smuggled from South America, she could lose her medical license. What would her parents think if she could no longer practice medicine? What if her illegal actions were exposed in her mother's last few months of life? Without her income, she and Andrew couldn't afford the mortgage on their house. Would she lose him, too? No, she wouldn't let anyone find out.

Now, on a wet Saturday night, it was time for step three. When the rotating surgeon, Dr. Sanchez, arrived at the hospital, Amy ducked into her SUV, swiped her employee badge on the kiosk, then nosed out into the shroud of rain. She drove two towns north of Delray Beach to Lantana. The rain slowed to a trickle when she pulled into a deserted strip mall bathed in neon lights.

If her med school classmates could see her now. Practical Amy, Amy who didn't trust anything that couldn't be proved in a lab, with one hundred dollars in cash she'd withdrawn from an ATM and a list on her Notes app to tick off: *Du zhong. Xu duan. Shu dui huang. Dong chong xia cao.* Amy's mother had whispered the name of each herb into the phone like a secret, and Amy had repeated their pronunciations and how to use each one. Her mother didn't ask whether Andrew was privy to the conversation. Maybe mother's intuition told her he wasn't.

A few hours earlier, she'd stolen a moment to duck into the hospital bathroom, where she pinched her skin between her fingers and plunged the needle into her abdomen, her phone buzzing on the porcelain sink. Someone always needed her, urgently, so she'd locked her injection kit in her office drawer and had run down the hall, toward whatever chaos awaited her. A drunk driver had T-boned a sedan carrying a mother and her four children. Amy was fed the facts: twelve-year-old boy. Unrestrained. Unresponsive.

Amy commanded people, and they flowed, a single entity. Among the voices and the needles, the monitors, the chatter, Amy felt it: the room slowing around her. Her movements were sharp, decisive, while her thoughts were steady. Amy hadn't lost a single patient since she'd started at Boca General. She was at her peak. She was in control of the room. Of her life.

In the strip mall parking lot, the rain pattered her windshield, and she glanced at the clock. The store closed in ten minutes, and she had to get back to the hospital. She shut her car door and darted toward the shop. She felt like a general, lining up her men before she began her attack.

She glanced around, looking for anyone who might recognize her in her green scrubs. Then, through the shroud of rain, across the street, a valet jogged from a gray Audi toward Lombardi's Steakhouse. Amy's head cocked to the side. It looked exactly like Andrew's car. But it couldn't be, could it?

CHAPTER THIRTEEN

Saturday, April 8
Andrew

Lombardi's Steakhouse was warm and cozy on the rainy evening, the rich mahogany booths bathed in intimate sconce lights. As instructed, Andrew had driven up the rainy highway to a restaurant two towns north, their anonymity solidified with each passing mile.

Kathryn shrugged off her blazer and set it on the booth beside her. She tapped on her phone, frowned, then placed it face down on the table and scanned the wine menu. Andrew took in the way the light in the room made her skin glow. She wore a stack of bangles on one wrist and a heavy gold watch on the other. He pictured the girl he'd known all those years ago, with her bright laugh, her long, sun-kissed hair. This Kathryn was stiff; she appeared to carry herself with an air of confidence, even when the occasional signs of discomfort peeked through her strong exterior. From what he could tell, Kathryn surrounded herself with a safe cushion of isolation. Amy had been his second chance—why hadn't Kathryn found hers?

"I'll have the filet mignon with the Kona-coffee rub. Medium rare. Steamed vegetables and potatoes on the side." Kathryn handed the waiter her menu. "And a glass of Silver Oak cab."

"I'll have the same. Medium, with an iced tea."

When the waiter walked away, Kathryn recalibrated. "When did you stop drinking?"

Andrew folded his napkin onto his lap. "Twenty years sober next February."

Kathryn's eyes widened, a blush rising in her cheeks. "I can cancel my order—"

"Don't worry about it, Kathryn. I'm fine. And when you're meeting your estranged ex to discuss your secret love child, wine might be necessary."

Kathryn stared at him. "Drew . . ."

He let his smile break across his face, and Kathryn returned it, a spark of relief in her eyes, and her shoulders relaxed. The waiter brought her wine, and she held up her glass. "Well, cheers to that." Andrew held his iced tea aloft, and they clinked glasses. Kathryn's eyes drifted to the ceiling tiles above. "What is it with all the restaurants playing Frank Sinatra, like, exclusively?"

Andrew focused on the music floating above the din of the restaurant, grasping the bouncy tune, before the lyrics caught up with him: "The Way You Look Tonight." He and Kathryn locked eyes. They remembered.

The first time he'd leaned in her ear and whispered *I love you*, they'd been dancing, the magic of "The Way You Look Tonight" swimming in the room. She'd stopped. They'd never said these words to each other before, and for a moment he thought he'd upset her.

"I love you, too, Andrew." She had given an embarrassed smile before he kissed her.

Now Andrew looked at Kathryn across the table as he took in the memory, reliving the delicious magic of first love. He hadn't felt anything that magical in twenty years. "We were something else, weren't we?"

Kathryn's gaze dropped to the table, and her smile fell. "We were. We were crazy about each other. But we were just kids; there was no way we could have known how everything would turn out." Sadness lingered in her eyes.

The room bustled around them, and he saw it again: the weight of her decisions and how carefully she tried to conceal her regret. It was there, clear as day, always present, always hidden.

The waiter set their dishes on the table, steam rising between them, and they ate for a while, lost in their own thoughts.

"How are your parents?" Andrew asked. He'd gotten along with Kathryn's family and still felt a sting at all his unreturned calls to their house.

"My dad passed away ten years ago." She snapped her fingers. "Heart attack. Just like that."

"I'm so sorry." Andrew was genuinely surprised. His parents were alive and healthy, and he realized how fortunate he was.

"Thank you." She straightened, set down her wineglass, composed herself. "My mom sold their house and moved to Naples. She got married again, which is so strange to me. But she's happy. They live in one of those fifty-five-plus communities, and they play pickleball." She shrugged. "And you?" Her words were clipped now. "How's your family?"

"My parents are doing well. They're retired. My brother moved to Myrtle Beach, and he has two boys."

The previous fall, Andrew and Amy had gone to visit his brother, Timothy. On their first evening together, they had all gone down to the beach for an evening walk while Tim's kids skidded across the waves on their boogie boards. At dusk, Tim had called out to his boys, and they'd charged at him, leaving their small footprints in the sand, and Tim had wrapped their squirming bodies in a giant rainbow beach towel. The image had hit Andrew like a slap, along with the realization that his younger brother was living the very life he'd planned with Kathryn, while he and Amy stood on the sidelines, spectators in dry-clean-only clothes she'd purchased for the trip.

"Andrew?" A man turned the corner, his voice jolting Andrew from his reverie.

A frantic heat spread from his chest to his face as the Rolodex in his mind spun, trying to place the man's face and how he fit into his life, and whether he knew Amy.

"Charles?" Andrew asked as the man stepped into the intimate glow of light Andrew shared with Kathryn.

"How's it going, stranger?" Andrew's client, Charles, clapped a hand on Andrew's shoulder. He wore a linen shirt with a busy palm-leaf print, his face pink from, presumably, too many rounds of golf and too much bourbon. He motioned to Kathryn. "So this is the missus?"

Andrew reached for his water glass as Charles extended his hand in Kathryn's direction. Instead of a handshake, Charles kissed the top of Kathryn's knuckles, his eyes tracing her clavicle, down the low-cut neckline of her dress. An ice chip lodged itself in the back of Andrew's throat, leaving a white-hot trail of pain when he swallowed. Charles hadn't met Amy, but if he did, how would Andrew explain the dinner with another woman? His thoughts spiraled, that familiar prickle in his fingertips.

"Just a friend. Kathryn." Kathryn's voice was laced with a jagged barb of warning. She was skilled at rebuffing lecherous men, Andrew noted.

"Well, I don't want to interrupt your dinner." Charles eyed Kathryn one last time. "It was good to see you, Andrew. Nice to meet you, Kathryn."

Charles disappeared into the background of the restaurant.

"Sorry about that," Andrew said, and a breath drained from him. "One of my clients."

Kathryn gave a small nod. "Are you all right?"

"Yes, I just—we have to be careful."

"Why?" Kathryn's nearly empty wineglass was perched between her fingers. "We're not doing anything wrong."

"No, we're not." Andrew went back to his dinner, his appetite diminished. He could have told Amy he was taking a client out. But lying seemed worse than an omission. And he couldn't shake the sticky-dirty feeling of watching Charles ogle Kathryn, that tickle of panic. "But I'm not ready to tell Amy about Max. About you."

Kathryn considered, then gave a small nod. Andrew pushed his guilt aside. Kathryn was right—he could eat dinner with whomever he liked. Amy had never shown him a shred of jealousy. If he had dinner with a female friend, she'd never question him. So why did this feel like a dirty secret?

As he ate, he took in the way Kathryn's graceful fingers held her fork. For a moment he pictured himself in a world where they didn't need to jump when people like Charles interrupted their evening. *This is my wife, Kathryn,* he imagined saying, savoring the envy in Charles's face. For a moment he allowed himself to exist in the place where they were a normal couple enjoying a night out, with twenty years of love and partnership between them.

He and Amy rarely went to dinner. They'd dated over breakfast, plates of chicken and waffles, Amy in her scrubs after a long shift. When Amy was home in the evenings, they basked in coziness. Now her schedule was so hectic, when she did eat breakfast in his presence, she ate oatmeal standing over the kitchen sink before she rushed off to work.

Andrew shook away the thought. "What's a nineteen-year-old doing with a car like that?"

Kathryn took a deep breath as she prepared to answer. "Max inherited some money. And a month ago he found himself in need of new transportation." Her voice was cold, with an edge of disdain. "He came home with that thing a few weeks back." She gave a resigned shrug. "At least its safety features are top of the line."

What Nick had said was true—Max was a spoiled rich kid. Kathryn's father must have left him money, and Andrew imagined Max striding into the Audi dealership with cash; it was every teenage boy's dream. "Lucky kid."

Kathryn dabbed her lips with her napkin and didn't elaborate.

Andrew remembered the way Kathryn had withdrawn when he'd pushed before, and he couldn't risk driving her away again. He leaned forward and laid out his question carefully. "Did Max have any difficulties growing up?"

Kathryn's eyes still held their trepidation from when she'd spoken of Max's car, and she seemed to consider her answer carefully. "Yes." Ice flushed Andrew's veins. "He had a bit of a rough patch, and for a while his behavior was . . . dangerous." Kathryn's tone shifted, and the color drained from her face. So what Nick had said was true. Then she rushed: "It was my fault; I sheltered him too much for too long." Her cheeks glowed. "He's better now, though some days speaking to him can feel like handling a live grenade." Her words slowed. "Still, it's like living in limbo. I'm waiting for him to do something, to make a choice. To go back to school, maybe."

"But he's better?" Andrew probed. Max's haunted eyes in the swimming pool photos flashed again, and he swallowed the lump in his throat. Something had to have happened in Max's life to affect him so deeply.

"Yes." Kathryn's shoulders slumped. Her voice was raw and honest. "I'm scared to push him. He's old enough to make his own choices, but I don't want anything to throw him off course."

"You mean like meeting me?"

"Yes." She turned the stem of her glass, rotating it in small degrees. "But I've been thinking."

"Hmm?"

"Maybe if we approach it the right way, I could introduce the two of you. Someday. Right now I feel like if anything upsets him, it could end badly." A ripple in her voice. "I've tried everything to get through to him, but he won't listen to me. Maybe if he demonstrates a little more emotional maturity, you might be the person who can get him to take his life seriously."

She held his eyes with hers, and something stirred inside him. Andrew had spent years blaming himself for Kathryn's absence, punishing himself, and now he felt her open up just slightly, and he thought there might be a sliver of a chance he might learn why she'd omitted him from their lives.

Kathryn's words held a loose promise of a future between them, in some form, and there was a beam of hope in this, too. Maybe she'd let him meet Max. And another spark: maybe it meant this dinner didn't have to be the last time they'd see each other. "I'm here, Kathryn. Now that I know, I'm not going anywhere. I can't. You understand that, don't you?"

Kathryn considered his words. Then she cocked her head, a blush to her cheeks, and he saw the Kathryn he'd loved all those years ago. Andrew shoved aside a fresh wave of guilt, letting the nostalgic magic of their memory of the love they'd shared settle over their table like a cloud, blended with the taste of what their life could have been, and savored it all. Kathryn's return to his life now held a hint of permanence, and he allowed an illicit excitement to creep into his heart. What he'd known for twenty years was true: their story wasn't finished.

CHAPTER FOURTEEN

Then
Kathryn

On the morning of her college graduation, Kathryn's parents, Sherry and Henry, made the four-hour drive to sit in the freshly repainted bleachers of the football field, sweating in the sunshine as the dean crawled down the list of graduates. Kathryn searched for her parents' beaming faces in the crowd as she collected her degree, and after the ceremony, she sat beside Andrew. Her parents treated them to a celebratory lunch on a brick patio at a decadent French bistro beside a bubbling fountain. Then, tipsy on champagne none of them could pronounce, Kathryn watched her mother's hand wave before their SUV turned the corner and disappeared.

She savored the feeling of her parents' unabashed pride, of providing them with a memory they could capture in a glossy photo, and promised herself it would be the first of a lifetime of milestones. After all, as an only child, any milestone she failed to reach would rob her lovely parents of a life experience. Kathryn had Andrew by her side, a degree in her hand, and a list of law schools to apply to. She pictured Sherry and Henry beaming as they witnessed Kathryn and Andrew recite their wedding vows, then as they cradled their first grandchild. She was standing at the threshold of her life, and the world was bursting with possibilities.

Kathryn moved her sparse belongings into Andrew's apartment and, free from the burden of school, they spent their time tangled in one another, the sun of late morning pressing against the curtains. In the evenings, Kathryn waitressed at a pizza restaurant, but when she was off, they spent their nights barhopping with their friends, returning home in the middle of the night, buzzed from a few beers and intoxicated by one another. They talked until the sun rose, mapping their plans to harness the love they shared and chart their course in the world.

"You'll be the best mom," Andrew said, wearing a wistful smile. He was sprawled on his bed, one hand resting beneath his head. "And I can't wait to be a dad. It seems like the coolest thing you could possibly do, like you get to create a whole person and show them the best things in life."

Kathryn's heart swelled.

"We have to have at least three."

"Excuse me? Are you pushing them out of your body?" Kathryn demanded with a laugh, then propped herself up on an elbow. "No more than two. No less than two."

"Okay, so two."

"Being an only child was—is—a lot of pressure. I'd never do that to my kid. Thank God for Harper; she's the sister I never had."

"I get it." Andrew rolled onto his side and fingered a loose thread on his bedspread. "That's how it is with Nick."

"But you have a brother."

Andrew pinched the thread, tugged it from the fabric. "Kind of. Timmy's eight years younger. He and his dad were always busy with his football practices. I was all about my grades."

"His dad? Your dad?"

Kathryn saw the hardening in Andrew's face, his jaw set. He shook his head, a quiver in his fingers as he yanked the thread from the bedspread, tearing a hole in the fabric. White fluff spilled out.

"What is it, Drew?"

"My dad." Andrew's voice wobbled. "My biological father. He ran off when I was two."

"Oh wow. I had no idea."

Andrew met her eyes. "My mom married Craig when I was five. He's all I know, really. He insisted I call him *Dad*, and he's been great to me, always, but . . . I always suspected it was more about him and my mom and their perfect image, this nuclear family, you know? He took care of me and Timmy, drove us around, cooked breakfast every weekend, made sure we did well in school. And I'm grateful for it. I saw the way he worked his ass off, and he never complained. He's the reason I am who I am. But when I found out about my bio dad, my mom just told me, 'He's probably passed out on the floor of a bar somewhere.'" Andrew's breath snagged, and he stuffed the fluff back into the hole in his blanket. "My mom and Craig and Timmy, we had such a normal, uneventful life, but I always wondered what would happen if someday he came back for me. I blamed the booze. They say it's a disease. So if he got better, he'd want to come back, at least check in on me, right?"

Kathryn didn't picture this sort of gritty pedigree for Andrew, with his expensive haircut, his gray collegiate crewneck. Andrew covered his face with a hand. "I've never told anyone this besides Nick."

His hand shook, and Kathryn reached out, weaved her fingers into his. "You can tell me anything."

"When I was thirteen, my mom told me he'd been killed in a bar fight." Kathryn gasped. Andrew's eyes were pink, glossy with tears. "I mean, yeah, he was a piece of shit. But until that day there was a possibility for him to show he cared. Then it was just gone." Kathryn was silent as Andrew palmed a single tear from his cheek. "Does this make you rethink having kids with me?"

"God, Andrew, none of that matters."

"Alcoholism can be genetic."

Kathryn shook her head. "We'll raise our kids with all the love in the world. I'm not worried about any of it." She tugged his hand closer. "Both of them. Three, maybe, as long as we can live on the beach."

"Near the beach." Andrew's smile broke through again. "In the general vicinity."

"*On*. Oceanfront. And I want a pool." She could see it then, their children licking drippy Popsicles. She could smell the chlorine, see the sparkling wedding band on her hand and the smoke rising from the barbecue. And Andrew. Always Andrew.

"You're going to have to be a hotshot corporate lawyer if you want oceanfront *and* a pool."

"I'm working on it." Kathryn laughed. "You'd better score a fancy finance job if you want three kids."

Andrew rolled his weight on top of her, his tongue slipping into her mouth, silencing her giggles. And like that, the cloud of his past dissipated.

Over the phone, Kathryn gushed to Harper. "I can't wait to bring Andrew to Delray so you and Luke can meet him." There was a giddiness in her tone Kathryn didn't recognize.

"He sounds perfect, Kat," Harper said. "They'll totally hit it off."

Hearing Harper's voice prodded Kathryn with a throb of homesickness. By her junior year, she'd grown weary of the smattering of dive bars in their small college town. She itched for Andrew to complete his final year of school. When she finished law school, they could afford a house in Delray, begin their lives near Lucas and Harper, so they could share a pitcher of strong mojitos at Cabana on Atlantic Avenue, double-date, savor a pan of paella. It was years off, but every day was a step closer.

But it seemed Harper and Lucas were miles ahead of them.

"I have news," Harper said, her voice wobbly, breathless. "Luke's dad died a while back. And, well . . . he left Luke some money." Harper's voice danced across the words. "Luke bought us a house."

"A house—where?" Harper had grown up with money, more money than Kathryn could comprehend. Maybe if Lucas was financially comfortable Harper's mother would loosen her grip on her daughter.

"In Delray. Near the beach," was all Harper offered. "You and Drew will have to stay with us when you visit. But there's more, Kat."

Kathryn gripped the receiver. "Tell me."

"Lucas proposed."

The words sucked the breath from Kathryn, and she sat up against the pillows. "No. Way. Harper—when—*how*? And what did Nora say?"

Harper fell silent for a moment. "She's livid. She hates Luke. But mostly because . . ." Harper's voice faded. "Well, I've been seeing someone . . . like a therapist. Since I started dating Luke," she rushed. "And he helped me see how much control my mom had over me. How that's not good. So I've been spending less time with her. And I'm on some medication, too."

Wow. It was a lot. No wonder Harper sounded lighter. But for the first time, the pieces clicked. Harper's ups and downs, the sharp accusations, maybe they'd never been about Kathryn at all. Harper sounded . . . free.

"Anyway, we're going to elope. In Paris. Two days from now."

"Two days? *Paris?* Holy shit. Congratulations on the engagement. And the house! I can't believe I'm not going to be there when you get married."

"I know, but I just want it to be us. To be romantic."

"I get it. I'm shocked. But I'm excited. More than excited—you're so lucky to have found Lucas."

"And you found Andrew. *We're* lucky, Kat. Hurry up. Move back down here, marry this guy, so we can live near each other and our kids can be best friends," Harper squealed.

Kathryn grinned. "I'm working on it. I just have to chill and work this shitty restaurant job while I fill out law school apps. But it'll all be worth it. We'll do it, Harper." When Kathryn spoke the words, the possibility of it all felt like a blissful dream. Everything she'd ever wanted, so close she could almost touch it.

In September, Andrew returned for his final two semesters, rising early each morning and shuffling around his bedroom in a rush before he darted out the door. Kathryn woke to the remaining heat of summer and Andrew's absence. It was like flipping a switch: one day she had all of him, and the next, he ducked into the apartment only to shower and sleep. When Andrew was home, he hunched at his desk, his single light aimed at the pages of his book.

Then his stepfather called. Craig had arranged an internship for Andrew, one that would make Andrew a shoo-in for a position at Craig's firm after graduation. Andrew grinned, but Kathryn read the strain in his eyes. "If I can make a good impression at the Gainesville branch," Andrew said, "I can soar at the Charleston firm. I'll be making bank, and fast." He pecked Kathryn's lips.

"But what if I don't want to move to South Carolina?" she argued. Leaving the state had never crossed her mind.

"Kat." Andrew locked eyes with her. "If I do this, I can afford our dream life, the kids, the pool, all of it."

"I want to live in Delray, close to Harper and Luke. And I'm going to be a lawyer; I won't need you to pay for our life."

Kathryn thought the matter was settled. But one evening she slipped her hands around Andrew and pressed a kiss against his earlobe, feeling his body stiffen beneath his T-shirt. Kathryn knew him, knew how quickly he responded to her touch, and she leaned in to kiss him in earnest.

Andrew drew back as if she weren't standing behind him and flung his notebook, the pages fluttering like an injured bird before it struck the wall. "These fucking notes make no sense," he shouted. "I have one hour to do this before I have to be at my internship."

Kathryn straightened. She hadn't expected Andrew's sudden burst of anger, had never seen him react badly to frustration before. "Calm down, Andrew. It'll be fine."

Andrew grimaced. "Kat. Sweetheart. I need to learn all of this. I'm not going to live on your salary."

"Who said anything about living on my salary?" she demanded.

Andrew jumped up and shoved his textbooks into his backpack. He snatched his notebook off the floor. "I need to get out of here."

"Where are you going?"

Andrew zipped his bag. "Somewhere I can focus."

The sting of rejection coursed through her like poison. "Really, Drew?"

A long sigh drained from him, and his shoulders fell. Andrew stepped forward to place a placating kiss on her forehead. "I'm sorry. But—do you want to be married to a jobless loser?" He tried to make his voice sound light, but Kathryn could still feel his words, like he'd slapped her. "I'm not going to be like my father. I need to do this right. For us."

"We don't need to re-create your mom and Craig's marriage," Kathryn said as Andrew closed the door behind him.

Kathryn settled against the headboard. She didn't like this side of Andrew. She found herself wallowing in his absence, in the long, lonely evening stretching before her, with so many just like it to follow. It was only September, and she'd already slid to the bottom of his list of priorities. They had eight months to navigate before he graduated.

When they'd started dating, it hadn't taken Kathryn long to notice Nick and the quiet way he watched her. She was familiar with the feeling of a man's eyes on her, just as she was practiced at ignoring it, but she had to admit there was *something* about him. His deep eyes were a warm chestnut that seemed to change with his moods, which was . . . not *unattractive*. When she'd moved into their apartment that summer, she'd often passed by Nick's bedroom door and seen him sprawled across his bed with a book in his hands. Sometimes his hands were spotted with paint, and he hung canvases in his room. With Nick, she found herself wondering what he was thinking, curious about the sides of himself he kept hidden from the world.

Kathryn and Andrew included Nick when they went out, though she sensed Nick's discomfort when the three of them were together. Nick had a pensive way of taking in everything around him, and occasionally she found she was the subject of his interest, but when she met his eyes, he didn't drop his gaze.

Kathryn knew Nick had every reason to be jealous of Andrew. Nick was racking up student loan debt while Andrew's parents seemed to have no issue funding his education and expenses. She'd never seen Andrew stress about rent or gas; on countless occasions she'd seen him put a 2:00 a.m. pizza on his credit card, and he often picked up the tab for friends, and for Nick, who averted his eyes while Andrew scribbled his name beneath a generous tip.

As fall wore on, Andrew spent his evenings at his internship or at the library. Kathryn often came out into the living room in the evening, where Nick sat watching TV. One night she dropped onto the couch next to him. "Can we watch *Friends*?"

Nick glanced over at her. "For the love of God, no. I'm not watching that crap."

"Please?" she begged, reaching out for the TV remote.

Nick rolled his eyes and handed it to her, and she flicked between channels. For a while they watched the show in silence, and she felt his presence, the palpable sensation of sharing a space with a relative stranger. Nick sipped his beer and kept his eyes on the screen until ten minutes into the show, when a sudden laugh burst from him. Kathryn's eyes shot to the other end of the couch, and she jutted a finger. "See? *Friends* is *hilarious*."

A smile cracked across his face. "Fine, it's clever." He drained the remainder of his beer.

Kathryn rose and pulled two bottles from the fridge, handing Nick a fresh beer as she took a seat again, this time a few feet closer to him. They clinked their bottles together.

On their evenings off, she and Nick watched *Friends* while Andrew studied at the library. Sometimes, Kathryn looked to the other side of the couch and found him looking at her instead of the television, but she brushed it aside. Andrew was everything she'd imagined her college boyfriend to be: he was confident and good looking, and he came from a stable family. He was focused and studied hard, and her parents adored him. All summer she'd felt a magic with him she'd never felt with anyone, but, as fall wore on, she realized no matter how much she longed for the Andrew she'd known in the summer, Andrew didn't look at her the way Nick did.

One quiet evening alone in Andrew's bedroom, a crash from the other side of the wall jerked her attention from the novel in her hands. She rapped on Nick's bedroom door, and his voice called out from the other side. "It's open."

Nick sat in the middle of his bedroom between towering stacks of books. His bookshelves were empty. "Did I wake you?" He glanced up. "Sorry, I didn't realize you were home."

But she was always home. Always there to collect the mail, her law school rejections stacking up by the day. She'd brought them up to Andrew, and he'd offered an infuriating, "Don't stress about it, babe."

Kathryn leaned against Nick's doorframe. "What are you doing?"

"I found this bookcase outside by the trash." It was a cheap-looking particleboard piece, placed against Nick's wall. "I'm rearranging my collection."

"Need help?" Before he could respond, Kathryn took a seat beside him on the rug and pulled a book from the top of the stack. "Yuck. So many classics. I only read them when they were required."

Nick didn't answer. With an old T-shirt, he dusted each book before he sorted them into stacks around him. Kathryn plucked another book from a pile and let the pages run between her fingers. "Robert Frost. I always liked this one."

Nick glanced up from his work.

"We discussed it in ninth-grade English. '*Two roads diverged in the woods.*'"

"'*In a yellow wood,*'" Nick corrected gently.

Kathryn nodded, pulling the book close to her. "'*I took the one less traveled by, and that has made all the difference,*'" she finished. "I love that the difference isn't explained. We don't know if it's good or bad."

Nick frowned and nodded, considering her words.

"That's what I told my ninth-grade teacher, anyway, and she gave me an A." Kathryn shrugged and set the worn book back where she'd found it.

"Don't do that," Nick said.

"Do what?"

"Don't dumb yourself down. Ever." It was the first time she'd heard Nick speak so assertively, and the flash in his deep eyes stirred something in her belly. "You're going to be a lawyer, Kat."

"I'll only be a lawyer if they let me in, and it's not looking promising."

"You'll find the right school." Nick said it with such confidence, while Andrew seemed concerned only with his career. Without looking up, Nick asked, "Are you going to marry him?"

The abrupt question silenced all of Kathryn's thoughts, and she pulled her knees to her chest. "Andrew? I don't know." But the thought was there. Sparkling. "We've only been together seven months."

"Do you want to marry him?" Nick asked. "Or someone like him? Have a couple of kids and a house in the burbs."

It was exactly what she'd planned. She balked. "Why do you ask like it's a bad thing?"

Nick shrugged. "It's not. It just doesn't seem like you. You shouldn't settle." He went back to his book stacks. "You're too smart."

"Life with Drew isn't settling."

Nick responded with a soft grunt and continued with his project, but Kathryn's mind circled back to the picture of the life that stretched out ahead of her. Some might consider it predictable, she conceded, but it was a life some people could only dream of. For her, for Andrew, it was attainable. "You don't want a family?"

"Someone to share my life with? Sure. Kids? No."

"Never?"

Nick shook his head.

"Why?"

"My dad remarried. My mom was . . . a less-than-ideal parent. I was shuffled between their houses like a piece of luggage." She saw his shoulders tense. "It felt like they had to tolerate me until I turned eighteen and moved out. I never even had my own room."

"So you don't want better for your kids?"

"I want to enjoy my freedom. To travel, to explore the best of life: food, books, music. Sex." Nick dropped his tone, low, husky. Sexy. "I want to live for myself, not go through the motions, acting out commercial holidays."

Kathryn considered this. "I've always wanted a family." She thumbed through a book absentmindedly. "I'm all my parents have, so there's this immense pressure to give them the white wedding and the grandkids. My childhood was so . . . lonely. That's the only word I have for it. Holidays were boring. I opened my gifts alone. I got exactly what I asked for, but I had no one to share it with, you know?"

Nick kneeled and began sliding books onto shelves. "Wait until you go to Drew's house for Christmas. They all wear matching pajamas." Nick scowled. "They have brunch with cloth napkins. His mom buys a new cardigan for the occasion each year. It's like a goddamn magazine."

"It sounds nice." Kathryn imagined her children, a boy and a girl—and maybe the third Andrew teased her about—gathering for Christmas with their grandparents, she and Andrew watching them tear open gifts. Maybe living in South Carolina wouldn't be so awful. But if she and Andrew lived in Delray, visiting Andrew's family once or twice a year in South Carolina would be special, a place where they'd paint memories. The picture wasn't generic; it was warm and welcoming, happy, and secure. It was what she wanted. Wasn't it?

Or were she and Andrew sketching a life they were conditioned to desire?

The freedom Nick spoke of, the indulgence in music, food, carnal pleasures . . . something stirred in Kathryn. She'd always derived joy from these things. Why deny herself?

"There are studies on only children, you know?" Nick said. "Like you, like me. They're often overachievers, stubborn, independent. But, also, they're not afraid to take risks, to challenge stereotypes, to live for themselves."

"Huh." How would it feel to skip out on law school? If she didn't get accepted to the schools she'd applied to, would she find a measure of relief? Could she surprise everyone and live a wild, indulgent life like the one Nick desired? Could she throw the duty to please her parents aside, live without any burdens? Spend her time exploring the world, making love to men who looked . . . like Nick?

Nick motioned for her to hand him the last few books spread on the rug. Kathryn wiped her sweaty palms on her shorts before she did, and he worked them onto the shelves. "Done."

They regarded their work: the spines organized by color. "Wait, check this out." Nick jumped to his feet and flipped his light switch, plunging them into darkness, revealing hundreds of glow stars smattering the ceiling and walls. He settled onto his back on the rug, and Kathryn followed his lead, letting her eyes adjust. Nick's room fell away, leaving a vast expanse of stars, like a clear summer night. She dropped her head to the side and found Nick looking back at her, his eyes soft. And she pictured the lush life he had planned for himself, long hours in bed with a book or writing in the weathered leather journal she'd seen on his nightstand. She imagined rainy days, lattes, travels to the castles of Ireland.

Then she saw it, bright, visceral: her body wrapped in a sea of blankets beside him, one bare foot brushing her leg. She saw his strong body above hers, tipping her head back to meet her mouth. Time didn't matter; the pressures of the outside world didn't exist there. It was just the two of them, sharing the hours, the years, as they came. Nick held her gaze. He was close, and she could feel his breath on her skin, which sent a ripple through her, to the deepest part of her belly. In the darkness she thought she saw him tilt his head toward her, a movement so slight she was sure she'd imagined it, and wondered how his full lips would feel on hers when they parted.

Nick sat up and flicked the light switch, returning the world around them to reality. "Thanks for helping me," he mumbled, then walked into the hallway, leaving her to wonder if he, too, had imagined a life together.

CHAPTER FIFTEEN

Thursday, April 27
Amy

Spring break would be the death of her, Amy mused as she scrubbed her fingernails beneath the rushing tap. Her shift had ended six hours before, but as she was bracing to leave, the ER had exploded with activity. The patient fated to meet her was wheeled in. Golf cart accident. Blunt-force trauma to the chest. Six hours of saving him from his own drunken stupidity. Another win.

Amy's body had adapted to layers of exhaustion, but she was near delirium when she stepped into her warm kitchen that evening to a waft of roasted potatoes. "Dinner's almost ready," Andrew said in that way of his, soothing her worries. He planted a kiss on her forehead, and she devoured the meal he'd made. She was foolish to think it had been Andrew's car at Lombardi's Steakhouse that rainy night. This was the man she loved, nurturing and gentle.

She set her fork on her clean plate. She couldn't remember a time when she'd been so ravenously hungry. "My schedule might get more intense over the next few months. They're shifting some people around." She dabbed her lips with a napkin.

Andrew frowned. "You're already working seventy hours a week, maybe more." Then a shift in his expression, and he lifted his iced tea. "But if you can handle it, I'll hold down the fort, no problem."

Andrew's adaptability was one of his sexiest qualities. Yes, he'd make an excellent father. Beneath the table, Amy smoothed her shirt over the physical evidence of her own secrets.

At first, the bruises were tender, but after a few days they faded to a dull, sick yellow. Earlier that week, when she was in the shower, Andrew had cracked the bathroom door, and her heart had skipped. He'd loved to meet her there, their mouths on each other before he lifted her against the tile. What would he say about the bruises? But he'd just quipped, "Need the floss," and closed the door behind him, leaving her alone in the steamy space, relieved and disappointed.

"How are things at work since you turned down the promotion?" She hadn't brought it up since their fight, but maybe it was time to clear the air. Andrew's shrug was resigned, but his face remained smooth. Maybe he'd let it go after all. Andrew was a natural caregiver. Ultimately, she could picture him finding fulfillment in their home. She saw him throwing a football in the backyard with a boy who shared his sandy-blond hair, and smiled.

At work Amy sipped the bitter teas made from the strange herbs she'd bought, swallowed the large tablets, mixed powder into her smoothies, and tried not to feel guilty about her secrecy. It would all be worth it.

That night, after Andrew brushed his teeth and slipped in the bed beside her, he leaned to peck her good night. The kiss deepened, and then he was leaning into her, his strong body, the man she remembered. The man she craved. Amy clicked the light off before she pulled her shirt over her head and thought, See? Everything is going to turn out beautifully.

CHAPTER SIXTEEN

Monday, May 1
Kathryn

"You look lovely this morning, honey," Kathryn told Emmy as she reversed into the street. Emmy had curled her hair and donned a pale-blue dress dotted with delicate flowers.

The back of Emmy's neck flushed pink, but she smiled. "Thanks. You do, too."

Kathryn considered her own fitted dress, the way her perfume blended in the small space with Emmy's—was that Chanel? Maybe, like Harper had, Emmy bloomed when she escaped Nora. "I have an after-hours meeting today." Kathryn cleared her throat. "Then I'm meeting a friend for dinner."

"Busy day," Emmy mused.

Excitement brewed when Kathryn thought of meeting with Andrew that evening. They'd agreed to a late dinner after her dreaded networking event. She preferred when Andrew drove. Sure, she didn't want nosy people like Regina seeing her come and go late at night, but she'd originally asked because she needed at least two glasses of wine at their meetings, and driving home with a buzz was ill advised for someone whose son had totaled his car just a few months earlier. But there was something about sitting in silence beside him as he cruised home down the highway, the streetlights strobing the intimate space between them. It was a tiny sliver of the life she'd imagined with him that she hadn't lost. "You're right—I do have a lot on the agenda today. And we both look good—want to grab an iced coffee before I drop you off?"

Emmy's smile lifted. "Yeah, sure."

With coffee on the horizon, Kathryn accelerated up the street.

Emmy turned to Kathryn. "I have a weird question."

The engine purred. "Okay."

Again, Emmy flushed. "I don't remember anything about when you lived with my family. And my mom isn't exactly . . . open to talking about it." Kathryn gripped the wheel. This could go in a million different directions, all of them painful. "Anyway . . . I . . ."

"What is it, Em?"

Emmy's grip tightened on her phone in her lap. "Max and I, we're not like . . . related or anything, are we?"

Of the millions of directions Emmy's questioning could have gone, this was one Kathryn hadn't anticipated, and adrenaline pulsed through her. "Did Harper suggest that?"

Emmy's eyes widened. "No—never. I just . . ."

Kathryn narrowed her gaze on the road. Of course Harper had. "No. You and Max are absolutely not related."

Emmy faced the window. "Okay. You guys, you and my mom, you just never talked about what happened."

Kathryn's mind reeled. The girl was right. It had been nearly two decades of this. It had gone on too long. It was time to have a talk with Harper, even if that meant loosening a stone on the wall they'd constructed so long ago.

Emmy

Guilt bloomed in Emmy at the secrets she held from Kathryn. Kathryn was nice, shuffling her to school, buying her iced coffee, but the way she'd tensed when Emmy brought up Kathryn's falling-out with Harper left Emmy with more questions about her past than before.

On the nights Kathryn came home with takeout in tow, the three ate dinner together at the kitchen table, like three actors on a stage, each playing their parts. The three developed a silent cadence to their parallel secrets. Kathryn asked Emmy about school and danced around inquiring about Max's daily activities. Then, after Kathryn loaded the dishwasher and they retired to their respective bedrooms, Max and Emmy shot each other flirty texts from their separate worlds, just yards away. But as the weeks slipped by, a new blooming concern: What would happen with Max when her time in Florida was up? And Emmy's thoughts shifted when it came to her mother. Now she answered Harper's messages with short answers. I'm fine, just enough to keep Harper from asking her to come home.

Because being with Max was more than she could have imagined. And, though she continued her countdown to her eighteenth birthday, she no longer felt like a prisoner hashing her days until freedom. On the nights Kathryn went out, the world was theirs, a blur of long drives up the winding, blue coast, of Max's limbs intertwined with hers in the back seat of his car, and late nights sprawled on the trampoline beneath a starry sky. Their secret spot, beneath the line of catamarans that rested in the sand on the beach, their masts rising into the moonlight, the waves crashing with the rhythm of their bodies, cloaked in darkness.

When they were home alone, they found each other. Whether it was their clandestine afternoon hours in one of their bedrooms, or passing the time in idle ways—her delicately painting her fingernails at the kitchen table while Max chopped vegetables at the counter—his presence made her feel complete. The day after Emmy had asked Kathryn about her mother, she and Max were stretched on the couch together, and Emmy had dozed on Max's chest. The rattle of the garage door woke her and they shuffled to opposite sides of the couch just as Kathryn came through the door.

"Hey, kids." Kathryn kicked off her shoes and let her bag and jacket fall in a heap on the floor. "What smells delicious?"

Max's brow dipped when he eyed her mess. "I made pasta sauce."

"Wonderful, we all get to share dinner." Kathryn beamed and raked her fingers through Max's hair as she passed. He jerked his head from her reach. In the kitchen Kathryn flipped the light switch, and Emmy pressed her shoulder into the sponge of the couch cushion, observing Kathryn's movements as she lifted the lid on the saucepan, a cloud of steam rising around her. A tight skirt hugged her curves, and her cream blouse was unbuttoned just enough to show a subtle hint of cleavage. Her gold necklace swung like a pendulum near the surface of the sauce. Kathryn reached into the cabinet above the stove for a bottle of wine and a glass, then fished in a drawer for the wine key, which she used to expertly uncork the bottle. Kathryn moved with a grace that struck a chord in Emmy—something she'd never seen in her own mother, a confidence in who she was.

Emmy considered this woman and her secrets. Guilt pulsed inside her; three weeks had passed since the encounter with the man in the car. When she'd woken the morning after, at her father's beach house with Max, she'd questioned her own sanity. It had been dark in the car; how closely could she have seen the man?

But his image was imprinted in her brain.

When they'd left her father's house after that stormy night together, the morning had been sky blue and bright. Max cruised north along the winding road that hugged the coast, the ground still wet from the rain. They settled at a café on the water, where wicker fans churned the air above aging bamboo furniture, the windowpanes blurred with salty sea spray. "Do you have any idea who your father is?" Emmy dared.

Max had been looking at his menu, drawing circles on her open palm, and his finger stilled. "Nope." He folded his arms and leaned back in his chair.

But the man's face returned to her mind. She couldn't let it go. "Have you ever asked Kathryn?"

"Of course." There was an edge to Max's voice. "First, when I was ten or so. That time, she sat me down and said he was someone she'd dated. That was pretty much it." Max's eyes fell to his lap. "Then when I was sixteen. It was one of those fights that started about one thing—me staying out all night or something—and then we were yelling about everything. She accused me of keeping things from her. I threw that right back in her face, that she'd never told me anything, not why we moved out of your dad's house, not why she practically kept me locked inside the house while I was growing up." Max's face shadowed, and Emmy saw a ghost of the hurt little boy he harbored inside him. "Then I asked her who the hell she'd slept with, if he even knew about me or not. I kind of accused her of being . . . promiscuous." His jaw tightened. "She got weird after that. Distant. She'd never done that before. That was when I started drinking a lot. Enough that she might notice. One day I ditched class. I was a straight-A student. But that day I got wasted, then decided it was a good idea to go to my afternoon classes. That's what got me kicked out." His face shadowed. "Zero out of ten, do not recommend."

"God, Max." Emmy reached out, and he let his hand fall into hers. Emmy thought of Kathryn passing through the house. Some days Kathryn was buoyant, giddy even. Other days it was as if the weight of the world sat upon her, but she was always distracted. Kathryn rapped on Emmy's door to check on her; she sent texts. Emmy pictured the elastic tension between Kathryn and her son, the way they moved around each other. If she told Max what she suspected and he confronted Kathryn, only to find out the whole thing was a misunderstanding, it could be catastrophic for Kathryn and Max's relationship. And if she was right about what Kathryn was hiding—it could be worse.

"Then . . ." Max scratched his nose. "The morning after my car accident, she woke me up and gave me this weird look and said, 'I think I know what this is all about, and I want you to know you came from two people who loved each other, and there's nothing wrong with you.'" His face screwed up. "Like what the hell does that mean?"

Emmy took this in. "That's it?"

"I just assumed he's dead, or a drug addict or something."

She hated the weight she saw settle on Max's shoulders.

In the kitchen, Kathryn balanced her wineglass between her fingers, and Emmy again considered Kathryn's evasiveness when it came to Harper. And the way she dressed up for whomever she was meeting for dinner after work. All of it had to be connected. Max hid his secret with Emmy in plain sight, and Emmy realized, maybe that was something he'd learned from Kathryn. And that insight told her all she needed to know: Kathryn was hiding a secret, too. A big one. One that could hurt Max. Emmy suddenly wished it weren't true.

"Max." Kathryn approached. "What have you been up to?"

"The usual," Max mumbled. "I had my appointment with Dr. Hennessey this morning."

Kathryn sipped her wine. "How'd that go?"

Max didn't take his eyes off the TV. "We had a breakthrough. I'm cured."

Kathryn scoffed, then looked to Emmy. "Sweetheart, can I talk to you for a moment?"

Panic pulsed. The man in the car had to have told Kathryn about the incident. Was Kathryn about to confront her? Or, worse, had Kathryn noticed anything between Emmy and Max? Was the blissful bubble she was living in about to burst?

She followed Kathryn as she padded up the stairs and into her bedroom, where Kathryn closed the door. Kathryn's bed was placed squarely in the middle of the far wall, littered with throw pillows, and above it hung three white-framed pictures of Max as a small child. A paper fan in a wooden frame hung on the opposite wall. "Sweetheart, I spoke with Harper today." Kathryn's expression hardened. She set her wineglass on her nightstand and worked her hair into a bun. "She said you've been ignoring her texts."

"Kathryn," Emmy snapped. "She's never been a mother to me. Not like you are to Max." Kathryn swallowed. "So, yes, I got tired of it and ran away. But she didn't try to stop me from leaving. She hasn't come back for me. She hasn't done anything to make up for seventeen years of being a shitty mother, of letting Nora talk to me like I'm trash. So she's going to have to try a lot harder than a few texts."

Kathryn's intense eyes narrowed as she processed this information. "That"—Kathryn wrapped her arms around herself—"makes me sad to hear." Kathryn sighed. "But being a parent, it's tough, Em. Life changes people. What happened to your dad and your mom and me—we're different people than we once were, okay?"

It wasn't okay, and Emmy ached to know what Kathryn was referring to. Something shifted in Kathryn when she wasn't near Max, a vulnerability Emmy didn't see when Max was present. But now, Kathryn stiffened. "I know Harper's difficult to talk to, believe me. But she cares for you more than you realize. She just isn't equipped to show it. Do you understand?"

Emmy broke Kathryn's penetrating gaze and didn't respond. Kathryn strode away, working the buttons on her blouse, and stepped to her closet. Hangers rattled.

"She wasn't always like this, you know?" Kathryn said as she returned in her black lace bra. "Harper was . . . she was so happy to be your mom."

This prodded a nerve. Another piece of her life just beyond the periphery of Emmy's memory, of Harper's gentle kisses, of bedtime stories. A different person than the one Emmy knew. It occurred to Emmy that she'd been dressing and undressing in a locker room full of girls her entire life and never gave it a second thought, but she couldn't remember a single instance of Harper going about the private parts of her day in her presence the way Kathryn did. She didn't know her mother at all.

"So then why doesn't she like me now?" Tears thickened Emmy's voice.

"She loves you. And she loved Luke." Emotion snagged Kathryn's tone. "Losing you, too, might be more than she can handle."

Emmy couldn't answer. She tried to swallow past the knot in her throat.

"My house is yours, Em," Kathryn said, and her tone dropped. "Now and always. But under one condition: you need to talk to your mom." Kathryn turned, and Emmy saw her brush a tear from her cheek before she disappeared into the bathroom, then the rush of the shower severed their conversation.

Kathryn's guilt and prodding worked, and the next afternoon at lunch, Emmy concealed herself in a shady spot outside the cafeteria doors and called her mother. "Emmy?" Harper answered on the second ring.

"I'm just calling to say I'm fine," Emmy hurried. "If you care."

"Of course I care." Harper's tone was raspy. Relief. And a sadness that mirrored Kathryn's. How had these women hurt each other so deeply?

Emmy squinted into the line of palm trees in the distance. "Well, I'm okay, so you can stop harassing Kathryn." So much had changed since Emmy had left Nora's house. Her magical moments with Max bloomed in her mind. She'd started having sex. She felt like an adult, wondered whether Harper would recognize her when—or if—they saw each other again. She ached for a mother she could share these things with.

"I didn't call her, she called me," Harper said. So her mother hadn't tried to woo her back home via Kathryn. "But you can come home if you'd like."

It was laughable. Emmy couldn't imagine being away from Max for a moment.

"We can go shopping, we can get you a new car."

A wave of disappointment. Harper hadn't changed. "I don't want a new car—you can't fix everything with money," Emmy snapped. "I'm not going anywhere—Kathryn's so nice, she cooks, she eats dinner with us, she's involved in Max's life." It was a stretch from the truth, but that wasn't the point. "I love it here."

"Okay," Harper said, resigned. "Could we maybe have lunch someday?"

Emmy sighed. She had to give Harper just enough that she wouldn't cut her college funding and wouldn't make her go home. "Maybe. I'll think about it." Guilt stroked her, but she hung up, and pushed her mother, and Kathryn, from her mind. With her time ticking by, she wanted to enjoy it with Max.

The following evening, Kathryn returned from work shortly after five. "I'm going to dinner. Use my card to order pizza?" she said as she passed by Max and Emmy, seated in their designated places on the couch, then traipsed up the staircase. Max leaned forward to meet Emmy's eye, his lips lifting into a smile that held the promise of the world, an evening of freedom, as they'd become accustomed to each evening when Kathryn ducked upstairs to shower, when the house filled with the whir of her blow dryer and a hint of spicy perfume.

Max pressed Emmy into the couch cushions, and her hand snaked across his back. When he was close, all thoughts of her mother evaporated. "Want to go out tonight, or stay in?"

Emmy thought. She wanted to put on a dress, curl her hair. Girly things. "Out," she said. He kissed her, deep, and she nearly changed her mind. "We're going to get caught."

Max's breath was warm on her ear. "No, we're not." A ripple ran through her.

But there was a tug of apprehension in Emmy when Kathryn reversed out of the driveway and disappeared. She had to tell Max what she suspected. She couldn't keep things from him, but she didn't want to hurt him, either.

That evening, Emmy found herself beside Max and Javi at a table on the lawn of an old house, renovated into an artsy restaurant. The bartender was buddies with Javi and slid their drinks across the bar, his eyes panning the crowd for the manager. Inside, reverberation from an electric guitar cut the night before the band found their rhythm, and music carried out onto the lawn. An ancient banyan tree reached its arms protectively overhead, strands of twinkle lights wrapped in its branches. Max sailed beanbags effortlessly through a cornhole board, while each of Javi's slapped against the wood. Emmy sipped her third mojito—cold and strong—and Max caught her gaze, and his smile widened. In her rum-induced haze, she found herself overwhelmed with happiness; her life had melted into a sort of dream.

Afterward their mismatched footsteps scratched the brick sidewalk of Atlantic Avenue, Max's and Javi's laughter booming off the dark storefronts as they passed, orange neon CLOSED signs glowing on the boys' faces. Max's arm was draped loosely around her waist, and Emmy struggled to follow the story the two boys recanted in alternating bits. A group of them had gone out on a boat, and they'd been drinking all afternoon, and one of them had tried to pee off the back of the boat—their story lost in the boys' overlapping voices. Javi stopped in the middle of the sidewalk, doubled over, one hand clutching Max's arm. Tears spilled from Max's eyes as he struggled to deliver the final words of the story—something about the direction of the wind—before they both melted into hysterics, and their laughter rang out into the nearly deserted street.

Their energy faded as they walked the few blocks home through the stillness of their neighborhood. Under the yellow cone of a streetlight, while a cloud of bugs circled beneath the dome of glass, they said good night. Javi pulled Emmy into a hug. "I've never seen him like this," he whispered into her hair. "You make him happy."

Emmy squeezed Javi's hand gratefully before he walked away. "I don't think you realize how lucky you are to have a friend like Javi," Emmy said while Max unlocked the front door.

Max's crooked smile lifted. "He'll do, I guess."

Emmy didn't want to break that smile, never wanted to be the bearer of news that would hurt him.

The following Saturday, Emmy slipped behind the wheel of Max's car, and he climbed in beside her. She cruised up Ocean Avenue, beside the stretch of rippling blue water, testing the engine's response. When she was comfortable, she cranked the radio and floored the gas. The car was effortless, elastic, as it zoomed up the narrow, winding stretch of road, the trees hugging a canopy above them. Max gripped his seat and shouted, "Damn, girl. Take it easy." Emmy laughed and accelerated again, her hair blowing out the open window as she whipped around hairpin turns. "Be careful at this bend," Max cried over the wind and music.

"You think I can't handle this?" Emmy punched the gas as she approached the turn, and the tires screeched, clearing the narrow curve. Her heart thudded, sea air salting her lips, and Max turned to face her. He shook his head and, without a word, Emmy continued up the road, sailing over a bridge, where she peeked at Max. His eyes had drifted to the horizon, and wind whipped his hair back. Emmy took him in, the smoothness of his forehead without its usual worry lines.

She made a sharp, illegal U-turn at the Palm Beach County line and headed back the same way they'd come, rolling at the speed limit, their faces dewy with sea spray. The sky was a dusky lavender when Emmy pulled into the vacant public lot and parked, letting the clicks of the settling engine fade before they climbed out of the car.

Max's fingers laced hers, and they made their way through the dunes and dropped into the sand a few yards from the water. The breeze stirred the warm night, and the moon rose in front of them, glowing against the watercolor streaks of sunset at their backs. Emmy worked her toes into the sand. "I talked to my mom this week. She hasn't changed at all."

"I'm sorry." His frown was genuine, knowing.

"Not that I'd go home anyway. But . . . I have a question." She wrung her hands, and met Max's eyes, glowing in the iridescent twilight. "Would you consider coming to Washington with me?"

Max's stare locked on her face.

"I mean, you don't have to," she rushed. "We could see where this goes . . . but I thought maybe you could look for a culinary school." It was stupid, embarrassing. They'd been dating only a few weeks.

A pensive breath drained from Max, and light flickered in his eyes. "Yeah—I mean yes. If you're okay with that. I'd—it would be awesome to go with you."

Emmy's heart soared. Max didn't plan to let her leave with nothing but a loose promise he'd visit. They weren't going to swap a few awkward texts, then let their love reduce to an awkward exchange if they ever saw each other again. He was serious about her, serious enough to move across the country. It was happening. Really happening. To *her*. "I can't think of a better birthday present than to pack up your car and get out of Florida." The warm bubble of excitement swelled in her chest, blotting the sting of her conversation with Kathryn, of her tangled feelings about Harper. "Wait—we're really doing this?"

Max draped an arm over her shoulders. "Yeah. I mean, it'll be strange to leave Javi. Before you, I just assumed I'd spend my life . . . well, like my mom does, dating people, but not seriously. But you made me realize I don't want to be anything like her. You made everything make sense. So, hell yeah, we're doing this. I want to go wherever you go." When he pulled back, a childlike grin grew across his face. "How many weeks?"

"Five weeks and four days." Emmy pulled her phone from her pocket, and the screen glowed to life at the tap of her finger: 9:14 p.m. "And three hours. Not like I'm counting or anything." They giggled, and she nestled her head beneath his chin and watched the waves crash on the sand, safely in his grasp. The world was warm. Peaceful. Right. Max had articulated her feelings with precision: all she'd ever known was solitude. In him, she'd found a partner. Promise. "If Harper wants to find me, she's going to have to come all the way to Washington." The minimal likelihood of that happening prodded Emmy, but she wasn't going to let anything spoil her buoyancy.

"Forget our parents." Max shifted in the sand. "They've had so much control over our lives. We don't need them. Let's figure it out on our own. I have money, you have school. We have this."

This. Emmy closed her eyes and soaked in his words. Max was right—nobody mattered except the two of them. Their future was wide, theirs to navigate together.

But that word *parents* niggled her. Emmy didn't want to pop their bubble, but she couldn't plan a future if she was hiding things from Max. She pulled away to look at him, anxiety coursing through her. "I need to tell you something."

Max's brows narrowed. "What?"

"Something weird happened. I don't know how to explain it." Emmy hesitated, sorting her thoughts. "The day we went to the beach house, a man came to pick up Kathryn, and I got into his car. I only saw him for a few seconds, but it was obvious—he looked exactly like you."

"What does that mean?"

"It means he looked *exactly* like you. The same eyes, the same nose—like, everything." Emmy nibbled her lip. "I freaked out and ran back into the house. But a few seconds was enough. Whoever Kathryn's been going out with at night, I think he's your father."

Max's brows knitted. "Why didn't you tell me?"

Shame surged. Emmy dropped her gaze. "I didn't know how, and I second-guessed it. But I had a conversation with Kathryn, and she totally locked up—"

"I remember." Acid laced Max's tone. "I saw that car." His forehead narrowed into an M. "Kathryn's been acting squirrely. I knew she was hiding something."

"But wouldn't she say something to you if he's going to come so close to the house?"

Max fell silent, and Emmy couldn't imagine the thoughts churning in his mind.

"Of all the fucked-up shit she's done, this is the worst." His voice was raw.

Emmy thought of Kathryn's green-eyed gaze, the way Emmy had watched her heart break when she'd urged Emmy to make peace with Harper. "She must have her reasons, Max."

Max didn't answer. He pushed his toes deep into the sand, his gaze hard.

"Are you upset with me?" Emmy asked. Their future had held promise just moments ago. Would this ruin it?

"With you? No." Max reached for her hand, pulled it close.

Emmy hated the idea of Max hurting, hated that she could read it on his face. Night blanketed the landscape. Over the cobalt water, the moon reflected off the rippling surface in a long V, and the only sound was the low boom of the waves.

"This is just so . . . her." The venom in his voice thickened. "She gives me shit about what I do, while she's running around keeping secrets. It's been like this my whole life—you've been in our house for weeks and she doesn't nag you. Instead, all of her attention goes to this dude, whoever the fuck he is."

Emmy let Max's anger settle. This was the reaction she'd dreaded. "I didn't mean to come between you and your mom."

Max faced her, squeezed her hand. "You couldn't, Em. This has nothing to do with you. It's all on her."

Emmy absorbed this. He was right, but she was still desperate to soothe him. "I'm not going to tell you I know how you feel. But I know what it's like to wonder about the other half of you, to feel like a missing puzzle piece nobody talks about. I don't know what made my mom the way she is, and . . . you don't, either."

Max gave a small nod.

"It's crazy that decisions they made—decisions we may never understand—affect all of us, decades later."

Max's gaze fell, unfocused for a pensive beat.

"What are you thinking?" She watched him return to the moment.

"I'm thinking there has to be a way to catch them, so they can't lie anymore."

Emmy drew a circle in the sand, mulling his words. "We could."

"I can." Max's eyes narrowed. "I will—I have to. I don't have any other choice."

"We. Whatever we do, we do it together."

CHAPTER SEVENTEEN

Then
Kathryn

On Andrew's twenty-first birthday, Kathryn awoke to find his bedding pushed aside, an indent on his vacant pillow. It was the first of their birthdays since they'd met, and while drifting off the night before, Kathryn had imagined when morning came, she'd wake him with a deep kiss. Or slither beneath the blankets and surprise him in a more creative fashion. They'd make love; then she'd cook breakfast and he'd jaunt off to school with a smile on his face.

Instead, an empty bed. So much for wild birthday sex.

Andrew emerged from the bathroom, a toothbrush dangling from his mouth, and Kathryn propped herself up, raking her fingers through her hair. "Happy birthday, babe."

"Happy midterms day," Andrew said through a mouthful of foam.

"I know. But please, *please* promise you'll come home at a normal time tonight," she begged.

Andrew ducked into the bathroom, and Kathryn heard him spit, then the rush of the tap. He popped back into the room. "What's 'normal,' Kat? I have midterms for all five of my classes this week, and my internship."

She leaned into her pillow. "Seven? Jason and the rest of the guys said they wanted to get pizza before we go out."

Andrew tugged a hoodie over his head and grunted.

"They're *your* friends," she snapped.

"Fine," he groaned. "I can't do pizza, but I'll be home by eight; then we'll hit the bars." He leaned in for a kiss, mint on his breath, then slung his bag over his shoulder.

That evening Kathryn globbed a cucumber mask onto her face, then shaved her legs and pumiced her feet. She stepped into a lacy lingerie set, then styled her hair into long waves. When she zipped the formfitting red dress she'd tucked in the back of her closet, she smoothed her hands over the fabric before the mirror. This would certainly get his attention.

It was 8.32.

Kathryn ignored Nick's double take when she padded into the living room, shaking a bottle of nail polish. He took a slow swig of his beer while Kathryn dropped onto the couch. They let a *Friends* rerun cover their silence as she layered three coats of glossy red polish onto her nails.

The bouncy tune that accompanied the final credits marked the time: 9:00.

"He'll be here," Nick muttered.

Kathryn huffed a breath and sat back against the couch cushions.

At nine thirty, the door swung open, and Andrew dropped his bag to the floor beside the doorframe. Kathryn's stomach dropped at his shadowed expression. "I got a fucking D on my statistics midterm," Andrew lamented as he marched to the kitchen. "I haven't gotten a D on anything in my fucking life. My dad is going to kill me." The refrigerator door slammed, followed by the hiss of a bottle being opened and the clank of the cap on the counter. "I had to beg the professor to let me retake it. I'll have to work around my internship hours, and this time I need to study hard."

Kathryn crossed her arms, and Nick tilted his head, eyeing her warily. Andrew reappeared, carrying his mood into the living room.

"You can't study tonight," Kathryn said. "It's your birthday."

"Fine." Andrew waved a hand in surrender. "Fuck it. I need a drink. Let's go."

The three of them piled into Kathryn's car. None of them spoke, a current of electricity vibrating in the confined space. At the bar, a half dozen of their friends cheered when they arrived, and Kathryn perched on a barstool. The room teemed with people, and Nick and Kathryn nursed their beers while Andrew's friends' fists pounded the sticky table as he tossed back the rounds of birthday shots they ordered. A crack of pool balls cut through the suffocating chatter. Kathryn squirmed in her too-tight dress. After a few hours, she touched Andrew's shoulder. "It's getting late; we should head home."

"If I'm going to skip studying to drink, I'm going to make it worth it." His voice had an edge to it, making the back of her neck prickle. "You're the one who wanted to come out in the first place."

"I'm tired. And you have midterms tomorrow."

"I realize I have midterms, Kathryn," Andrew snapped, his tone full of liquor and venom.

She told herself his reaction stemmed from the liquor. And he'd had a bad day. Not that it was an excuse. "Andrew . . ." Her voice trembled.

Kathryn shuffled back, and Andrew took one step closer. "Let me celebrate my failures and get fucked up in peace. It'll be my birthday present. Go home. I don't care." His words silenced the chatter of the group, and a staticky energy bounced between them.

The red dress burned like a rash. She was foolish. Desperate.

Nick's fingers slipped around Kathryn's arm. She blinked away the burn of tears, white-hot mortification rising in her chest. She yanked her arm from Nick and bolted for the door, desperate to escape the neon signs and tinny country music.

Outside, the street was deserted. Silent. The door swung open, and Nick followed her out onto the sidewalk. She walked away. "Kat," he called, his footsteps quickening. "Wait up."

Kathryn marched on without a word. When she climbed into her car, Nick rapped on the window. She unlocked the door, and he ducked into the passenger seat. Kathryn turned the key, and the engine roared to life. "I want to go home. Let him bum a ride or get a taxi. Or walk. I don't care."

They didn't speak as she drove, and when she killed the engine, their silence settled. They stared ahead out the windshield under the yellow glow of a streetlamp. Nick broke the quiet. "He was drunk. And pissed about school. He didn't realize what he was saying."

"We shouldn't have come out. I knew he wasn't in the mood." Kathryn hung her head. "Things have been different lately. When he's stressed—I don't know, it's like he goes *inside* himself, like I'm not even here."

"He's crazy about you, Kat." Bitterness floated just above the surface of Nick's soft words.

Kathryn recalled the Andrew she'd known in the summer, the way their love eclipsed everything else, and her throat clenched. Her tears broke free, and now she let them, hot as they flowed down her face.

Nick squared his shoulders. "You know what?" His voice was suddenly forceful. "Fuck that. Fuck him. You *should* be upset. I've seen him do this before, snap at people when he's drunk."

Kathryn had known only a happy, tipsy version of Andrew. What did Nick know that she didn't?

"He's a spoiled brat who has never met a consequence in his life, and what he said to you was fucking disrespectful, and I should've punched him in the face."

"Nick—"

"He has no right to humiliate you in front of other people." Nick straightened, anger flaring from his intense stare. "He's had everything handed to him. And he doesn't realize how lucky he is. He has *you*."

His words landed between them, and Kathryn was too tired to pretend she didn't know what Nick meant. Andrew was the first man she'd ever loved, and she did love him. Truly. Madly. Intensely.

And she had been certain he loved her, too. But his words from the bar rang in her ear with a fresh wave of hurt. And this man beside her, the one who had followed her from the bar when her boyfriend had not, the one who had turned his head to regard her beneath the canopy of stars in his bedroom, who held a glimpse of a life she'd never considered . . . These boys were giving her whiplash.

She yanked her keys from the ignition.

In their apartment Nick flicked on the light, and Kathryn slumped onto the couch. He sat beside her. "I should go to bed," she said, but didn't move. She couldn't bring herself to stare at the walls alone.

"You can come to my room," Nick offered in the same husky tone he'd used the night they'd organized his bookshelves. His anger had abated, leaving her mind to churn with bits of what he'd said, the fire in his eyes when he'd defended her, and the way he'd watched her at the bar, his leather jacket hugging his arms when he lifted his beer to his lips.

The minute stretched. "I don't want to be alone," she admitted.

In his deep eyes, she saw the desire he'd concealed until she was ready to let him in. She stood and walked into Nick's bedroom. He followed. She slipped her shoes off and sat on the end of his bed, the mattress sinking when he settled beside her. Nick didn't speak, didn't object when she leaned over to kiss him, his full lips parting to make room for her, or when she shed the red dress, revealing her lingerie. A sharp gasp from Nick, then he caressed her skin, his palm brushing the lace, and drew her mouth to his.

They shifted on his bed, his body hovering over hers. When she opened her eyes, he asked a wordless question. She didn't have time to examine her life, had no desire to weigh her dreams against potential heartbreak. For the first time she gave in to indulgence, to what she craved, with no regard for anything else. She nodded, and in Nick's eyes something flashed. Relief, maybe. And longing, the same she'd seen every time he looked at her, before he tore her lingerie off and pressed into her in one swift, controlled movement. Unlike Andrew, who had always been gentle, Nick was powerful and assertive, and it awoke something in her, something she craved in the moment. His skin smelled of leather when she kissed the middle of his chest. Nick gripped her wrist and squeezed. "Too hard?" he panted into her ear.

"No," she gasped back, then pleaded, "Harder." He squeezed her wrist until it almost burst with pain, but in a strange, delicious way, and she unwound, clasping Nick's hair in her fist as he followed her lead. He collapsed beside her. Kathryn's adrenaline dissipated, a flame blown out.

She felt . . . sick. What the fuck had she done? What if Andrew had walked in on them? Was that what she wanted, to hurt him as deeply as he'd hurt her?

Nick leaned in to kiss her cheek, then settled on his side. Kathryn was still, frozen, until his breathing came in soft snores.

A flutter of noise at the front door, Andrew's key being forced into the lock. She heard the metallic clink of keys on pavement and a muttered *fuck* from the other side of the door.

Blinding panic ripped through her.

Kathryn snatched her scattered clothes from the floor, sprinted to Andrew's room, and stuffed them in the hamper. She darted to the bathroom and clicked the lock behind her, hands trembling.

"Kathryn?" Andrew slurred from the bedroom, and she threw the shower handle, water spraying violently into her face. She lowered herself onto the cold porcelain. Sobs burst from her. She dry heaved, and for a few moments she thought she might vomit into the tub.

If Andrew called for her again, Kathryn didn't hear. Instead, she cried until she was hollow, aching with exhaustion, then shut off the now-cold tap. Gingerly, she stepped from the tub and dried herself. Nothing but silence from the opposite side of the door. When she entered the darkness of the bedroom, Andrew's snores rose and fell. Kathryn felt around inside the dresser and withdrew a T-shirt that she pulled over her head, then crawled onto the mattress. Andrew rolled onto his side, the sick-sweet smell of liquor emanating from his body. His hand thrashed on the sheets, searching, until he found hers and clutched it tight.

The following day, Andrew returned—albeit hungover—to his studies, as if the night had never happened. He seemed oblivious to the shift in the dynamic inside their apartment, blind to Kathryn's despondence. She wore a hoodie to cover the bruises Nick had left on her wrist, and Andrew didn't get close enough to question them. Kathryn spent her days in bed, with no interest in emerging from the depressed state she deserved to endure alone.

One morning she padded down the hall and turned the corner, bumping into Nick's chest, and his eyes locked on to hers. He was wearing nothing but a pair of sweatpants low on his hips, his face inches away. "Kat, please. Talk to me."

"Nick, listen. What we . . . it never should have happened." The memory of his body rising above hers, the way he'd bit her bottom lip, flashed in her mind. "Don't tell him," she pleaded.

"You know I won't." Nick placed his hand on her arm, and she drew a sharp breath, but this time he was gentle, his rich scent hovering between them. "But we can't just pretend it didn't happen. That it wasn't—we were fire together, Kat."

His words sent a shiver down her spine. "I love him, Nick. It was a mistake." She jerked her arm away and pushed past him.

In the following weeks, Kathryn vowed to be patient with Andrew's distraction. Guilt simmered when he reached out for her in the night or when he weaved his fingers with hers while he read in bed, in the moments their love was how it had once been. Maybe it was just a blip in their love story. An indulgence on her part. Maybe their future wouldn't collapse. She made a silent pact to bury her betrayal, the deepest secret she'd ever carry, where it would never see the light.

When Andrew announced his plans to return home to South Carolina for Christmas break, unexpected panic spiked in Kathryn. It had been only two months since she'd slept with Nick, and she couldn't imagine smiling at Andrew's family.

She called her mother, thinking maybe a trip back to Delray Beach might do her good. She was desperate to get away from the boys, to sort through her feelings with the fresh perspective only distance could provide.

"Oh, honey, you haven't been home in almost a year, and we figured you'd be going home with Andrew for the break, so we booked a *senior*"—Sherry whispered the word—"cruise. No one under fifty, so I'll look young, and there won't be any of those DJs or wild pool parties where girls take their tops off."

Kathryn rolled in bed with a groan.

"I told the girl next door I'd pay her twenty dollars to water the plants, but I suppose you could stay here and look after the house."

"No, it's fine. I just wanted to check and see that you're fine with me going with Andrew's family."

"Is everything okay, dear?" Sherry's question was long and drawn out, and Kathryn needed to get off the phone before her mother sensed anything was amiss.

"Yeah, Mom. I'll talk to you soon. Love you."

Kathryn hung up and called Harper, who asked, "You're going to stay in that crappy bachelor pad for Christmas?"

"I guess," Kathryn moaned. "I just can't imagine putting on a show in front of his family." She'd confided in Harper about the distance she'd felt with Andrew since the summer ended but couldn't bring herself to confess what had happened with Nick.

"Come home anyway. You can stay with us—you can see the new house. We're going to the stuffy country club Christmas dinner with my mom, and you're welcome to join. I promise it'll be the most uncomfortable situation imaginable."

Kathryn pictured the string quartet, the terse waiters filling champagne flutes under Nora's glare. "I'll think about it."

On Friday afternoon, Andrew burst into the bedroom, a toothy grin on his face, and snatched Kathryn into a hug. "I did it, babe—a 4.0 GPA." He beamed, reaching for a high five. "One semester to go, and I'm totally going to crush it."

Kathryn gave his hand a smack and mumbled, "Congrats."

"Please come home with me for the break?" He leaned over to place a kiss at the base of her part. "It's our first Christmas together. My folks are expecting you."

Kathryn examined the carpet and picked her nails. "My parents need me to house-sit."

That was it. She'd go home to her empty childhood home and process everything that had happened. Maybe she would have dinner with Harper and Lucas. But could she confess everything to Harper, or would Harper think she was a slut? Guilt throbbed in her belly as she watched Andrew pack his things. She almost stood and stuffed her clothing into his bag, but a throb of guilt gave her pause. Years later she'd look back on those few seconds and wish they'd played out differently. That way, nothing would have turned out the way it had.

Andrew plopped onto the bed and wrapped a heavy arm around her, pulling her face close to his. "What am I supposed to do without you for a week?"

Something inside her cracked. He did love her. This man held her future in his blue eyes, and she'd betrayed him in the worst way, one that couldn't be undone. Kathryn yanked her gaze from his and tried to swallow past the knot in her throat, tears prickling.

For two days after Andrew left, Kathryn wallowed in his bedroom. She heard Nick come and go at odd hours but avoided him until late Christmas Eve. She was on the couch, numb from a bottle of cheap merlot, when he came home. In the flickering light of the TV, they locked eyes from across the room.

"I figured you would've gone home with Drew." Nick cracked a beer and settled at the other end of the couch.

"I couldn't stomach their wholesome, happy faces in their matching pajamas on Christmas morning, given . . . everything."

Nick grunted but didn't press for more. She switched the channel to a generic Christmas movie. On the screen, two absurdly attractive people appeared to own an entire wardrobe of red and forest green. For ninety minutes, they battled a ridiculous misunderstanding that culminated in a perfectly worded confession of love in the final scene, and a kiss in a gazebo as artificial snowflakes danced around the town square. The credits rolled. Kathryn's tears burned. She loathed the movie. Every fucking second of it was sickening. This was not how life worked. Sometimes the two beautiful people don't figure it out; life wasn't a happy ending in the making. It was gritty and ugly and confusing. The picture of the life Andrew wanted with her was as artificial as the movie, and if she forged on into a life with him, every second of it would be a lie. Their relationship was tainted. Rotten.

"You okay?" Nick asked, and when Kathryn blinked her tears away, he was staring, his mouth an O of concern.

She shook her head, an aggressive *no*, then slid to the other side of the couch and cupped Nick's face in her hands. He still wore the look of confusion as she leaned in and kissed him. Then he gave in, pulling her close, matching the desperation of her need to feel something better than the mourning she already felt for the life she'd almost had with Andrew.

Kathryn woke to dawn peeking through Nick's curtains, the merlot raging a war inside her brain. Her existence felt cheap. Grimy. Empty.

Nick was awake, staring into the corner. His paintings were hung, soft shapes in deep hues, forest green and cobalt. And red, like blood. They made her anxious in a way she couldn't pinpoint. "What are we going to do, Nick?"

His jaw, shadowed with stubble, tightened. "Let's not pretend there's a choice."

"What does that mean?"

Nick tilted his head to look at her. "You know what it means, and you know what you want. You just feel shitty right now."

"I love him. You love him, too."

Again, Nick's jaw squared. "Kat, I work at a bar. I have the kind of mom that doesn't even want me home for Christmas. And the kind of dad that thinks a punch to the jaw is a sufficient punishment for getting a C in chemistry."

Shame swelled in her gut.

"But guys like Drew always win. The blond, rich boys. And if it's not him for you, it'll be someone else who can give you the life you want."

"He hasn't always had it easy, Nick. His dad abandoned him."

"Yeah, and after that he won the rich-stepdad lottery."

Every Christmas Kathryn's mother prepared a ham for dinner, and that afternoon Kathryn attempted to re-create the recipe from memory, sipping more merlot, which managed to dull the fog of self-loathing. Nick insisted the meal was delicious, but Kathryn couldn't taste it. They ate outside at a patio table, where they remained until the sun bled into the horizon.

When night fell, they slipped back into Nick's bed, and as she tugged her shirt over her head, Kathryn wondered how her life had changed so completely since the magical summer she'd shared with Andrew.

When Andrew returned a few days later, he met her in his bedroom, fresh faced, blue eyes glittering. He was well fed and rested. He'd thrived without her beside him, without her dulling his light. Andrew lifted her off her feet and carried her to his bed. They collapsed in a pile, and his mouth met hers, his tongue dancing, sparking her desire. "I missed you so fucking much," he said when he pulled away, his weight pressing her into the mattress. Then he buried his face in her hair and breathed her in, his voice muffled when he asked, "Promise we'll never spend a week apart again?"

He undressed with fervor, oblivious to her aching guilt as she followed his lead, fighting tears as he tipped her head back when they came together, his mouth hot on her neck, when she realized she'd never again be able to give him all of her.

It was February when Kathryn realized something in her body might be amiss. At first it was a quick, suspicious thought that she brushed off. Concern struck her again as she was wiping tables at work late one night. *No. It's not possible. I'm just stressed.*

She rummaged through her purse, withdrew her calendar, and counted back the dates. She was a full two weeks late. Had she missed January without noticing?

Shit.

A woozy sense of dread. If it were true—she didn't allow the thought—it could be Andrew's. Or it could be Nick's.

The floor wobbled.

After her shift, Kathryn rushed into the pharmacy, avoiding the cashier's eyes as she swiped her card and snatched her purchase from the counter. Andrew was asleep when she got home, the box concealed under her sweatshirt. Kathryn decided to take the test in the morning. The whole *scare* was punishment for her behavior—she was sure of it.

Kathryn tossed, her nerves accelerating. The test was going to be negative. She could picture it in her mind. The rush of relief. The only possible option.

Or it would be positive. And then what? What if she was knocked up with her boyfriend's roommate's baby? Or a baby with the man she loved, whom she was cheating on? How would she know whose baby it was?

Why had she always been so fucking blasé about taking her pill?

She kicked the blankets to the end of the bed.

At seven, Andrew's alarm cut through the room. He stumbled around, gathering his things. Kathryn wondered if he knew she was faking sleep, but before he left, he placed a soft kiss on her cheek.

Kathryn dashed into the bathroom, locking the door behind her. She clawed the box open and dropped it on the vanity. Her hands quivered as she unwrapped the white stick. It didn't feel like a few grams of plastic could send her life rocketing into an unexpected—and unwelcome—new trajectory.

She couldn't look. Instead, she dropped onto the cold porcelain lip of the tub, screwed her eyes shut, and waited. Her knee bounced as she drew in shaky breaths, counting. One hundred and twenty seconds.

A little blue plus sign.

A guttural wail escaped her without warning, and she dropped to the floor, clutching the stick. Then hard, racking sobs of regret. Of realization. Of shame.

"Kathryn?" Nick's voice came from the hallway outside the bedroom. "You okay?"

"I'm fine," she shouted.

"No, open the door. Please."

Kathryn pulled open the bedroom door. She couldn't hide it, didn't want to hide it. She had to tell someone. She held the stick up for him to see, and watched the realization settle in his expression. He beckoned for her to follow, and they seated themselves on the living room couch.

"Have you told Drew?" Nick asked.

"No. I literally—" She motioned to the stick.

"Well—what do you want to do?"

The weight of the question hit Kathryn like a tidal wave. "I—I don't know. I haven't had time to think."

Nick leaned forward, palms pressed together. "Let's get out of here, you and me; we can find a place to rent."

Kathryn swallowed. "You told me you didn't want kids."

"I know. And I don't. This isn't ideal. But I can get a better job. Maybe this is the thing that pushes us into a life—"

"But what about what I want, Nick?" Her words echoed in the room.

"Yes, Kat. What do you want? What the fuck do you want?" Nick's tone pitched. "You have to make up your mind."

"I have bigger concerns. I don't know if it's yours. I don't know if it's his."

A bolt of jealousy in his eyes. Nick leaned back onto the couch, drawing a shaky breath.

"I'll . . . just . . . take care of it . . ." Her voice quavered.

"You're not going to tell him?"

"How can I do that? I'll have to tell him what we . . . I'll have to tell him everything." Tears spilled down her face. Waves of nausea rolled her stomach and she doubled over.

"Well, there has to be something wrong between you two, because you came back for more of *what we did*," Nick spat.

Nick's words left her with a grimy feeling.

All the control she'd had over her life slipped through her fingers, and she grasped for one thing—anything—she could decide on her own. Kathryn suddenly itched to get out of the room, away from the whole damn town. She got to her feet and ran down the hall.

"Where are you going?" Nick yelled, and she realized he'd followed her. He was always right behind her, and now it was suffocating.

"I'm going home for a few days."

"When are you coming back?" he demanded.

In Andrew's room, she dragged her suitcase from the closet and tore her clothing from the hangers. "I don't know. But you can't tell him. He'll hate me, but he'll get over me. But you're his best friend. If he finds out, he'll hate you even more than me. And you'll lose him."

"You're his girlfriend," Nick cried.

"Not anymore." She went into the bathroom and gathered her makeup bag. "Tell him my parents needed me to come home last minute. I'll call him in a few days and tell him I'm not coming back." She zipped her suitcase. It had taken only a few moments to gather everything she owned. "I won't tell him about us. Ever."

Kathryn dragged her bag down the hall, Nick in tow. She didn't deserve Andrew. She didn't deserve Nick. She uncoiled her key from her key ring and tossed it onto the table. Nick's eyes were pleading, helpless when she slammed the door in his face.

CHAPTER EIGHTEEN

Sunday, May 14
Andrew

Kathryn's long hair spilled down her shoulders onto the bare skin of her back. Her full lips were a deep garnet red, the same color as the dress she wore, and she drew him closer. His hand met her smooth skin, shattering the wall between them; he surrendered all control.

Andrew pressed his lips to the skin of her shoulder, and she faced him. Her dress was gone, and his fingers wound into her hair. His mouth traveled her, kissing her neck, her breasts, down her belly. Her hands were on his head, guiding him, and then he was above her, her tongue on his. They were together, moving as one, and Andrew could feel himself—both of them—climbing higher and higher. She called out, and he spiraled above her, then unspooled in circling waves of ecstasy. He tried to clutch her close, but she began to fade. *No.* He reached out, but she was gone.

Andrew bolted upright, surrounded only by the darkness of his room, the duvet in a pile on the floor beside the bed. Where was Amy? At work. Of course she was at work. Disoriented, more alone than he'd ever been. *"Fuck."* In the quiet, his heart thudded, his breath ragged. His eyes adjusted to the light as his dream swam in his mind.

"Fuck fuck fuck." He darted into the bathroom, where he attempted to clean himself. Relief, pleasure, and shame flowed through him. It was mortifying. *That* hadn't happened since he was in high school.

Andrew lumbered down the stairs, the harsh light of the kitchen assaulting his eyes. At the counter, he watched the coffee maker spit, the liquid collecting in the carafe, all while lost in his dream, trapped between the warmth of the fantasy and his harsh, unforgiving reality.

"Andrew?" Amy's voice sliced his thoughts. She stood at the entrance to the kitchen, her face weary and worn, wearing her scrubs and socks. Her crooked name tag hung where it was clipped to her top. She smelled, as she always did, like medical hand soap, and the scent cut through the kitchen to stir an aching nostalgia, a longing for something he wasn't aware he was missing. Guilt surged through his system. Going out with Kathryn, learning about his son, he could lie to himself, say he didn't want to hurt his wife. But the dream—so visceral, so raw. He couldn't rationalize the desire he felt for another woman. A throb of remorse. He ached to brush Amy's cheek with his thumb, to smooth back the flyaway strands of hair. But if their skin touched, would she sense a change in him? Amy cocked her head to the side. "Are you all right?"

The coffeepot hissed, drawing his attention. "Hey—yeah, how was work?"

"It was fine." Amy unclipped her name tag before she pulled off her top and headed into the laundry room. "Are you sure you're okay?"

"I didn't sleep well." Andrew rubbed his eye with a knuckle.

"My mom called last night." Amy's voice came from down the hall as he spilled coffee into a mug, her words waking him.

"Is she okay?" Andrew imagined the worst, that he and Amy would have to jet off to California. He pictured the awkward cross-country flight, his routine thrown off-balance, his wife devastated.

"Yes," Amy answered. "She's as fine as she can be." Flush with relief, he leaned against the counter to take a sip of his coffee, which scorched the tip of his tongue. He deserved it for his horrible thoughts. "My dad has a conference in Miami at the end of the month. They're going to drive up here that Saturday night for dinner."

"Saturday? Don't you have to work?" The surface of his coffee rippled when he blew on it, then dared take another small sip, his thoughts tangled in his dream.

Amy didn't answer. She came back down the hallway and into the kitchen, wearing her gray cotton boy shorts and sports bra. She looked different, with a subtle roundness to her belly and her face. Her breasts were fuller. Andrew wondered when the last time was that he'd looked, really looked, at his naked wife.

Amy shrugged. "I'll switch shifts, work Sunday night instead. That's Memorial Day weekend, so we'll need all hands on deck." She glanced at him like she had something else to say but then thought better of it.

Muted light crept through the windows, and between the heaviness of the weather and his vivid dream, Andrew was lost to reality. "What time is it?" he asked.

"Eight o'clock. If you're going for a run, you'd better go soon. It's going to rain." Her shoulders slumped in exhaustion. "I'm going to take a shower and get some sleep." She jogged up the staircase.

Andrew laced his shoes and crossed Ocean Avenue. His body was sluggish, and the dense, humid air had him doused with sweat within a mile. The waves were rough, slate gray, and raindrops pelted the sand. His dream passed through his mind on an endless loop while rain soaked his shirt. He pushed on, allowed his mind to drift, emotions and desires swirling fluidly. His heart pounded, as much from his thoughts as the miles of sand under his feet when he recalled Kathryn's smile, the way it gently pulled at her mouth, her chin cast down, her eyes narrowed on him like they shared a deep secret. Which, of course, they did.

At first their conversations had revolved around Max. Then memories seeped in. Old jokes, long forgotten. Now, when Amy worked nights, he sat across from Kathryn at one of Lantana's restaurants. His evenings weren't a stretch of loneliness any longer; for a few evenings each week, Andrew lived another life, one where he had a son. One where Kathryn hadn't broken him. Gone was the straight-backed Kathryn from their first meeting; beneath sconce lights, her smile beamed, like she wasn't conscious of every movement she made.

At their last dinner, they'd settled on a patio, Kathryn's elbow rested on the wrought iron, her chin propped on her knuckles. Her eyes reflected the twinkle of the low-hanging lights strung between the palms. He'd leaned toward her. "Do you remember that road trip we took?"

A faraway smile appeared on her lips, small at first; then it spread, tugged at the corners of her eyes. "That was not a road trip. That was an impulsive—and stupid—Saturday-afternoon drive."

"Come on. It was fun for a while," Andrew teased. "We sang along with the radio and took in all the beauty Central Florida has to offer. Like alligators and Yeehaw Junction."

Kathryn giggled. "Yeah, until we realized we were hours from home, and then that storm rolled in—I think it was the worst I've ever seen outside of a hurricane."

"You were terrified."

"Of course—we couldn't even see the road."

"I thought my dad was going to kill me for putting that shitty motel on my credit card," Andrew said. "But we were stranded in the middle of nowhere." The memory returned in bursts: the outdated motel decor, peeling off their wet clothes to hang in the bathroom, the TV with three channels, the flat pillows and their laughter. He remembered the way he'd kissed her, their bodies together. Their laughter rose in unison, and he said, "We were so stupid, so young and impulsive."

Kathryn's face split into a smile. "We called it our accidental road trip."

Andrew leaned across the table. "Don't you wish we could do something like that again?"

Kathryn's eyes locked with his. "You mean if we didn't have kids and jobs and . . . ?"

A wife.

The fluid moment—equal parts memory and fantasy—all but dissipated. But he could see in her face her thoughts were the same as his. They were both reminded of their obligations, but he had been sure she also wondered, for a moment, how it would feel to drive off into the night together.

His watch beeped, bringing him back to the beach. He adjusted course, pushed on for the final stretch of his run. And though the world was awash with gray, he felt it: color crept back into his life. Excitement. Something he hadn't felt in so long. The night he'd returned from dinner with Kathryn at Lombardi's Steakhouse, Andrew had taken the two orange bottles beside the sink and tossed them into the trash. With each day that passed, while his antidepressants and antianxiety medication faded from his system, he found the exhilaration of living a secret life was a far greater high than any he'd experienced. And, as the source of his intoxication remained undetected, his confidence bloomed. Andrew rode the days like the waves of the ocean, a power larger than himself. Mundane tasks passed in a haze, and his colleagues zipped by him in a blur as he waited for his evenings out, to be swept up in the wave once more, to surrender to the strength of the tide.

He recalled the way he and Kathryn had broken into a dance for a few moments on a restaurant patio. She'd laughed when he'd spun her, making the skirt of her dress sway. The red glow of the evening sun had caught her hair as she brushed it from her face. He thought of the way her long legs looked as she watched the night pass from the passenger seat of his car.

Another night, lost in conversation, the restaurant was empty, their table bare, save for her half glass of cabernet and Andrew's water, now mostly melting ice. With their bill paid, the servers rolled silverware in the corner and left them alone, and they were left to share their thoughts with each other.

The pressure and disappointment of his real life floated just above his shoulders, but he swatted it away. He wasn't doing anything wrong. He didn't touch Kathryn in a way he wouldn't touch any other friend:

A peck on the cheek. His palm on the small of her back as they maneuvered a crowd. Fingertips brushing her arm. And, with an outlet for his loneliness and their argument over his promotion in the past, he and Amy fell into a groove. He packed her lunch and cooked her dinner. He put their sheets in the wash.

Amy seemed content at her job. And Andrew? He certainly wasn't having an affair.

But with Kathryn he was important. Worthy of her attention. There were no expectations, just tapas and easy conversation. And with each evening together, Kathryn fed Andrew more details about Max, and Andrew absorbed each bit of information, like someday they'd all combine and form a complete picture of his son.

Near the end of his run, his house came into view. Andrew stopped, drawing ragged breaths. He was an impostor; he didn't live there and didn't know the man who did. If he'd completed grad school, it would have been his salary that paid for this stunning home. Instead, he'd married a surgeon. Somehow it felt like he'd cheated his way into this life.

Andrew worked his shoes off and went upstairs to shower. Stepping under the hot spray, he closed his eyes and let it run down his face, his hand flat against the smooth tile, riding the familiar, gnawing waves of guilt. Every minute that passed posed more danger that Amy would discover what he was hiding. He couldn't keep her in the dark much longer, but he knew the moment Kathryn and Max entered Amy's reality, the colorful dreamworld he was living in would dissipate. His time with Kathryn would slip from his fingers, and he'd be left with nothing more than the cold rooms of his house and a son who may never want anything to do with him. It couldn't go on like this forever, he knew. But, with each passing day, he was going to soak it in while he could.

The curtains in the bedroom were drawn, and Andrew moved silently around the space as he dressed. Amy's body was silhouetted under the blanket, small and vulnerable, a section of her hair coiled on the pillow beside her. Just one month ago, Andrew would have slipped into bed beside her and buried his face in her neck, taken in the smell of her, grateful she was the balm that soothed the wounds the world had left him with. Now, as he watched Amy sleep just a few feet away, the gap between his two lives felt more difficult to bridge.

There was a cushiony distance between Andrew and everyone in his life. Everyone except Kathryn.

◆　◆　◆

Amy

As Amy feigned sleep, her mind struck one thought like a dart. Bull's-eye.

On Friday night, as she and Andrew had piled into his car before the Hart Breast Cancer Research Fundraising Dinner, Andrew had held the car door for her.

It was a simple gesture. Benign. But it was something he'd never done before. Amy had always seen it as a sign of respect; they were equals. When had he picked up this habit?

They'd sailed wordlessly along the ribbon of nearly deserted highway in the dark. The Boca Resort opened ahead of them, uplighting on the towering palm trees, and the valet took Andrew's keys. Amy had picked a looser gown than the previous year, something to conceal the bloating caused by the illicit fertility drugs. She felt puffy, uncomfortable beneath the fabric. But Andrew looked dapper in his suit, his baby-blue eyes catching his baby-pink tie. Even the day she'd married him, she hadn't found him as handsome as she did that night. The glint in his eye also tickled something in her.

At these events, Andrew knew how to play the game, with his practiced eye contact, his unintimidating smile, his questions balanced, personal yet professional. Only Amy could see what it took from him, the red blotches on his neck. The fact that he'd be exhausted, despondent for the following days. Why did she ask him to attend these events she knew he loathed? He'd more than proved his willingness to please her years ago. But that night he seemed more relaxed. His conversation flowed more easily, and Amy raised an eyebrow at him over her drink.

It was nearly midnight when they drove home, Andrew taking his time as he cruised Ocean Avenue, the moon dancing on the surface of the water like a white, jagged lightning bolt. When the garage door lowered behind them, Andrew turned off the engine. He sighed out the energy of the night, his hand gripping the shift.

Amy tilted her head toward her husband in the darkness. "We're very different people, aren't we?"

Andrew lifted his eyes and said softly, almost with a hint of melancholy, "Yes, we are."

A beat.

"But I love you," Amy said.

"I love you, too." Andrew's gaze was earnest. She was certain he meant it.

And even more certain this wasn't a blip in their marriage—her husband had something to hide.

CHAPTER NINETEEN

Then
Kathryn

Kathryn was sandwiched between her parents at their polished cherrywood table, pushing green beans and cold mashed potatoes around with her fork, her mind spinning with her fight with Nick. And that word: *pregnant.*

She had raced down the highway in three hours, thirty minutes less than it usually took, when she wasn't driving like a crazy person, tears blurring the double yellow lines as they flew past her car.

"Honey, what's wrong?" Sherry asked for the fifth time—Kathryn had counted.

Kathryn forced herself to swallow a bite of meat loaf. "I'm fine, Mom, really. Just tired."

After greeting her parents that afternoon, Kathryn had gone upstairs to her childhood bedroom. Fading photos were tacked to a board above her bed, smiling faces of her high school friends. At one time, the moments frozen in those photos had felt invaluable, and she realized how much her world had changed since she'd first left home. Fresh shame washed over her. What if she ran into one of those friends in town or, worse, one of their judgy parents? Kathryn dropped onto her twin bed, knocking a stuffed giraffe to the floor, tears streaming onto her pillow.

On her way downstairs to dinner, she'd taken the phone off the hook in her parents' bedroom, knowing Andrew would call. She'd blocked his number from her cell. She wouldn't be able to ignore his calls and messages when they started rolling in. Now she glanced at the red, blocky numbers on the stove clock. It had been twenty minutes since Andrew was due home, and her stomach lurched at the thought of him finding her key abandoned on the table.

After dinner, Sherry sliced and plated two pieces of vanilla cake. The muffled sound of the TV spilled from the living room, where her father, Henry, sat on the couch. Thunder rumbled through the open screen door. Kathryn used her finger to bring a smear of buttercream frosting to her lips, sickeningly sweet on her tongue. She stared at the rainbow sprinkles scattered across her plate.

"Are you ready to tell me what this is all about?" Sherry asked. "Did you and Andrew have a fight?"

"No," Kathryn told her solemnly.

"You're not pregnant, are you?"

She hadn't expected her secret to be revealed so quickly, but hearing Sherry say the words made Kathryn draw in a breath, and the tiny blue plus sign strobed in her mind's eye. Tears burst from her before she had a mind to stop them.

"Jesus, Kathryn," Sherry scolded. "I expected you to be more responsible."

Kathryn dropped her face into her hands. "I'm going to call the doctor tomorrow and set up an appointment to confirm, but . . ."

"But what? You haven't told Andrew yet?"

Kathryn's shoulders trembled. "No."

"Why not?"

Kathryn didn't answer. "I thought you'd be supportive." She sniffled like a small child sent to the principal's office.

"Supportive? The timing is terrible. You've been applying to law school." Sherry's words stung almost as much as the disappointment in her face, and Kathryn cried harder at the reminder of the rejections she'd received; coupled with the raw demise of her relationship with Andrew, the plan she'd had evaporated like a mirage. "None of them will let me in, Mom."

Sherry huffed a resigned breath. "So what's the problem? It's early, sure, but you and Andrew can make it work. Maybe law school isn't in the cards."

"That's not it," Kathryn snapped.

Lightning flashed outside, then a clap of thunder, closer. Sherry lifted a brow. "It is Andrew's, isn't it?"

In her lap, Kathryn's hands trembled, and she whispered, "I don't know."

Sherry's jaw dropped. "Jesus, Kathryn."

The stress, the hormones—now that she knew that was what it must be—had left Kathryn teetering on the edge of a breakdown, and it was Sherry's judgment that nudged her off the ledge. Mortification rose in her belly, like a pot boiling over. Again, the sky lit up beyond the back door, and thunder boomed overhead. Kathryn shoved back from the table and dashed up the stairs. She zipped her suitcase and hauled it down the stairs, then out onto the porch and down the front steps.

Swollen raindrops spattered the driveway as she maneuvered her bag into the back seat. Her mother's voice sailed from the porch. "Kathryn. There's no need for theatrics. Come inside, let's talk about this."

Kathryn bit back tears, then slammed her car door and started the ignition. As her car idled, the rain came down in earnest, Sherry now reduced to a smudge of movement on the front porch. The weather matched her mood. Kathryn dialed Harper's number. "Come over," Harper said without hesitation.

Following Harper's direction, Kathryn wound down Ocean Avenue to the house number she'd been given: 228. Her tires rolled to a stop on the slick, deserted road after approaching the house on the east side of Ocean Avenue.

The addresses on the west side of Ocean were owned by the well-off residents of Delray Beach, who worked within the community. The owners of the houses on the east side, on the oceanfront, were rarely seen—second homes for the country's elite, those who held their privacy in the highest regard. *Harper lived here?*

Kathryn rode through the dark gate. The house was concealed in a shroud of rain, and only the glowing windows of the first floor sat before her. She climbed from her car. The back door cracked open, and Harper poked her head outside, ushering Kathryn into the warm, dry house, out of the storm.

◆ ◆ ◆

"So you're not going to tell him?" Harper brought her mug to her lips.

"I don't know. Not yet, anyway." Kathryn blew out an exhausted sigh and crumpled the remains of the tissue Harper had given her in her palm. For an hour, the details of everything that had happened had tumbled from her lips, from Andrew's birthday to fleeing her mother's judgment. She'd thought Harper's eyes might narrow in disapproval, that she might throw sharp words. But instead, Harper sat across the table, occasionally tugging her cream sweater over her shoulders, and listened. Now Kathryn was drained by the catharsis of her confession. Her eyes grew heavy, and her limbs felt like they were made of wet sand. She swallowed the last of her cold tea and set the mug on the table. "Enough about me. Can we talk about this house?" Kathryn gestured around the cavernous kitchen. "You said near the beach, Harper, not *beachfront*. Holy shit, this place is unbelievable."

Harper's face lit up, and her eyes sparkled when she smiled. "It's pretty great, right?" From the kitchen, five windows faced out onto the driveway. The rain washed against the panes, but the recessed lighting cast a warm ambiance into the room.

"And this thing." Kathryn reached for Harper's hand to examine the sparkling, emerald-cut diamond. "Was Luke's dad an oil baron or something?"

A secretive smile crept across Harper's lips from the other side of her teacup.

"Has any of this"—Kathryn again motioned toward the house—"warmed your mom's icy heart even a little bit?"

Harper shook her head. "She's livid about the elopement."

"She'll come around." Kathryn didn't believe the words when she said them.

"I doubt it. She said she doesn't recognize me anymore." Harper set her cup on the table, and the halo of happiness surrounding her flickered, as if Nora's cold grip had reached into the room.

Harper stood and set their mugs in the dishwasher, squinting out the windows to the black night. The lock clicked, and Lucas ducked into the room and slammed the door. Harper met him, dripping on the mat, and Lucas brushed his hood from his hair.

"Sweetheart, Kathryn's visiting for a few days." Harper draped his jacket on the hook next to the door.

Lucas's face widened into a grin. "Kathryn, it's so great to see you." He slipped off his shoes and came to kiss Kathryn on the cheek. Lucas's smile was like the warmth and safety of the house during the storm. The kitchen lights caught the cluster of gold in his left eye, glittering like stars.

Kathryn took in the first floor as Harper led her through the dining room. The house was decorated in warm wood, and the guest bedroom was tucked away off the dining room, with an inviting plush four-poster bed.

"There are clean towels in the bathroom." Harper switched on one of the lights beside the bed. "Get some rest. I'm worried about you and the b-a-b-y."

In the shower, hot water washed the day away. By the time she slipped between the sheets, an exhaustion she'd never known before tugged Kathryn toward sleep. And this new character forming inside her, barely more than an idea, was the last thing to flutter into her thoughts.

Kathryn awoke to the morning light slipping into the room between the palm branches, and before she'd moved from her pillow, an answer appeared with abrupt clarity, the way a word on the tip of her tongue would pop into her head: she was keeping the baby. It didn't matter if it were Nick's or Andrew's; it was *hers*. This baby was bigger than its circumstances.

Kathryn placed her hand over her flat abdomen. A spike of adrenaline brought her reality into sharp focus. She needed to see a doctor. She had to get a job and find a place to live. She needed to buy a bassinet, furniture, tiny onesies. *One thing at a time.*

Kathryn felt awkward approaching Lucas and Harper in the kitchen, but Harper's face lit up.

Lucas was standing in front of the stove, a spatula in hand. "Morning, sunshine."

Kathryn seated herself across from Harper, and Lucas opened a cabinet full of souvenir coffee mugs from the couple's travels: Paris, London, Oahu.

"What are we thinking today? Rainbows?" He set the mug on the table, a pastel rainbow with a smiling sun splashed on the front, then tipped the carafe, letting the heavenly brown liquid rise to the top of the mug.

"I filled Luke in." Harper slid a ceramic cow filled with cream across the table. Kathryn's cheeks burned, but Harper reached out and touched her hand. "There's no judgment here, Kat." Being with Lucas has changed Harper, Kathryn realized with a swell of gratitude.

Lucas set three plates of pancakes in front of them, and Harper caught Kathryn up on the details of their honeymoon as they ate. Kathryn welcomed their chatter as a pleasant distraction from the whirlwind of the previous day. The privacy of the property, and its larger-than-life opulence, not to mention the most comfortable bed she'd ever slept in, were a cocoon of safety from the events of the previous day. There was no way Andrew or Nick could find her here.

And Harper seemed lighter than ever. More focused. Lucas was good for her, Kathryn realized, and her heart throbbed when she thought of Andrew.

After breakfast Kathryn followed Harper up the wooden staircase to the third floor, home to Lucas and Harper's sprawling suite. The bed faced the windows to the east, and french doors opened to the balcony. The two women stepped outside; the water, layered in shades of blue, glittered below.

"I'm keeping the baby," Kathryn blurted.

"Wow, Kathryn." Harper's eyes widened with a sparkle of excitement. "That's amazing."

Kathryn sighed. "I hope so." The fresh idea of a baby still didn't seem real.

"I talked to Luke this morning, and we want to offer you the guesthouse." Harper's hair whipped in the breeze. "If you want it."

"I just need a few days to go look for an apartment."

"Stay awhile, if you'd like. Save some money. I'll have it cleaned later today."

The previous morning, when her life had been turned upside down in Andrew's bathroom, Kathryn couldn't have imagined herself living on Lucas and Harper's beachfront property. A safe palace for her and her baby. It was more than she could wrap her head around, far more than she deserved. "Harper, I can't thank you enough."

Harper beamed. "It'll be nice to have someone to talk to."

That afternoon, Harper led Kathryn across the driveway to the guest cottage, letting a long beam of sunlight fall into the space. A plush couch faced the living room windows, and french doors opened to a small bedroom tucked in the back. In the kitchen, Kathryn brushed the curtain aside, the ocean visible between the low-hanging palm branches. Underneath her big toe, the terra-cotta tile closest to the sink had been memorialized with a dog's footprint. Harper leaned against the doorframe, smiling as she watched Kathryn take it all in. "So do you think it'll do?"

◆　◆　◆

Two weeks later Kathryn sat across from her mother at a bustling pancake house, where she looked down at the Formica table and repeated, "I'm keeping the baby."

Sherry shook a sugar packet into her iced coffee, pensive, but Kathryn saw a smile creep across her face, along with the same excitement she'd seen in Harper's eyes. The judgment was gone. "You can come home. Dad and I would love to have you."

"Mom, don't take this the wrong way, but you and Dad have given me everything my whole life, and I'm kind of a spoiled brat. I can't come home and have you take care of my baby. I'm going to stay with Harper and Lucas for now."

"Staying with your wealthy friends is your idea of being less spoiled?" Sherry smirked.

"I'm just saying, I need to do this on my own."

Sherry nodded before her tone softened. "I'm not sure what happened between you and Andrew—and I don't need to know—but please talk to him. He's been calling the house every day, and I can't hold him off forever. He deserves an explanation, or closure, whatever you kids call it."

Kathryn set her face in her hands. "I will, Mom. I just have things to work out first. Please don't tell him where I am or . . . anything."

"This is not my news to tell, Kathryn."

Keeping Andrew in the dark forever wasn't part of the plan, but, inwardly, Kathryn knew what she was waiting for: she wanted to see her baby.

The first few weeks of pregnancy, Kathryn felt energetic and couldn't believe an enormous change was taking place inside her body. Eventually, she succumbed to morning sickness, keeping her in bed for days. The weather was gloomy and overcast during this period, which fit her mood.

With each passing day, she wondered what Andrew was doing, how he'd reacted when he'd come home to find her key on the table. Scenarios whirled in her mind as she lay in bed in the cottage. Had he been devastated? Or worse—relieved? Had Nick told him about the pregnancy? Did Andrew think she'd run away to have an abortion; was he furious with her?

Or had Nick kept her secret? Had Andrew moved on already, found someone else?

Kathryn snagged a job as a paralegal at a local firm and paid Harper and Lucas the small sum of rent they'd agreed on. She often picked up groceries or bottles of wine and left them in the kitchen of the beach house, anything she could offer as a token of appreciation for her friends' generosity. Harper often invited Kathryn over for breakfast, and on alternating Saturday nights they all had dinner together on the large sunporch facing the water, where their laughter carried over the waves. On these nights Kathryn looked out on the moonlight over the water and set a hand on her growing belly, and the ache for Andrew dulled to a throb.

The moment the doctor confirmed she was having a boy, battling images clashed in her mind: a dark-haired child with Nick's eyes, or her olive skin paired with Andrew's blond hair. She contemplated submitting a DNA test once he was born, but how would she pull it off? Did it even matter? She might never see Andrew or Nick again, and she'd love her son just the same. Sleepless, her hand on her belly, where her baby kicked and turned, partners in insomnia, Kathryn tried to picture his face. This tiny person was centimeters from her fingers, and the love that swelled within her at the thought of him felt as if it would break her. Kathryn longed to know who the other half of this person was, while she also wanted to keep him inside her forever, where she could wrap her arms around the globe of her belly, where there was nothing to hurt him.

Max made his pink-faced, screaming entrance on a late-September night. When Kathryn thought back, the memory evoked a haunting cocktail of elation and—was it regret? Certainly not regret for Max, the most perfect human she'd ever seen, her tears rolling onto his tiny head when she'd cradled him for the first time. It was as if no other version of this boy had ever existed; he just *was*, with a silky tuft of blond hair and brilliant blue eyes. A DNA test seemed laughable, if she had it in her to laugh.

The hospital buzzed with activity; nurses and doctors came and went, and the hallway outside her door was a parade of voices, balloons, crying babies, carts with squeaky wheels. On Max's first morning, Kathryn's parents came to meet him, followed that afternoon by Harper and Lucas. But when night fell, Kathryn found herself alone with Max for the first time. Somehow she felt truly alone, though she realized her life would never orbit around herself again.

Max was swaddled in his bassinet, asleep, a tiny oval in the pale light. When the night nurse came to help Kathryn hold Max to her breast, Kathryn clutched him, fresh tears spilling onto his tender head. *Mine.* Nothing would take him away from her.

The following weeks drained Kathryn in a way she'd never imagined possible. Her body, her sanity, her sleep; this tiny person needed it all. For a few bleak nights, bleary eyed and exhausted, she wanted to grab the phone and punch in Andrew's number, to wake him, to confess everything, then demand he make the drive south. She saw it: the harsh whispers, hurt eyes. And she saw Andrew holding Max in the dim light of the cottage while she drifted to sleep, relieved of the weight of it all. And maybe, when she woke, the sun spilling in on a new day, there would be softer words. Forgiveness.

Instead, she gathered Max in her arms and paced the driveway in the light of the moon until he settled.

During those first months, Lucas and Harper brought over foil-covered plates of food each evening. They sent their housekeeper to tidy the cottage once a week, making Kathryn feel spoiled and guilty, but her heart swelled with appreciation.

Days passed. Months. Max grew heavy. He was safe there with her. And every day Kathryn found something new to love about her new home, from the morning light filtering in between the palm branches to the sweet song of the ocean floating into the house. Kathryn returned to her paralegal work, and each morning she dropped Max off with Sherry. With a full-time job and a baby, Kathryn's schedule kept her busy and out of Lucas's and Harper's way. Exiting the gate each day felt like she was entering the *real world*. All day at work she longed to collect Max and let the branches of the weeping willow that hunched protectively over the front gate brush her car, the gate that opened to Ocean Avenue sliding shut behind her.

Max ticked off milestones with dizzying frequency; it seemed every day she collected him from Sherry he'd learned something new. Kathryn ached to freeze time; to savor Max's babble in the car seat behind her while she drove, chubby fingers at his wet gums, cheeks as rosy and pink as ripe peaches.

On a sunny March afternoon, Kathryn arrived at her parents' house and rushed inside. Max was seated in his pack-and-play, and his face split into a grin when he saw Kathryn. "Ma!" he burst. The one syllable shattered Kathryn, hard and unforgiving, like a slap: she realized she and Andrew could have had the future they'd planned together, with this little boy to bask in their love. But she'd ruined it. She slid to the floor as sobs exploded from her.

"Honey." Sherry entered, clutching a sunflower-print dish towel. "What's wrong?"

Kathryn shook her head violently. Sherry fetched her a glass of ice water, and after a few minutes, Kathryn composed herself and lifted Max, placing kisses on his head.

What have I done? She repeated the words as she drove home. *I have to call him.* Andrew would be angry—livid. Heartbroken. But she had to do it.

So she did. After Max settled that night, Kathryn unblocked Andrew's number with trembling fingers and dialed. The phone trilled over the sound of her hammering heartbeat.

"Hello?" A woman's voice.

Kathryn gasped.

"Hello?" the woman demanded. "Kathryn?"

Kathryn clocked the voice, the syrupy southern drawl. Lily, Andrew's mother.

"Mrs. Williams." Kathryn sniffed. "Is Andrew—I'm looking for Andrew."

"Andrew isn't available." There was a curl of venom in Lily's voice.

"Is he okay?"

"No, he's not." A frigid pause. "Andrew nearly threw away his future for you. I knew you were bad news from the start, knew you'd distract him from everything he worked for. That's what girls like you do."

Kathryn reeled.

"So you leave my son alone. He's getting his life back on track, and if he knows what's good for him, he won't tangle with another *hussy* like you." Lily hung up. Kathryn cried until the dawn light crept in.

The first time a man, another intern from her firm, expressed interest in her, Kathryn rebuffed his suggestion they get a drink. It was uncalled for. She belonged to Andrew. Then it struck her: she didn't belong to anyone. She was single. It was then she realized her love for Andrew wasn't a choice. It marked her permanently, a scar. Would it fade? Or was it permanent? And in that moment she longed to turn back time, ached for Andrew's tender touch, the way he found her beneath the blankets and folded his arms around her. She'd been given a winning lottery ticket to the life she dreamed of, and she'd destroyed it.

But she belonged to Max. He was hers alone to guide through the world.

From that day on, Kathryn sealed her life off from anyone aside from Lucas, Harper, and her parents. She kept a polite, professional distance between herself and her coworkers. She didn't make friends, didn't date. Kathryn found she was content to hide from the consequences of her decisions behind the heavy gate of 228 Ocean Avenue.

They celebrated Max's first birthday on the sunporch, and Kathryn snapped a photo of her son poking a finger into a blue frosted cake. That afternoon, in front of Kathryn and her parents, Max took his first steps. Lucas gently held Max's hand in his palm until Max pulled away, marching forward on his own. Kathryn's vision swam with tears.

But Lily's icy words jangled in Kathryn's mind. And the thought she clung to when she looked at Max: *mine.*

One evening Kathryn coaxed Max to sleep, then wandered down the path toward the beach, baby monitor clutched in hand. She closed her eyes and listened to the rhythm of the waves. Everything was calm. On her way back to her cottage, the warm light of the kitchen window spilled onto the driveway. Kathryn approached the back door, knocking gently.

Lucas pulled the door.

"I'm sorry, I thought you were Harper," Kathryn said.

"She went to bed early," Lucas said. Seconds ticked by. "Want to come in? I'm making some tea."

She didn't want to return to the cottage alone, so Kathryn climbed the steps. Lucas moved around the kitchen, gathered two mugs. Beneath the kettle, the burner glowed. Kathryn set the baby monitor on the table. "I have something to say."

Lucas lifted his brows.

"You're good for Harper," Kathryn said. "She's happy. She's . . . lighter than before."

Luke's smile bloomed. "She's good for me, too."

"Have you had many interactions with Nora?" Kathryn remembered Harper's childhood home like something from a fairy tale; the property seemed to never end. All white marble and pillars, a pool, a grotto. And they had staff; someone to cook, someone else to clean. Harper had a nanny and a tutor. But Harper walked the house, stiff, like she didn't belong. She didn't smile. Nora didn't allow messes; there were no pizza rolls to be microwaved in the kitchen, no globby nail polish for giving each other pedicures. So they spent time at Kathryn's house, where Sherry brought juice and snacks up to Kathryn's bedroom while they watched *Total Request Live*.

"Not really." The kettle whistled, and Lucas snatched it, filled two mugs with boiling water before he set them on the table. A smile lifted the corners of his mouth as he lowered himself into a chair. "But that WASPy old bitch doesn't scare me."

Kathryn choked back a giggle. "And how about your family?" She'd lived in this man's guesthouse for almost two years, but she didn't know him well, she realized.

Lucas wrapped his fingers around his mug. "I grew up in Miami. But both my parents died within a few years of each other. I had to get away."

"God, Luke. I'm so sorry."

Lucas offered a resigned smile. "It's okay."

"Do you have any brothers or sisters?"

"None I've ever met. It's just me. But my dad left me money. I needed a job for the summer while I waited for the estate to be settled, so I moved up to Delray. That brought me to the country club, which led me to you, who led me to Harper." A tiny smile lifted his lips when he spoke his wife's name. "And her mother, with her iced tea and her salad. Dressing on the side."

Kathryn smiled, then blew on her tea. "What happened to your parents?" She realized how rude her question sounded as soon as she said it. "Never mind—that's not my business. I'm sorry."

"No, it's okay." Lucas cleared his throat. "My mom came here from Brazil when she was a teenager. She grew up really poor. She met my dad; he was a businessman in Miami. But as it turns out, he had a family. Wife, kids, the whole thing. I was four when she found out, and she was devastated. But she never told them, and she never left him. She was in love with him."

"Did you ever meet him?"

"He took us out a few times. He'd come by and pick me up and we'd drive around. Seemed like a cool enough guy. But we lived in this shitty apartment, and my mom worked three jobs, and I was home alone more often than not."

Kathryn bobbed her tea bag in the steaming water.

"Anyway, my dad died when I was fifteen. Colon cancer. He left my mom all of his money. His wife and kids took my mom to court and tried to fight it, but it was there in his will, it was clear." Kathryn stared at Lucas's face in the dim kitchen light as he spoke. "Then my mom died."

"I'm so sorry."

Lucas shrugged, his eyes sad. "I wish I could have my mom back. All I can do is move forward, start my own family. And I don't want it to be anything like my childhood."

Kathryn gave him a soft smile.

Lucas twisted the string of his tea bag around his finger. "Have you thought about reaching out to Max's father?"

"Constantly," Kathryn admitted. "I just don't know how I could at this point."

"My mom raised me alone. I don't want that for you, Kathryn. Or for Max."

"Andrew's a catch. He's probably found someone who is more suited for him by now." She heard the bitterness in her words. Lucas frowned. "Think about it. For Max's sake."

Kathryn considered Luke's words as she stared into her tea.

Kathryn and Harper took long sunset strolls, the foamy surf rolling around their ankles, the salty sea air tangling their hair. But when Kathryn couldn't sleep, and the light in the kitchen window flicked on, she rapped on the back door of the beach house, and Lucas let her in, and they sat at the kitchen table, talking late into the night. Maybe it was the anonymity of the night pressing against the kitchen windows, but she knew anything she said over her steaming teacup would never leave the room.

And maybe echoes of Harper's judgment reverberated somewhere in the recesses of Kathryn's mind, but she never mentioned these evenings with Lucas to Harper.

Shortly after Max's first birthday, Kathryn went to Sherry's house to collect him after work. "A letter came for you, honey," Sherry said.

Kathryn regarded the envelope. Eckman Law School. It was one of the few schools she'd applied to after Max was born. She slit the flap. An acceptance.

A spark in the darkness. She might be able to give Max a shred of the life she'd promised before she'd conceived him. A pool. A safe home that was *theirs*.

Three months into her classes, in the kitchen one night, Lucas set their two mugs on the table and announced that Harper was pregnant.

"Wow, congratulations," Kathryn gushed, but a barb of hurt jabbed her. Why hadn't Harper told her the news herself? Her friend had been more tired than usual, less talkative.

"I don't want my kid to be alone all the time like I was growing up." Luke leaned his back against the wall. "I'm Brazilian; I want them to be surrounded by food and music and the ocean—the more people in the house, the better. Maybe we'll adopt, too, in the future?"

"Don't get ahead of yourself." Kathryn laughed, letting the magic of Luke's picture for his life settle over them. "Let me know how you feel about this one when you haven't slept in days."

Lucas's eyes were alive with possibilities.

"I guess I need to finally get out of your way." Kathryn was unprepared for the swell of unease that wrapped around her when she thought of moving. She'd be on her own—truly. Without the warmth of her friends or the safety of life on Ocean Avenue.

"You can stay, you know. You just started school. Most people our age live with roommates; what's the difference?"

"The difference?" Kathryn sputtered and motioned around them. "Most people our age don't have babies. And your kind of money, and houses like this one."

Lucas shrugged. "We're not like most people our age, that's for sure."

"I'm sure the neighbors talk."

Lucas's smile pulled at the corners of his eyes. "Fuck 'em. Let them think what they want. Let them think I have multiple wives and multiple kids. Let them think I sacrifice goats in the attic. I don't care." They both covered their faces to stifle their laughter, but Kathryn was awash with relief. *I don't have to go. Not yet.*

"Luke told you about the pregnancy?" Harper asked three days later as they walked the beach. Harper walked slowly, like her energy had been drained.

Kathryn couldn't lie. She nodded.

Harper didn't elaborate. She retreated into the upper levels of the house for days on end. Kathryn gave her space. She was too familiar with the harsh words Harper was capable of slinging when she was in a dark place, and too vulnerable to be Harper's target.

"Is she okay, Luke?" Kathryn asked one evening.

Lucas frowned, as if he didn't want to betray his wife. "She went off her meds. Her doctor said they were safe, but Harper . . . she doesn't want to risk it."

Some days Harper seemed like herself, and sometimes she was a recluse. One Saturday, Kathryn knocked on Harper's door, a Publix bag of candy and salty snacks in tow. She and Harper nestled in bed and watched TV, munched Twizzlers. They didn't need to speak much, just shared one more chapter of their lives together.

With law school and a full-time job and a toddler, the days melted into months in a dizzying haze. Kathryn rode Harper's ups and downs with her, but she couldn't help but feel a bolt of relief alongside her excitement when Harper went into labor and Emmy burst into their lives the fourteenth day of June.

Kathryn gave the couple space. She brought groceries, left them in the kitchen, took Max to the beach.

One afternoon, when Emmy was one month old, Kathryn knocked on the door, and Lucas yanked it open, cradling his daughter. His eyes were red rimmed and bleary. "Luke? Where's Harper?"

"She went away for a few days to rest." In his granite expression, Kathryn understood. "She needed time to adjust to her medication. Having a baby, it's been hard on her."

"But she's back on her meds?"

Lucas nodded, and relief swept Kathryn. "The doctor gave her something new."

Kathryn reached for Emmy, offered the one thing she'd fantasized about when Max was a newborn. "I'll take her for a few hours; you sleep."

Lucas nodded gratefully.

Lucas and Kathryn developed an unspoken cadence to sharing childcare and prepping meals, even after Harper returned home. Harper's moods seemed to stabilize, but she slept often. The medication, Kathryn guessed.

Kathryn still woke every morning with Andrew on her mind, but he existed at a safe distance, like an old memory. After Emmy's first birthday, Harper seemed to find her footing. Her moods no longer came and went like the tides. Harper bloomed; she chatted with Kathryn, their feet in the warm sand, the sun on their faces. Harper carried Emmy on her hip, kissed her small fingers. The kids spun around them, splashing in the surf on the blinding-bright afternoons of their childhood. This was the life she'd always thought she'd share with Harper, Kathryn thought with a bubble of gratitude.

Kathryn enrolled Max in kindergarten the summer before his fifth year, and as she filled out the address on his school forms, she realized with a lurch how much time had passed. Max needed his own space, his own bedroom. She needed to make a home that was her own, not a borrowed escape from reality. Leaning against the reception desk at Max's future elementary school, she realized her life would never be as dreamy as it was behind the stone wall of Lucas and Harper's home, but there was no way she could know just how quickly—and permanently—their collective time together was about to spiral to an end.

CHAPTER TWENTY

Sunday, May 14
Emmy

Emmy woke in the back seat of Javi's Jeep, a rolled sweatshirt beneath her head, the first light of dawn creeping in on the heels of the night. They'd spent the evening in Miami at one of the clubs owned by Javi's parents, and Emmy had drifted off on the hour-long ride home up a nearly deserted I-95, and when she half woke, Emmy recalled the evening in flashes, sweaty bodies writhing against hers, arms in the air, the music pulsing deep inside her body, lost in a trance of rum-induced freedom.

It was almost too easy to lie to Kathryn, who seemed dreamy those days, her faraway thoughts painting a faint smile on her lips. Emmy had said she was staying with Maggie again, she recalled with the same tickle of guilt she felt when she appeased Harper with vague texts.

Emmy's eyes crept open. On the front console, Max's and Javi's tan arms rested side by side as they yelled to one another over the cool rush of morning air. Since she'd told Max about the man in the car, a heaviness hovered over him. As each day loomed closer to enacting Max's plan to expose Kathryn, Max grew more introspective; Emmy caught him nibbling his bottom lip, his brows pinched. But her vision of the future morphed like a kaleidoscope. She pictured Max, relieved of this weight, their hands entwined, watching sailboats glide across Lake Union, a world away from their parents' mistakes.

Four more weeks.

Emmy straightened as Javi pulled into the beach lot. The boys' flip-flops slapped the pavement as they unloaded their surfboards and jogged toward the water. Still tangled in her dreams, Emmy settled into the sand, a blanket hugging her shoulders, and watched the boys crest a wave. After his fifth ride in, Max clutched his surfboard and ambled across the sand, shaking the water from his hair. "You ready for your first lesson?"

Emmy peeled her dress over her head, then followed him into the chilly water. Max guided her onto the board, and she tried to find her balance on the wobbly surface, her feet gripping the knobs of wax. The board lurched, and she crashed into the water, which chased away the cobwebs of the liquor that hung in her brain. She surfaced and spit brine. "How do you make it look so easy?"

"Don't say shit like that to him," Javi called, bobbing a few feet away. "It goes straight to his head."

Emmy treaded water and watched Max mount his board, his hair slicked back, before he glided to the shore on a swell.

Javi sat on his board, his feet dangling, and smirked. "I told you."

"I'm starving. Let's get some breakfast and come back," Max said, then dove beneath the waves.

In the car, Javi pulled on a faded orange tank top, and they swung around the drive-through at Good Burger.

Back at the beach, Javi parked beneath the shade of a tree, and Max distributed their iced coffees. Emmy fished in the bag, handing Max a greasy sleeve of hash browns. Families had arrived at the beach to lay claim to their spots for the day, spreading sun-faded towels and opening coolers stuffed with crushed ice and soda cans. Javi peeled the foil from a breakfast burrito while Emmy let a spoonful of strawberry milkshake melt on her tongue.

"How can you eat that shit for breakfast?" Max asked.

"It's delicious." Emmy leaned over to spoon milkshake into Max's mouth.

Javi bit his burrito. "Listen, you two. Can I eat my fucking breakfast without you rubbing your lifestyle in my face?"

But Max's smile reached only half-mast.

Javi turned to Max. "You're one to talk, Maxwell, eating that greasy shit. You're getting flabby." He pinched Max's belly. "I've had to hit the gym without my spotter."

Max reached for Emmy's milkshake and forced a spoonful into Javi's mouth, then said, "I have something to tell you."

Javi wiped his face with a napkin. "Please don't propose to me right now. I look rough, and I haven't even finished my coffee." He sucked his straw.

Max shoved Javi's forearm. "Asshole. Listen. I'm serious." Max's tone downshifted, and the change caught Javi's attention. "Emmy's been accepted into UW, and we're planning to head to Washington the second week of June."

"*We?*"

"We," Max repeated.

Javi stared at Max for a long time. "Washington? That's a big step. Huge." The two boys shared a look. "Our deal stands."

"Okay, Dad." A spike in Max's tone.

The two boys fell silent. Emmy's stomach lurched. What did Javi know about Max that she didn't? "What deal?"

Max's body tensed, and he released a defeated exhale, the kind that came only before a confession. He shifted to face her. "After I got expelled, I started partying a lot more. Then, a few months ago, Javi and I went out one Saturday night, got fucked up. I dropped him off, but I guess I decided I wasn't ready to go home, so I sped up Ocean and skidded out on a curve. I don't remember. But when I came to, there was glass everywhere, and there was a light pole where my passenger seat was . . ." He shuddered. "I was alone in the dark. And it was really quiet." Max's Adam's apple rose, fell. "I was crying because I couldn't find Javi. It took a few minutes to remember that I'd brought him home. If I hadn't done that . . ." His voice dissolved.

The waves crashed. "It's cool, man," Javi whispered.

"No, it's not," Max snapped, tears snagging his words. His head hung, and he drew in a shaky breath.

Max and Javi exchanged another look, and Max apparently conceded. Javi turned to Emmy. "When I found out he'd nearly killed himself, I lost it. But when I found out Kathryn literally took him to the threshold of rehab, and this stubborn jackass refused help, I was pissed. Really pissed."

Emmy hated the idea of anything hurting Max, and the thought of how close he'd come to losing Javi made her shiver.

Javi turned his gaze to Max. "So I forced him to make some promises. He swore he'd keep his drinking to a normal amount, and if he ever felt like he was losing his shit that way again, he'd get help."

"So that's what you were arguing about at your house," Emmy said to Javi.

"I didn't want him to get hung up on anything—or anyone—that might send him spiraling again. *Anything*." Javi looked to Max. "So. The deal stands."

"I got it," Max said. "I'm good, Javi. My life is different now." There was a flicker in Max's face, and his mouth lifted.

Javi smirked. "Look at you, *smiling* and shit. I never thought I'd see the day." The clouds in the car parted. "You're practically an old married man. Gotta get you some dad jeans to go with your Birks and socks. You know, Washington style."

Max's brows narrowed. "Javi—what if you came with us?" Silence fell. Emmy hadn't anticipated the offer. And, looking at Max's face, he hadn't, either. He looked at Emmy. "I didn't ask you—I'm sorry."

But a thought spread over her. She wanted Max happy, wanted him surrounded by people who loved him. In the ghosts of her memory, Harper had been happy with the family she'd built, with Kathryn and Lucas. Maybe fate would fare better for her, Max, and Javi. "No, it actually makes sense," she said. "I'm going to live in the dorms; you'll need a roommate."

Max's smile cracked open, and the darkness in his eyes lifted.

"Wow." Javi stared out the windshield. "I'm flattered, but a throuple isn't really my style." Max shoved him. "I mean, it's a lot to think about. My mom will lose her shit. But . . . why not?"

Max's smile was gleeful, and Emmy's heart swelled. It was falling into place. Maybe Max's past behavior was a rough patch, but their collective future was as bright as that morning. Max leaned back to plant a kiss on her lips, deep, drawing her in, and they ignored Javi's *Okay, gross*.

The boys returned to their burritos, and Javi asked, "I take it Kathryn hasn't found out about you two lovebirds yet?"

"Fuck no." Max wiped his mouth with the back of his hand. "She wouldn't let Emmy stay if she did."

"There has been a development," Emmy said.

Javi glanced over his shoulder and cocked an eyebrow. "Oh yeah?"

Max motioned to Emmy with his chin between bites. "Tell him."

Emmy leaned forward. "Kathryn has someone new. Or someone not so new."

"What happened to the cop?" Javi asked.

"I don't know," Max said. "But Emmy bumped into this new dude about a month or so ago, and she said he looked just like me."

Javi straightened. "What does that mean?"

Max balled his wrapper. "It means exactly what I just said."

Javi scrunched his nose. "Maybe you're not a test-tube baby after all?"

Max shrugged.

"Is he good looking?"

Max grunted. "I said he looked like me, didn't I?"

"They drive the same car," Emmy added.

Javi chuckled. "Well then, cancel your *Maury* appearance, that's all the proof we need." He grinned. "Have you considered asking Kathryn about him?"

Max squinted. "Are you really suggesting that? You've known me—known her—for, what, fifteen years? When has she ever been forthcoming with anything?"

Javi shrugged. "Point taken."

Max tucked a foot underneath his body. "We have a plan to catch them."

Javi's eyes scanned the ocean, where a few pelicans danced over the surface. "Is that really what you want, Max?"

Max's face darkened, and he looked up at Javi, then nodded. "What other choice do I have?"

Javi locked on to Max's eyes. "We've got your back, dude, no matter what comes from this." He motioned to Emmy, who nodded in agreement, with a swell of gratitude that someone loved Max, and understood him, as much as Javi did. Javi turned to Emmy, then back to Max, and cocked his head to the side. "So what do you have in mind?"

CHAPTER TWENTY-ONE

Friday, May 19
Amy

Amy found her husband standing in front of the open refrigerator, his shirt adhered to his body with sweat, his back still heaving from his run. "Good morning," she said, catching the jerk of his shoulders when she startled him.

Andrew reached for a bottle of water before he turned to face her, letting the refrigerator door fall shut. "Morning." He cracked the cap and discarded it on the countertop.

Amy had gifted him an expensive thermal water bottle, yet he chose to drink out of the cheap plastic ones they stocked for guests. Andrew leaned against the fridge, downed half the bottle in one swig, took a deep breath, and asked, "Did you sleep well?"

Amy set a hand on her hip. "I suppose. It's nice to sleep in my own bed. It's hard to nap at the hospital." She'd clocked more hours than usual that week, and guilt snagged her. But people needed her, even if her husband did, too. She anticipated his next words, his gentle yet persistent suggestion she dial back her hours. Seconds ticked by.

Hmm. It wasn't even a word. Just a noise, deep in his throat. The nape of Amy's neck prickled.

Andrew hadn't been the same since that morning when they'd fought in the kitchen. Sure, for a while, he'd seemed relieved. But then something else had replaced the friction between them. The changes were subtle, the kind of shifts noticeable only in retrospect. It wasn't things that happened more, but that happened less. A touch. A look. They occupied the same space, but their circles found fewer reasons to overlap. They used to chat about everything, nothing, before they fell asleep, or while they had their morning coffee. Now they read on their individual devices. And the things Amy had always asked him to do—put his running shoes away instead of leaving them by the back door, make the bed, collect the mail—were now all checked off without fail. Andrew's shoes were nowhere to be seen, the bed was made, hospital neat, as if it had never been slept in, the mail stacked in a neat rectangle on the counter.

But the night she'd spotted his car at the steakhouse, something had planted itself deep inside her. A seed of suspicion that bloomed every day. Now all her husband's actions were divided into one of two categories: the behavior of the Andrew she knew, the Andrew she'd married, or the actions of someone who held a secret. This *hmm* hashed in the latter column.

In the kitchen, Andrew's eyes darted around the room; he was nervous, like he was anticipating her next question.

"You stopped taking your medication?"

His Adam's apple bobbed. "Yes."

She'd spotted the bottles at the bottom of the bathroom trash back in April, the tablets rattling inside when she'd examined them. She'd given him time to raise the subject, but he'd never breathed a word to her, a *physician*. Amy took him in, the toned body she'd once reached for without hesitation. He seemed jumpy, recently, on edge. "Don't you think you should have a discussion with your psychiatrist before making that kind of decision?"

Andrew straightened. "Amy, twice a year I pay that man one hundred and fifty dollars for a ten-minute slot so he can write me a script. He never even makes eye contact. I hardly think he cares."

"What if your symptoms return?"

Andrew's gaze fell to the countertop before he answered. "I'm tired of taking them. They make me numb. I'm sick of it." The vulnerability in his eyes prodded her. Deep inside, she craved the caress of his fingers on the back of her neck, on her arms, everywhere. But she couldn't get distracted.

At work Amy carried on, soothing her patients, pacing the hollow hospital corridors in the dark hours of the night, while she sorted her thoughts. She needed to use her brain, to separate her emotions. Feelings couldn't be trusted. Only evidence could be relied upon.

Naturally, she'd formed a plan. It had taken a few shifts for the opportunity to present itself, but one evening the hospital was uncharacteristically quiet, her schedule briefly overlapped Dr. Sanchez's, and Amy was allowed a rare indulgent break. Instead of napping or brewing coffee, she slipped into her car and cruised up the highway to Lantana.

She felt foolish. She'd never imagined chasing a man around the dark streets. But this was her life, her partner, she thought as the halo of streetlamps passed. Everything he did affected her. And she spotted it: Andrew's car in the lot at Angelo's Bistro, the restaurant's loopy logo glowing red in the darkness. This time, without the camouflage of a deluge, Amy was certain it was his car. That custom color: Amethyst Gray. Confirmed by his plate.

Amy spent her life reading charts, facts. None had ever struck her like a hot iron.

That fucking car had been the first clue that she and Andrew hadn't been on the same page. Amy had expected him to choose something safe and practical, like her Volvo SUV. Instead, Andrew had selected the sleek sedan, adding every feature the salesman pitched without hesitation, his face split into a grin like a child set loose in a toy store with a hundred-dollar bill. Amy had been tucked into the back seat on the test drive, nausea swelling as Andrew engaged in a pissing contest of increasing machismo with the salesman. His custom paint job had delayed the delivery of his vehicle by a month. What was wrong with regular gray? "Do you know how dangerous colors like that are in low light?" Amy had growled when the salesman was out of earshot. "One rainy day you're going to get T-boned. I work in the ER. I see it all the time."

Andrew had rolled his eyes, leaving Amy feeling like a nagging wife. A title she'd never imagined for herself. At the finance desk, a shrine to etched-glass accolades, Amy had sat with her arms and legs crossed, bathed in the assault of aggressive air-conditioning. She had clutched her opinions to herself while inwardly, swirling questions seeded themselves in a place she didn't dare visit.

After spotting Andrew's car at the bistro, Amy stomped the gas on the empty stretch of highway, and the exquisite engine responded; her car sailed over the curves. She knew the consequences of speeding— logged in the back of her mind like bloody Polaroids—but she didn't care. Had she missed something in him when they'd dated? Andrew had checked all the boxes. He came from a good family, worked hard. She considered the documentary she'd watched about the wives of serial killers, how they each claimed they saw no signs the man they shared their beds, their bodies, their children with, were monsters. Had she married a philandering narcissist? It wasn't possible.

Amy couldn't lie to herself; her heart yearned for the man she'd fallen in love with, longed for the vulnerability he showed when he drifted off with his head nuzzled to her body. But this was her life, and maybe her one chance to get what she wanted, and she couldn't let him ruin it. At her age, she was out of options. Amy had jerked her car back into her assigned space and trotted back to the sterile halls of Boca General, a scummy film tainting her view of her marriage, of the entire life she led.

Now, in the kitchen, with her reactions in check, Amy cocked her head and examined him when she asked, "What do you do at night while I'm at work?"

Andrew's movements were slow, and he stepped forward, resting his forearms on the island. He collected the cap, examined it between his fingers. "Sometimes I spend time with Nick. You know, grab some chicken wings at Bru's Room. Watch a Heat game."

He tossed the cap back onto the marble, and it landed with a click. Amy's eyes followed his movement, and his finger found the cap again, flipping it over with his finger. *Click click.*

Silence hummed between them, and Andrew's eyes lifted, as if he expected her to speak, but the only sound was the click of plastic against the marble. *Click click. Click click.*

Amy was aware there were things she didn't know about her husband when she'd married him, but she'd never imagined him to be a liar. And a terrible one at that. Chicken wings. Bullshit.

It was time to form a new plan, one to expose what Andrew was hiding. In the meantime she'd let him dig himself deeper into his own mess while she waited for the right moment.

CHAPTER TWENTY-TWO

Wednesday, May 24
Kathryn

The soft rap on Kathryn's office door shattered her daydream. Addie, her intern, peeked into the room. "Kathryn? You have a visitor."

Heat blazed Kathryn's cheeks. She'd been lost to time as a decidedly *not* work-appropriate daydream played in her mind while she stared at the waving palm fronds out her office window. Her eyes flicked to her laptop screen, the cursor flashing in silent beats beneath a half-written email. Had Andrew come to see her? Her heartbeat skipped. Maybe her thoughts had summoned him. Kathryn wasn't the only one blushing; Addie's cheeks were rosy when Nick nodded and he strode into the room, a coffee in each hand. Kathryn swallowed her disappointment.

"Iced vanilla latte?" Nick lifted a Deja Brew cup, condensation running down the plastic. The drink looked creamy and delicious, and in his uniform, Nick looked good, too.

In a few strides Nick was in front of her, and he set the coffee on her desk. "Thank you," she mumbled, and he leaned forward to take her face in his calloused hand.

When he pressed his lips to hers, Kathryn jerked her head to the side, and Nick's reaction was instant. He recoiled, his square jaw tense. "What is it?"

"Nothing." She drew back. "It's just . . . you could've called before you dropped by. I have a lot going on."

Nick stood straight, and his eyes panned the room, at the mahogany molding, the gold desk set her colleagues had gifted her when she'd made partner. "Yeah. You look swamped."

Kathryn snapped her laptop shut and placed her elbows on her desk. "Did you come here for a reason?"

Nick strode to the other side and seated himself. "You haven't been by lately. I wanted to check on you."

"I'm an adult, Nick. I don't need anyone to check on me. I've been busy."

Nick hitched a brow. "Yeah, I hear you have."

Kathryn's face warmed, and she crossed her arms.

"Drew tells me things, you know."

"I don't have to explain anything to you. Or to anyone." Nick's eyes were hard, but Kathryn found she didn't care. Since that Friday in late March when she'd spun around in Starbucks and Andrew had rocketed back into her life, along with the portrait they'd once painted for each other, her life had spun on its axis.

Over their dinners, she was finally able to share stories about Max, even if they were just snippets of their better times, and Andrew absorbed every word.

After Andrew had announced he wasn't going to share the news of Max with his wife at their first dinner, she became a persona non grata at their meetings, which suited Kathryn. There was something there, emanating from him; something she recognized. The sadness of solitude. An ache for a person who offered only slivers of their time. The very feeling that had first inched into Kathryn's relationship with Andrew all those years ago. And she wanted to soothe that ache for him.

Each time they met, Andrew greeted her with a kiss on the cheek, as he would with anyone else. And each time they parted, he pecked her cheek, but sometimes his lips lingered, brushing the corner of her mouth. Kathryn found herself craving this moment the entire evening. She inhaled, savoring his lingering scent on her dress. His cedar cologne shrouded her with a comfort she hadn't felt in decades, like coming home.

As their connection deepened, the more Max seemed to pull away. She couldn't introduce the two, not then. Maybe someday. But the idea of Andrew's presence in her future sparked a glow inside her. Men had gawked her entire life. But no one looked at her the way Andrew did as they'd sat across from one another those last few months. Something flickered between them, the embers of a flame that had never burned out entirely.

"Anyway." Nick drew her back to the present. "To answer your question, I did come here for a reason." He passed his coffee from one hand to the other. "Something's going on."

Andrew's face was the first to flash in her mind. Had he come to his senses? Or had his wife learned about her and Max and forbidden Andrew from seeing her again? Had he sent Nick to sever ties with her? "What is it?" Kathryn demanded.

Nick leaned forward, gripping his cup. "You know that light pole your kid knocked out when he wrecked his car?"

Kathryn nodded, her pulse ticking.

"Well, he's not the first, as you know. He just got lucky. Speeding on that stretch of road is for someone with a death wish."

Kathryn had driven past the sharp curve on Ocean Avenue more times than she could count. A spot on the grass was memorialized with three black-and-white signs, like morbid lollipops, displaying the names of the lives it had claimed. An invisible vise on her throat blocked her swallow.

"Well," Nick continued. "The city is reviewing the accidents at that location so they can update the placement of the light poles and signage . . . you get the idea. When they got to my report, discrepancies were noted."

A flush of panic burned Kathryn's chest. "Was Max's name listed on the report?"

Nick's mouth dropped open. "I could lose my job, Kathryn." The words landed flat between them. "I was already placed on leave due to an investigation of an incident last year. Now an inquiry has been ordered, and I will be questioned about the details of the accident. The meeting is next week." A beat. "Of course I had to name your kid in the report. And the ownership of the vehicle. But that's not going to be a problem, Kat. Without new developments, the worst he'll face is a ticket. But they're going to ask me questions. Like why I let him walk when the accident was clearly his fault."

A knot braided itself inside Kathryn's stomach. "Nick . . . I think we should . . . cool it for a while."

"We've been . . . cooling it," he sneered.

"For good, then."

Nick's body stiffened, and the side of his mouth twitched. For a moment he didn't speak, just drew a breath, then released it, controlled. "You're unbelievable."

"It doesn't look good. I'm his *mother*; if someone found out about us, it would paint you in a bad light—"

"Like I lied on a report to cover for your drunk kid just because we occasionally fuck?"

His words hit her like a slap. She hadn't heard him speak this way in decades, and part of her believed this side of him to be long buried. "Nick—"

"Save it, Kathryn," he spat. "What is this to you? Am I just a distraction—someone to drink with, someone to screw when you're bored, someone to bail out your kid when he's in a jam?"

"That's not it." Even as the denial spilled from her, she realized that was exactly what their relationship was. "I'm just asking for some time, some space. To figure out our own lives, to let all of this settle."

"To let what settle, exactly? My situation at work, or yours with Drew?"

Her memory dragged her back to the day she'd told Nick she was pregnant. She was twenty-two again, sitting on that dumpy couch in Andrew and Nick's living room, Nick begging she choose between the two of them. And what had changed in two decades? Time and space hadn't tipped the scales in Nick's favor, and he seemed to realize it. They were still tangled in a delicate web, and someone was going to get hurt.

"None of this is his fault, Nick."

"No, it's not." Nick's brows knitted, sweat beading his hairline despite the air-conditioning. "What do you expect is going to happen with him, Kat?" He leaned forward. "Andrew is married. He loves his wife."

"Really? They don't have a family and she's never home." She regretted the words as soon as they spilled from her; she'd allowed Nick's words to spark defensiveness in her, betraying Andrew's secrets.

"You don't know the whole story," Nick said. "You only know the side he shows you, but I've been there with him for the last two decades. I know him."

Kathryn's eyes broke away to the bright sky outside her window. "Andrew and me . . . our situation is different."

"I know it's different. It's always been different. You two have something *special*." Nick's lips twisted. "Something I can't touch. You'd think twenty years would have changed things, but it hasn't. You two, you're—you're like some sort of addiction to each other," he stammered. "But neither of you can seem to get your shit together and commit; you just leave me . . . bouncing between you whenever it's convenient."

Kathryn didn't reply.

Nick exhaled. "I have a question."

She didn't meet his eyes. "What?"

"If Drew had never moved here, would you have told him?"

"About Max?" Kathryn's gaze dipped to the rug beneath her feet. "Probably not. I had no reason to."

"Are you ever going to tell him the truth? About how unsatisfied you were with him back then. That you came to me to find your *satisfaction*. And because of all that, you thought the kid was mine?"

She met his hard eyes. "I was never dissatisfied. I was young and confused."

Nick rose, along with his voice. "And what's changed? You were indecisive back then and you're still indecisive. You had a choice, a safe, basic life with Andrew. You and me, we could've traveled the world. I would have given you anything you wanted, and you know that. But you couldn't choose, and you ran away, and now what do you have?"

"What do I have?" She waved her hand around her office. "I've worked my ass off to get here." She stabbed her fingertip onto her desk. "I have a healthy son, a beautiful home, and I'm not going to let you minimize it."

"Yes, Kat. You have a lot of *stuff*. But you don't have what you want. Drew is living the life you wish you had down on Ocean with another woman. Only you don't seem to realize he's not an option for you anymore." A wave of air-conditioning drifted in the room. "What's the best-case scenario for you, Kathryn? How do you imagine all of this will end?" Nick's unanswerable question buzzed around them. "Drew deserves to know. You can't just give him half-truths."

"I'll tell him when I'm ready. He needs to hear it from me. Not you. If not for my sake, then for his." If Andrew learned the truth—that he'd been betrayed by the two people he'd trusted with his heart—it would shatter him. She'd lose him for good this time.

And so would Nick.

Nick knew it. His glare dissipated. A surrender. He swept a hand down his face. He was beautiful, and her heart ached for him. She couldn't give him the partnership he craved. And from his expression, Nick knew it, too. The swell of remorse that rushed through her was so familiar she almost welcomed it, her punishment the only constant when it came to Nick and Andrew.

The decades she and Andrew had spent apart hadn't solved any of her problems, had instead provided the perfect environment for her secrets to bloom. She had to bury that secret, could never let it come to light. Their lives had grown complicated; there was far more at stake. But was it worth the risk, worth hurting the people they'd hurt, worth the lives they'd destroy if they chose to fight for the love between them?

Nick's face softened, the lines in his forehead melting away, and when he closed his mouth, a trace of a smirk appeared on his lips. Kathryn expected anger in his movements, the same vitriol she'd seen flash in his eyes. Instead, he spun and left with the grace of a ballerina, as if he'd never been there, as if he didn't want to leave any trace of himself in her life.

CHAPTER TWENTY-THREE

Then
Kathryn

The first sign of trouble came to 228 Ocean Avenue on a Saturday morning just after Max's fifth birthday. Thunder shook the walls in the middle of the night, and Max slipped into Kathryn's bed and pressed his face to her chest. When the rain glided out over the ocean and the world grew still, they drifted off, the residual fog keeping the morning sun at bay, the cottage cool and dark.

Later she made her way across the wet driveway and found Lucas sitting at the kitchen table. Harper bounced around the room, topping off their coffee mugs. These were the mornings Kathryn cherished, when she could leave her responsibilities outside the door and bask in the companionship of their patchwork family.

Max and Emmy scurried from room to room until they burst into the kitchen, a tattered book dangling from Emmy's fingers.

Lucas pulled his daughter into his lap, where she squirmed out of his grip. "They're stir-crazy."

"Let's take them to the zoo." Harper grinned. "I don't remember the last time we all did something together."

"Zoo!" Emmy shrieked, her ringlets bouncing onto her cherubic face.

Kathryn looked at her son and ran her fingers through his hair. It seemed Max was growing before her eyes, and she wanted to press pause, to cling to every minute she had with him. "That sounds wonderful."

The zoo was mostly deserted, the air heavy with the earthy smell of wet dirt and the barnyard smell of animals. The three adults lagged while Max and Emmy ran along the pathways, laughing and pushing each other into puddles.

At the otter exhibit, the creature dipped beneath the surface of the water to tease Max through the Plexiglas. A grinning Max pressed his hand, which had just begun to lose its toddler chubbiness, against the glass. When the otter swam away, climbing up a branch in its enclosure, Lucas lifted the boy so he could get a better look.

Max's eyes were wide with wonder. "Mama, look."

Kathryn regarded Lucas, holding her little boy, and her heart swelled. He'd always been nurturing with Max, guiding him, teaching him new things, though at a respectful distance. When Emmy had arrived and Lucas stepped into the role of a father, he became more hands-on with Max. Now five, Max craved male attention, and Lucas obliged. To Kathryn's relief, Max hadn't yet asked why Emmy had two parents while he had one, and why he didn't have someone to call *Daddy* like Emmy did.

Kathryn realized how fortunate she and her son were to have Lucas, and guilt tugged deep inside her when she pictured Andrew in his place, Max perched on his hip, sharing the same messy blond hair, the same inquisitive expression.

Did I do the right thing? Max was happy, yes. It occurred to her that she was living a semblance of the life she'd once fantasized about with Andrew: she had a brilliant child with Andrew's blue eyes, her career was finding its footing, and the beachfront home she lived in exceeded her wildest dreams.

But it didn't belong to her. This was Harper and Lucas's life. Kathryn's reality was a distorted version of the one she'd once imagined, like a dream where everything was upside down, familiar, but unrecognizable. And it was penance for what she'd done to Andrew.

At the end of the day, the five of them slid into a booth at an Italian restaurant, and the kids nodded off, Max first, head slumped against the wall beside them. Emmy followed shortly thereafter, nodding off in Lucas's arms, her sweaty hair stuck to her forehead.

Kathryn draped a sweatshirt over Max and devoured her lasagna. When she looked at Lucas, he squinted, brows narrowed in what looked like anguish.

Harper's fork dropped. "Is it happening again?"

Lucas gave a weak nod.

Harper was shrill. "This is the third time this week."

Lucas kept his eyes screwed shut and didn't respond.

"I'm taking you to the emergency room," Harper said.

Kathryn had never heard Harper speak so assertively.

"No, I'm fine," Lucas argued, his voice weak, and pressed his fingers to his forehead. "I just want to go home, get some sleep."

Harper drove home, Lucas slumped in the passenger seat, Kathryn tucked between the sleeping kids in the back, fingers of apprehension twisting her thoughts. Quick, suspicious memories flashed in her head; things that had meant nothing at the time suddenly bubbled into a dark, swirling paranoia.

Lucas had been less patient, sometimes snapping at the kids for being noisy. Kathryn often saw the light on in the kitchen long past the time Lucas normally went to bed. When Kathryn came to the beach house to drop Max off before her evening classes, she'd noticed Lucas's eyes were shadowy, the lines around them more defined.

What else had slipped by her unnoticed? Her stomach twisted.

That night Kathryn thought she could hear arguing through her open window. She tossed until well after midnight, then rose to get a glass of water. Across the driveway, the kitchen light glowed. Kathryn rapped on the door. Lucas opened it without a word but stood at the top step.

"Are you okay, Luke?"

He nodded, his response as weak and unconvincing as it had been at dinner.

"Let me make you some tea," she offered, stepping into the kitchen.

Lucas sat and, in reversed roles, Kathryn set about filling the kettle. "How long have you been feeling this way?"

"I've had migraines come and go for the last few years."

Kathryn tried to let this explanation soothe her, but concern still tugged at her. "Have they gotten more intense lately, more frequent?"

Lucas didn't answer.

Kathryn sat across from him. "Harper's right. You should see a doctor."

Lucas's eyes were sunken, and Kathryn wondered when he'd last slept through the night. He gave a resigned nod, then settled against the wall.

This man had changed her life permanently. Allowing her to live on their property had saved her when she'd needed it. It gave her a place to hide, to heal, a family when she'd needed one. He'd been a confidant, a partner in insomnia, and, for a period, a partner in parenting. She scrambled to find the words to sum up how much she loved him. Instead, Kathryn reached out, setting her hand on top of his. Lucas rolled his hand, and Kathryn gripped it. She held his warm, golden eyes with hers, and squeezed his palm. She clung to him, love coursing through her fingers, a love she had no words for.

"Luke?" Harper's voice cut the space, and Kathryn looked up to see Harper, half of her face illuminated by the light of the kitchen, the other half obscured in the shadows of the house. Harper's gaze fell to their hands. "What are you doing?" she demanded.

Kathryn recoiled, yanking her hand from the table.

"Having some tea," Lucas said.

Kathryn shoved her chair back and rose. "I was just going home." She tossed her steaming tea into the sink, then dashed out the door and down the steps. The familiar, grimy feeling at Harper's accusatory glare followed her across the driveway, the same one she'd felt in that electric-pink bikini all those years ago, after she'd slept with Nick, and at Andrew's mother's pointed words.

◆ ◆ ◆

The following morning there was a harried rap on the cottage door. Kathryn opened it to the brilliant sunlight and to Harper clutching Emmy's hand. Emmy was still dressed in a nightshirt, her hair messy, as if Harper had snatched her from bed.

Relief washed over her, and Kathryn squinted. "Hi, Harp."

"It's Lucas—his migraine is worse."

Kathryn shielded her eyes, caught Harper's expression; the fear from the previous day now encompassed Harper's entire being. The back door swung open, and Lucas ambled down the steps. He didn't move like the Lucas she knew, as if he didn't trust his own movements. Dread coursed through her; he was pale, his face gray and hollow.

"I'm taking him to the ER." Harper nudged Emmy into the cottage.

Kathryn lifted the little girl and watched the couple climb into their car and drive away.

She cooked breakfast for the kids, then walked them down to the shoreline. At the edge of the breaking waves, Kathryn lowered herself into the sand while Max and Emmy splashed and shrieked around a cluster of seaweed. Lucas's house towered behind her, solid, but their existence there was fragile.

When the kids were worn, she plopped them in front of cartoons and paced the beach house, stomach roiling. By dinnertime, there was still no sign of Lucas and Harper. Kathryn made pasta for the kids, then watched the sun set through the kitchen window while she washed dishes in warm, soapy water.

There was so little she could hold on to in this life; everything seemed to have a way of slipping through her fingers.

She took Max and Emmy back to the cottage and ran them a bath. Kathryn tucked the kids, clean and in their pajamas, into her bed and read them picture books, one story after another, relishing the smell of their strawberry shampoo on their damp hair. "Read another one." Max's sweet, sleepy voice came from beside her. Emmy had drifted off, her small body curled next to Kathryn.

Everything is fine. No news is good news. But the sinking feeling in her belly remained.

When Max drifted off, Kathryn reached for a novel from her nightstand, which she read until drowsiness overtook her. She was awakened by the sound of tires crunching on the gravel. She glanced at the clock: 11:35.

Terror gripped her. Why were they home so late? She heard voices, two of them, unmistakable, but Lucas's tone had an edge to it, harsh and angry. Harper's voice was naturally soft, but now her words were pointed. Kathryn couldn't hear what they were arguing about, but it lasted only a few seconds before the car door closed and footsteps approached the cottage. Kathryn leaped from her bed.

Harper pulled the front door without knocking, and their eyes met. Worry overrode any shame Kathryn held from the incident in the kitchen the night before, and her words came out in a breathless rush. "Is everything all right?"

For a second Harper didn't say anything. Her red eyes were puffy, her expression wide, like she didn't know where to look. "Everything's fine." She moved across the space and scooped Emmy into her arms, buried her face in her daughter's hair, and drew her in. Finally, she looked at Kathryn, and her voice trembled. "Thanks for watching her." Harper stood in the doorway with her back to Kathryn for a moment before she turned around and said, "It was a bad idea to have you come live with us. I should have known after what you did with your boyfriend's roommate."

Harper's blade-sharp words gouged Kathryn. "It's not like that, Harper."

But Harper turned, her hair swaying behind her back. She hitched Emmy on her hip, and Kathryn watched the two disappear into the house.

CHAPTER TWENTY-FOUR

Then
Andrew

It began on a February afternoon in Andrew's final college semester. He'd returned from class to a particular stillness in the apartment. Maybe Kathryn and Nick were both out. Maybe one or both were reading or napping. There was nothing to alert him anything had changed, and he let his bag slide down his arm to the floor. He spotted the brass key where it rested on the woodgrain of the table, and collected it, puzzled. Kathryn had streaked red nail polish across the metal so she'd know which one opened the apartment door. Now it was orphaned from her cluttered key ring.

Nothing in the kitchen was different, and the living room was in its usual state, so it took Andrew a second to feel the weight of the key in his hand. Then it registered in his mind, jarring, like an alarm.

In his closet, beside Andrew's selection of T-shirts, the rail was lined with bare hangers, though the space smelled like Kathryn. He yanked his dresser drawers open to find they were vacant. His stomach dropped, and he darted to the bathroom, where the vanity was nearly empty, home to just his toothbrush and a curled tube of toothpaste, squeezed from the top no matter how many times Kathryn had scolded him for it. He threw the shower door aside, and his fears were compounded by the soap-scum rings left behind by a half dozen bottles he'd never understood. Andrew sank to the floor, something tearing inside him, like the time he'd ripped apart a baseball, the tough material resistant, strings snapping, never to be whole again.

At twenty-one, Andrew had little experience with which to compare his first heartbreak. He'd walked the line; his grades had set him in his teachers' good graces. Everything he did made his parents beam. For as long as he could remember, he'd dutifully followed the path laid out for him, believing it would be the key to everything he'd wanted for his future, which, over his last year with Kathryn, had been a vivid picture. He convinced himself he'd overridden the faulty wiring, his drunk father's only legacy.

"Did she say anything to you?" Andrew demanded of Nick in the kitchen when he came home that evening. "Did she say where she was going?"

"She said she had to go home for a few days." Nick dodged his gaze.

"Then why is all of her shit gone?"

"I don't know, Drew." Nick pulled a Hot Pocket from the microwave.

"Her phone is disconnected or something. Let me try with yours."

There was a flicker in Nick's face. A pause. "No. She obviously wants to be left alone." He ducked into his bedroom, shutting the door.

That night Andrew unscrewed a half-empty bottle of rum and tossed back three shots. Warmth crept through his body; then the anesthetic sensation set in, leaving a detached, comfortable numbness. He dialed Kathryn's parents' house repeatedly, heavy apprehension in her mother's voice when she told him Kathryn wasn't home. He downed the remainder of the rum. The acute agony of his heartbreak was still present, just at a manageable distance.

The next morning Andrew woke to the cold tile and harsh reality of his bathroom floor. He'd vomited during the night. His head throbbed, and his body ached worse than it had when he'd had the flu. The shattered picture of his life came into focus.

He drove to the liquor store.

The days passed in a blur. Sometimes Kathryn's avoidance felt cruel and calculating, other times entirely his fault. He called her best friend, Harper, to no avail. If Harper knew where Kathryn was—which Andrew suspected she did—her well-mannered, evasive voice told him she'd never betray her friend.

The school year culminated while Andrew teetered on the edge of functionality. Every night he drank until he blacked out, and he dialed Kathryn's parents' house until her mother took the phone off the hook, but as the semester wound down, his squeaky-clean reputation meant none of his professors noticed his tardiness, or the decline in the quality of his papers. He told himself he was hardly the first student to come to class hungover the last few weeks before graduation. He was skidding fast, and when the semester culminated, free from the restraints of any responsibility, Andrew let himself slip beneath the surface of the raging sea, preferring to watch the storm from below, where everything around him fell silent. There was something poetic about it, he thought in a haze. He'd finally found a single thing in common with his real father.

As the year wore on, his tolerance for alcohol soared, and Andrew discovered liquor was more effective on an empty stomach. His breakfast consisted of eggs and dry toast, but the rest of the day, in lieu of a meal, he tossed back a few shots. When he was hungry or felt the taunting stab of heartbreak, he did another shot. By the end of the summer, his ribs jutted from his sides, and his clothes hung on his frame.

"You look like shit, dude," Nick mumbled one night as they crossed paths in the hallway.

Andrew balled his fist. He itched to smash Nick's face into the wall, but Nick disappeared into his room. Instead, Andrew stepped on the bathroom scale. At the beginning of the school year, he'd weighed 190 pounds. Now, between his bony toes, the number read 162.

Andrew avoided visiting his family until their requests grew insistent, and he gave in on Thanksgiving, carefully rolling shooters into the T-shirts in his bag. When his mother, Lily, fretted about his weight, he explained he'd recently battled the flu, and she said she'd *fatten him up* and went back to her chardonnay. By the time they sat down to dinner, everyone was tipsy, and nobody noticed Andrew's trips to the bathroom to drain the liquid from a tiny plastic bottle. Andrew watched his mother, seated beside Craig. They were a pair. Well matched. Dull. There was no flame that roared between them like there had been for him and Kathryn.

Every evening before Nick returned home from his training at the police academy, Andrew hauled the trash, clanking with glass bottles, to the recycle bin.

The scale read 143.

It was like driving down a twisting road with his eyes closed and his hands off the wheel. It was only a matter of time until he crashed and everything went dark. A fantasy he welcomed.

He was nothing. Would never amount to anything. Just a privileged boy from a chilly family. If he vanished from the world, it would be the best thing for everyone. Andrew's parents would mourn their idea of him, but they didn't know him, and they had another son. Craig's real son. They'd move on. Nick might be sad, especially if he was the one to find him, but having a dead best friend might be the kind of tragic backstory girls would swoon over. When Kathryn heard . . . Andrew doubted she'd give it a second thought. But he was too chickenshit to do the deed himself. Instead, he punished his body, starved it, drowned it with poison. It was only a matter of time until one of his organs failed, and each time he drifted off in a haze, he hoped, when everything faded to black, it would be the last time.

One evening Nick came home late. The shades were drawn, the room bathed in the pallid light of the TV. Andrew had been drinking since late morning, since his eyes had fallen on the date on his phone.

It had been one year since Kathryn left. She'd been gone longer than they'd been together. It was absurd, Andrew told himself. Their relationship had been a summer romance, and though it had blazed white-hot through the fall and winter, it had ended, as relationships do. He got blackout drunk by noon.

The jab of Nick's finger woke him. "Get up."

"Get the fuck out of here." Andrew moaned.

"No," Nick snapped. "Get up." Something was different in Nick's tone, and Andrew jerked upright. They locked eyes. "Enough of this shit," Nick spat. "You need to forget about Kat. She's not coming back. She's obviously happier wherever she is than with you—"

Andrew lunged, a move so unexpected neither of them saw it coming, and his fist met Nick's face with a sickening crunch. Nick stumbled, his hand searching his cheek, where a red wound, like a smashed piece of fruit, oozed with blood, and for a second the two men froze. Then something blazed in Nick's eyes, a sharp narrowing Andrew didn't recognize. In a flash of motion, Nick's head slammed into Andrew's torso, sending the two of them to the ground, and beneath the haze of drunkenness, for a moment Andrew was convinced he was dying, unable to draw a breath. His back was pinned to the hard floor and the room whirled. Nick lifted his fist, rage still flashing in his eyes as blood dripped down his face. The image of Nick hovering over him, heaving ragged breaths, would be frozen into Andrew's memory for the rest of his life. A side of his friend he'd never met.

"Get your shit together, Drew, or get the fuck out of my life," Nick panted.

They held each other's gaze for a second that melted into an eternity. The energy drained from the room as quickly as it had erupted, and Nick climbed off Andrew and rose to his feet. He stormed from the apartment, rattling the walls as he slammed the door. Andrew dragged himself onto the couch and stared at the ceiling until his hammering heartbeat slowed.

Long hours passed with the intermittent lucidity of a bad dream. Andrew drifted off, only to be jolted awake by a determined pounding at the door, dredging his consciousness to the surface. His sweaty body ached when he dragged himself from the couch to open the door. The intense morning light seared his eyes, and it took him a moment to focus on the two figures at his doorstep. When Lily and Craig entered his apartment, they crossed the line between their polished, controlled life and the reality their son was living.

A weight, pregnant with disappointment, drowned the room as his parents packed his belongings and cleaned the apartment. The clanking sound of empty bottles and cans collected into a trash bin roiled Andrew's stomach more than his hangover. He was buckled into the back seat of their car like a child, every available inch of space taken by the trash bags used to hastily transport his things.

Back home, Andrew's parents arranged a counselor for him. He attended meetings. Was matched with a sponsor. His parents monitored his every move, painstakingly concealing his secrets along with their shame. It seemed his hometown was teeming with high school classmates and his parents' friends, so Andrew shut himself in the house. When his brother called, he passed the phone to Lily; the last thing he needed was for Timmy to remind him he'd turned out to be the good one, that Andrew had surprised no one by becoming the fuckup of the family.

Andrew had always been social and wasn't prepared for isolation to become his sole companion, but when he itched to call Nick, biting resentment chased away the thought. Nick was a traitor who got him trapped in his parents' house like a prisoner.

Andrew's first panic attack ambushed him on Lily's fiftieth birthday. It was an uneventful dinner at a white-tablecloth steakhouse, a twinge of anxiety behind his parents' smiles as they chatted with their sons. Andrew's mouth was dry, and he sucked down three iced teas. While Craig retrieved the car from the valet, Andrew dipped into the men's room, then accepted a mint from the hostess and stepped out the door. He scanned the lot for Craig's car. Or Craig. Or Lily. Or Timmy. But none of the faces in his line of sight were familiar. It was fast, merciless, his breath locked in his chest, his heart drumming in his rib cage, a strange, tearing sensation gripping his diaphragm. Andrew dropped to his knees, certain he was going to die right there on the worn red carpet in front of horrified patrons.

Panic attacks. Triggered by a sense of abandonment, a psychiatrist dryly declared the following afternoon, and sent Andrew on his way with two scripts to curb the worst of the symptoms.

Two weeks later, Andrew rose early. He'd scoured the internet for remedies for his panic attacks. A crowded gym was out of the question, so Andrew laced his sneakers and broke into a sprint on the deserted street. The first week, his body ached in protest, and he pushed on until he was panting for breath. But each day, it got easier.

Andrew ran each morning at dawn when it was unlikely he'd bump into anyone he knew, offering fellow runners only a polite nod. He loathed the idea of being lumped in with the kinds of people who trained for marathons: the pushy types who tried to make him feel like whatever he was doing wasn't good enough. Andrew had encountered these people when he'd joined the gym in college; they'd wanted to know what his fitness goals were and were fiercely insecure and competitive, their brows furrowed in frustration when he'd explained he didn't have any goals.

What are my goals? he thought as the pavement passed beneath his feet. *To never pick up a drink again. To never again see the disappointment in my parents' eyes when they realized the child they'd loved and supported and given absolutely everything to is an alcoholic.*

He was just running. Unless he was sick or stayed up too late the night before, Andrew ran every morning. This new addiction overtook him, a healthy one this time. He found his thoughts of Kathryn softened around the edges, to the point where he could examine them, and he could remember the love he'd given—a lifetime's worth—without feeling like it had been wasted.

One year after Andrew's parents had intervened and, Andrew had to admit, saved his life, Craig arranged a job interview with a business acquaintance in West Palm Beach. Though the offer Andrew received felt sticky with nepotism, it also offered atonement to Lily and Craig, and he accepted. A glimmer of hope for his future. He made the drive from South Carolina down to Florida, and moved into an apartment downtown, where he basked in his freedom for the first few weeks, running the streets at dawn each day. But as the weeks wore on, Andrew realized that as a sober man in his midtwenties, his social life had vanished. When his coworkers jaunted off to happy hours, Andrew found himself alone in his apartment, a depressing box of macaroni for dinner.

A seed formed; he needed to feed himself and was tired of pasta and frozen pizza. Andrew scoured culinary websites and each evening taught himself a new recipe, taking on more-complicated techniques. His weekends were filled with excursions to gourmet grocery stores, and he savored his creations on his balcony, watching the sunset fall behind the skyline.

Having no one in his life morphed his perspective when it came to Nick. Maybe his having reached out to Andrew's parents wasn't an act of betrayal, but a last resort, to save Andrew's life. Nick had been a victim in the fallout of Andrew's relationship with Kathryn, he realized. He called Nick and invited him to spend the weekend in West Palm. When he arrived, their conversation was cautious, but in Nick's voice, Andrew could hear relief, knowing their friendship hadn't been destroyed. The two men stayed up talking late, their conversation finding the connection they'd once had. Nick was navigating a breakup, he said; he was searching for a job. Andrew suggested he apply nearby. Maybe they could be roommates again. A fresh start.

Nick agreed, seemingly sensing Andrew's isolation. When he moved in, Nick made the perfect guinea pig for Andrew's culinary experiments, offering an honest opinion and, sometimes, a helping hand.

I'm here, Nick's presence said without words. *This will get better.* Andrew was indebted to Nick for saving him, for guiding him through loneliness. Nick julienned carrots while Andrew whisked a roux beside him. And, in a silent pact, it seemed they agreed to avoid the subject of Kathryn Moretti forever.

◆ ◆ ◆

Saturday, March 27

Andrew knew what a hangover looked like. At their Saturday lunch, Nick was in the grips of the head-pounding kind, the kind that left him answering questions with grunts between sips of coffee. But greasy Cuban sandwiches and caffeine seemed to satiate his friend, and Nick donned his sunglasses as the two walked to his rumbling Mustang, to-go cups in hand.

"Where's your cruiser?" Andrew asked.

Another grunt from Nick. "In the shop." Liquor seeped from Nick's breath and body, twisted Andrew's stomach, the smell dredging up vivid snippets of vomit splashing a toilet basin. A ragged shudder passed through him.

They rolled with the traffic through downtown Delray. Storms were slated to swoop in that afternoon, and though the day was still bright, the wind made the treetops dance, and a rushed energy emanated from the lunch crowd. There wasn't an empty table in sight. At the railroad crossing, Nick glided to a stop, and the wooden arm dropped a few inches beyond the hood of the car.

"What are you doing later?" Andrew asked. His excitement tickled at the thought of another evening with Kathryn. Apparently Max was out for the evening, and she'd invited Andrew to collect her. Each day they weaved their lives closer together.

"I gotta shower. Have a nap. I have plans tonight."

"Plans?"

Nick's brows narrowed above his sunglasses. "Plans." He didn't elaborate. "Your kid has a new girlfriend, you know."

"Max?"

Nick nodded. He was strange, the way he kept some information close when he was loose with other details. But this news was a surprise to Andrew. "Kathryn's never mentioned a girlfriend."

Nick paused, then gave a dismissive shrug. "She's staying with Kat. They're all over each other in his car. They're especially fond of the public beach lot."

Andrew's thoughts spun to sort this new information, and a flash broke into his mind of the girl's perplexed eyes in his car that rainy evening. The girl who lived with Kathryn and Max. Andrew was certain Kathryn didn't know what was going on between the two, and a tickle of amusement rose when he realized he knew something about his son that she didn't. "Huh."

Another shrug from Nick. "I know you see her. A lot."

It took Andrew a moment to realize Nick meant Kathryn. Warning bells chimed, and minutes slipped past as the train rolled by, rattling the car. Andrew looked at his best friend, at his shadowy expression. After actively avoiding the topic of Kathryn for nearly two decades, the moment she'd appeared in their lives again, rumbles of a storm had crept back in between them. He shoved it down deep. If he and Kathryn grew closer, he'd reach a tipping point where no one could come between them again.

The train rattled off, and the gate rose. Nick broke free of the downtown traffic and sailed over the bridge, the car vibrating as they drove across the grates, invisible at their speed, like they were flying over the waterway. Andrew's phone vibrated against his thigh. A spark of excitement. Andrew swore he saw Nick's face shift at the sound. No, he was being paranoid.

On Ocean Avenue, Nick made a sharp turn into Andrew's driveway. "Well, have a good night," Andrew said as he swung open his door. Outside, the air was heavy, salty. Unsettled.

"Yeah." Nick nodded. "You too."

Andrew shut the door. Slate-gray clouds peeked over the treetops, palm branches whipping in a violent gust. He darted up the steps to his house, rushed to duck for cover before the storm rolled in.

CHAPTER TWENTY-FIVE

Saturday, May 27
Kathryn

A violent storm rattled the windowpanes that afternoon, and outside her bedroom window, the world had fallen into midnight darkness. But just as it had come, the front rolled out toward the ocean, leaving a salt-tinged humidity in the air as Kathryn wrangled her hair in the bathroom mirror.

She checked the time: 5:55. As good a time as any to enjoy a glass of wine before her evening with Andrew. Setting her phone on her nightstand, she padded down the hallway, but from the top of the staircase, Andrew's face appeared in her line of sight, and her heartbeat sputtered. The wrongness of it, of him, standing in her living room, hands tucked deep in his pockets. Her fingers were an inch from the banister, her steps frozen by a bolt of panic. It was invasive, like he was an intruder. "Andrew, what are you doing here?"

He flinched. "You—your message said to come in." Confusion crumpled his face.

Fear spiked. Where was Max? Relief washed over Kathryn when she recalled seeing him speed away from the house earlier that afternoon, but she had no idea where her son had gone or when he'd return. She needed to get Andrew out of her house.

Andrew withdrew his phone, held it up. "You said to come inside," he echoed.

Kathryn bounded down the staircase. He smelled freshly showered, with a dab of cologne somewhere. The smell she adored. But now it was a warning sign, blaring. They'd exchanged a few unremarkable messages, and she'd anticipated their regular Saturday-evening dinner, but he was an hour early, and she was certain nothing she'd said had invited him into her house. In front of Andrew's slack stare, Kathryn's heartbeat hammered. Andrew's fingers sped to tap his passcode, and they leaned over his screen.

Kathryn: Dinner?

Andrew: You name the place.

Kathryn: Pick me up. 6? Just come in when you get here.

Andrew: You sure??

Kathryn: Yes. He's not home. It's fine.

She hadn't sent any of those messages. Her eyes broke away and met Andrew's. Silence crackled.

As if on cue, the front door swung ajar, startling both of them. Max stepped inside, shutting the door behind him.

Andrew's gaze fell onto his son before he took one step back, his eyes circles of apprehension. He'd certainly imagined meeting his son, but not in this way. Kathryn watched the muscles in his neck clench as he scanned Max head to toe and swallowed.

Kathryn's eyes flashed to her son, taking in the two men in front of her with the same sense of helplessness as watching two cars collide. Max appraised Andrew. Pain shadowed his expression, and his eyes broke away.

A hot, stabbing throb deep within Kathryn; it was the sum of all her fears combined. Everything she'd worked so hard to prevent for twenty years now torn from her control. Panic blazed, the stabbing sensation now twisting, jagged.

"Max." Kathryn stepped toward her son before his stony expression stopped her feet on the rug. Heat enflamed her face and chest. "Max, this is Andrew. Andrew . . . this is Max."

The two locked eyes again. Max swallowed, then Andrew, their movements mirrored in one another. A staticky beat, then Andrew jerked forward. "I—it's nice to meet you." His voice barely audible.

An eternity stretched while the three of them stood, frozen. A violent whack from inside the ice maker made them all jump.

"I think the three of us should sit down and talk." Kathryn's voice was just above a whisper.

Max strode beneath the archway that separated the living room from the kitchen and dragged a chair from the table before dropping into it. Kathryn seated herself across from her son, and Andrew followed. "Max, I know what you must be thinking," Kathryn started.

"I promise, you have no idea what I'm thinking." Max's voice quavered.

Kathryn withdrew into her seat, like she'd been smacked by her son's words. "Max—"

"Kathryn." Andrew set his hand on top of hers. "Let me try to explain."

"No, this is my—" Kathryn pleaded.

"Just let me try—"

Max's eyes fell on Andrew's hand and, as if Max's gaze had burned him, Andrew retracted it, tucked it beneath the table.

Max stood and yanked the fridge door. He withdrew a beer bottle and let the door slam behind him. The clink of metal jingled as Max riffled through the silverware drawer; then came the hiss of the cap, which he let fall into the sink. Max turned back to the table and took a long drag from the bottle before he set it down and sat, rod straight, his fingers laced before him on the woodgrain, like a student about to begin their lesson. "I don't care which one of you decides to talk, but I feel like I'm owed an explanation," he said, the effort to keep his voice steady evident in his tone.

Max's face was stony, but his eyes were pleading, and Kathryn's heart cracked under the weight of her guilt. It didn't have to come to this. None of her best- and worst-case scenarios had produced this result. They should have been a team, a family. Instead, in her son's cold expression, and Andrew's desperate one, she saw only the culmination of her mistakes. And, as she'd feared, Max was paying the price. The decades' worth of worry and energy she'd spent trying to shield him from the consequences of her decisions lay wasted. She'd waited too long to give her son the truth. And why? Because of her deep-seated shame? Because she cherished her indulgent evenings with this version of Andrew? Because she relished their secret life. It was selfish. These failures were hers and hers alone.

Max, Andrew, right in front of her, it was all too much, and Kathryn bowed her head and pressed her fingertips to her temples. "Of course you are, sweetheart—" The chime of the doorbell. Kathryn looked to Max, then Andrew.

Kathryn rose, her legs trembling as they carried her across the floor, the electric snap of danger rising in the space. She turned the knob and light spilled into the room. Nick stood silhouetted in the brightness beyond the doorway.

Max's voice came from over her shoulder. "Hoo-boy. Here it goes."

A fresh bolt of panic. "Nick," Kathryn snapped. "This isn't a good time—"

"I got your text—" Nick said.

"Nick?" Andrew's voice prickled the nape of her neck. Kathryn turned to see him rise from the table. "What are you doing here?"

Nick leaned into the room. "Drew?"

Kathryn's head snapped back to the kitchen.

"Wait—you two know each other?" Max asked.

Andrew's face paled. A twisted giggle rose from Max's throat. "Oh wow, this is even better than I thought."

Kathryn turned back to Nick, who folded his arms and said, "You told me to come get you at six."

241

The puzzle pieces snapped into place: the texts. Andrew. Max. The precise timing of Nick's appearance. Kathryn spun; Max's mouth twisted into a smirk. "Really, Max?"

Max leaned back in his chair, arms crossed over his body, the beer bottle clutched in his hand. "Maybe you accidentally sent a text to the wrong boyfriend, *Kat*."

Time beat in silence. Their collective gaze shifted to Max, and Nick brushed past Kathryn, who took a step back, her hand still gripping the door. Nick stepped closer and jabbed a finger at Max. "You. You did this."

The strange smile pulled at Max's mouth. "It's been a while since I've seen you around. I thought maybe my mom had dumped you."

Crimson flushed Nick's face.

"What's he talking about, Nick?" Andrew demanded.

"Max." Kathryn shut the door. "That's enough; this isn't a game." She marched back to the table while Max's laughter pitched, filling the room, which buzzed like a live wire.

Andrew leaned across the table. "Cut it out."

Silence enveloped the space.

"I don't need this bullshit," Nick spat. "You can fuck off, all of you."

"Jesus, Max," Kathryn cried, panic rising. How had Max gotten her phone? Andrew and Nick glowered at each other, and her stomach twisted. "Was all this necessary? If you had questions, you could've asked me."

Max's smile evaporated as his eyes narrowed onto Kathryn's. He slammed the beer bottle on the table. "Ask? It's not my job to ask!"

Kathryn sucked in a breath. "Max—"

"You let me go my whole life wondering about—about this other *half* of me, and you've never said a word. You let me wonder if he was dead." He waved a hand at Andrew. "If he was in prison, if he had a real family and wanted nothing to do with us, with me—"

Kathryn's eyes broke away.

"And then one day this dude who looks *just* like me shows up in our driveway, and not only do you not say a word—you go running off with him a few nights a week. Like I won't notice. Like I'm stupid. For months. Who does that? What the actual *fuck*?"

Kathryn gaped. When Max spelled it out, her actions weren't just selfish; they seemed downright sinister.

"I told you this would happen." Nick crossed his arms. "I told you I didn't want to be involved."

"Shut up, Nick," Andrew barked, shoulders squared, and panicky heat rose to the top of Kathryn's head.

Max leaned in, facing his mother. "So here's your chance. Keep up your lies. Tell me he's not who I think he is."

"He is, Max." Kathryn's vision swam with tears. "Andrew is your father."

Max nodded, and his gaze fell to the table between them. His lips moved, as if he were about to speak, then stopped. He pushed back and bounded up the staircase. The slam of his bedroom door ricocheted through the house.

Kathryn scaled the stairs two at a time and rapped on Max's door. "Max, open up, please," she begged. "Talk to me."

She wasn't aware of Andrew's presence behind her until he spoke. "Let me try?"

Kathryn rounded on him. Andrew was close, too close, backing her into the space between his body and Max's bedroom door. "No, you need to get out of here. Now."

"You can't keep him away from me forever, Kathryn—"

The gravity of the last few minutes fanned a fire within her that erupted into an inferno. The bruised feelings of Nick and Andrew were her fault—always, it seemed—but the heartbreak in Max's expression eclipsed all the mistakes she'd made in her life. Now they were all tangled in the web she'd spun, and she had to get Max out of it. "Yes, I can," she cried. "I can and I will if I have to. This"—she waved at Max's bedroom door—"is exactly what I was trying to avoid."

Emmy's bedroom door flew open, and the girl crossed the hall, her eyes round. She brushed past Kathryn and Andrew and knocked on Max's door. "Max, it's me. Open up. Please."

A pulse of silence. Kathryn's mind whirled, wondering what Max had seen when he'd had her phone. It was all there, in black and white. Not only would her texts have confirmed Max's suspicions about Andrew, but they would have revealed all the times she'd slipped into Nick's bed after a long day.

"Max," Emmy begged, and knocked again. Max yanked his door, and all three jumped.

"Sweetheart, listen—" Kathryn pleaded.

Max's face was crumpled, his eyes narrowed on Kathryn. "I don't want to talk to you. And I definitely don't want to talk to *him*." He jabbed a finger an inch from Andrew's face. Then Max reached for Emmy's wrist, she slipped inside, and the door closed again.

Kathryn faced Andrew. "You need to get out of here." Her words stabbed him, she could see in the way his brows pinched. She stomped down the staircase. "You too, Nick. Out."

When Nick came into her line of sight, his arms were still crossed, his stance wide.

"I'm going to ask you one more time. What the fuck are you doing here, Nick?" Andrew demanded over her head.

Fear crept up her spine. She was there, physically between the men, her secrets tearing through the thin film that had contained them all those years.

"I'm out." Nick held up his palms. "This is your mess, Kat. You can deal with your shitty kid and his little girlfriend that you let *live with you*, and all the fucked-up shit going on in your world. And you got yourself sucked into it, Drew, after I warned you not to."

Nick strode across the rug and threw the front door open, then slammed it behind him. A wave of muggy air rolled into the room, and Nick's absence filled the space, like a ghost. Andrew's chest heaved, but Kathryn's mind spun. Max. His girlfriend?

Nick knew everything that went on in town.

Moments snapped into place. Bits of conversations. Max's expression when he looked at Emmy from across the dinner table. The orchestrated six feet of space between them on the couch. The particular stillness of the house when she came home each evening. Kathryn rarely saw Max and Emmy interact. She'd been stupid, blind to it all. For months. Max wasn't being unfriendly to Emmy; he was hiding something. The same way she'd hidden Andrew. It all screamed at her, if only she'd been paying attention.

Andrew shook his head no. But Kathryn's feet were already moving, taking the steps two at a time to Max's bedroom door once more. "Max. Emmy. Get out here. Now."

A pulse of silence. Whispers from the other side of the door? Then Max yanked it open, his face stony.

"Come downstairs." Kathryn padded down the steps into the living room, this time lava flowing through her veins, hot and slow. Max descended the staircase, flanked by Emmy, her cheeks aflame. Kathryn motioned to the couch. "Sit," she ordered.

Kathryn hardly noticed Andrew, a statue on the living room rug.

Emmy perched on the edge of her cushion, while Max shot Andrew a glare before he slumped down. Kathryn stood before them, and for a moment all she could hear in the dense silence was the thud of her own heart. Max's and Emmy's eyes burned onto her as she drew a steadying breath. "Tell me what the game is: you two hide out in your rooms when I'm home? You don't address one another in my presence, but as soon as I leave . . ." Her words hung in the air. Mortification flowed. She'd allowed herself to be blinded by Andrew.

"You wanted us to get along." Max leaned back, folding his arms.

Kathryn looked to Emmy, where she knew she'd find the truth. "How long has this been going on?"

Emmy swallowed.

"What does it matter?" Max barked.

Kathryn drew a long breath and shifted to her son. "It matters, Maxwell, because she's an underage girl living in my house." She looked at Emmy. "How long?"

Emmy's voice was small. "It started a few days after I got here."

"Around the same time this sperm donor"—Max waved an arm at Andrew—"showed up in our driveway."

Another wave of mortification. Kathryn took an unsteady breath.

"Kathryn," Andrew interjected. "Maybe everyone should take a break—"

Kathryn silenced him with a palm. She exhaled through her nose, then reset. "I find it to be extremely . . . disrespectful"—she looked to Emmy—"that you two hide things from me while you're together in my house."

"Kathryn, I'm sorry," Emmy burst, her cheeks aflame.

Kathryn saw the girl's hand flutter. Emmy's instinct was to reach for Max, and Max's to reach back. He weaved his fingers between Emmy's, and they clung to each other.

"Babe." Max's tone dropped and from his side profile, Kathryn watched tenderness transform his face. "It's okay. We have nothing to be sorry for."

She'd imagined lust, the thrill of secrets. But in Max's and Emmy's actions, recognition swept over her: the two were besotted. The kind of love she knew too well, the kind that framed the perception of life going forward, the kind that resulted in crushing heartbreak. This was the thing that would shatter her son. A bolt of fear.

Max turned to his mother, fire blazing behind his eyes. "You're such a hypocrite." His lips curled. "You sneak around with this dude." The floor creaked when Andrew shifted. "I'm an adult, Emmy's of age; she can have sex with anyone she wants to."

Kathryn watched embarrassment flow over Emmy.

Max tightened his grip on Emmy's hand and turned to her. "Come on, baby." He jerked a thumb toward the staircase. "Let's get our stuff.

Let's go." Emmy sat, frozen. Max looked at Kathryn. "We're going to Washington. Together."

The floor spun beneath Kathryn's feet. "You can't leave," she hissed.

"Why the hell not?" Max cried. "I can do whatever I want, and you can't stop me. You don't know how it feels to be in love. You've never had a lasting relationship. You run around fucking whoever you want while you kept me locked in the house my whole life."

Kathryn's eyes flicked up to Andrew's. Everything she'd been hiding her son from had been useless. Andrew was there, witnessing the fallout of her failures as a mother. Her son was closing her out. Every bit of power was inching away. Her armpits pricked with sweat, panic rising. And Harper was going to lose Emmy.

Kathryn looked at the girl. Maybe she could reason with her, stop the two from leaving. "Honey, you're young and you think you're in love and I get it—I've been there. But you weren't here a year ago when Max was kicked out of school. You weren't here when he almost killed himself driving drunk. You think you know him, but you don't. This is what he does; he's reckless. First, it was drinking; then it was drugs, and now it's you. But you need to think about this before you run off to another state with a boy. You're going to get hurt."

Emmy's head jerked. "Kathryn, no—"

"You're still seventeen for three more weeks." Emmy's eyes were round with fear. "You need to go back home to your mother."

But Max's voice overpowered hers when he leaned forward and boomed, "This is bullshit. You can't make her go back there. Harper doesn't care about her." Max stood. "She's almost as bad as you are."

Kathryn's face ignited, and Max's expression confirmed he'd struck his intended target.

"You want to talk to me about keeping secrets? About being reckless?" Max leaned over his mother. "You're the one who's running around with your sloppy leftovers from twenty fucking years ago." His eyes ping-ponged between Kathryn and Andrew. "Have you run out of dick in this town and now you're making the rounds again? Isn't it uncomfortable for you to look at his face? Isn't he just a reminder of the worst mistake you've ever made, or at least a reminder to use a condom this time around—"

The crack of Kathryn's palm on his cheek silenced the room. Emmy and Andrew gasped in unison. Regret swept Kathryn, a tidal wave. Her hand burned. Max's eyes welled.

Kathryn covered her mouth. Max deserved a better mother than the one he'd gotten. She'd failed him. Completely. And now Andrew saw she was the worst mother in existence.

Max's eyes narrowed, his voice granite. "You're right. I am fucked up. But I've learned from the best." He strode from the house, the slam of the front door rattling the floorboards, and Kathryn collapsed onto the couch, her face in her hands. There was tearing deep in her diaphragm as she tried to suck in a breath but couldn't. She opened her eyes to catch Emmy's shape disappearing out the door.

Max was gone. Despite her best efforts, he'd slipped from her grasp.

CHAPTER TWENTY-SIX

Saturday, May 27
Emmy

Emmy's eyes adjusted to the sunlight, and the crest of Max's shoulders were all she could see from where he was hunched on the curb. Emmy lowered herself beside him and snaked an arm across his back. "Max—"

Max's head jerked up, his eyes red and teary. "I can't believe her." One side of his face was a delicate pink where Kathryn had slapped him.

Emmy blew a long breath. Their plan was a disaster. She'd told Max she'd stay in her room while he confronted his mother and Andrew, but when she'd heard him storm up the steps to his bedroom, her heart had shattered, and she'd blown their cover by rushing to his rescue.

"Babe," Max said. "Let's leave right now. I have the money. Pack your things, and we'll go to a hotel or something. We'll figure it out. We can get married," he blurted, a light tremble to his lower lip. "Whatever you want, we can have."

Married? Emmy's thoughts spiraled. She grasped to find the control in herself that seemed to be slipping from Max. This wasn't the confident Max she knew. She dropped to the wet asphalt between his knees and reached for his hand. "Max, I have three weeks until my birthday.

Let's take a step back, let everything settle; then we can decide what we're going to do."

"A step back?" Max jerked his head side to side. "No—it shouldn't be like this. My mom can't control our lives."

"She can control *my* life right now because I'm still seventeen, so if I can't stay here, I have to move back in with Harper and Nora."

"I won't leave you alone here with *her*." Max pointed at the house.

"It's a matter of *weeks*, Max. Go to a hotel. Or stay with Javier. We'll talk when this blows over."

"No," he growled.

"You talk about marriage, which is *ridiculous* at this age—"

"We don't need to get married *now*; I just want you to know I'm in this for life—"

"You can't know that—you're nineteen."

Max's eyes were stormy. "*I* know that."

So this was the ugly side of love. The consequence the romance novels never charted, when passion rages white-hot and burns, leaving everything in its wake charred. Like a mother unable to love her child. No, that wasn't going to happen to her. Emmy pushed herself up and stood over Max. "Fine. If you're going to be stubborn, if you can't give me a breather, time to think this through, if you force me to go back to Nora's, we're finished."

From the curb, Max stared up at her. "You're breaking up with me?"

"I didn't say that," Emmy yelled, her frustration ripping at the seams.

Max climbed to his feet. "Yes, you did. So that's it? It's that easy to walk away from what we have?"

"It's not *that*, Max. I love you. You know I do. But you know the situation I came from, and you're forcing me to go back there when you said I'd never have to. So if it's easy for you to break the promises you make—we can't be together." Tears blurred her view of him. "Or you can let me stay here, give me three weeks. Let's be honest with Kathryn—"

"Because Kathryn has been so honest with me?" Max snapped, his eyes welling.

"As soon as I turn eighteen, we'll go to Seattle," she pleaded. "But I need a break from you. From all of this right now."

The front door opened, and they both looked up. Andrew's tall frame loomed in the doorway, and he closed the door behind him. Max gave Andrew the finger with both hands, and Andrew frowned but strode toward them, undeterred. "Max—" Andrew started.

"Really?" Max snapped. "Can't you see we're in the middle of something?"

Andrew hesitated. "I just thought we might have a talk."

"Dude," Max cried. "Seriously. Fuck off."

Andrew acquiesced, turned, and ambled to his car. He backed from the driveway and drove away.

"Emmy, please." Max's chest heaved. "Don't make me go anywhere without you. I don't want to go back to being without you." Emmy saw it in his eyes, the pain he'd endured, the raw hurt and unanswered questions, and his fear he'd return to what he'd been for so many years: alone. And she saw his love for her. Kathryn was right: she was an addiction to him, and this frightened her. She wasn't going to end up like Harper. She wasn't going to let Max end up like Kathryn. She'd take this burden for him, shatter her own heart, before Max sank in deeper, before it was too late. "I can't do this, Max. I just can't. I'm going to Washington by myself."

Max looked as if he were about to speak, then raked his hands through his hair. In a few swift motions, while Emmy watched, helpless, he marched away, climbed into his car, and backed into the street. He sped off, the engine roaring until he was out of sight.

Emmy dropped back onto the curb, the emotions of their fight cascading down on top of her. She dropped her face to her hands, hurt, regret, heartbreak rushing in relentless waves. And once again she, too, found herself alone.

CHAPTER TWENTY-SEVEN

Saturday, May 27
Andrew

His mind racing, Andrew zoomed around Delray for thirty minutes, scouting Nick's regular haunts: Duffy's, Bru's Room, Flannigan's. The memory of Kathryn striking Max soured his stomach. The pain in the boy's eyes. He'd finally met his son, and the boy hated him.

And ugly, dark suspicions. Kathryn had insisted she and Nick had just gone for drinks. Was it more, had they slept together? The thought spotted his vision with red, and Andrew gripped the wheel. Then he spotted Nick's black Mustang, tucked in a corner spot at a dive bar at the north end of town, and jerked his car into the lot. He killed the engine, then darted through the puddles left behind by the storm. The place was dim, the walls adorned with dusty nautical paraphernalia and rusted license plates. Nick was at the far end of the bar, and Andrew slid onto the stool beside him. He pictured Nick's hands on Kathryn's bare skin, and swallowed the acid that rose in his throat. "We need to talk."

Nick was nonplussed by his presence, and tossed back a shot, then set the empty glass on the bar. In front of Nick, a beer sweated against the worn wood. The astringent smell of tequila floated on the air. Andrew salivated.

Andrew dropped his voice. "What the hell is going on between you and Kathryn?" The idea of Nick and Kathryn together, Nick's hands on her dress, her skin, kissing her, braided into a twisted version of his dream, Nick in his place—and crimson rage again seeped into his vision.

The bartender dropped a coaster in front of Andrew. "What's your poison, my good man?"

Andrew's eyes traced the backlit bottles behind the bar, the amber and gold. Smooth. Magic. A craving for relief. Andrew waved him off with an unsteady hand. "I'm good, thanks."

"Not that it's any of your fucking business, Drew." Nick's dark eyes blazed. "But there's absolutely *nothing* going on between me and Kathryn."

Relief? Disbelief? "Then why did Max lure you to her house? Have you two been 'going out for drinks' the entire time you lived here?"

"What does it matter how often we go out?" Nick barked. "You have no claim over her. It's none of your business."

"It is my business!" Around the bar, heads snapped in their direction. Nick waved them off, and Andrew again lowered his tone. "You're supposed to be my best friend. But for *two years* you knew I had a kid, and you never breathed a word. You knew she lived in town when I moved here. What the fuck? What else do you know that you're not telling me?" Nick's glare wavered. "Why does your loyalty lie with Kathryn?"

"My loyalty?" Nick's eyes locked with his. "What about yours? You sure as hell haven't been considering Amy while you're sneaking around."

Andrew swallowed. "Don't bring Amy into this. Kathryn and I have a child together."

"I thought we were past all this, Andrew. We're not twenty-two any-more. But we're still fighting over the same shit." Nick took a drag from his beer, and Andrew's stomach clenched. "I told you in the beginning I wasn't going to get in the middle of the mess you two made."

Andrew heaved a breath. "Then don't get in the middle of it. Leave Kathryn alone."

"Fuck off, Drew. She doesn't belong to you." Nick's voice was thick. "And you have bigger problems," he taunted. "Max knows now. He's pissed off, and you have no idea what he's capable of."

Again, Max's face flashed. His shape disappearing out the front door, away from Kathryn. His distraught eyes as he stood in the street, fighting with his girlfriend. Andrew knew that pain, that panic. It was a vein that ran deep within him.

"You have a secret kid in the same town as your wife." Nick let out a twisted giggle. "I told you to tell Amy at the start. I told you not to marry her if you were still pining over your ex—which you swore you weren't. Some bullshit that turned out to be. I told you Amy deserved to know you nearly killed yourself with booze once, and there's a good chance you'll do it again if something in your life goes tits up. But you ignored me like you always do. And now you're carrying on with Kathryn." He snorted a breath. "You're in deep shit. And you'd better not come to me when all this blows up—because I promise you, it will." Nick lifted his drink to his lips once more.

Andrew wiped his sweaty palms on his thighs. He had to get to Kathryn. Had to get to Max. This was spiraling out of control, and it was only a matter of time before the tidal wave reached Amy.

CHAPTER TWENTY-EIGHT

Saturday, May 27
Kathryn

For the second time that day, Andrew appeared in her house. Only this time it wasn't jarring. She craved him, his comfort, his smell. Kathryn lifted her head from her tearstained pillow, and he was there, in her bedroom, in her space. Andrew looked taller, his shoulders squared, his neck a blotchy red, but his movements were controlled when he closed the bedroom door and strode toward her. "May I?" he asked, and when Kathryn nodded, he lowered himself onto the foot of her bed.

"I'm sorry, Drew. About all of this." She tucked her feet beneath herself. "Max shouldn't have had to resort to cornering us. It's all my fault."

"Maybe I can reason with him when he calms down." Andrew's eyes were pleading.

"Andrew, no." Kathryn shook her head at the thought of her son's wounded eyes. This wasn't Andrew's to fix; it belonged to her alone. Her eyes darted to her phone, face up on the bedspread, dark. She'd called Max three times, each instantly rejected. So she'd sent a text: Max, please talk to me. Nothing.

After she'd heard Max's car speed down the street, Emmy had dashed to her bedroom and locked the door behind her, ignoring Kathryn when she'd knocked.

Andrew inched closer and reached across the bed, but didn't touch her hand. Andrew didn't want to touch her after he'd seen what a terrible mother she was. Tears sprang to her eyes once more. "I *hit* him. I've been so judgmental of Emmy's mom, but I'm the worst mother in the world." Kathryn let her face fall into her hands. "Oh God. Harper. She's going to kill me."

A tick of silence. "You had to have had your reasons." In his tone, Andrew sounded as if he was convincing himself. But he shuffled closer. "Raising him on your own must have been tough. But . . . you're not alone in this anymore." His words throbbed like a bruise. "I'm here now. I don't want to be in the dark anymore—we're past that point. I want to know all of him. Even the gritty parts. Especially those. Please. Tell me where it went wrong."

Kathryn palmed a tear from her cheek. "It was all because of Lucas and his money." She failed to veil the bitterness in her tone. "Harper's husband. Her Lucas."

"Money?" Andrew's brows arched. "What money—how much?" She glanced up. Andrew's shoulders drooped, and he mumbled, "I'm sorry—that's not my business."

Kathryn cleared her throat. "Lucas left a trust for Max that matured the day he turned eighteen, in the fall of his senior year of high school. That's how Max bought that car." She stared at the far end of the room. "I know Lucas meant well, but I worked so hard to protect Max, and the minute he got access to that money, he's had no limits. He got access to a massive amount of cash before he was emotionally equipped to handle life."

"This Lucas"—Andrew scratched at the bedspread—"that's who you went to see the day you left? Was there . . . something between you two?"

Kathryn's neck snapped to face Andrew. "No. It wasn't like that." She swallowed and pushed herself up against her pillows.

"Then please. Tell me."

Kathryn's throat was tight. "Really, it all went wrong when Max was five." A resigned sigh. "But please listen to the whole story before you judge me."

Andrew nodded.

Anxiety coursed through her, and she took a long, grounding breath. "The day I left your apartment . . ." Kathryn's gaze fell, then lifted back to his face. "When I told my mom I was pregnant, we got into an argument, so Harper invited me over for the night. She and Luke had this incredible house right on the beach, and I stayed there. I rented a cottage on their property. That's where I lived when Max was born. We all became a kind of family, especially after Emmy was born. The kids adored each other." Kathryn swallowed. Her mouth was dry. "The years just kind of slipped by, and we were so *happy*. I thought it was a sign I was doing the right thing for Max." She closed her eyes. "Then everything fell apart." Her voice shrank. Andrew reached out, slipped her hand in his, squeezed. *I'm here. It's okay.*

Kathryn started to talk.

◆　◆　◆

Then

For weeks after Harper and Lucas had gone to the doctor, the couple's cars came and went at odd hours, leaving the beach house still, its dark upper windows looking down at Kathryn like ominous eyes. Kathryn's nerves buzzed, and she tossed at night, imagining what Harper might have seen that night in the kitchen, Kathryn gripping Lucas's hand. And all their late nights together, the raw vulnerability of their conversations. Lucas was never anything more than a dear friend. How could she make Harper believe her? Would she lose her best friend over a misunderstanding?

One overcast Saturday night, Kathryn waited in her living room for the kitchen light to flick on at the beach house, and when it did, she crossed the driveway and rapped on the door, heart thudding. The Lucas who appeared stole her breath. The handsome man was gone; now his face was gaunt, and his T-shirt hung on his bony shoulders. Kathryn gasped, all thoughts of Harper whisked away. "Luke—what's going on?"

Lucas paused before he ushered her inside, and electric anxiety coursed through Kathryn as she dropped into a chair. Lucas lowered himself delicately across from her and drew a long breath. "It's not good, Kathryn." He broke her gaze. The room was still. "I need something from you," he rushed. "I need you to promise you'll look out for Emmy. I don't know if Harper can handle raising her." His eyes flicked upward to meet Kathryn's, an unfamiliar desperation in his expression. "I'll make sure you have access to whatever you need—money, a lawyer, anything—so you can make sure Emmy's okay."

"Luke, back up—"

"No, Kathryn, I need you to listen."

Something significant was coming. She could hear it in his voice and see it in his hands, as both were unsteady, and Kathryn steeled herself.

"You need to promise me, because in less than a month I'll be dead."

His words sucked the air from the room. "That's not funny, Luke." Her voice was small.

Lucas's shoulders dropped, and he shook his head slowly, his eyes hollow, resigned. "You have no idea how much I wish this were a joke." His bony hands rested on the table; his eyes didn't look like his own.

"Luke, tell me what's going on," Kathryn whispered.

"A tumor. In my brain. It's grown rapidly, growing as we speak, and it's already spread to other organs." Lucas's eyes held hers, and they said more than he could have. "Harper and I saw a slew of doctors, and they all said the same thing: in its location, it's inoperable."

Kathryn read his surrendered expression: there was nothing any of them could do.

"It's the worst, having all this." He motioned to the walls around him. "Millions. And I'm just . . . helpless."

His expression would stay etched in Kathryn's mind for the rest of her life. Lucas wasn't sick; he was *dying*. "There has to be something the doctors can do. *Something*."

"We've—*I've*—opted out of any kind of treatment. It won't help." Again, his eyes spoke the truth. "I didn't know how to tell you, I'm sorry, and Harper's been—" Lucas's voice wobbled. "I don't know what to tell Emmy." His voice broke, and for the first time since she'd known him, Kathryn watched Lucas crumple. Lucas was light and life and happiness, and now he sat before her, his shoulders trembling, tears spilling onto the draping fabric of his shirt.

Kathryn had spent countless nights sitting at this table, drinking tea, hashing their day-to-day problems, and now she clutched Lucas's hand in hers like she could keep him there forever. He was warm to her touch, but defeat hung in the room, everything she had slipping from their control.

"I'll make sure you and Max are taken care of. You may not want to reach out to Andrew, and I can't make you, but I'm not going to let you go through what my mom and I did." Luke's eyes narrowed. "It's important to me that my daughter can depend on you. Can you give me that one last thing?"

Kathryn gripped his hand so hard it must've hurt, and she promised.

Over the following weeks, Harper and Lucas locked themselves on the upper floor of the beach house. Their cars came and went. Sharp voices floated on the ocean air. The handwritten note Kathryn had left in the kitchen with bags of groceries went unanswered. *If I can help with anything, I'm here. I love you.*

One afternoon she returned to the cottage to find Harper pacing the driveway, Emmy beside her.

Lean Harper was frail. Her face etched with anguish. "Luke's at the hospital. I need you to watch Emmy." She drove away.

Kathryn lifted Emmy and placed a kiss to the girl's temple, relishing her sweet smell. Berry bubble gum. Emmy wrapped her velvety arms around Kathryn, and they regarded the house, Luke's broken palace. Columns of sunlight beamed above, the rush of the ocean on the salty air. The song of gulls.

That day stretched longer than any Kathryn could recall. She let herself inside the beach house, where the children skittered off, and searched for something to occupy her mind. She stuffed a vase of dead lilies into the trash, then moved to the living room, where, beyond the panoramic windows, the sun sparkled on the waves as if nothing had changed, and the indifference of the world felt like a kind of cruelty. The children's voices came from the hallways of the upper floors, disembodied, like the laughter of ghosts.

That evening she took the kids for fast food, then put them to bed.

In the dark, she peered from the cottage to the empty house. She expected the light to flick on, Lucas's silhouette in the kitchen. The smell of coffee in the morning, Emmy's sweet toddler chatter, Harper crooning a response. Swallowing tears, she realized she'd taken those moments for granted; they'd never exist again outside of her memory.

Harper returned the following morning, alone, eyes wide and unfocused. Kathryn didn't need to hear the words; she knew Luke—larger-than-life Luke—no longer inhabited this earthly plane. Harper fell into Kathryn's arms in the driveway, her thin body trembling. "I'm so, so sorry," Kathryn whispered between her own sobs. The tragedy of all of it was overpowering; Harper left to live the remainder of her life without the man she'd planned to share it with; Emmy wouldn't know Lucas as she grew. Luke's dreams for a loud, lively family blown out as effortlessly as a birthday candle. A ripple effect of lives decimated by a single rogue cell that divided, multiplied, a tiny event blooming beneath the surface until its catastrophic consequences. Their makeshift family, shattered.

In the days that followed, Kathryn and Harper existed outside the structure of time. Kathryn learned grief could be physical, like an open wound. It was indifferent; life offered no other option but to forge on. It ravaged Harper; Kathryn watched her fade to nearly nothing. Her clothing draped her small frame. Harper didn't venture to the upper floors; instead, she and Emmy lived in the downstairs guest room. Kathryn curled beneath the duvet with Harper and held her as she wept. It was Kathryn who eventually climbed the staircase and let herself into Harper and Lucas's sprawling suite. The space was frozen in time, the bed unmade, Emmy's toys discarded on the rug. Harper's and Lucas's nightstands were littered with neon-orange pill bottles, glasses of water, alien-looking medical devices. Kathryn let herself into the bathroom and scanned the pill labels for Harper's name. She found what she was looking for, beside Lucas's and Harper's toothbrushes, charging side by side, and a bottle of Infants' Tylenol. Kathryn handed the pills to Harper. "Please remember to take these." But Harper offered only a distracted nod.

Harper's mother, Nora, came to the house each day, something she'd never done while Lucas was alive, and swatted Emmy away whenever the little girl appeared. As Nora ordered a crew of movers from room to room, Kathryn realized the woman seemed determined to extract Harper from the ruins of her marriage as efficiently as possible.

Kathryn toured several properties beneath the hopeful gaze of a Realtor. She felt nothing but numbness at the sight of each one. The two-story home on Cherry Street checked her boxes, she recognized through her haze: the neighborhood was neat, just steps away from the high school Max would attend soon enough. The bay window in the living room allowed the butter-yellow morning sun to fill the space. In a twenty-four-hour flash, the offer she'd placed had been accepted, her closing date secured. But the thought of vacating 228 Ocean Avenue sliced a place deep inside her heart. In the cottage, Kathryn boxed their belongings. Then she inked her signature on the closing documents for the Cherry Street house. Maybe Harper and Emmy could join her; they didn't need their family to break apart.

Nearly all of Emmy and Harper's belongings had been transported from the beach house under Nora's eye. "Come stay with me and Max, Harp," Kathryn urged.

Harper's eyes were dull. "I can't, Kat." There was no life, no fight, left in her voice. Had she been taking her medication? "Nora's right; it's time I went back home."

So it was just the two of them: Kathryn and Max. When she brought Max to pick a bedroom as his own, he shook his head. "I don't want to live here," Max howled, fat tears streaking his cheeks. "When Lucas comes back, I want to go home. With Harper and Emmy."

His words stabbed her. *Home.* The people they had loved were their home. "I know, baby. Me too. But this is going to be our home now."

Max looked at the blank wall, resigned, his small body shaking. Kathryn held him. She had no words. In his sweet blue eyes she could see the darkness of the world had seeped in, despite her best efforts to protect him.

While Max was in school, Kathryn set about unpacking their belongings. Maybe she could make the place feel welcoming. She peeled away a section of newspaper to reveal a pastel rainbow and a bright yellow sun beaming back at her. Her fingers touched the cool ceramic of the mug Luke had given her, and in a moment she was transported to her first morning at the beach house, the day she'd decided to keep her baby. She stashed it on the top shelf, where Max couldn't reach it, the painted smile disappearing when she closed the cabinet door. It was then that she felt it: she was alone. No one would come to save her with a beautiful, comfortable property, with friendship, with a refuge. It was up to her to create a place in the world for her son.

The following morning Kathryn was summoned by Lucas's lawyer. Perplexed, she pressed the phone to her ear. "What is this regarding?"

"It's best if we discuss it in person."

A swell of unease. "I can come by this afternoon before my son gets out of school."

Two hours later Kathryn was seated at a refined oak desk where the lawyer penciled a circle around a figure Lucas had designated for Kathryn, and then for Max. "No." It was the only word that came to her mind. "I don't want it. I don't want a penny of Lucas's money."

The lawyer's expression didn't shift. "These were Mr. Silva's wishes."

Kathryn sped to the beach house, punched her code in at the gate. At the end of the driveway she threw the car into park beside Harper's and darted up the steps. She yanked the kitchen door, and, inside, her eyes adjusted to the light, and she spotted Harper, hunched at the kitchen table, her face in her thin hands, a glass of water before her. "Harp," Kathryn began. "I had no idea Luke was going to do this. I'll wire the money to you, every penny—"

Harper dropped her hands. Her face was pale. Streaked with tears. "How long was it going on, the entire time you lived here?" Harper's voice was that of her mother's, Nora's. Icy.

Panic coursed Kathryn's veins. "It was never like that."

"I knew there was something going on between you two," Harper snarled. "Do you want to take my daughter, too?"

"Harper, there was nothing between Luke and me, I swear. You have it all wrong."

"It's been like this since we were seventeen. Since you bought that slutty pink bikini to parade around in front of Sam," Harper spat.

Kathryn's mind spun. "Sam?"

"The lifeguard. You knew I liked him." Harper's voice trembled. "I should've known then. And after what you did to Andrew."

Kathryn gasped. "It wasn't like that—you're always accusing me of things, things that aren't true, Harper. Luke needed you, Emmy needed you, *I* needed you, but you weren't consistent with your meds—"

Harper rose with a guttural shriek, snatched the glass from the table, and lobbed it at the wall. Shards of glass and water showered the room. Harper rushed to the cabinets and snatched anything her trembling hands could grasp, which she slung at the wall, ceramic and glass cascading between screams. Kathryn stood, a frozen witness to Harper's destruction of the memories they'd shared.

"Mama?" Emmy's voice came from the doorway, and the space filled with silence. Harper looked at her daughter, chest heaving. Harper ran to Emmy and lifted her. Kathryn swallowed, tears choking, then darted across the kitchen, broken glass crunching beneath her sneakers. The screen door slammed at her back, and she vacated 228 Ocean Avenue for the last time.

◆ ◆ ◆

Andrew

Darkness had settled outside, and Andrew watched the reflection from Kathryn's bedside lamp in her eyes. He had no words. Kathryn's story wasn't what he'd anticipated, and the energy in the room had drained, like the aftermath of a panic attack. This was not the Kathryn he'd encountered at Starbucks, who had grabbed him by the arm, led him, always. With her legs tucked beneath the skirt of her dress, she looked small, defeated. He longed to pull her close, to take it all away from her.

Kathryn's jaw tightened. "I thought I was doing the right thing by staying with Harper and Lucas. Max was surrounded by people who loved him."

Andrew grasped what she was saying: her friends had made it easy to stay away from him, from whatever she'd sensed that made her want to run from him. The dulled nostalgia of far-gone happiness gleamed in Kathryn's eyes, and he grappled with the idea of this couple, Harper and Lucas, whom he'd never met, who inadvertently had so much influence over the course of his life. Kathryn had blossomed in the time after she'd left him, while Andrew had been living in a parallel universe, drowning himself, wallowing in his own weak self-indulgence to the point it had nearly killed him.

Kathryn drew a ragged breath. "But, in the end, Max lost the only people he knew as his family, and he'll never be the same because of it. He was so little, he didn't understand, and he became so withdrawn. He grew up at age five. And we never quite connected again—" Her voice broke. Swollen tears spilled down her face, and she pressed her eyes closed. Andrew clutched her hand, and she squeezed as if clinging to him for life. "I can count on one hand the number of times Harper and I have spoken since."

Andrew read her face: she'd lost both her friends at the same time, both painful and permanent.

"I have no interest in making friends. Acquaintances, sure, but I never let anyone get close to me. I sheltered Max. Too much. I feared running into you, but also I didn't want to connect with anyone. Didn't want him to, either. So he went wild when he was a teenager, filled his life with superficial relationships, with drugs and drinking, and it got so much worse when he got the money. And it *hurt*. I didn't know what I'd done wrong. But I realized all he'd ever learned from me was how to keep people at a distance. How to be alone."

She shuddered. A band of silence.

"Max would have been better off if you'd been in his life. If I'd stayed with you, none of this would have happened—he wouldn't have become the person you met today." She jabbed a finger into her chest. "I failed him."

"There's no way you could've known that." Andrew's voice came out in a hoarse whisper.

"But it's true. And I live with that guilt every fucking second."

Andrew watched sorrow settle over her, her lashes wet with tears, and wondered if she'd ever done this, ever let herself feel this, before. Time had passed, but the weight of her pain and regret was raw, exposed. Tears spilled faster than Kathryn could wipe them away.

Andrew nudged closer, draped an arm around her shoulders, pulled her into him, and she curled against his body. That word, the one that governed all of Kathryn's choices—*guilt*—settled between them. But what had he done that had led her to abandon him? High-voltage fear buzzed on the other side of that question; would he lose her when he knew, this time permanently?

He never wanted to leave, he wanted to hold her there, in the intimacy of her bedroom, forever. But he couldn't, and when he told her he had to go, she nodded, resigned. "I'll walk you out."

She left the front door open and walked barefoot down the sidewalk to the driveway. Beside his car, Andrew turned to face her. He took her against his body, and Kathryn melted into him, as if his arms were the only thing keeping her from sinking to the ground. In the humid night air, the fire of excitement that had raged between them was gone, replaced by the dull sting of her open wounds, finally laid bare.

Kathryn took a small step back. "Thank you for listening." She dodged his gaze. "I'm sorry this night was a disaster."

"Kathryn . . ." Andrew pressed his lips to the top of her head, inhaling the scent of her shampoo and what remained of her warm perfume, drawing it, drawing *her*, into himself. "It was nice to not have to face something alone for once." The words surprised him, both that he'd spoken them aloud and that they held the truth. Kathryn's shoulders dropped; then she fell into him once more, squeezed. Andrew kissed her hairline, then released her, stepped back to place a light kiss on the soft skin of each cheek, slow and gentle. When he was finished, he pressed his forehead to hers and said, "Max will come around. Try to get some rest." She nodded against him, and when she stepped back, her fingers traced down his arm, brushing his hand down to the tip of his pinkie.

Kathryn nudged a shoulder toward her house. "I'm going to try to talk to Emmy first."

"Can I come by and see you in the morning?"

Kathryn's small smile answered, and that familiar excitement sparked within Andrew once more. The night had been a catastrophe, but they'd weathered it. It didn't mark the end of them, whatever this was. He watched her pad to her house and close the door behind her back.

CHAPTER TWENTY-NINE

Saturday, May 27
Kathryn

In the hallway a light flickered in the crack beneath Emmy's door. Kathryn knocked.

Emmy's voice came softly. "It's open."

Kathryn turned the knob, and the girl sat up and adjusted her pillows against the headboard, her face white in the glow of the muted TV. "Can I talk to you for a minute?"

Emmy's eyes were red and puffy, and she gave a weak shrug. "Sure."

"Where's Max?"

Emmy sniffed. "Javi said they're together."

A weight lifted from Kathryn. Max was safe; he just needed some space.

"Kathryn, I didn't mean to disrespect you, or to cause problems between you and Max." The words tumbled from Emmy; then she hiccuped and fell silent.

"Honey, calm down. Take a breath." The mattress shifted when Kathryn lowered herself onto its surface. Every movement required more effort than she had energy for.

"But I don't want to go back to live with Nora." Tears snagged Emmy's words.

"I'd never make you do that." Relief washed Emmy's face, and her shoulders dropped. Mortification flowed again when Kathryn recalled the argument. "Earlier, I said a lot of horrible things I regret deeply. I'm the adult here; I should know better than to bite back in anger that way. And I'm sorry you were there to witness that." A flash of Max's eyes. Devastated. Kathryn swallowed.

"Max is angry because you've never been honest with him about his father—"

The knife in her diaphragm was back. Gouging. Twisting. "Andrew has nothing to do with this." Kathryn's voice came out in a gravelly whisper.

"He has *everything* to do with this, Kathryn."

It crashed over her, waves on a seawall. Kathryn closed her eyes. Emmy was right. Her body trembled before the tears came. Shuddering sobs. Kathryn dropped her face into her hands. "It's complicated with Andrew," she cried. "I never explained the situation to Max, and that's my fault. Max shouldn't blame Andrew."

"But Max doesn't know that."

She breathed into her fingers. "You're right."

A beat of silence. Kathryn cleared her throat. "I've sent him to all the best therapists. Nothing seems to have worked."

"Have you tried going with him? He might have some things to share with you."

Kathryn had never considered this. Why had she been so blind all along? "I can do that." Emmy's maturity was remarkable. Harper had done a better job than she had. "But Max does have a history of being impulsive, and he doesn't react well when things get tough. In the past, his behavior has been concerning. Dangerous, even. I don't want you getting your heart broken, but I don't want him to get hurt, either. Do you understand?"

Emmy nodded, tears tracing her cheeks. "We broke up. I mean, I think we did. I didn't want to. I love him," she sobbed.

A sigh emptied from Kathryn. "Oh God. I'm sorry, honey." She thought of the way Max had clutched Emmy's hand on the couch. "I never thought he'd let anyone in, really in. I thought he'd learned that from me."

Emmy shook her head. "No, that's not Max at all. He's sweet and funny and he's . . . happy. We're happy together." A flicker of light in Emmy's face. "And he loves Javi." Emmy palmed a tear from her cheek. "But when he's upset, he withholds love from himself, like a punishment. And I'm pretty sure he learned that from you."

Kathryn bit her bottom lip and let this wash over her. That was all her son had taken from her. But that flicker in Emmy sparked a thought: maybe Emmy was good for Max; maybe her son could be happy. Kathryn thought of the way Harper had transformed when she met Lucas.

Kathryn sighed. "Having you here has stirred up so many memories. I told your dad I'd take care of you, and I haven't done a very good job." Her voice was thick, and she cleared her throat. "But also memories of your mom. She was so different back then."

"Nobody ever told me that, either. I don't know what happened. Max and I both grew up with these things nobody talked about, big things, formative things that are just blank for us."

This had never occurred to Kathryn, that these gaps were holes the kids had filled on their own. Another teary sigh. "You're right, Em. I need to talk to Max. And maybe if you make space for Harper, she'll talk to you, too."

Emmy took a ragged breath. "Fine."

Exhaustion gutted Kathryn, but she reached over to squeeze Emmy's hand. "Get some sleep. We'll talk in the morning." She rose and pressed a kiss to Emmy's forehead before she closed the bedroom door behind her.

Kathryn fell onto her bed and stared at the ceiling. It had been the longest day she could recall, and she knew she wouldn't sleep that night. But there was a modicum of relief; hiding Andrew from Max was in the past. And speaking of Lucas and Harper had been painful, yet cathartic.

It was ten thirty. She dialed Harper's number. It rang once. "Kathryn, what's wrong?"

Kathryn propped herself up. She hadn't considered what she'd say. "Everything's fine. Emmy's fine." But her own voice was scratchy. It was clear she'd been crying. "I—I have something to tell you."

When Kathryn froze, Harper asked, "Well, what is it?"

"Emmy and Max . . . they've been seeing each other. I just found out today."

"Haven't you been keeping an eye on her?" Harper's voice was sharp.

"Harp, I—" The tears came again. "I've been distracted, okay? Yes, I kept an eye on Emmy, but she's eighteen in a few weeks, and she said she was with her friend, Maggie."

"Maggie moved away a year ago," Harper said.

Fresh embarrassment flowed. Harper had entrusted her with her child. Lucas had entrusted her with his child. And what had she done? Neglected her. Allowed the girl to witness the culmination of years' worth of mistakes come to a head at her house. Emmy had witnessed her reducing her son to nothing, a thought that now made bile rise in Kathryn's throat. "I was distracted with my own things."

"With Andrew?"

Kathryn shut her eyes. "Yes."

Harper sighed on the other end of the line.

After Lucas had died, after Harper had severed their relationship, Kathryn hadn't let a man touch her for three years. The coldness of her solitude had felt like an appropriate punishment for her transgressions, for everything she'd allowed herself to lose. When men asked her for

a date, her refusal was automatic, practiced. One evening, when she'd
settled in at her firm, one of the newbies, Tad, asked her out for an after-
hours drink. She'd become so accustomed to saying no, his request felt
almost invasive. But Max was at a sleepover, and an endless stretch of
a lonely evening at home loomed in front of her. Besides, Tad worked
one floor beneath hers. If she didn't want to see him again, he could
easily be avoided.

After a dinner over contrived laughter and three martinis, Kathryn
and Tad slid into his BMW in the nearly vacant parking garage, and
his lips crashed into hers before he slipped his hand inside her blouse.
She'd set her red-bottomed heels on the floorboard and leaned into him.

Three weeks later, Kathryn was about to pass off an envelope des-
tined for Tad's office to an intern. Instead, she decided to deliver it
herself. She rode the elevator down and knocked, catching Tad's smirk
when she stepped into the room. Kathryn shut the door behind her,
and Tad loosened his tie. Then she spotted the framed wedding portrait
on his desk. Tad's toothy smile was caught mid-laugh, his blond wife
beaming at the camera. Kathryn leaned in close to him, her palms flat
on his desk and asked, "Do you have children?"

"What are you talking about?" Tad's eyes darted toward the portrait.

"It's a simple question, Tad. Do you have children with that
woman?" Kathryn pointed a manicured nail at the photo.

"No." His voice wobbled. "Not yet."

"Then tell her."

His brows knitted together. "Excuse me?"

"Tell her, you piece of shit. Before you waste any more of that girl's
life. Or I will. And I'll have you fired for sexual harassment." She strode
from the room.

After that day, Kathryn scoured for wives and children on the
social media profiles of any man who offered to take her out. When
she was certain they weren't scumbags, she made bubbly conversation
over drinks, laughed at dumb jokes, but never told them where she
lived, or about her son. In the end, the men were all the same: generic

and ultimately boring, and she left most of them with a polite peck on the cheek. If the conversation flowed, if she felt a hint of what was supposedly called chemistry—or if the bite of loneliness was particularly sharp—she let them take her back to their place for the evening. She realized sex didn't need to leave life-altering wreckage in its wake; it could simply be a transaction, a momentary distraction from the crushing emptiness in her life.

When she returned to her silent house, Kathryn often passed by Max's bedroom and pushed the door open without making a sound. She never dared enter, but sometimes she slid down the doorframe onto the floor, letting the soft rhythm of his breathing soothe the sting of her isolation. She hadn't let anyone get close to her until Andrew returned to her life.

In her bed, with the phone pressed to her ear, Kathryn longed to hear Harper say something to soothe her. Maybe it was having her secrets exposed, opening up to Andrew that evening, taking down the stones that made up that wall she'd built one by one; maybe it was the culmination of all her failures, but Kathryn felt something inside her crack open. She'd spent so many years harboring animosity for Harper, bitterness over their lost friendship. Getting over heartbreak was difficult, but getting over losing your best friend? That was a grief Kathryn had never steeled herself for. Harper was alive, grieving for Lucas, suffering the trials of motherhood, all just a few miles away, and Kathryn had never reached out. Suddenly, the bitterness seemed fraught. The loneliness they'd endured alone suddenly so absurdly trite.

"Look, Harper," Kathryn said. "I want to make one thing clear. I loved Luke with all my heart. But I loved him the same way I loved you, as a friend. You two were a fucking fairy tale. I'm done with everyone judging me. Luke didn't have the luxury of time; he had to make his choices fast. All he had was his money, and he did what he thought was best for his daughter. And that was asking for my help, so you wouldn't be alone. And I fucked that up. I wasn't there for Emmy, and I certainly haven't been there for Max."

Harper didn't speak, but Kathryn could hear her breathing into the phone.

"Motherhood is hard as fuck. And I'm failing at it. Miserably. I've been failing at it since Max was five."

"So am I," Harper said. "I'm sorry, Kat. I'm sorry you're having a hard time, and I'm sorry for my distance."

A swell rose within Kathryn. "This would be easier with a friend. What do you say we leave it all behind us? We were so much better when we were on the same side."

"Yeah." Harper's voice was just above a whisper. "Okay."

"These two pain-in-the-ass brats of ours aren't making life easy." A teary laugh broke from both ends of the phone, along with a warm swell of possibility. Kathryn might have her best friend back, her confidante, with whom to share the ups and downs of life. Quick, bright flashes from the summers she'd spent with Harper peeked into her thoughts, of glittering pools and lounge chairs, the greasy-coconut smell of tanning oil.

"There's so much I have to tell you," Harper said.

Kathryn tilted her head against her pillow. "Harp, you have *no idea*."

"I left Joshua," Harper blurted.

"What?" Kathryn sat up. "Why?"

"It wasn't fair to him. I didn't—I'll never love anyone the way I did—" Harper's voice broke. "I know Emmy doesn't want to be around Nora, so I'm going to get my own place. Maybe she could come with me for the summer."

Maybe Kathryn could bridge Emmy and Harper's relationship. A shred of atonement for everything. "I'll talk to her in the morning."

"Thank you," Harper said. "This thing with Max, do you think it's serious?"

"It seems so," Kathryn said. A *hmm* from Harper. "You raised a sweet kid, Harper. Luke would be proud."

"Thanks." She heard Harper swallow. "So tell me about Andrew."

Kathryn thought of the way his eyes held hers that evening, and the way he lingered when he touched her. His kisses in the driveway. Andrew had given her a small part of his life, and she clung to it. Maybe the dreams they'd once dreamed on those afternoons so long ago weren't dead. "I love him, Harp. I always have."

CHAPTER THIRTY

Saturday, May 27
Andrew

After Kathryn disappeared into her house, Andrew stood beside his car as the minutes rode by. How could he return home as if nothing had happened? He had to tell Amy about Max now that his son knew, but the thought made him queasy.

A low thump of music interrupted the night, and the blinding headlights of a rugged Jeep swept the driveway and rolled to a stop. Andrew paused. Muffled voices came from inside the car, and the dome light flicked on before the passenger door slammed. Max stood, illuminated by the headlights, his long shadow cast against the garage door, staring at Andrew's car.

Kathryn had been a shell of herself that evening. With the magic of secrecy zapped, their relationship felt bare, vulnerable. Andrew ached to put her back together. To make it right. And above all, he wanted Max to know he cared, so he didn't grow up feeling like discarded leftovers from another man's life.

The driver of the Jeep said something Andrew couldn't hear, but Max waved them off, and the car reversed into the street. When the music from the Jeep faded as the car disappeared down the block, Max turned, then headed toward the front door.

"Max," Andrew called, and Max turned. Andrew drew a steadying breath and lowered his voice. He took a few tentative steps closer. "Can you and I talk for a minute?"

Max squinted into Andrew's unforgiving LED headlights. "I'm just here to get my stuff."

"Listen, everyone's had a long day. Can we go for a quick drive?"

Max leaned his weight on the foot farthest from Andrew. "I'm not going anywhere with you."

"Please. I'll bring you back when you want me to."

Max was rooted in place, but his eyes turned up at the house, where a light glowed through the gauzy curtains in the upstairs windows. "Fine," Max huffed. Andrew opened his car door and climbed in, and after a moment Max followed, dropping into the passenger seat.

In silence, Andrew backed into the street, gripping the wheel. A few months ago, he had no idea this person existed. Now his son was seated beside him as he coasted down the dark road. Max was larger than Andrew's imagination had allowed, a grown adult, tall, filling the intimate space with his presence. Andrew could smell him, sweat and liquor, with something more, a note of familiarity.

"Nice car," Max said acidly. "You could've sprung for the Prestige package, but . . ."

Andrew frowned. Max was a mouthy little shit. He pulled into the empty lot at the public beach, a place he knew was familiar to Max, where his son might be comfortable, and shut off the engine.

Max rolled his eyes. "Long drive."

Andrew climbed out of the driver's seat. Max followed, and their footsteps scratched the sandy concrete. The streetlights were dimmed around them, as not to affect the hatching sea turtles; a glowing moon illuminated their surroundings. They sat together on a bench, Max putting an arm's length between them.

In the moonlight, Andrew examined Max's face, the shape of his lips, the slope of his nose. He was young and handsome, but his eyes were lost and defeated.

"You're married," Max observed bluntly, looking down at Andrew's hands, flat on his thighs. ·

"I am." Even the confirmation felt disingenuous.

"But you're dating my mom." The words were harsh with accusation.

"No." Andrew shook his head. Max had effortlessly struck Andrew's most guarded chord; where did he stand with Kathryn? Or Amy? "We've just been catching up. We have a complicated history."

Max straightened. Andrew pressed his hands together and let the rhythmic boom of the waves wash over them. He didn't want to push Max too far. Andrew now understood where some of the boy's hurt came from. Now that his son knew who he was, there was no way he could fade into obscurity again. Maybe in time they could overcome their differences. "Listen, I brought you here so we can talk alone. About you, and me, and what that might mean. What you did, confronting your mother, myself, and Nick—I'm not saying it was okay, but you shouldn't have had to resort to cornering all of us to get some answers."

"How do you know the cop?"

"Nick? He's my best friend." The words burned.

Max's face pinched. Then he exhaled a grunt. He turned to Andrew. "Okay, so where have you been for the last nineteen years?"

"I—I didn't know . . . ," Andrew stammered, buying himself a few seconds. He'd expected the question in one form or another, but it still caught him unprepared. A flicker of surprise crossed Max's face before his jaw hardened. "I had no idea about you. This whole time." Andrew took a deep breath. "Your mom and I were together in college. I loved her—like really loved her. But she left me, and we lost all contact. I never knew she was—about you. I tried to find her; I promise. But I didn't try hard enough. When I moved here a few months ago, just down there"—Andrew motioned down the beach, where his house sat—"I ran into her. It wasn't until then that she told me."

The unfairness of it all stung. The breeze rustled the trees around them. Max's brows furrowed. Andrew could see that Max had never considered that all his anger may have been misguided. "I'm sure you hate me—and you have every right—but I wanted to talk to you tonight because . . . I wanted you to know I didn't choose this. I didn't have any say. I wouldn't have stayed away from you. I know how that feels, and I would never have let you live that way. I would have chosen you. And I know we just met, but I think, at the very least, you deserve that explanation from me."

Max appeared deep in thought. Andrew raked a hand through his hair, a rush of regret at recalling all the nights he'd called Kathryn's parents' house and was blown off. How easily he'd given up. If he'd gotten into his car and gone to talk to Kathryn face-to-face instead of diving into a bottle of rum, maybe he could've been involved in his son's life. Looking back on all his mistakes, this overshadowed everything. If he had just changed that one little decision, he could have saved the little boy who sat beside him, now a grown man, paying for decades' worth of other people's mistakes. If Andrew had only tried one more time instead of surrendering to his own weakness, Max wouldn't be who he was. Broken.

"Don't blame your mom," Andrew said. "I don't know her reasons behind everything she did, but I've spent a lot of time with her lately and I know she thought she was doing what was best for you. That's always been her intention."

Max blinked, his face hard. *So here's Kathryn.* Physically, their son was all Andrew, but the way Max expertly held on to the things that broke his heart—this was Kathryn.

"I'm sorry. We failed you in so many ways, intentional or not, and you deserved better. You deserve better."

Remorse stabbed him, powerful, blinding. Andrew balled his fists. He yearned—more than he had for anything in his entire life—to turn back time, to catch Max before the world had hurt him. Andrew couldn't articulate the depth of his regret, could never atone for the fact that neither of them would ever know what could've been. Andrew cleared his throat. "That's not all I brought you here to talk to you about. I heard you fighting with Emmy."

Max's head snapped toward Andrew, and his voice dropped several octaves. "I'm not discussing Emmy with *you*."

"Listen—you don't have to. I'm not going to tell you I know how you feel. Maybe you two will be fine. It's just—when my relationship with your mom ended, I had no idea how to handle it. I let everything fall apart around me. More than that"—Andrew hung his head—"I wanted to die, Max. And I very nearly did. I see a lot of myself in you, in your reactions, and I don't want you to go down the same road I did."

Max again turned his face toward the glowing moon.

"As much as I wish I could tell you it gets better, for me it didn't, not for a long time," Andrew said. "If I hadn't gotten professional help, I wouldn't be here. I would have hurt my parents, and everyone who loves me."

A tear traced Max's face, and he rushed to brush his cheek. Andrew reached over and set a hand on Max's shoulder. The boy tensed but didn't pull away. It was a tiny move, but it was monumental. For as long as he lived, Andrew knew he'd never look at anything the same way. And once again, Andrew recognized himself in his son in the most unsettling way, beyond the physical. Something mirrored in the two of them. He was certain Max had inherited the darkest parts of himself. But also he'd taken from Andrew his capacity to love with everything inside of him. It would be his greatest trait, but if Max wasn't careful, it could also be his downfall. Still, if Andrew could pass anything to his offspring, it would be this.

And a realization dawned on Andrew, his son's presence touching something deeper inside him than anyone in his life had before. Maybe his love for Max, or any child he brought into the world, would be far greater than the fragile fear he'd let govern his decisions until that point. He'd give his life for this person he hardly knew, of that he was certain. It was his purpose, sewn into his story decades, maybe lifetimes, ago.

In that moment, Amy and Kathryn didn't exist. Andrew didn't think of himself—the only thing that mattered was that Max knew he was present, that the two of them weren't so far apart after all.

And with all his heart, he hoped he'd been brought into his son's life for a reason, that he'd gotten to the boy before it was too late.

CHAPTER THIRTY-ONE

Saturday, May 27
Amy

Amy knew when to call time of death. It was a last resort, when all hope had been exhausted, but it was an instinct. Her duty. Still, each time, it gave her pause. Was there anything more she could do?

The morning she'd told Andrew she'd changed her schedule to accommodate dinner with her parents, he'd been zombielike, so distracted she was certain he hadn't heard her. But that evening as she sped home from work, she'd nearly convinced herself she'd come home to Andrew standing in the kitchen, laying out plates, a blooming bunch of pink lilies on the table. Three months ago, this was the man he'd been. Without nagging or prompting. Andrew would kiss her parents on the cheek and wrap his arm around Amy's waist.

As Amy drove home from work, the streets were glossy in the wake of a storm, the sangria sky aglow, and she bubbled with hope. But the inside of their house was still. Amy was rarely home alone, and this time she walked the space, considered the rooms in the absence of her husband, imagined how it might feel if that absence became permanent. The only evidence of him were the water droplets on the shower door and a trace of his cologne in the air.

Her phone chimed, and her heart sputtered. Andrew? But it was her mother, Elena, calling to announce they were passing Fort Lauderdale. Amy had thirty minutes to pop a bottle of chardonnay in the fridge and shower before their arrival. "Actually"—Amy lifted her tone so her mother wouldn't know she was lying—"my shift ran late, and Andrew got called to a client meeting." The lie was grimy. "Can you and Dad pick up some Thai food on your way over?"

When they hung up, Amy pulled up her call log, scanned for Andrew's number. She scrolled back, past the dozens of calls from her colleagues. Her parents. When was the last time she'd spoken to her own husband on the phone?

Amy showered, her blood boiling. She'd had an appointment with Dr. Cassidy the previous Wednesday. Amy had sat in her car in the parking garage beforehand, wrestling her emotions. She wanted Andrew there, holding her hand, but the warm, swimming happiness that fantasy gave her made her despise herself. She'd never needed anyone. Amy had snatched her purse off the passenger seat and jogged to the bank of elevators.

Still, it was Andrew's face that flashed in her mind when Dr. Cassidy confirmed she was, indeed, pregnant.

"It's still very early. There are no guarantees, but we'll check back in a few weeks." Dr. Cassidy beamed. "Like I told you, sometimes these things just take time to happen naturally."

Though she couldn't take credit for anything, the doctor's eyes were fixed on another glowing testimonial for her website, and Amy rested her hand on her abdomen and let Dr. Cassidy bask in her success. Amy would never tell her—or anyone—her pregnancy was attributed to a seedy backdoor shop in Miami.

Then Amy had wept in her car. Waves of elation rolled over her. She'd done it. She was going to be a mom. She'd *won*.

But she longed to share this moment—this joy—with the man who had vowed to stand by her side through better or worse. They'd gone through *worse*; was she weak for aching for him when she got to experience *better*? Her love for him was embedded deep inside her, she realized. Love was sticky, semipermanent. She couldn't just unlove Andrew at will, despite the rage his absence, his indifference, ignited inside her.

So she'd decided to kill two birds with one stone: she'd announce her pregnancy to her parents in person and surprise Andrew with it at the same time. But with Andrew absent from the house, she couldn't break her news. She had to tell him about the pregnancy before she told her parents; it was only right. But he'd robbed her of the gift she'd ached to give her mother.

Amy dressed, and her parents' rental car pulled into the driveway, catching the rosy glow of dusk. Then her house was full again, of voices, of a long hug from her mother, a peck on the cheek from her dad, Thai food wafting from paper bags. The clink of silverware, chardonnay spilling into three glasses.

"Will Andrew make it in time for dinner?" Amy's mother asked as she laid flatware on the table.

"I'm not sure." Amy gave Elena a sweet smile, but mortification raged inside her. And she spotted it: the same look she'd seen in her mother's eyes all those years ago, the same hardening Amy had felt since the evening she saw Andrew's car in that bistro parking lot. Amy hadn't expected the wallop of pain that came with having her suspicions confirmed in her mother. It was mortifying.

Amy allowed herself a tiny sip of chardonnay. Though it was hardly enough to rest on her tongue, guilt rose, but the wine was perfect—cool and crisp.

Andrew was out, doing whatever he did when she was at work, gallivanting about like a man with nothing to lose. It had gone on long enough. It was time to face her husband and his obvious—almost painfully deliberate—deception. A girlfriend? How cliché. But something niggled her. Selfish men had affairs. Dumb, vain men had affairs. That wasn't Andrew. And she still sensed his love for her in the way he examined her when he thought she wasn't looking. This was bigger than a girlfriend.

But unease stirred in her. When she confronted him, would that be the end of their marriage? If it was, would Andrew choose to be a father? Or would he pick whatever drew him to the midlevel restaurants of Lantana?

Amy allowed herself one more sip of chardonnay before she dumped the glass down the drain when her mother's back was turned. She seated herself at the table, piled her plate with noodles. It was time to gather one more piece of evidence, to draw a final, indisputable conclusion. Then she could call it, one way or the other.

After hugging her parents goodbye, Amy backed her car out of the garage and parked it a block away, then walked back to her house under the glow of the moon. Andrew had assumed she was working, that he was free to do whatever he pleased with his evening. And without her car, he wouldn't be aware of her presence in their house until she was ready.

She curled beneath the comforter in the downstairs guest bedroom. Sleep wouldn't come until she heard him. Until it was time.

Andrew's footsteps trudged inside and up to their bedroom just after midnight. Amy waited, adrenaline pumping with each of her heartbeats. *I hope whatever it is, it's worth it, Andrew.*

But for the first time in her life, Amy was frozen with fear. Indecision. When she confronted him, her marriage would be ruined. Her vision for the life she shared with the man she loved would evaporate. Instead, hot tears rushed down her cheeks. Relief. Heartbreak.

Fear.

She sobbed into her pillow with her husband one floor above her, a world away, oblivious to her presence.

CHAPTER THIRTY-TWO

Sunday, May 28
Andrew
1:00 p.m.

Amy hadn't returned from work. Andrew's nerves gnawed at him as he imagined sitting her down and telling her about Max, but he had no other choice. His palms sweated. So when noon passed and her car was still absent from the driveway, he couldn't ignore the relief her absence brought, and Andrew's plan adjusted: he'd promised to visit Kathryn. Maybe in the daylight, speaking to her would offer some clarity on the events of the previous day; then he would break the news that would shatter his wife's world.

He sent Kathryn a text: Did Max come home? Can we talk?

He's still not home, Kathryn responded. Then, yes.

So much promise in one word.

Andrew showered and dressed, then backed from the driveway and watched cars battle for parking spots along the beach and cruised past the now-full public lot. In the sunshine, the beach was a different universe from the place he'd shared with Max the night before.

Andrew let himself into Kathryn's house. In the kitchen, the table where Max had confronted them sat vacant, the chairs pushed in, uniform. After their conversation on the beach, Max had asked Andrew to let him out of the car at a house a few blocks from Kathryn's, and he'd watched Max's broad shoulders disappear into the night. Andrew clung to the scraps of their conversation beneath the moonlight. Kathryn had twenty years of memories, but these belonged to him.

The roar of the TV floated from Emmy's room, and Kathryn, dressed in a cream sweater with her hair pulled into a messy bun, popped her head into the hallway and ushered him inside. A vanilla candle flickered on her dresser, and Andrew closed the door behind them. A single empty wineglass sat on her nightstand. "How was your night?" he asked.

"I didn't sleep much."

Her bedroom was no longer a strange space to him. Andrew came to the end of her bed and sat down. Laced his fingers. "Neither did I. I stared at the ceiling all night. Alone." He'd spent so many nights that way. His house still, silent. Their conversation that evening had pinballed in his mind, and he'd felt Kathryn, his arms around her on her bed. What did he want from life? If there were no consequences, what did he truly desire? The answer burned into him, and he'd punched his pillow and turned onto his other side. His bedroom hadn't felt like his own. Things couldn't continue the way they were. He was flying too close to the sun. But the thought of losing Kathryn gave him that same swimming feeling of an impending panic attack. He knew what his life was without her, and the thought of returning to that existence felt like slipping back into sleep after jerking awake from a nightmare; a fear of returning to a terrifying void. The thought of losing Amy itched. But he'd gotten a glimpse of the life he and Kathryn had planned. And he could give Max what he never had, a father who stood by him. He was standing at the precipice of something, and whichever way he favored, one side would bloom, while the other would be reduced to ash.

In Kathryn's room, Andrew beckoned for her to come closer. When she did, he reached out and took her hands in his. "Kathryn, where do we go from here?" Kathryn drooped, uneasy. Andrew dropped her hands and rose. "I'm here. With you. I shouldn't be doing this, I know that."

"Drew . . ." Trepidation laced her tone.

Kathryn eyed him, taking one tiny step back. Without thinking, Andrew reached for her, and when he did, Kathryn fell into his arms, and he wrapped them around her, as if pulling her closer could somehow shield them from the reality of their lives, from everything that was keeping them apart. When he pulled back slightly, she met his eyes, and without taking a second to think, he met her lips with his. Her response was immediate; she surrendered, parting her lips, and he drew her in greedily. Fire had sparked between them the moment he met her eyes at Starbucks and had grown with every hug, every secretive phone call, every smile they'd shared; now it ignited, raged between them.

They moved as one, took a step closer to her bed, where his mouth broke away from hers momentarily, pressing her against the bedpost as he slipped a hand under her sweater, her skin velvety and warm. He pulled her sweater over her head, losing sight of her for a moment, and when she came back into view, her mouth met his again. He kissed down her neck and chest, and she sighed a soft, desperate noise of encouragement. Kathryn gripped his hair before she ran her hands down his body, stopping where he was hard beneath his jeans. She reached for his belt.

A flash in his mind. Amy. Sunlight glinting off his grill in the backyard. His home. The beep of Amy's car when she came through the door, chased by a swell of relief that she'd returned safely.

Andrew gasped and jerked back. "Kathryn, stop." Her hands fell away, and he took another step backward. "We can't." He fastened his belt with trembling hands.

Kathryn covered herself with one hand and snatched her sweater off the bed with the other before she yanked it over her head. "Why not, Andrew?"

"Because I'm *married*."

Her face flushed. "And? That didn't matter a moment ago. It hasn't stopped you from anything you've done over the last few months."

An exasperated sigh burst from him when Kathryn struck the raw nerve reserved for his guilt. She was right. But he couldn't lose Amy. "That's not fair. You don't know the whole story." Arousal coursed through him. He'd never wanted someone so badly, like if he didn't have her, he might burst. Desire was chased by white-hot frustration.

"You can't honestly tell me you don't feel anything here," Kathryn spat. "Like you said, you call me every time your wife leaves the house. You two must be *blissful* if you're spending all your time with me."

Kathryn's words prodded him again. She'd reduced his actions down to the core of his dirty secret, that he desired her. And that his wife's absence stung. "Is this what you wanted all along?" he demanded. "After all this time you want me again?"

Andrew watched her face bloom with anger. "Don't put this on me," she cried. "I didn't expect to run into you that morning. But when I did, I knew it was time. I owed you an explanation about our son. Our past. But you wanted to get together again and again each week. I never told you to hide this from your wife—that was your choice. I'm not with anyone, Andrew. You are. I never pushed you into this."

"It's not that simple," Andrew snapped, pacing. That familiar tingle, electricity dancing in his fingertips. "She's . . . she's never there. And you are."

Kathryn's lips parted. "So I'm a convenience to you?"

"No. I—there's something here, Kathryn. I feel it, and I know you feel it, too."

Kathryn's jaw hardened in confirmation. Battling images. He wanted her. And part of him feared this more than he'd ever feared anything. But it was impossible. A fantasy. The hurt he'd cause was too much to fathom. If she'd stayed with him, life would have been different.

Exasperation spiked in him. "You just left one day. You *disappeared.* I deserved to know you were pregnant, and you had a million opportunities to tell me. There were days when you thought about it—I know—don't tell me you didn't." He paced, his molten rage flowing through his entire body.

Tears spilled from Kathryn's round eyes, but she stared, absorbed each blow he dealt, like she'd been waiting for it for decades.

"When he was *born* you didn't call me. Just because you had room-mates or friends or whatever, you didn't think I should know?"

Kathryn's eyes broke away when Andrew mentioned Max's birth. He'd struck a nerve.

"You stole twenty years from me. Every milestone, every birthday. All of it. You made a conscious *choice* to keep all this from me. You made that decision for all three of us, and I can never get that back. And why? I wasn't a drunk—at least not at that point. I didn't hit you. I would have made a good father. I would have supported both of you. Always. I just don't get it."

"I'm sorry." Kathryn's shoulders quivered as she cried. "You're right."

"I know I'm fucking right." His pace quickened. "You act like I shouldn't have moved on, which is absurd. You chose to stop loving me all those years ago, and now you make me feel bad because I built a life, because I found someone to spend it with." His feet paused on the rug, and he turned to face her. "Then, one day, you're standing right in front of me again, out of nowhere. And *God*, you're beautiful. And yes, I've enjoyed our time together. It's so *easy* between us. But that's not our reality, and now other people stand to get hurt here. I love my wife." He ran a drenched palm down his face. "And I don't know if I've loved you this whole time or if I fell in love with you all over again, but all I know is I now find myself in the impossible situation of being in love with you, too, Kathryn."

Kathryn looked up at him, defeated and distraught, and whispered, "I love you, Andrew."

The words rang in the room.

"But you made your choices," Andrew said. "And there are no sec-ond chances. It's twenty years too late for us."

Kathryn swallowed through her tears, then tugged the sleeves of her sweater over her hands. Her voice was hard when she spoke. "Then there's your answer. Go home to your wife. This is your clean break, and I'll never breathe a word. You can pretend none of this ever happened, that Max and I don't exist. I won't call you. When I see you at Publix, you'll just be another fucking stranger to me." Crimson blotches dotted her neck.

Her words severed his patience like the snap of a frayed rope, and he met her cold stare. This was familiar, someone shoving him away. He shoved back. "Fine—that's exactly what I want." He opened his hands. Closed them. That tickle spreading. His face, hot, while his body trembled. "For you, for all of this, to just disappear." He waved an arm at the space around them and saw Kathryn flinch.

He'd meant for the words to hurt her—to slice into the raw place where her words had stabbed him—but the reality of what he'd said—of letting Kathryn go, of letting Max go—came into focus; the tingle surged up his limbs, gripping his throat, and a gray, swimming sensation filled his vision, like he'd slipped beneath murky water. Without his medication, the feeling was overpowering, and Andrew tried to draw a breath, tried to chase away the chills shaking his body, to grasp for control.

Something you can see: the fear emanating from Kathryn's eyes; the heartbreak, the loneliness, all she'd ever known.

Something you can hear: the blood rushing in and out of his shattered heart.

Something you can taste: bile, metal, salt.

"If that's what you want, then leave." Kathryn's voice a brash whisper.

"Kathryn—"

"Leave!" she shouted, her voice breaking as tears spilled down her face. "Get out of my house right now! Don't ever speak to me or my son again."

Color slipped back into Andrew's vision, anger overriding his panic. He threw his hands up. "No, not yet. Tell me *why!*" His voice boomed. "It's all I've wanted to know for twenty years. Tell me what's wrong with me. Tell me why you chose this instead of the life we planned—"

"Because I didn't think he was yours!"

Andrew stopped, rooted to the floor, and squared his body to face her. "What do you mean?"

Kathryn crumpled, tears rushing down her face. "I'm so sorry."

Andrew stared, mouth ajar. "Not mine. Then *who?*"

Kathryn shook her head. "I . . . wasn't sure. It could have been you. But . . ."

"Who else?" Andrew's voice reverberated off every surface.

Kathryn hung her head and choked a sob.

Pieces snapped together in Andrew's mind; things that hadn't made sense suddenly came into focus; old memories took on new meaning. He locked on to her eyes as scalding, poisonous rage flooded every cell in his body. "Nick?"

It couldn't be true. His brain rejected the thought.

But Kathryn sat before him, racked with sobs, wordlessly confessing the things that had been right there in front of him the entire time, things he was too blind to see. "When?" Andrew shouted. "Were you two"—he couldn't say the word, couldn't think it—"the entire time we were living together?"

Kathryn lifted her gaze. "God, no. Just—" Her voice fell, barely audible. "That Christmas when you went home."

"Just the once?"

Kathryn's eyes broke away, her cheeks slick with tears, and shook her head. Subtle, but speaking volumes of jagged truth. "And on your birthday."

Andrew froze, statue still. Cold betrayal washed through him.

Kathryn broke, her body trembling with sobs. "Andrew—"

"Don't." He held up a hand. A suffocating tension filled the room. Reality blurred, his entire life a kaleidoscope, shaken. "I need to get out of here." His words were barely audible. "I need to never see your face again."

Andrew turned and marched out the door. His movements were automatic; he didn't think as he started his car, the engine roaring to life. His pulse ticked in his ears as he backed into the street and shifted into drive. Stevie Nicks's voice blared from the radio, and Andrew stared at the screen for a moment, taking in the words as she sang about picking up the pieces and going home.

Kathryn. Nick. Since the very beginning.

It was as if Stevie's voice—as if the entire universe—was mocking him for his blindness. He punched the radio until the music abruptly muted, leaving the screen broken, distorted with blobs of black. Andrew didn't care, he wrapped his hands around the steering wheel and sped up the street.

CHAPTER THIRTY-THREE

2:00 p.m.
Kathryn

Shame, embarrassment, loss—they hit Kathryn in waves. She relived it all, every word shot back and forth.

Andrew had transformed the instant the depths of her betrayal seeped in; his eyes grew hard, ice blue, and she hardly recognized him. For a moment, she thought he might do something—smash a lamp or punch the wall, or worse, hurt her—but he hadn't. Instead, with all the anger knocked out of him by her confession, he'd walked away from her life for the last time. She'd finally lost him, just as she'd always known she would.

The sharp chime of her phone jarred her from her thoughts. A flicker of hope as she reached across her bed to collect it. Maybe Andrew was willing to let her explain.

Javier Quintero. Apprehension swelled, and she cleared her throat. "Hello?"

"Kathryn?" Javi's voice, hesitant.

Kathryn's pulse doubled. "Javi? What's wrong?"

"I'm not trying to scare you; I just wanted—is Max home? He got pretty messed up. I haven't seen him like that in a while, and when I woke up, he was gone. His car is gone. He's not answering his phone. I'm worried."

"I'll call you back." Kathryn hung up and rushed down the hall, where she threw Max's bedroom door open, hoping to see him sleeping off a hangover under his comforter, but his bed was neat, his room eerily still. Her heart thudded. Javi would never betray Max; if he was concerned enough to call, she needed to find Max quickly.

Her call went straight to voicemail in her trembling hands.

"Emmy!" Kathryn dashed across the hall and swung the door open. "Have you heard from Max?" she yelled over the TV.

Emmy scrambled for the remote, muted the TV. "No, why—what's wrong?"

"He took off from Javi's early this morning."

Emmy's eyes widened.

"His phone is off."

Emmy covered her mouth, the fear in her expression fueling the sinking feeling in Kathryn's gut.

"I'm going to drive up Ocean to look for his car. And I'll call the hospitals." Kathryn pointed a finger at Emmy. "Get Javi, go anywhere else you think he might be."

Emmy jumped from bed and pushed her feet into her sandals.

"If you find him, if you hear anything, call me immediately." Kathryn walked away, leaving Emmy's bedroom door ajar, then darted down the staircase and ran out the door.

CHAPTER THIRTY-FOUR

2:15 p.m.
Andrew

In the stretch between Kathryn's house and his own, Andrew braced to confess his sins to his wife. Knowing the full extent of what had transpired with Kathryn would crush her, but he had to tell her about Max. Amy was the only person he had in his corner, the only one who hadn't lied to him. His stomach twisted for having betrayed her. He had to set things right.

With each passing mile, his anger roiled. Nick. Kathryn. It was right there the whole time, and he'd been blind to it—maybe he hadn't wanted to see what was laid out in front of him. Amy's car was in the garage, where it hadn't been that morning. He parked and marched up the steps, tremors still quaking his hands after Kathryn's confession.

"Amy?" he called, his voice echoing into the silence. A cool unease stirred in the house, and his stomach dropped. The hair on the back of his neck prickled. Andrew scanned the downstairs. The appliances hummed against the smooth tile and white walls.

He took the stairs two at a time. Andrew saw her, sitting on the bed in the dark, her back to him. She didn't move when he entered. "Amy? Why didn't you answer me?"

Amy turned her head to the side. She'd been crying. Ice coursed from Andrew's head to his fingertips. He scrambled through a list of all the things she could have found. Had she gotten ahold of his phone while he was asleep? His mind raced with horror at the thought of Amy reading his text messages. He couldn't think of any in particular that were incriminating, but he'd gotten careless. Had someone they knew seen him out with Kathryn? "Amy—"

She rounded on him, her face cold, hard. Expressionless. "Who is she?"

Andrew held his wife's gaze, while two and a half months of dinners and laughter with Kathryn spun in his mind. His hands in her hair, kissing her. He swallowed, painful, like a jagged rock was lodged in his throat.

A flare of rage rushed across Amy's face, and she screamed, "Who is she?"

"Amy—it's not what you think." Stupid. The most clichéd line he could deliver. The words of a guilty man.

"Is it someone you work with?" Amy demanded.

Andrew shook his head. "No. No. It's not like that."

"You're a fucking asshole."

Andrew had never heard Amy speak this way, and her words struck him. She darted past him and went down the stairs, her small feet barely making a sound on the steps.

Andrew turned and trailed her but stopped on the landing at the top of the stairs. "I need you to listen to me," he called.

"Leave me the fuck alone." Amy disappeared into the kitchen.

Andrew bounded down the stairs until they came face-to-face in front of the island. The same location as their first fight. "That's not fair—you won't even give me a chance to explain."

"You don't even try to hide it." Amy was screaming. Unglued. "You stay out late. 'Chicken wings and a Heat game'?" She mocked his voice. "You think I'm stupid."

"I don't think you're stupid—"

"You didn't show up last night." Rage was splashed across her face. "I told you weeks ago my parents were coming to dinner. And you didn't even dignify me with an excuse. Do you know how embarrassing it is to know my husband doesn't even care enough to *lie* to me?"

Dread spread, a cold, slow poison. His memory flashed back to the morning Amy had mentioned her parents were coming into town. She hadn't said anything to him about it since. "You set me up."

"Set you up? I told you we had plans, and you were too distracted with—whatever it is you do—to show up."

Mortification bloomed, blending into a toxic mix with Kathryn and Nick's deception. With his own. The gradient layers of their lies, and his sympathetic nervous system in overdrive, his body ticking like a faulty engine, ready to blow.

"What is it about me, Andrew? What am I missing here? I picked out this house for you. For us. I stuck myself with needles so I could have a family. With you."

Needles?

Amy stabbed a finger to her chest. "I give you all of me, literally—my body, my life, *all of me*. I'm faithful to you and I put you first—"

"You do *not* put me first. You put your job first, and you always have."

Amy's eyes widened.

But the gates opened and all reason slipped away. He stepped closer, the crosshairs narrowed on his wife. "You don't want a family with me; you want me to get you pregnant. There's a difference. I tried to warn you. It's not a good idea. Depression and addiction are hereditary. And my father—not perfect fucking Ken doll Craig, my real father—was an alcoholic. And so was I. I wouldn't eat for days so I could get as fucked up as possible. I was suicidal. I wanted to die, and I would have if Nick and my parents hadn't intervened. When I got sober, I started having debilitating panic attacks. I spent our marriage heavily medicated, and you knew that. But you wanted a trophy husband. And I look the part, don't I?" He waved his arms. "I look good in a suit at your boring benefit dinners. I do as I'm told. You want your perfect house and your perfect husband, then a perfect baby—but what if it's not all so perfect, Amy? What if your kid is fucked up like I am; are you going to bury yourself in work and avoid him like you avoid me?"

Max's face, lost and distant, illuminated by the moonlight, sat forefront in Andrew's mind.

Amy recoiled, like she was disgusted by the very sight of him. "What's gotten into you? You should've told me all of this."

Andrew narrowed the gap between them. "I told you I wanted to consider adoption, but that didn't fit your vision of your picture-perfect life, so you blew me off. Like you blew me off when I wanted to grow in my career. Why, so you can run off seventy hours a week and leave me here with a baby, in this empty fucking *mausoleum* of a house?" His voice thundered on the hard surfaces of the kitchen. "Here's a thought: maybe your body refuses to give you a baby because it knows you're too selfish—too *cold*."

A sharp gasp from Amy.

Then, deafening silence.

Sick, instant regret crept into Andrew. His thoughts shifted, and he saw Amy not as the target of his anger, not as a roadblock, and not as a powerful professional. She'd always been tough—stronger than he'd ever be—but now she looked small, delicate, destroyed.

By his words.

Amy was right. She'd given him all of herself. Everything she had, everything she'd worked for, she'd committed to sharing with him. And he'd lied to her, sneaked around behind her back. He'd let himself fall in love with another woman. He was worse than Kathryn. Worse than Nick.

"We're done, Andrew," Amy whispered.

Ice pumped his veins. No, if she'd just let him explain, tell her about Max, tell her what happened with Kathryn all those years ago. "Amy, please . . ."

"I hope it was worth it."

"No." He drew a breath, a sharp pain in his windpipe. "I need you to listen. There's so much more to this than you know." Then the tingle started in his fingers, and at the crown of his head, vibrating downward, clenching his throat, his diaphragm. This time, he was too weak to fight it.

Amy kept her eyes frozen on him, and she gave a nod. "Yes, there is much more to this than you know." A flicker of a smile on her lips. "I want you gone when I get home from work tonight."

Amy turned and marched up the stairs. Andrew clutched the countertop, tried to suck in a breath, jagged tearing ripping apart his rib cage. He doubled over, straining to form his wife's name on his lips. But she was already gone.

CHAPTER THIRTY-FIVE

2:15 p.m.
Emmy

Emmy jogged the half mile to her father's house and spotted Max's car in the driveway. A cocktail of relief and apprehension rose in her chest. With trembling hands, she worked the keypad and stepped inside. The house was dark. Deathly still.

"Max?" Her voice echoed in the upper levels. The wood floor creaked underfoot as she made her way through the dining room. At first, nothing seemed out of place, and then she spotted it: a crumpled blue blanket on the couch by the sunporch window, the shape of a person underneath. The shades were drawn. Emmy pulled the fabric aside, exposing the creamy skin of his shoulder, cold and clammy to her touch. "Max, are you okay?"

With a groan, Max's head rolled to the side, his eyes red and irritated, and in a raspy whisper, he said, "I feel like shit."

Emmy dropped onto the couch and ran her hand down his back, which was damp with sweat. "How much did you drink?"

"Just let me be," he groaned.

"You know I'm not going to do that." His fingers found hers. It felt like a lifetime had passed since she'd touched him. "Let me help. I'll get you some water and run you a bath."

Max squeezed her hand.

In the bathroom upstairs, Emmy turned on the faucet, letting the water spill into the basin. "Brush your teeth," she instructed, clouds of steam rising in the room, and Max complied. She'd never seen him look so tired, like he'd aged five years overnight.

When the tub was full, Max slipped into the warm, bubbly water and closed his eyes, and Emmy slid down to sit on the tile beside him, her back against the wall. Max was safe. He was there with her. But apprehension welled; she'd heard Andrew and Kathryn fighting. Would things ever be good for any of them again? "Where are your clothes?"

"Downstairs in the dryer."

"What the hell happened today? Javi called when you went missing. Kathryn is out looking for you. We need to call them; everyone's worried."

"My phone is dead. Don't call my mom yet. I don't want her to see me like this." The water sloshed as Max ran a hand down his face, then shut his eyes. "I'm sorry being with me isn't like your books. No happy ending here." He opened his eyes to look at her for a brief second before his gaze went unfocused. He closed them again.

"You're still high." Emmy hung her head. "Jesus, Max. What did you take?" His jaw tensed. "Max, please."

"Just something to help me sleep," he whispered. Max's arm hung off the side of the tub, and bubbles dripped from his fingertips. "Right before you got here."

Emmy pressed her forehead to the cold porcelain and closed her eyes. This was worse than she thought. And she couldn't escape it. She was caught deep in the web of the ugliest side of love.

CHAPTER THIRTY-SIX

2:30 p.m.
Kathryn

Kathryn pounded on Nick's front door until he yanked it open. "She lives," he said, and frowned. "Jesus, what happened to you?"

Kathryn knew it was clear she'd been crying. "I need your help," she pleaded. "Max is missing."

Nick turned away, and Kathryn followed him inside. The room was stale in the flickering light of the TV; dishes sat in the sink and take-out containers littered the counter. Nick dropped onto the couch, his eyes locked on a screeching car chase on the screen. "Okay." He drained his half-empty beer in one swallow. "What do you want me to do about it?"

Panic buzzed through her. Every minute was a waste. "Please, Nick. You know where he hangs out. Do you have any idea where he might be?"

Nick answered with a grunt. "Sorry, I'm swamped."

"Really, Nick?" Kathryn lifted her chin. Nick was paler than she remembered, and his face had gone unshaven for days. "You're just sitting in this dump, drinking by yourself?"

Nick's eyes snapped to her. "I got fired. The discrepancies in the report of your kid's accident were my second strike." His voice was flat, and Kathryn's anxiety ticked up notches with each long, stifling second. "So forgive me if I don't want to go chase him around town today." On the TV, two cars collided and burst into flames. "Call Drew. Maybe you can do some detective work and solve this one together."

"Nick—"

"Or did you two have a fight?"

The sting of tears threatened her eyes, and she blinked them away.

"Of course you did." He turned back to the TV. "So if you don't need anything else, fetch me a beer on your way out."

Kathryn stood, frozen in place.

Nick rose and brushed past her. He yanked the refrigerator door, glass bottles clanking. "I'm sure Drew'll be by in a little bit to gripe about it." Nick popped his beer cap. "He makes me keep tabs on that shit kid of yours, just like you do." He lifted the bottle to his lips, then shook his head. "If you're half as infatuated with him as he is with you, I don't know what either of you is going to do when his wife finds out, because it's only a matter of time."

Kathryn swallowed. She'd shattered Andrew with her words, had broken his heart—and her own—one final, permanent time.

Nick reassessed. "Unless that's exactly what happened today?" He stepped closer, stopping a few inches from her face, sweat and yeasty alcohol emanating from his body. He reached out and stroked her cheek with the back of his finger, the cool glass bottle brushing her skin, raising gooseflesh. "I don't know what you see in him, anyway. He's spoiled and indecisive, always waffling between one thing or another—is he a drunk or not? Is he in love with his wife, or with you? But you and I, we keep coming back to each other, can't you see that?"

Nick leaned forward, pushing his lips to hers. Kathryn backed away, putting one hand to his chest. He grabbed her by the wrist, forced her back against the wall. A bolt of pain shot up her arm, along with fear—scorching and primal—in the shock of his sudden violence. Fire blazed behind his eyes, his hand, a viselike grip on her wrist. "Nothing has changed in twenty years, Kathryn." Her wrist seared in agony.

"Get the fuck off me, Nick." Kathryn's adrenaline spiked. She jerked her arm and slipped from his grip. "You need to get your shit together," she said, her voice shaking. She threw the door open and bolted out into the courtyard, toward her car. An explosion of a glass bottle cracked against a wall from inside the apartment.

CHAPTER THIRTY-SEVEN

3:30 p.m.
Andrew

Andrew paced the first floor. The only sound in the house was the soft hum of the air conditioner and his aimless footsteps. His panic attack had finally receded, and he was empty. Amy was still locked upstairs.

He considered going for a run. The hot, salty air and pounding of his heart always made him feel in control. The beach was the place where he found peace. But he didn't deserve peace; he deserved to wallow in the misery he'd created, and exhaustion ached every fiber of his body. Pacing, he cycled from anger to remorse, guilt to rage, to utter disbelief. His house was pristine—glass and steel—but around him, his life was in ruins. Amy's words spiraled: *We're done*.

And it was his fault. His alone. Sure, if Kathryn had started with the truth about everything back in March, she could have spared everyone a lot of heartache. But he'd gone willingly into her world the moment she'd opened the door to him. The wound Kathryn had left him with two decades before had been ripped wide open and exposed. And now, with her gone, he'd certainly lost Max as well. All of it was splashed with the acid of his best friend's deceit.

When Andrew thought of Nick's decades-long betrayal, his rage seared white hot. The life Andrew lived—his entire existence—had been set in motion by a lie that had finally come to light. But his own selfish actions had cost him his wife, too. The damage was irreversible.

He'd lost everyone he cared about.

Waves of self-loathing, of self-hatred, washed over him, penetrating the deepest layers of his being, where they belonged.

But Amy deserved the truth. Their marriage was over, but she needed to know about Max.

Andrew padded up the stairs and opened the bedroom door to find her lying on her side, facing the far wall. He couldn't tell if she was sleeping or awake. "Amy?"

She didn't answer, just shifted her weight on the mattress. Andrew walked around to her side of the bed, and in the dim light he saw her eyes were open, her cheeks streaked with tears. He sat, placing his hand on her bare foot. "There's something I need to tell you."

Amy propped her head up in her hand. "From here on out, our only communication should be handled through lawyers."

"This is my house, too. Where do you want me to go?" Andrew heard the entitled whininess of his response, and the space between them filled with the obvious answer before Amy spoke it.

"Go back to wherever you spent your time this morning, where you've been spending all your time." Her face twisted with fury. "Go where you keep all your secrets." Her words boomeranged around the room. Andrew watched her anger morph into heartbreak. Fresh tears spilled down her cheeks, and she settled back on the pillow. "Now please leave me alone. I need to check in at the hospital in an hour, and I'm expected to be prepared to perform surgery at a moment's notice. I can't be distracted."

Andrew stood and went to the top of the staircase, his options forking before him.

Without the protective emotional padding of his medication, he'd felt everything that day. The love, the desire, the rage, the betrayal.

And for the first time in what felt like forever, an itch crept in, one he desperately wanted to scratch. He could picture their liquor cabinet with photographic clarity: three bottles of chardonnay lined up beside a bottle of Grey Goose, three-quarters full. Two bottles, one of rum, one of whiskey, the latter still sealed. He'd memorized the labels with startling precision.

There was nothing stopping him from going downstairs, cracking a seal, spilling liquid into one of the fancy crystal tumblers they'd received from some well-intentioned wedding guest who knew nothing of his past, nothing of the monster that existed inside him. The thought of the satisfying burn in his throat made him salivate.

Andrew pounded down the stairs. He passed the kitchen without looking at the liquor cabinet, then sprinted to the garage, where he dropped into the driver's seat and pulled out his phone, smashing the call button next to Nick's name as he reversed out of the driveway.

Nick answered. "Right on time, Drew."

His voice was slurred, and the back of Andrew's neck tingled. Nick was drunk. "Where are you?" Andrew demanded, weaving between lanes of traffic. "We need to talk. Right now."

CHAPTER
THIRTY-EIGHT

4:00 p.m.
Emmy

Emmy fished Max's clothes from the dryer and took them upstairs before she helped him out of the tub. She waited for him to dry himself, then pull on his jeans and T-shirt before she said, "Let's talk."

Max stood with his back to her. His breath rose and fell. Water droplets dripped from his hair onto his shirt, and he nodded.

On the couch downstairs, Max leaned back against the cushions. "Max," Emmy began, and huffed a defeated breath. "All I asked you for was a few weeks. For some time and understanding, and you couldn't handle that. Now you've made an even bigger mess."

Max closed his eyes. "I'm sorry, Em."

"I just want to undo the last twenty-four hours." Her voice wobbled. "To go back to the way we were. I was so happy; we were so happy."

"Me too." His feeble laugh touched a nerve somewhere deep inside her, and she felt her resolve melt. "I love you, Emmy," he whispered. "Most people go their whole lives and don't find what we have. When I thought I was losing you, I lost it."

Emmy leaned in and buried her head in his chest and inhaled his familiar scent, and the soft bubble bath that lingered on his skin. "I love you, and I want you to know that. I hate to see you hurt like this." She took a shaky breath into the familiarity of the warm space under his arm. "But I'm not going to sit here and watch you get drunk and run around and do . . . whatever you've been doing."

Max was still, and Emmy weaved his fingers between hers. His hand was damp. "Listen." She sighed. "I know you haven't had it easy. Your mom has never been honest with you. You've had some shit happen to you that isn't fair. But that's not an excuse, Max. That wasn't a reason to act out the way you did in high school, and it's not a reason to act the way you are now."

Max didn't move.

"Are you awake?"

"Yes." His voice was soft, but he opened his drowsy eyes.

"It's your call. You can get it together, and we'll figure out our lives, or I can walk away. It will kill me—" Her voice broke. "I will never love anyone the way I love you. Nobody will ever love me like you do. But I will *not* sit by and watch you self-destruct."

"Emmy, you're the only thing I want." Max's voice was like gravel.

Tears rolled down her cheeks. "Then don't ruin it. I need you to be stronger. This can't be the way you react when things get hard. I need you to find some direction. I want to figure life out together."

Max's tears spilled down his face. He pulled her close and kissed her softly, their lips salty. "My life would be wasted if I didn't spend the rest of it with you," he whispered.

Emmy nodded, her forehead to his. "We're going to go home and talk to Kathryn. First thing tomorrow, you're going to get help. You're going to go for as long as it takes, and you're going to get better." She started to believe the words as she spoke them. For the first time in a week, a flicker of hope. "And I'm going to wait for you."

Max nodded again, more tears falling down his face.

"I'll wait forever, do you understand?"

Another nod, and a raspy, "Yes."

"But before I met you, I planned to move to Washington alone." She took a long, shaky breath. "And that hasn't changed. I'm leaving on my birthday. And when you're ready, you can join me. But not until you're ready. Because once we're together, I want it to be for life."

She pulled him close, feeling his body tremble as he whispered, "I will, I promise."

"I need to know you're strong enough to handle whatever comes our way. Because there will be times when I'm going to need you to be strong when I'm not. I need to know you can handle it. Start by taking care of yourself. Start here."

"I will," he whispered.

"In the meantime, I need to learn to do things on my own so that I can do it by myself if I have to."

"You won't have to. I'll be there. I want the happy ending." He kissed her.

She wrapped her arms around him, and he clutched her to his chest. "Can we stay here for a little while?" he asked. "I'm so tired. I just want some time with you before we have to be apart."

"Yeah, for a little while."

Max drifted off in her arms. Emmy meant everything she'd said; she'd never love anyone the way she loved Max, and she had no doubt he loved her more than anything else in the world. She'd take him back into her life when he recovered; she'd be ready for him. A glimmer of hope existed for their future. She had to be prepared in case he failed. But in that moment, all she could do was hold his body to hers.

CHAPTER
THIRTY-NINE

4:00 p.m.
Amy

From the bedroom, Amy had heard Andrew slam the door to the garage. He'd sped down Ocean Avenue, away from her, maybe for the last time. This house was her castle, her monument to the life she'd built—and it was all crumbling down.

She'd stayed awake most of the night imagining when, and how, she'd confront him. Should she go upstairs, wake him? Or sneak his phone from the nightstand, gather evidence?

She'd drifted off in the early-morning hours, then woken late, after noon, and decided to confront Andrew then. They were adults, she thought as she climbed the stairs. But their bed was vacant, and the audacity of Andrew's behavior struck her. She'd been mistaken, she realized, mortified. He didn't love her. He was the type of simple, dumb man who'd had the audacity to have an affair. He'd been out with *her* the night before, and he was out with her again?

What did this woman give him that she didn't? Who was this woman who had the balls to pursue a married man?

Amy stopped herself. It was easy to hate the woman, but that took the blame off Andrew too easily.

He'd come home midafternoon, his eyes red, his energy like a live wire. It wasn't the fight Amy had expected; it wasn't like in the movies when characters confronted their cheating spouses and tossed their belongings from an upper window before weeping into a pint of Ben & Jerry's. She hadn't anticipated the agony she'd feel the moment he confirmed her suspicions. And she certainly hadn't expected the swell of love she felt for him when he'd gaped at her, as if it hurt him to hurt her, as if all of this stemmed not from lust or selfishness, but from some unresolved wound he'd been concealing. Her mind spun.

Now, in his absence, the house was suffocating. Amy waited, expecting an emotional breakdown. She expected to sob, to cry, to let go. She'd assumed her anger might guide her when she confronted him, would power her through the necessary steps to sever their relationship. Instead, she was empty. The idea of being alone with her thoughts—with the certain tidal wave of crippling emotion sure to arrive shortly—terrified her. She didn't have anyone to call, and even if she did, she had no interest in discussing Andrew's transgressions with anyone.

The room was dark; she'd tugged the curtains closed when she'd retreated to the bedroom after their fight, but sunlight peeked through a gap in the fabric, the final hours of a beautiful sunny Sunday. The beaches and restaurants were no doubt packed with people, oblivious that Amy was living the worst day of her life. She craved nightfall, for those people to retreat back to their homes, for the day to be over.

Amy glanced at the clock. She needed to check in at the hospital, needed to be ready to take control of the trauma ward, buzzing with fifty or so bodies all focused on one goal, all looking to her for direction. Somehow it seemed easier than the dissolution of her marriage.

Amy went into the bathroom, flicked on the light, appraised herself in the mirror. Her face was blotchy, eyes swollen. She blew her nose and ran cool water from the tap, then washed her face and smoothed cream onto her cheeks. After brushing her hair, she pulled it into a ponytail. There was work to be done, and she wasn't going to let anyone get in her way.

CHAPTER FORTY

4:15 p.m.
Andrew

Shattered glass sparkled in a pool of yellow beer on the tile inside the door of Nick's apartment. "What the fuck is this mess?" Andrew barked.

"You can thank your girlfriend for that," Nick spat, walking toward the kitchen.

Andrew sidestepped the puddle, the shards of glass and stench of stale beer kindling to his rage. His patience with everyone in his life had all but expired, and Nick's mention of Kathryn set his anger to a boil. His quick strides closed the distance between Nick and himself. "You're supposed to be my best friend, Nick. And you let me live a lie—you let me *humiliate* myself—for my entire fucking life."

Nick's eyes locked on Andrew's. "It's about time you saw what was right in front of your face."

An image of Nick with Kathryn flashed through Andrew's mind. "You've made me feel like a fuckup for all this time—"

"You were always so fucking oblivious," Nick shot back. "I tried so hard with you, with both of you. But you know what I realized a few weeks ago? Neither of you ever gave a shit about me unless you wanted something. At least I got to *fuck* Kathryn. But you? You're so self-absorbed, so wrapped up in your own bullshit—"

Andrew grabbed Nick by his shirt, pushing him back against the kitchen counter. "Did you move to Delray for her?"

"What is it to you?" Nick barked.

"What did you think was going to happen? Did you think you'd get a job here and she'd fall in love with you?"

"Fuck you, Andrew!" He saw it in Nick's eyes, what he'd been blind to all along: his jealousy. It was all-consuming. His best friend was in love with Kathryn Moretti.

Andrew suddenly understood why Nick hated that Max looked so much like him: he was a reminder of everything Nick couldn't have. "You didn't learn about Max two years ago. You knew this whole time. You thought he was yours, didn't you?"

"I knew he was your little clone the second I saw him. Then he became a drunk, acting like a weak, spoiled little shit, just like you did—" Andrew's grip tightened, his knuckles white, but Nick didn't stop. "You're just a spoiled rich kid who went on a binge when your girlfriend fucked your best friend and then took off—"

Andrew shoved Nick, who stumbled back into the kitchen, knocking a cluster of empty beer bottles off the counter. Glass shattered around them. "You two fucking deserve each other," Nick spat.

They were interrupted by Andrew's phone. Andrew thrust his hand into his pocket, and both men looked at the screen. *Kathryn.* Andrew sighed and took a few steps back, leaving the argument hanging between them.

Andrew answered. "Kathryn?"

"Andrew." Her voice was breathless. "It's Max. Emmy called me. Something's wrong with him. They're at her father's house down on the beach. I need you to go help her, see what's going on. I drove up north, where he likes to go. I thought he might've gotten into an accident again. I'm turning around now, and I'll get there as fast as I can, but I need you to go over there—228 Ocean."

Andrew had never heard Kathryn's voice sound this way, desperate and scared. His feet were already crunching over the broken glass. He darted out the door into the sunlight.

He didn't see Nick behind him until Nick bellowed, "Where the fuck are you going? What's wrong with Kat?"

Andrew yanked his car door. The engine roared to life, and he grabbed his seat belt. "It's not Kathryn, it's Max."

Nick pulled the passenger door and dropped into the seat beside him. Andrew met Nick's bloodshot eyes. There was no time to fight with Nick. Andrew slammed his door and shifted into reverse. He sped along Ocean Avenue, the tension in the car palpable as he scanned the heavy gates, searching for the address Emmy had given them. His eyes fell on the brass numbers 228 peeking between the trees, and he slammed on his brakes, then made an abrupt turn through the open gate. It was only a few miles from where he lived, maybe just short of the distance he regularly ran, but he'd never noticed it.

Andrew took in the towering three-story house. This was where Kathryn and Max had lived. All the windows were dark except for one on the second floor. Andrew opened the back door, which Emmy had left unlocked, and Nick followed him inside, into the kitchen.

"Max, Emmy?" Andrew called out. They passed into the dining room.

Emmy came down the stairwell, her face pale in the low light. "He's upstairs. Follow me."

At the top of the wooden staircase, a triangle of light poured into the hallway. Emmy entered the bathroom first, followed by Andrew, then Nick. Max was slumped next to the bathtub, eyes closed, his head resting on his hand on the pristine white porcelain. He was pale, sweat seeping through his shirt. Andrew's pulse quickened, and he knelt to jerk Max's shoulder. "Max?" Max's limp body shook under Andrew's hand. Andrew's palms itched, panic spiking. He turned to Emmy. "How long has he been unconscious?"

"I don't know. He was talking to me before, but he wasn't himself. So I called Kathryn." Emmy's voice was rushed but small. "I thought he was just sleepy. Hungover, maybe. But then he came up here and threw up. And then he passed out, just before you got here, and I couldn't wake him up . . . Is he going to be okay?"

"Max?" Andrew said his name forcefully, then lifted his wrist off the cold tile and found a weak pulse. Max was breathing, Andrew noted, but his skin was cool. "What did he take?" Andrew demanded.

"Javier said Oxys, probably . . . Should I—should I call someone?"

"When did he take them?" Andrew looked from Max, to Emmy, then back again.

"An hour or so ago, maybe. But he could've taken more when I went to get him a towel, or when I went to get his clothes from the dryer." Her voice faded before she whispered a lost, "I don't know."

Andrew turned to Emmy. "Yes, go downstairs. Call 911. Make sure the front gate is open. We need help. Fast."

Emmy froze, her eyes wide, and she turned from Andrew to Nick. Nick stared down at Max but said nothing. Max's eyes fluttered, a quick flash of blue; then they closed again.

"Max." Andrew shook Max harder but got no response. He turned to Emmy and cried, "Now, Emmy. Hurry."

Emmy sprinted down the stairs, and Andrew turned back to Max, trying to lift his head. He shook Max and called his name, then turned to Nick, desperate. "Nick, I need help. What do I do?"

Nick jerked a shoulder. "There's nothing you can do. He's as good as dead."

Andrew's head snapped up. "No. He has a pulse, he's in and out of consciousness. He's overdosed, and he needs help quickly. Should I do CPR?"

Nick's footsteps shuffled on the tile, unsteady. "What a surprise," he slurred.

"Nick, please," Andrew pleaded.

"I should've seen this shit coming. I guess he really is your kid, Drew." Nick swayed. "Not like there was any question."

A dizzying spike of panic. Nick wouldn't be any help, as drunk as he was. "Nick, if we don't help him, he could die. I need you to tell me what to do here."

"You were the only one she ever wanted," Nick muttered.

"Nick—"

"I was never anything more than a distraction."

"This isn't about Kathryn. Focus, I need your help!"

"That's all she ever wanted. And you, too—you only wanted what you could take from me." Nick swayed again, taking his hand off the doorframe.

Andrew spun back to his son. Where were the paramedics?

A laugh rose from Nick, small and hollow, and a chill ratcheted through Andrew. "Yeah, Drew, I'll help. I'm always around to help. I'll help put an end to all this bullshit." Nick reached into his holster, took his firearm off his belt, and aimed directly at Andrew.

The bathroom spun, a dizzying sensation Andrew numbly recalled only from the darkest moments of a drunken haze. But this was different, raw fear. "Nick." He spoke his best friend's name in a whisper and met his eyes. "What are you doing?" His pulse ticked, white-hot panic rising in his limbs, and he held out his palms. "Please. Put the gun down and let's talk about this. Max needs help."

Nick turned the gun from Andrew, then aimed at Max, calm and with intention. The room exploded with an earsplitting noise.

A scream cut the air, and it took Andrew a moment to gather the scream had come from himself before he dropped to his knees, ears ringing. He crawled across the floor toward Max. Blood poured from the red spot that appeared on Max's side and pooled onto the black-and-white tile floor. Andrew grasped his son and yanked him into his lap. Thoughts boomed in his mind like fireworks, millions of shards of useless information he'd once received, first aid in an emergency. It all slipped away from him, and Andrew grasped only two thoughts: press on the wound, stop the bleeding. He was helpless as he lifted Max's shirt. A small hole just above Max's waistband, like a tiny open mouth, spewing blood. Andrew laid his palm over it and pressed into his son's flesh, blood oozing between his fingers.

A flash of movement caught Andrew's attention, and he looked to Nick, who now backed up to the doorframe, his eyes round with horror.

"What the fuck, Nick?" Andrew bellowed.

"I'm sorry, Andrew. I'm sorry." Nick's voice came out in no more than a whisper.

Andrew clutched Max and watched Nick back away from them. In the hallway, flashing red and blue lights appeared, faint on the wall.

"I'm so sorry." Nick's voice came from the doorway. His hands trembled, and he lifted the gun one more time.

"Nick—" Andrew screamed.

The shot rang out, silencing the beach house.

CHAPTER FORTY-ONE

5:00 p.m.
Emmy

Three men in the house. Two shots—Emmy screamed these words into the receiver, and an eternity passed while she waited, helpless. She looked up at the house. She had to go in. Had to see what had happened. Max was inside.

Two shots.

The wail of a siren sailed over the trees, and an ambulance sped into the driveway, spraying gravel behind it. Then it seemed every emergency vehicle in the area trailed behind the ambulance, cars flying under her father's old willow tree, officers jumping from their cars, guns drawn. A mass of bodies dressed in black moved across the driveway, the world bathed in oscillating blue and red. Her heart thudded in her ears as she watched her father's castle burst alive with chaos and light.

One of the officers pulled Emmy to the other side of his car and knelt on the gravel beside the guesthouse.

Then she saw him; Andrew came outside, hands above his head as instructed, and a half dozen men ran past him into the house. At the bottom of the steps Andrew allowed the officers to pat him down, and Emmy bolted toward him. Andrew was pale, his body trembling, his shirt soaked with blood, and when her eyes met his face, she knew.

Three men. Two shots.

"Max—" It was all she could say before Andrew pulled her to his body.

"Andrew—" the officer who had grabbed her started.

"Officer Grace." Andrew panted, holding his palms out. "Jake. It's me, Andrew. Nick's friend." He knew the officer. "I have her now. But it's Nick." He waved at the house. "He did this. And I need to get to the hospital as soon as possible. The boy inside, he's my son."

A scratchy voice blared from the officer's radio.

Andrew faced Emmy. "Emmy, get in my car. I need to talk to the police."

She shook her head, still clutching him. "Is Max—tell me!"

"They're going to take him to the hospital. Get in the car. I don't want you to see this."

The hospital. A swell of hope: at the hospital there was help. Emmy climbed into the passenger seat, her breath ragged, the passage of time unreadable as she struggled to catch a glimpse of what was going on, yet terrified of what might be revealed through the pane of glass. Andrew spoke to a cluster of officers and motioned to Emmy inside his car, his movements erratic, panicked. A swell of nausea roiled, and she fought it; she didn't have time to get sick. Whatever Andrew had said, it worked. He jogged toward the car and jumped into the driver's seat just as the ambulance roared onto Ocean Avenue.

"They're coming to the hospital with us. We may not have much time." Andrew's voice wobbled, and he sped down the driveway and turned onto the road without looking in either direction. He flew around the blind corners. A police car trailed behind them.

The flashing lights of the ambulance disappeared into the distance. "Fuck!" Andrew shouted, startling her. Emmy's eyes scanned the road ahead. Every second that passed was a waste.

Andrew's knuckles were white on the wheel. "I need you to call Kathryn."

"I can't." She almost couldn't get the words out.

"Listen. She's on her way here, but I need you to tell her to meet us at Boca General. I don't want her going to that house."

Emmy imagined Kathryn coming onto the scene, seeing the flashing lights as she approached. Her worst nightmare. Andrew took his eyes off the road and turned to her. "Please," he begged.

Emmy nodded, her phone clutched in her hand. In the intersection ahead, the light flicked from yellow to red. Andrew slammed his brakes, and the tires skidded on the pavement, his arm shooting protectively in front of Emmy as they were both thrown forward in their seats. The car came to a stop, just short of the intersection, and he drew his hand back and slapped it on the steering wheel. "Fuck. *Fuck!*"

Seconds dragged on for an eternity.

"Come on!" he shouted.

"Can I ask a question?"

Andrew turned to her, his face sweaty and pale.

"That other man—he's dead, isn't he?"

The fear in Andrew's face, which had not changed since he'd come out of the house, answered for him. "Yes."

"OhmyGod," she cried.

The light switched green, and Andrew floored the car through the intersection.

CHAPTER FORTY-TWO

5:20 p.m.
Amy

Amy jumped as her phone vibrated on her hip, slicing her thoughts. She glanced at the message and, abandoning her cup of coffee, bolted through the heavy wooden door, where the triage nurse met her in the hallway, keeping pace with Amy as she delivered information. "Incoming, two minutes. One male, teen, GSW to the abdomen. Unresponsive. Pulse is faint. BP dropped during transport. Intubated at the scene."

All Amy's experience told her it was grim. "How long since the incident?"

"Less than ten minutes, but he's critical. OR Five is prepped, we'll bring him right there. You need to scrub in immediately. The paramedics said the family and the cops are on their way," the nurse said. "Full moon tonight, it's going to be a shit show."

A flurry of activity from the ambulance entrance caught her attention, and as Amy turned the corner near the walk-in desk, someone shouted her name. Andrew. Her anger flared; he couldn't show up at her job just because they'd had a fight. Their domestic drama didn't belong in the hospital. *You're going to get me fired.*

Andrew called to her again, his voice strange and desperate. Fear gripped her. Had he been drinking? Amy pushed the heavy double doors to the waiting room open, and Andrew ran to her.

"Andrew, are you all right?"

Blood soaked his shirt and pants. "Amy." He grabbed her arms. "A boy just got here. I need you to help him."

"Are you okay—what's going on?"

Andrew was pale and sweaty. "You need to go now," he pleaded.

"Were you in a car accident? They said it was a GSW—"

"Amy, please. Help him." His body was trembling, and his grip on her arms was so tight it hurt.

"Andrew—"

"Andrew!" a woman cried, running through the double doors. "What happened—where is he?" She gasped, anguish painting her face.

A teenage girl ran to them, rushing to answer the woman's questions, but her words were lost, the three talking over one another. Two police officers strode in, and one nodded to the other when they spotted Andrew. Amy had witnessed this scene countless times: desperate families grasping for answers, living the worst moments of their lives, when only hours ago—minutes, perhaps—they'd been blissfully unaware of what awaited them. But her husband didn't fit into this picture.

"He's going into surgery right now—" Andrew stammered. The woman howled, then fell against Andrew's arms, clutched him as if the entire world would fall apart if she let him go. But Amy watched Andrew stiffen; then he turned, locked his gaze onto Amy, like she was the only person in the room. "Amy, please. Fix this. Fix him."

"Dr. Williams." Amy's head snapped back to the doors behind intake. The triage nurse called out, "OR 5 is ready. You need to scrub in."

Amy looked back to Andrew and the women, and the officers behind them. But she had to go. She was being called to her place, to the OR, away from her husband. She turned and ran down the hall.

CHAPTER
FORTY-THREE

The Following January
Andrew

Andrew woke somewhere between night and the dawn of a new day. This had become his routine; the world slept while he was awake.

He slid out from bed and descended the stairs, switching on the light above the stove. When his coffee finished brewing, he clutched his steaming mug and stepped barefoot onto the front stoop, sinking onto the top step. The remaining night air was cool and heavy, and it clung to his skin. Crickets chirped in the yard. On the horizon the inky abyss was beginning to give way to a subtle orange glow, and Andrew watched the light spread wide across the ocean, reaching into the sky. It was then, as he did every morning, that he allowed his mind to drift.

When he was alone, he saw it again; the bathroom of the beach house flickered in his mind like scenes from a movie. His breath grew ragged and his body quivered.

Occasionally he'd reach for his phone to call Nick, a force of habit—he couldn't bring himself to delete Nick's number.

Andrew attended therapy twice per week, sometimes with his wife, mostly by himself. Some days Amy allowed him to address only her in therapy, where she sat with her legs crossed away from him as he confessed to the aching loneliness he'd felt, his perceived abandonment. And of the moral battle he'd lost, of his jealousy and his selfishness. Andrew didn't try to justify his actions, but he couldn't deny it was cathartic to let the events slide away from his conscience. And it happened slowly, the shift between him and Amy. In ebbs and flows, she started to let him in.

There were moments she pitied him, he could see, as she wiped a tear off his face with her thumb. Some days she didn't flinch when he rested his head on her shoulder and set a hand on her growing belly. Sometimes Amy wore the same resigned expression she had when she'd entered the waiting room at the hospital to face Kathryn, Emmy, and himself. The night Amy closed the circle of secrets that existed between all of them.

Amy confessed things, too: that her performance during that surgery had been hindered by everything on her mind, by the image of another woman clutching her husband in the waiting room. And the boy's face on the table before her, illuminated by the brilliant lights, so similar to her husband's that her hands had quivered when she'd lifted her scalpel. How the blade had slipped, a millimeter at most, a catastrophic measure of space. She'd pressed her eyes closed as she recounted those moments, the deluge of blood, the cacophony of warnings from the monitors.

Two weeks after that night, Amy had resigned from Boca General. She'd accepted a position at a private surgery center where there were no surprises, just scheduled, routine procedures. Now she was home with Andrew more often, where Amy gauged him, as if waiting to see if his honesty was a permanent shift. But he didn't falter. His transparency became a near default. He detailed his whereabouts at all times, shared his feelings even if they were raw. He considered her in every action. And, in return, she let him, never pulled away. Sometimes she let him reach for her in bed, even just the brush of his fingertips.

Often, when Andrew couldn't sleep, he went down to the beach and sat on the bench, always sitting to one side, leaving space for someone next to him. There he spoke to Max. To the void beside him, he atoned for everything that had hurt his son, the unfairness of it all, though his words floated away out over the restless waves. But on that warm morning, Andrew didn't dare venture far from the house, in case Amy needed him. Instead, he watched the sun rise, yellow fading to orange to deep, endless blue, bringing with it a new day, a new beginning.

Amy's parents had flown into town, and Amy's induction was scheduled for the following day, when they would finally meet their twins, a boy and a girl. That morning, before he'd slipped from the bedroom, Andrew had considered Amy, sleeping on her side, a pillow between her knees. Under the blanket her full belly was visible, and she'd looked relaxed and peaceful.

For the first time in a long time, Andrew felt a glimmer of excitement. His coworkers had thrown him a half-baked baby shower the previous Friday before he started his leave. They'd plated a sheet cake in the conference room while Andrew withdrew snarky onesies from pastel paper bags. When Andrew shared the gifts in the warm kitchen that evening after work, Amy's mom had stretched two onesies over Amy's belly, and the four of them had laughed, Amy's smile reaching her eyes. Andrew thought of the first time he saw Max, how he'd seen himself in his expressions, in his mannerisms, how he'd loved him then. How he'd love these babies, too.

Andrew waited for Amy to wake. The previous morning, as they'd sat together drinking coffee, Amy's parents shuffling around them, Andrew had regarded his wife as the warm yellow sunlight spread through the kitchen, glowing on her face. He realized then he'd been right about her all along: Amy was the sun coming through after the storm clouds had moved on, even if the storm was one he'd brought on himself.

Emmy

Emmy did leave for Seattle as planned on her eighteenth birthday.

Though nothing was how she'd planned it.

That day, Harper had led Emmy through the front door of the place Emmy had promised she'd never set foot in again: Nora's house. The mansion was as cold as she'd remembered, with the same eerie stillness in the marble hallways. But this visit was different.

In the private waiting room at Boca General, Emmy, Andrew, and Kathryn had huddled together in a teary, bloody haze as they waited for any word on Max's fate, each second ticking by, impossibly long. The group was bound together by secrets, tragedies, influences from the universe none of them could comprehend. The police had returned and shuffled Andrew from the room.

Then, behind her tears, Emmy didn't see her mom, but she heard her. "The security company called me and—" Then Emmy felt Harper's arms around her, pulling her close, their two hearts beating together. "Emmy," Harper sobbed. "Thank God you weren't hurt."

Kathryn wound her arms around Harper, cocooning Emmy between them. Their future was perilous, but Emmy had this. These women. "That poor, sweet boy," Harper said over and over. "I can't believe any of this happened; he didn't deserve this."

Now Harper's arm was wrapped around Emmy's shoulders once more. Inside, Emmy was gutted. The idea of facing the days ahead, let alone a whole lifetime of days, was an impossibility. She let herself be led inside. She knew now that her mother understood how it felt to be broken in a way that could never be repaired.

Nora's heels clicked on the cold, hard floor as she approached. "I heard what happened at the rental house," she said. "Horrible. Just horrible." Nora cocked her chin. "Maybe now you'll consider selling that house, Harper. Nothing good has ever happened there."

"Mother," Harper said, her voice stronger than Emmy had anticipated. Harper gripped Emmy's hand in hers. "We're just here to get my belongings."

Before they'd left the hospital, Emmy had turned to her mother. "I need to get out of here. Out of Florida."

Harper had nodded. "Let's go. The two of us. Like we should've done years ago."

At Nora's house, Emmy and Harper spent the next fifteen minutes yanking Harper's clothing from velvet hangers and stuffing it into a suitcase, which they zipped, then closed in the trunk of Harper's car. They couldn't hear Nora's words, just saw the woman shrink into an insignificant smudge in the rearview mirror as they drove away.

They drove toward Seattle, taking turns at the wheel, letting silent hours settle as miles of pavement disappeared behind them. At a café in Georgia, Emmy set a coffee mug on the counter alongside their two sandwiches. In Colorado, she did the same. "I want a mug from each state," Emmy explained when Harper watched the cashier wrap the mug in butcher paper.

"Your dad used to collect mugs. Did you know that?"

Emmy shook her head. But when they climbed back into the car and drove on, chasing the sunset, Emmy asked how Harper had met Lucas. And about their wedding. And their life together in the sunny years that sat just beyond the horizon of Emmy's memory. Harper obliged. The mugs had opened a door for her to speak about the man Emmy knew only in theory, the man she must have loved before she understood what love was.

When they arrived in Seattle, Harper and Emmy found a second-floor apartment of warm hardwood and exposed brick overlooking a tree-lined street, and Emmy arranged their mugs on a shelf in the kitchen. For the following months, the two women drank frothy lattes each morning while the cool, soothing rain traced the windowpanes.

Emmy and Harper grew to know each other in a way they never had: Emmy realized maybe her parents weren't the source of all her flaws, of all her scars; maybe there was a thread of each of them living inside her. And she'd learned she'd been right about Max from the start, that they had found in one another what Harper and Lucas had: a love that was timeless, fated. Infinite.

A love that had been shattered by tragedy. Her mother had survived. So would she.

Emmy knew this. But still, at night, when she was alone in her room, when missing Max felt like it would physically split her in two, Emmy's tears spilled onto her pillow. She realized how hard it must have been for Harper to raise her while she ached for the man she loved with all her soul, the man she had to find a way to love, despite the unfairness—the *permanence*—of his absence.

CHAPTER FORTY-FOUR

January
Kathryn

Kathryn's car rolled to a stop at the crest of a circular driveway. Though the manicured grounds and bubbling koi pond gave off a resort-like feel, the squat, aggressively modern building made Kathryn uneasy, and she was grateful this would be her final visit. Max's car rolled to a stop beside hers, and Kathryn climbed out into the sunlight. Javi joined her, pocketing Max's car keys. He glanced at his phone. "Noon on the dot."

As if on cue, the pristine glass doors of the clinic glided open, and Max strode down the stone pathway, a backpack slung over his shoulder. Kathryn's heart swelled when she saw him in the beam of sunlight falling between the trees. He looked healthy, even better than he had the week before, when she'd come to attend their therapy sessions. He'd gained weight, and when his eyes fell on Javi, his face split into a grin.

"Maxwell!" Javi called, and jogged to meet Max at the end of the driveway. Javi reached out tentatively. "Can I?"

Max nodded and dropped his bag. "Yeah, yeah, it's all right."

Javi pulled Max into a hug that lifted him off his feet.

Kathryn approached. "You look good," she said.

Max gave her a shy smile. "Thanks."

When Amy had entered the waiting room that fateful night, Kathryn had finally met the woman she'd known only in theory up until that moment. Kathryn's life—her entire reason for being—hung perilously in the balance. Though Amy's face was dewy with sweat, her forehead creased with exhaustion, she was beautiful. Andrew ran to Amy, begged her for the news that would change all their lives. Amy told them how she'd nearly lost Max more than once. How she'd fought to bring him back.

"Thank you" was all Kathryn could form through her sobs.

Amy swept her scrub cap from her head. "This is what I do." Then she'd turned away.

After a grueling month in the hospital—a time Kathryn hardly remembered—Max had spent six months in rehab. Six months of lonely nights in an empty house, longing to hear his noises on the other side of the wall. The rush of the shower. A fork on porcelain. But he was safe, she consoled herself. Healing. And each week, during their therapy sessions, she got to see him, touch him, watch him change. Now, seeing Max in front of her was like looking at a dream.

Kathryn had shown up each week for her session with her son. It went against her instincts, everything she'd ingrained in herself. Kathryn knew how it felt to have her secrets laid bare. Still, she told her son who she'd been before him. How he'd come to be. How he'd changed her.

How she wouldn't change a single thing about who he was.

Max's blue eyes held steady. Sometimes a flicker. But he absorbed it all.

And in return, behind tears, Max confessed that the guilt of nearly killing Javi was one he couldn't escape. His words were a twisted dagger to Kathryn's heart, the burdens her son carried. Nothing Kathryn had ever experienced hurt like Max speaking badly of himself. She longed for him to see himself as she did—perfect. She ached to absorb all of it for him. To absolve him of the agony of the human experience.

Max had requested Andrew's presence for their last two sessions.

Andrew's level voice had filled the respectful silence as he described his life until that point: the year he'd spent drowning in Kathryn's absence, how he'd wanted to end his life. And how grateful he was that he hadn't.

Over the years, all the times she'd thought of Andrew, Kathryn had never imagined he'd spent the days from the last time she saw him to the moment he got in line behind her at Starbucks fighting a battle of wills just to survive. She'd never considered the loneliness of his sober years or the bond he'd grown with Nick. A sharp picture of Andrew formed. And she loved him more deeply.

He'd said his recovery had felt like taking a steering wheel and holding it steady in the direction he wanted to go, even when he felt he was too weak to go on. When he said this, the therapist leaned forward, the cap of his pen pressed to his lips. "I find that analogy interesting, Andrew. You felt like you had let go of the wheel and crashed, because that's exactly what Max did when he felt his most hopeless." Kathryn's attention moved to Max and Andrew, wearing a shared expression, taking in each word. "I think it's important for both of you to remember when you feel like you can't see the road in front of you, you need to take it mile by mile. Nobody is going to drive for you."

In front of the clinic, Max pressed a finger to the hood of his car. "Wow, I haven't seen *you* in forever."

Javi clapped. "I'm going to take a walk around the, uh, gardens. See what this place is all about."

Javi walked away, and Max leaned against the side of his car.

"Javi put your bags in the trunk," Kathryn said. "Our house sold so fast, I'm sorry you didn't get to say goodbye."

Max looked at the ground. "It's fine. Probably for the best. Delray . . . maybe I'll go back someday, but I'm glad you're getting a fresh start."

"That's what I thought, too." A heavy beat. "Max, I'm so sorry. About everything—"

"Hey, Mom. It's . . . Let's save it for therapy, okay?" But the sides of his mouth lifted. Kathryn stepped toward her son and pulled him into a hug. He was there: solid and alive, in front of her. She tried not to think about those lost hours when his fate rested in the hands of Andrew's wife.

In the sunlight, Kathryn buried her face in Max's neck. He slipped his arms around her and held her close. Finally, she let him go.

"Javier," Max shouted. "Let's go."

Javi appeared from the other side of the koi pond and tossed Max his car keys before climbing into the passenger seat.

"Are you sure you don't want to come home, even for a few days?" Kathryn asked.

Max smiled over the roof of his car. "Thanks, but Javi found an apartment close to where Emmy and Harper live. Emmy said she'd come over for pizza when we get there." The gravel scratched under his shifting feet. "We'll see where it goes after that."

Javi rolled down his window. "Like I'd ever let you pick out furniture by yourself."

Max climbed into the car, and the last sound Kathryn heard was Max's and Javi's laughter as they pulled away. She merged onto the highway and headed toward her exit, a few towns north of Delray Beach.

The morning she'd moved, Andrew's car had pulled up at her house just moments before she drove away for the last time. He'd reached up and dragged down the rolling door of the moving truck, and it had crashed beside them. Then he'd clutched her to his body. "Maybe in another life it would have been different for us," he'd whispered, and her body shook as he'd held her against his chest, his tears falling into her hair. He'd kissed her where her hair parted.

They hadn't said goodbye, because that wasn't what it was. They spoke occasionally, though their communication had become sporadic after Max had left the hospital. It would never be the same; they were bound together, irrevocably changed, but the unspoken message between them was clear: *I'm here. I'm not going anywhere, though this will never be anything more.* She had to be okay with that. She had no choice.

Kathryn called Harper as she cruised I-95. "He's headed your way," she said after Harper answered. "I tried to get him to stay, but he and Javi couldn't get out of here fast enough."

"Well, you know how stubborn we were when we were young," Harper said.

Kathryn felt a bittersweet smile spread across her face. "Keep an eye on him for me?"

"I will, Kat."

Her son was a few miles ahead of her on the highway. Over the years, all the times she'd felt Max pull away, she'd tried to reach across the void, only to find he'd already slipped from her grasp. Now, while the space between them grew, she felt closer to him than ever before. Max was off to set into motion his own imprint on the world, to make his own mistakes. And, for the first time since that morning twenty years before, when she'd sped along the same highway, running from the consequences of her choices, Kathryn felt confident in her son's future, comforted by the fact that Max was putting miles between himself and the wreckage of his parents' decisions.

As the midday sun rose, Kathryn decided to go home, make herself a latte. It was time to adjust to that vacant house, to the new town, where she wouldn't bump into Andrew, or his wife, or their babies. She took the off-ramp to the beginning of a new chapter she might chart alone. But she found she was comfortable with this notion, comfortable in her solitude, for the first time in as far back as her memory could reach.

ACKNOWLEDGMENTS

Writing can be a lonely venture, a path paved with self-doubt and rejection at every turn. But the luckiest among us find our people, people who get it, people who make the rough days easier and celebrate the wins. This book exists because I found my people.

First, thank you to my husband, Lex, for your unwavering support that borders on insanity. Thank you for believing I had something when I showed you my first rough chapters. Thank you for cooking and cleaning, doting on me, and wrangling pets so I could see my dreams through. You are my everything.

To the world's best agent, Michelle Jackson, who cold-called me on a freezing Sunday in January and made my dreams come true. Thank you for seeing my vision. It's your passion for this story that brought it to life.

To my critique group, Let's Cross the Finish Line (#LCTFL!): our inception was serendipitous. Without these brilliant women—Audrey D. Brashich, Brianne Somerville, Jessie Wright, Jody Gerbig, Katy Mayfair, Mary Taggart, and Natalie Derrickson—this book would not exist. Your insight, support, friendship, and humor keep me going, and you've given me the kind of writing family I could only dream of when I began this journey.

A very special thank you to my friend Kathryn Turner. You're an amazing human for so many reasons—you've been a sounding board, a therapist, and an editor. Thank you for your openness and honesty, and your willingness to read more drafts than anyone should ever be subjected to. Words aren't enough to convey how much I appreciate you. You are an inspiration to me every day.

Thank you, Ivan Scott: You were a supporter from the start, you've talked me off a cliff more times than I can count, and you taught me everything I need to know about cliff-hangers. I couldn't have done it without you.

Thank you to Shannon Evans, for your brilliant insight and encouragement.

Thank you to Bianca Marais, a true servant of the writing community. You, CeCe, and Carly have connected me to the greater TSNOTYAW community online. When I felt disconnected from my passion, your voices brought me back into the game. I have no idea how many books are out in the world because of your guidance, but your feedback on my submission package is the reason my book is out in the world.

To my early editors, Mari Ann Stefanelli, Hannah Mary McKinnon, and Tory Hunter: thank you for your guidance.

Thank you to Melissa Valentine at Lake Union Publishing for giving my story a home, and to Carissa Bluestone and Tiffany Yates Martin, the world's best (and most patient) editors, for your dedication and insight. Writing is solitary, but publishing takes an army, and the Lake Union team was just that—everyone poured their hearts into making this book what it is today. Thank you to my LU pub siblings for walking me though this first year; it's an honor to debut alongside you. What a wild ride it's been!

Last, but certainly not least, to the forty-plus beta readers who read my manuscript in various states of disarray, and who took time out of their busy lives to provide feedback and encouragement: each of you has your fingerprints on this story, and I cannot thank you enough.

Find your people, and never give up.

—Robin

ABOUT THE AUTHOR

Robin Morris has had a lifelong obsession with books and cats. She works in finance and is a certified book editor, a literary agent assistant, and an author of fiction and nonfiction. Robin was born in Colorado, resided in Palm Beach County as a young adult, and lives with her husband and two crazy cats. For more information, visit www.authorrobinmorris.com.